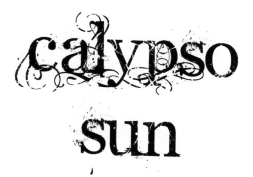

calypso sun

Alexander Frail

DAVNTLESS

DAUNTLESS PUBLICATIONS
Calypso Sun
Alexander Frail

Copy Editors: Ivan and Christa at Kirkus Reviews
Cover Design: Tracey Doyle
Cover Art and Painting: Annelise Mahoney
Interior Design: Alexander Frail and Tracey Doyle

The author thanks Annelise Mahoney for the Dauntless logo's beautiful design.

Published by Dauntless Publications and Alexander Frail
ISBN: 0692604146
ISBN 13: 978-0692604144

For

Eileen,

Ken,

and Joan

There is no song for the rabid dog.

—Minaerva Royce, *The Fires of War*

1

Old Broken Things

The death of a hero. In the beginning, it was; in the end, it shall be.

Jon stoked the flames. The fire had been softly dying underneath the whisper of the wind. His eyes examined the spears of fire, licking up and up and up. He prodded the logs. Fire lashed out at his knuckles. Jon recoiled silently. Not even the licking flames could melt the frown off his face.

Hidden within the flames was the letter, crumpled and blackened like a squashed spider on its back that had shriveled up to die. First the edges charred, then the body. It made a popping sound as it burned.

The burning logs gathered at his feet withered under the breath of flames. Jon wondered how long he could stare at them before he would go blind. Not long. Especially with sight so poor to begin with. My lord. He could barely see across the camp.

Flames ate wood. They could not survive without the wood, and yet the flames ate it up with abandon and no regard for their impending demise. Fools they were. Couldn't they see they were eating the last of life?

My lord. But that's how it began, with the death, the last of life. Then it shall end with the death of the hero, with Jon's hand, and the blue-sapphire cloth that she wrapped for him.

"My lord," someone said.

"Hmm," Jon hummed.

"Priest wants you. There's a boy down by the river. Priest needs you to be present for last rites," the man explained.

Jon looked up at him. He could see the man's impressive shoulders hunched slightly through the smoke's haze, though he couldn't make out the face. The firelight should've gleamed on the man's breastplate, but instead it was swallowed up by the mud caked to the metal. A shame. Jon would've hoped for more from these brave people.

Jon massaged his chin, peering back into the fire. "I'll come."

"He doesn't have long before he bleeds out. Arrow or something got him in the neck."

There were other men circled around him. In the gathering dusk, their shadows were growing pillars that stretched across the camp. Jon listened to their shifting feet crunch the gravel ring around the muddy circle in which he sat prodding the fire. The pace of their feet quickened. As they waited, they grew more anxious, perhaps frightened, at what Jon would do. He kept rubbing his chin, running his finger along the sixth day's stubble. What a man would pay for a sharp blade to cut hair and not throats.

The ground smelled like men killing men, women killing women, all of us killing all of them. Blood sunk deep into the soil. For years, for generations, it had seeped into the beige earth to turn it the color of beets, to kill the vegetation, to ruin the name of the two brothers. My lord. It made Jon sick.

"My lord," the man repeated.

"What is the boy's name?" Dinian, Jon recalled.

"My lord?"

"The name, damn it." Jon pounded the log he sat upon. The men's feet shuffled away from him.

Dinian, he repeated in his mind. My boy's name.

Yes, the boy's name was Dinian. Such a cute boy. He didn't have long before he starved, since there was no milk. Still, when Jon found the newborn in the woman's arms eleven years ago and she asked if Jon wanted to hold him, he said, I don't think that would be wise. You hold the boy for now.

Milk, my lord, the woman replied. The boy needs milk before he starves. There's no milk. I'll talk to the other ladies, but I'm no milk mother. Maybe one of the other girls.

That's okay; the other ladies will know what to do, he assured her.

Here, hold him, the woman said.

I shouldn't hold him. I don't think that would be wise.

Here, she insisted.

H-hi there, D-dinian. I'm J-j-jon C-carrow, he stuttered like a fool. Shhh. Uh, shhh, D-dinian; there, there.

Good, he listens to you, my lord. You sure you aren't the father?

No, I'm not, Jon stated.

Shhh, well, all that matters now is we get him to the sea. He must enter Mehsani's Light, the woman said.

"Mehsani take him," the soldier with the dingy breastplate snapped. Suddenly Jon found himself again in the present; he sighed. Too often, especially as of late, the past bubbled up and took him hostage.

"Hmm?" Jon hummed as the present returned to him.

"Mehsani, I said," the soldier spat. A thick glob of spit hit the flames with a pop and broke Jon's reverie. "Mehsani take that boy. Let him burn with the rest of the scabs."

Jon shot to his feet. The soldier backed away as Jon rose like a shadow leaping out from under the mattress to petrify a child. He imagined that the fire crackling softly at his feet threw an ethereal halo on the canvas of his tent behind him. Then he looked down, and there was his hand on the hilt of his blade where he saw the blue-sapphire cloth that Payton had wrapped around the handle, streaking between his fingers like three rivers. She'd wrapped the cloth around the handle when they sat in the Mire slapping their necks before the mosquitoes could bite. My Lord, was it already two months ago when the country did not have promise and this dispute had no end? Not like now,

3

where there was an end, *is* an end, with his hand closed around the blue-sapphire hilt that she wrapped. Jon swallowed and yanked his hand from his sword.

"I didn't know you still took offense to that word, Lord Carrow." A wicked grin broke across the soldier's face. As the firelight waxed and waned on the man's features, Jon recognized the man. Jasin. "Scabs. You've heard the stories."

"I've heard, yes."

How could he not have heard the stories? Three centuries had elapsed since the two brothers, Faedelin and Mehsani, forged this nation. Faedelin for the North, Mehsani for the South. Faedelin for the Sunburst, Mehsani for the Red Hook. Faedelin founded the University at Trowbridge, Mehsani built Sumara. The lessons were drilled into every skull that passed through the University at Trowbridge. The trick wasn't remembering the stories, but praying you could forget them and move along.

Jon wished he lived in some other place, where the legacy of the two brothers didn't linger in discourse like the smell of sleep on morning breath. He regarded the Sunburst on the chest of his followers, though a wry grin broke on his face at that thought; not only did their suspicions about him make them tenuous followers at best, but the emblem of Faedelin on their chests brought to mind only his days of fighting beneath the Red Hook, the image of traitors.

Even now, look at this horde standing round Jon Carrow's fire. The clump of Northern soldiers wore frowns in concert, as if prepared to kill him as much as they were ready to die for him. Jon disliked the conceit of the North. Yet here he was, their dubious leader.

"Back away from Lord Carrow," a voice snapped from beyond the shadows of the fire dancing its way to death. Edric Coyle, the sole fighter Jon trusted, sauntered out of the night. "He'll take offense to any word he finds suitable to be offended by." He shoved past the young soldier Jasin, who stared down Jon. "Is that clear?"

Coyle stood just a fingerbreadth away from Jon so that Jon could smell it on the man's breath coming like heat from a furnace so he must be back on it again like a fly zipping back into the same damn lantern again and again and again and just not this night for Faedelin's sake make him strong and shut that damn mouth like a furnace, Faedelin, just stop it all, my Lord. It's soon now. It's restless down in the valley, down in the Narrows.

"M'lord," Coyle mumbled, "there's a boy choking on blood down by the stream. A Mehsanic scribe. Was this side of the river to speak with some Faed priests." Coyle shifted uneasily on his feet, mud squelching beneath his boots. "Faed priest already there."

"I'm going now, Coyle." Jon pushed past the circle of men that had accompanied Jasin to his campsite. Four steps later, he turned around. "Jasin, you recall what we discussed the other day?"

The man who had said "scabs" gritted his teeth. "Yes." He added, "My lord," as an afterthought.

Jon nodded. "Good. You're with me tomorrow morning, Jasin. And polish that damn armor. Make it shine for all to see."

Why should I make it shine? Jasin had asked three nights ago.

Make it shine, make it shine, Jon answered.

Why?

Make the damn thing shine so the hosts of Braeland, the defenders of our country, can see your bravery, Jon commanded.

Why me? he asked.

Because the North needs a hero, Jasin, and you're just the man.

And Jon had a job for this man, just the job indeed. Jon truly had the job for this piece of shit who called him a scab and spat at him while he was trying to put right the things that went wrong. The most important job of tomorrow morning. It'd be him flying the banner high for everyone to see.

Make it shine and be gone, he ordered the soldier.

Yes.

Excuse me?

Yes, my lord, Jasin added reluctantly.

"Yes, my lord," Jasin echoed in the now.

"Good," Jon replied.

The firelight illuminated Jasin's pretty face. A face too pretty for the fields or the books or the army. Simply too pretty. His face was accented by two malachite irises laced with impossibly bold and dangerous eyelashes.

"Good," Jon repeated. He whipped around before he could see the man's face droop or more words could come tumbling out of that loud mouth.

"Faedelin's cock, it's hot right now," Coyle said with a sigh. The giant man took long steps, but Jon matched him stride for stride. "Not even the night gives us a little respite."

"It's the clouds."

"What?"

Jon jabbed a finger skyward. "More clouds, more heat. Tonight's cloudy."

They were walking through charred tents and overturned caravans with their goods spilled out over the riverbank, which was moist from the rain two days prior, and the swelling river, which was swelling because of the bloated corpses that dotted its face, and beyond that was the skeleton of the city, all bones and no heart. It stank everywhere.

Coyle groaned. "I don't know how you can do it." He mopped the sweat from his brow.

"Do what?" Jon asked.

"Sit in front of that fire on a night like tonight. Faedelin's cock, it's hot."

Jon shrugged. "Soothes me."

He saw the congregation before he saw the boy or the river. Their heads hung solemnly. Someone had lined the riverbank with torches that puffed away in the bleak night and whipped in the wind that plastered Jon's cloak to his back. Underneath, his sweaty skin begged to breathe. If only they made a cloak that would breathe better.

The priest was giving last rites. Must not have been able to wait for Jon. "We ask that the Lord Faedelin take our lost brother and accept him in his lofty sky above. This boy has sinned in life under the lies of the usurper Mehsani, the false brother of Braeland, but this boy has given that life in the name of Faedelin, the true founder and purest brother of Braeland. We ask that Faedelin accept this boy into the Light."

Coyle let out a sigh.

Jon never grasped the point of these circular rites. He wondered if anyone listened to them. He glanced at the sky. Are you up there, Faedelin? Do you hear the priest? Have you accepted this boy? Please, please, accept him. Just so you know, we'll have hundreds more to send you by morning, so please speed this one up, oh Faedelin.

The men parted so Jon could approach the dying boy. A Faed priest, whom Jon recognized as Father Gaebriel, was kneeling over the four-foot-long body that had ceased twitching and now stared emptily at the smoky sky. A stake was shoved into the boy's neck, which was the color of beets and running like a broken tap. His temple was colored with a violet bruise.

Father Gaebriel glanced up at Jon, nodded at him, and continued the prayer. He began by pouring water over the boy's bruised head. "Let the waters of renewal wash away the scum of Mehsani and those wicked teachings. Accept our brother into the fold. Adorn him in the Light." The priest traced a circle of yellow ointment on the boy's forehead and gave the circle teeth for sunrays. "Praised be the name of Faedelin."

"Praised be the name of Faedelin," the congregation echoed sleepily.

Jon crouched beside the dead boy, who had since passed on to Faedelin or Mehsani or Whothefuckever. He flicked the stake sprouting from the ruined throat and sighed, "Hmm." He glanced at the priest, whose face was redder than that stake adorned in blood. He might eat those lips if he wasn't careful; however, it was a miracle on par with Faedelin's ascension that the priest hadn't already consumed his lips while spouting platitudes for who knows how many decades. His lips might've made an appropriate garnish for those truisms. Jon turned his eyes back to the boy.

"I'd heard it was an arrow," he finally said.

"My lord?" the priest puffed out, but how he had saved enough air to puff out those words was anyone's wager.

"My men said an arrow caught the boy through the throat." He flicked the metal again. "That's a stake."

Father Gaebriel swallowed, and his great big throat ballooned like a toad's. "This soul has just left us, and you're concerned about arrows and stakes?"

"No, I'm concerned about the differentiation between arrows and stakes, Father. I expect accurate reports from these men. As a man of Faedelinity, you'll understand that discipline in Faedelin's army is paramount."

The priest gaped at him. For once, a Faed priest without a word to say.

"The boy," Father Gaebriel finally managed, "was struck by a horse. That is where he got that awful contusion, and in his stunned state, he fell upon the stake and passed on."

"Okay, let's wrap this up," Jon said, rising to his feet as he brushed the blood off his fingers with his pants. There went the priest's face again.

"My lord, Faedelin's Light is no parcel to be wrapped."

Coyle thundered forward and brushed past Jon so that the lord nearly stepped on the dead boy. It was on his breath. Had the man been sipping out of sight while Jon dealt with this mess?

"Whining to that prissy cock won't stop the scabs." Coyle slid out his blade so that just an inch of metal danced in the firelight. "Sing your dirges, but the dance is what counts."

The priest's eyes looked as if they might pop out of his head onto the boy's body, and the men all shifted in the squelching riverbank, which wept because of the coppery drink it had been given in such generous servings during the past six days.

Jon stepped forward and grabbed Coyle's arm. "Enough to come, Edric. Enough to come."

Coyle slid the blade back.

Father Gaebriel cleared his throat. "What, ah, what should I tell the boy's commander, my lord?"

Jon's eyes were scanning the far side of the river, where black silhouettes skulked between the orange globes lining the shoreline. How many were there? All these men, all these women, come to the riverbank crying as it drank blood, and all these men come to that riverbank for the two brothers who lived and died hundreds of years ago.

Finally he shrugged. "What's the one thing people love more than anything?"

The priest gaped at him.

"A hero," Jon said. He leaned over to pick up a dirty cloak that had been swept into the myriad of debris. He took a moment to shake it out before placing it over the dead boy. "Make him a hero."

We need a hero after all, Tomathy Carrow pontificated oh so many years ago.

"Yes," Jon said. "Make the boy a hero, and maybe then his mother and father will be able to accept his passing. Go," he said with a snap of his fingers. A few soldiers, the names of whom escaped Jon, scampered off to the last bridge where the emissaries met.

Be brave, son, Tomathy said to a young Jon.

Why do I have to be brave? he wondered.

The North needs a hero, Jon, so here are you and I. Tomathy Carrow and his brave son Jon. I know what your mother says; we've talked about that, but here we are, boy. This is a moment to make our names.

But Robert gets to stay, Jon whined. I don't understand.

All will be made clear, my brave boy, Tomathy promised. My brave boy, look at you all grown up and blond like me. Those blue eyes, though, I don't know where those came from.

Jon, look here: there are two houses that were built by two brothers. That's right, Faedelin built the North and Mehsani built the South. Right now the road between them is too wide to walk across, but see, you and I, we're building a bridge so that those houses can walk across.

How come you can't just walk across the road? Jon asked.

No, no, Jon. It's not, um, it's not a road. It's a river, he struggled to explain. Okay, so, we're building that bridge because we need the houses to come back together. So the father in one house gets the son of the other. Do you understand now? It's so the houses can talk together again across the river.

You could swim, Jon suggested.

What?

The river. Why can't we swim?

No, damn it. Okay, look, boy—sorry, no, don't cry. Look, chin up, shoulders back. Carrow boys are brave boys. Stop it. Stop it. Stop it.

When will I see you again, Dad?

The silence that followed Jon's question gnawed at him.

Dad? he repeated.

Silence. Twenty-four years later, the silence still chilled Jon Carrow. I just don't understand, he pleaded. Robert is still with Mom, and I'm only nine.

Jon, you are a brave boy, his father said impatiently, and this country will always thank you for it. There will be peace now, and not since Faedelin's death has there been peace, Jon.

But then Jon found himself hoisting the Red Hook of Mehsani and calling out Mehsani's name. The bridge that he was supposed to build collapsed, and all else went to ashes. His title, his legacy, his name: they were all cloaked in the blood of better men. It was true. Jon cut down Iayn Darrion, the Hero Knight of the North, because the sun caught Darrion's eyes. Nothing more. Jon hadn't been strong enough, and now here they were. The world rests at the nadir of a long breath.

There will be peace, my boy, that liar promised. You just have to wait and see. Be brave. Carrow boys are brave boys.

Wait and see, wait and see. When the fuck was he going to see? Jon had been looking for twenty-four years, throughout a childhood in the South, a tenure in the North, and all he could see at this point were the ghosts dallying in his wake.

Carrow boys are brave boys, Tomathy Carrow stressed.

"Ghosts," Coyle murmured.

"Hmm?" Jon hadn't noticed Coyle walking in stride with him from the riverbank.

"Ghosts," he repeated. He took a bite of an apple. Juice bubbled up on his lips and foamed down his bearded chin. An apple in these parts was a gem in vat of excrement. "At least that's what the Faed priest says."

"Indeed," Father Gaebriel concurred as he caught up with them.

Only then did Jon realize they had walked half a mile away from the dead boy into the shadows of Alaveren. The Holy City's towers pointed upward like jagged fingers, cut out of a black and smoky sky. Many of the great foundations suggested monumental towers far taller than the ones that remained.

"The ghosts are restless tonight," Father Gaebriel explained. "Spirits are everywhere in the Holy City. Lady Payton said as much earlier this afternoon. Ghosts and spirits are everywhere."

"Well, fuck."

"I'm sorry, Lord Carrow?" the priest asked.

Jon felt a rush of heat sear his backside. He spun around and took off down the road toward the riverbank and the dead boy. Coyle and the others shouted after him, but he could not stop. It felt as if someone had pressed a torch to his cheek. Sweat poured from him and sucked his cloak closer to his flesh. Then he came to a black mass hollering into the smoky night as a conflagration roared in front of him, sending a column of smoke to the heavens. There's your offering, Faedelin.

"Burn, you scab!" some of his soldiers shouted. Then Jon realized that screaming was also coming from a man trapped within the fiery maelstrom. It seemed like a big barn at first glance, but the high steeple belied its modest veneer. Most of the temple's steeple had already fallen into the flames. And within the flames a burning scarecrow thrashed against the barred windows that would not break. Jon glanced up at the sign above the door. A great red shepherd's hook was etched on it. The Red Hook of Mehsani.

"Fools," Jon hissed. The heat of the campfire he could abide, but not this.

Coyle caught up with him, and even amid the burning temple and flesh, Jon could still smell the liquor on Coyle's breath, and how did the man survive with so much of it in his belly?

"Coyle, hang the men responsible for this blaze and for the death of that prisoner. There was supposed to be amnesty." The burning scarecrow inside the flames had fallen.

Coyle nodded solemnly, then went to round up the Northern men who had broken Jon's order. Around the burning temple men danced and threw bottles of liquor into the storm. They hollered and laughed before Coyle got them.

11

Jon backed away. He slumped down on a bench in front of a gutted building. Coyle's unit, a band of scraggly men Jon rarely noticed, even when they walked behind him, helped circle around the lawbreakers and marched them away.

Within minutes Jon was left alone in front of the burning Mehsanic cathedral. He thought back to when the followers of Mehsani, the Southern-born, and those of Faedelin, the Northerners, could inhabit this city without locking one another in churches and burning them down. The scabs, the Mehsanics, the Southerners—all names to induce bile in the mouths of the North. Watching the flames, Jon reflected that this peaceful dream he envisioned hadn't taken place in almost three centuries. A wonder anyone remained to fight.

Jon rolled up his sleeve. A black heron was tattooed on his forearm. The symbol of House Carrow. He hadn't lived with his father and mother and brother for more than nine years before he was sold to the South in a sign of good faith. Then he was a Carrow in name only. But the ink lingered, a premature sign of his allegiance, which would be stripped from him in a rotten deal with the South.

The fire drew his attention. Weren't they all like the flames? They sought symbols and omens and cut one another apart because of their meanings. They'd orgasm for Faedelin or Mehsani, the two brats who began it all. The two brothers were dead. Yet their children continued the fight for three hundred years until Jon Carrow could sit in front of a burning cathedral in a broken city.

He watched the building fall apart. With a chilling roar, the flames ate the wood. Fools that they were, they danced as they died.

2

The Necklace of Squirrels

Fraternizer. Conspirator. Traitor. Ghost.

He woke gasping. It sounded like someone who had just been choking and was only now breathing for the first time and gulping down air like water. Sweat dribbled into his eyes and darkened the hem of his pants from navy to black.

The night rolled a breeze across his campsite. Jon shivered. As his breathing slowed, he glanced at the moon, a thin scythe set in a velvety sky. By its position, he judged he'd slept barely half an hour. With a grind of his teeth, Jon thumped onto his back to gaze at the heavens.

His days of youth in Sumara hadn't woken him in months. They had rested quietly beneath a shimmering surface like a lake under the moon. Lurked far out of sight, far out of reach. Those memories were the twinkling sugar of stars, so gorgeous to catch a glimpse and so sweet. Perhaps you could taste them, but then you would overdose and retch for days. Then the memories catalyze the time in the South, and they burst forth to shatter that shimmering surface so that you cut yourself on the shards because you aren't ready for it to break. And then you wake choking for air.

Sumara. The city protected by the Light. Its name left a foul taste on his tongue, like the bitterberries down south that wrapped like a green thorny noose around Sumara. Jon remembered the city on the cliff as the sea crashed on its face and the salt misted up over the precipice and dried out his tongue. The Stone Drum, the great fortress of the South, reared out of the city like a sleeping monster's backside, its head and legs buried in the houses and marketplaces. Sumara.

They say that when Mehsani gazed upon the spot he cried. Not tears of sorrow or pain, but tears of joy. He dropped to his knees before the exiles and prostrated himself toward the sea. Mehsani knew. That was the spot.

Some spot. It stank like brine and baked nearly through winter. Jon remembered his pale skin peeling within the first week he got there. His first sunburn in his nine years. Lord Mavogar comforted him. Said skin peels so it grows back thicker, so it won't peel again. His skin must've forgotten to thicken, since it peeled for the next twenty-two summers.

Lord Mavogar had been generous *(Fraternizer)* and welcomed him *(Conspirator)* into his great house by the sea and into the Stone Drum that had kept the Faed armies *(Traitor)* subdued for generations. That was long ago. Years before the omens and spooks and that damned fox *(Ghost)*.

Ghost Ghost Ghost.

The trip to the forest had done Jon in. That damned fox. And it was the squirrel necklace wrapped around his throat that had lured the fox, not his bad spirit and spite for Mavogar. It was the squirrels. No one went near Jon after that fox attacked him. But it was the squirrels that the fox had attacked, not Jon. He was only wearing the squirrels. It was always the squirrels.

A hungry fox sees a ring of dead squirrels. It's a smart beast. Winter is on its way, and game is scarcer. Does it run away? No. It steals the squirrels and frames Jon, and the priests say it's an omen.

Lying down too long did no one good. You didn't want to feel trapped. Jon's back curled up, and his arms wrapped around his knees. A fire was crackling nearby. Coyle stoked it with his sword. He saluted Jon with his beer mug, which was the successor of many predecessors, Jon was sure. He nodded back.

"In the two months I've known you, you haven't slept inside once. Not even tonight, huh?" Coyle barely opened his mouth to enunciate the words. His finger pointed up. "No more clouds. It's chilly."

"I'm not fond of closed spaces," Jon replied. Confined sleeping quarters brought back the nights they tortured him with the chant.

"Not fond of much, m'lord. What do you like?"

"Sleep. As with much in life, we like what we can't get."

"Worried about tomorrow? You know I'll be with you," Coyle reassured him.

"No, Edric. It's not that." He glanced at the man. Forks of flame bobbed in front of his face, bright as midday, and Coyle licked his lips like a sloppy dog staring down a steak it couldn't eat. "It's nothing."

Jon's thumbs rubbed circles into his temples. His eyes pressed shut. When he was younger, before he was sold to the city of Sumara, they drew the heron in ink on his forearm. Everlasting evidence of his allegiance to House Carrow. To conquer the pain he tried to squeeze his eyelids together and rubbed circles into his temples and thought that that would crush the aching into nothingness, like an anvil to an egg. The magic was gone.

Jon traced the black heron tattoo on the inside of his right forearm. Three pale scratches had obscured its head, wing, and leg. When the tattoo had raised too many suspicions in the South, he had taken a razor blade to the ink, trying to flay the heron mark. After he fled Sumara two years ago and found himself back in the North, it wasn't the tattoo of his house that stoked suspicion, but the scars he left from trying to remove it. Jon grimaced. Every motion he'd ever made was an attempt to avoid suspicion, but those attempts only added holes in the trust people put in him.

"Did you hang those men?" he asked Coyle.

Coyle slurped the last of his beer and burped. "The church burners? They're the newest fruit on your tree, m'lord. Still, how will that look? You, of all people. Hanging Faed men for burning a Mehsanic man. People will talk. Where does your heart stand? Not good, m'lord," Coyle pointed out.

Not a fox, not a heron, not a shepherd, just a fucking ghost. His days in the South were clawing back.

"They broke my law. They hanged for it," Jon stated.

Coyle held up his hands as if Jon was training an arrow on him. "I'm an upstart farmer who was given a sword and could swing it good. Don't mind me."

Jon's fingers kept tracing those circles.

"Especially given tomorrow, I find it strange, that's all."

"Enough, Coyle! Faedelin's dick, shut the fuck up!" He pounded his fist into the ground for effect. "Shut"—*pound*—"the"—*pound*—"fuck"—*pound*—"up"—*pound*. It took the breath from his chest. "I granted amnesty to any Southern prisoners. Those men took it away." Jon clambered to his feet. "They hanged."

Coyle raised his eyebrows, but followed it by shrugging indifferently during a long swig of ale. The fire crackled unbroken for a full minute. Jon slipped into a shirt that was unbuttoned to the nipples and let several scars peek out. They were purple-and-white worms etched across milky soil. He buttoned up.

"I'm going for a walk along the river." It flowed gently beside them. The rest of his men still drank up the hill in the skeleton of the Holy City. He could hear the frivolities echoing down toward the water. Coyle motioned to go. Jon held up his hand and said, "Stay."

"Yes, master," he responded with a smirk. "You going to speak with Tallhart?"

"No. Enough talk with her this afternoon."

"Hey, she gave you what you wanted."

"Mostly. She said Lanair and Jem have to design the treaty. I got the tower, though."

"Can't have it all, despite being Jon Carrow."

Jon rolled his eyes. "Just watch the river."

"Ha! Outnumbered, demoralized, and hungry to boot. They won't ambush."

Coyle turned up his mug, and for a heartbeat while observing the man's impressive seven-foot frame, Jon contemplated having him along. Few would dare fuck with Coyle's cocktail of farmer's endurance and warrior's physique. Then Jon said, "Just watch the far bank." He'd need it quiet.

Jon stepped over the log adjacent to Coyle, but his foot landed crookedly on a stone stabbing out of the mud. It was a cobblestone. Jon often forgot that three hundred years prior, the city reached down this far and even across the river and into the fields beyond. The common folk might have washed their clothes in this river atop properly placed cobbles. Now it was mud.

The riverbank spat out from the sides of his feet every time they pressed down. Brown flecks dotted his pants to the knees. They made them crusty and stiff.

Murmuring distracted him from his walk. It came from a tent up the slope a little, but not yet at the jagged ending of the cobbled city. He ambled toward the maroon sheets that concealed a swaying lantern within the tent. It reminded him of the Mire two months ago and the thing he saw beneath the bogs. The inexplicable lantern that filled him with light after an epileptic fit of flashing beneath the skin of the earth. Jon leaned in to listen.

"We ask Faedelin to guide us tomorrow," the murmuring went. "We ask Faedelin to bless our Lord Jon Carrow and our Lady Payton Tallhart, who watch over us and lead us into the good battle. Adorn them in the Light, Faedelin."

He barked out a laugh. Faedelin listening to Jon Carrow's name and sparing some of his Light for Jon Carrow. Fools, they were.

"Lord Carrow?"

A young soldier came up from behind Jon, who jumped. "I'm sorry, Lord Carrow, I'd never mean to scare you."

"It's fine. What's your name?" Jon asked.

"Daemon, my lord."

"Daemon. I'm Jon Carrow," he responded, stretching out his hand.

Daemon's eyes bulged, and he took Jon's hand like a young child grasping some mythical artifact. Some of the men had that expression when meeting him. Others lathered their palms with spit before shaking his.

17

"My lord, will you join us for a round of prayers?"

Jon smirked. "Better not. Probably won't get heard if I'm in there."

"My lord?"

"Pray, Daemon. Get some sleep, too."

"My lord?"

"Yes?"

"Could you, would you mind, I mean, telling us the story of how you took the capitol?"

Jon eyed the young man.

"What I mean is, the men have all heard the whispers. You sailing in under cover of night, Lady Tallhart swooping in from the north and scaling the walls of Trowbridge. The last stand of Lord Alaryn Tanogar. I think the men would love to hear it from you."

Jon frowned. "Sounds like they've already heard quite enough." He walked away from the man before he could protest.

The river lapped north. Its soothing susurrus ambled through the shadow of the city of Alaveren in the east and the mountains in the west and under the last bridge arcing like a dark collarbone two hundred paces away. The last bridge. It felt like a forbidden place to Jon.

Forbidden, the priest declared. This boy is forbidden from the House of Mavogar.

Forbidden? Why? Jon asked once his sentence had been passed.

Yes, forbidden. I am sorry, Jon, but this is the way it must be, Lord Mavogar replied.

He's just a boy. Barely thirteen, Alaryn Tanogar pleaded on Jon's behalf.

The priests have spoken. Mehsani has spoken, Lord Mavogar coldly declared.

Jon momentarily shook the memory loose and crouched on the soil. He squinted across the river where most of the torches had been put out. Tattered flags rippled in the breeze, flashing the Red Hook of Mehsani every few seconds. All else was shadows. Somewhere in those shadows was the boy. His boy. Dinian. Jon stuck his finger in the mud and made the curving hook of a shepherd as chills crawled up his spine. It was forbidden.

Forbidden, Lord Mavogar of Sumara declared.

Mehsani has spoken, and the Great Shepherd knows all, that fucking priest chirped.

But the boy is barely thirteen, Alaryn repeated. How could he possibly be an omen?

Enough, Alaryn, Mavogar snapped. If the priest says that the fox's assault on Jon was an omen against my family, I'll not have him living underneath my roof. The Lord of Sumara glared at Alaryn, his cousin, with eyes like live embers, and he turned them onto Jon, who was tracing the likeness of a shepherd's hook on the stone of the hall.

Jon, look at me, he commanded. You have been like a son in this house. A Northern son in a Southern house for four strong years. That is no small feat. Be proud, Jon. I know Lord Tomathy would agree, but the time is come.

But Lanair gets to stay, doesn't he? Jon muttered.

Of course, Mavogar answered. Lanair is my boy.

I don't understand. I always have to go, he cried.

Jon, do you know my house's emblem? That's right, the Red Fox. And the red fox you saw today was the spirit of Lanair, of me, of House Mavogar, of Mehsani himself. It saw you and attacked you. It is an omen. Its attack speaks of bad things on my blood should you remain under my roof. The priests have spoken.

No, it was the squirrels, my lord, I swear it, Jon pleaded. The fox wasn't attacking me. It was going for all the squirrels around my neck.

Mavogar sighed. Alaryn, would you explain to him now?

The old man stuttered, Uh, y-y-yes. I—uh, h-hello, Jon. You are going to live with me now, do you understand? I've been a man of the sea, but now you and I will be family.

But Lanair gets to stay, the young Jon whined.

Mavogar thumped his fist on the throne. Lanair is my boy. Lanair is a Mavogar, and you are not. Hereby, you are forbidden from my house.

19

The tears streaming down Jon's face were unstoppable. Mavogar and Lanair stood up on the dais looking at Jon, pitying Jon, hating Jon. It was the squirrels, but no one would listen because Mehsani had spoken and those priests opened their traps filled with nothing but hot stale air. Nonetheless, that stale, hot, acidic air somehow polluted Lanair's mind, and any connection Jon believed their shared was tainted. So rather than defense, Lanair provided him with abandonment, and sent tears torrenting down Jon's cheeks.

Mavogar rested his hand on Lanair's shoulder. The boy was Jon's height, was Jon's age, but looked down on Jon because he was on the dais next to his father and had a sudden glint of contempt in his eyes, and where was Jon's father?

Nowhere.

Jon, Lanair said earlier that day. That was before the sentence was passed. Before he glared at Jon with contempt and loathing. Like the days they used to wrestle together in the salt mist of the sea.

Yes, Jon replied.

Let's go hunting.

Are you sure?

Of course, but Father says we need to return before nightfall, Lanair warned.

What are we hunting?

Squirrels.

Lanair?

Yes?

I'm frightened of your father, Jon said. He gets angry whenever I do anything wrong.

Relax, Jon. You're like his son, and you're like my brother. Let's go.

Okay.

Maybe we could wrestle like we used to. Jon, remember that by the sea on Father's pavilion? You and I used to wrestle.

Maybe.

Jon followed Lanair out of the stables with the horses whinnying softly under their thighs. Lanair looked at him and said he liked the feel of the hard saddle in between his legs and asked Jon if he agreed. He shrugged. He said he guessed so. The breeze rippling over them was magnificent, and winter had only just begun to touch the air and make the trees blush.

Hours later in the forest, he found the prey. There, Lanair said, and pointed at the squirrel.

I see him.

Kill it.

Lanair rested a hand on Jon's back to help him balance as he aimed at the squirrel hanging off the tree. The arrow took it in the throat so he didn't cut up the good meat.

Nice shot.

Thanks, Jon said, but why does Father have us killing squirrels? He's rich. We could have a much nicer meal.

It's so if we get lost. Father says you might not always have to hunt for your meals, but you might not have the coins to pay for them, either.

That makes seven squirrels today, Jon noticed.

Father'll be so pleased. Here, add it to the collection.

Jon put the freshest squirrel on the necklace he'd been making on a tether round his throat. He listened to Lanair, and he made a necklace of the squirrels. They kept skulking through the forest as the sun slid down from its zenith and became a molten orange ball.

Jon smelled the musk from the red fox deep in the forest but kept going because Lanair insisted, and then it erupted from the brush with a flash of orange. The beast could've been a bear cub for its height. It pinned Lanair to the ground. He was screaming, barely holding the beast away with his forearm. Jon didn't even think; he drew an arrow and shot it, but missed the fox. Then the beast saw the necklace of squirrels, the free dinner late in autumn, and bounded toward Jon. It tackled him, but he wrenched his knife out of its sheath and planted it in the beast's heart. Its snapping jaw got lazy, then it stopped. Its body slumped onto his, and for five minutes, Jon lay there under the fox not realizing the omen that it had been.

Jon.

What?

We should go home, Lanair suggested. He was slightly thrown by the incident.

Are you okay?

Are you?

Yes, Jon replied.

Me, too.

Let's go.

"Whoa, girl, slow down!" some men shouted behind Jon, who had a vague grasp of the now.

That long-ago day, Jon walked back to the city of Sumara leading the horses on with a free hand. He was not riding them because he didn't want to get there any quicker than he already was.

"Faedelin's balls, she's loose!" the men screamed. Hooves thundered toward Jon, who was unaware while lost in the reverie.

When Mavogar interrogated Jon, the story of the fox attacking him came out but not the one of the squirrels that were around his neck since the priests opened their mouths. So Jon was kicked out of another home. First House Carrow and then House Mavogar. He moved in with Alaryn.

"Whoa, girl, whoaaaaa!"

"Whoaaaaa!"

"Lord Carrow, look out!" a man screamed.

Jon glanced behind him. A horse was charging toward him from where the cobbled roads left off above. He rolled sideways to avoid the descending hooves. Then he sprang to his feet, waved his hands over his head, and shouted over his men. "Whoa, girl, calm down! Calm down, calm down!" he bellowed.

The horse snorted and stomped several feet away. Men charged after her with swords drawn and arrows trained.

"No!" Jon shouted. He ran between the mob and the horse, who had slowed down. Her neck was bent toward the river, and she began lapping the water. "She's okay. She's okay."

A footsoldier, whom he recognized as Eames, stepped forward, his shirt disheveled and pants unbuttoned. His belly fat smiled below the hem of the shirt. "I'm sorry, m'lord. She got away from us suddenly. Broke her tie and all."

"That's okay, Eames," Jon assured him. "I guess the priests are saying the spirits are unsettled tonight; maybe the spooks got to her."

Eames scratched his head. "I don't mean to question you, but what are you doing down here all by yourself? Scabs could shoot you down."

Jon snickered. "I know only one person who could hit me from this far, and she's fighting for us."

"As m'lord says."

"Eames, take the mob back to camp. I'll handle the horse."

"As m'lord says."

The disgruntled drunks trudged up the hill. Another beer would probably do them good, though most of them had to hang on to their belts to keep their pants from sinking to their ankles. Perhaps another beer wasn't the answer.

Jon crouched back down. The horse was still lapping the river. It whinnied and snorted softly between drinks. Jon's hands rasped as each dry, dirty palm scraped against the other.

"Know how to ruin an eye?" Jon asked the horse. "You take their head, peel back their eyelids, and press them close to a candle as it wanes. A nice, slow, tantalizing process. They'll have poor eyesight when you're done with them, I'll tell you that.

"The ironic part is that you hold them there, pressed to the flame, to get the answer, but the more answers they give you, the longer you feel the need to trap them. Pressed to the flame, what can they do but answer? When you hear it, though, you'll wonder what other answers the candlelight can reveal. So you keep holding, holding, holding them there.

"And though their vision grows poor, they won't go blind. No, no, uh-uh. At best they've got blurred outlines of things that once were clear. At worst, you spell out an answer for them, whereas you sought it first, and it's a simpler solution than the one you needed: a quick four-letter panacea to make the candle go out. They won't even need the eyesight you tried to steal. They've got the new solution. Kill."

23

Jon had lowered his voice to speak in a soft, calm, monotonous murmur that seemed to fill the muddy ground and the sleepy camp around him with warmth and muted the clanging of pots and mugs and the chatter of soldiers and the crackling of torches. Slowly, the horse wandered toward him and stopped beside him. He scratched the horse's leg, and it whinnied.

"There, there, girl. You're okay, aren't you? Yeah, you're just fine, girl, we're all just fine." His gazed at the far side of the river. "We're all just fine. Once the candle goes out tomorrow, we'll be damn near perfect."

Come down by the waters, Lanair told Jon decades ago. They were eleven, and it was two wonderful years before the necklace of squirrels.

I can't swim, he replied to his adoptive brother.

Don't worry, we won't fall in. Just going to wrestle. Come here. Alaryn taught me some moves.

Okay.

"We're all okay, girl. We're just fine," Jon told the horse.

So, ready. Place your foot there and—

He pinned Jon to the ground in a flash. Despite his youth, Lanair's muscles had begun to catch the sunlight and throw shadows, and the girls were looking at him, even if he hadn't started looking back yet. The mud squished up around their shoulders as he held Jon down.

Come on, Jon, I know you're strong. I've seen you practicing swords. No one's stronger than you. I've seen how you move. I've watched you move.

Get off, Lanair. Get off.

Push back.

But how could Jon fight? The breath was being choked out of him, and he felt lightheaded, but then Lanair released his throat while staying pressed on top of him and gently breathed into his face so Jon could smell the lavender Lanair had been chewing. Lanair's onyx hair draped in front of those hazel eyes, and even though he had stopped, Jon could feel it. He could feel Lanair pressing his pelvis, tightening, and he smiled as his palm flattened on Jon's breast, which was naked in the sunlight.

Jon.

Lanair.

Jon, I think we should do this more often.

What?

Wrestle. It'll build strength, build character. We'll grow together as brothers.

Okay.

Lanair took his palm away.

Wait, Jon said.

What's wrong? Lanair asked.

Mind putting your hand back?

He smiled at Jon, and tenderly, his palm kissed Jon's breast.

Okay, Lanair said.

"We're okay, girl. We're okay," Jon said to the pacified horse.

Thanks, he replied years ago.

"We're okay, girl," he repeated to the horse. He clenched a fistful of mud and chucked into the river. Jon stood up, then jumped as he turned around to face the group of soldiers looking down at him. Eames's face hung agape. The lot of them were wide-eyed and openmouthed.

"How did you calm her down like that?" the fat man asked.

"A calm voice diffuses a tense moment," Jon responded, handing over the reins to Eames. "Better than knives and loud voices, anyway. Good night, boys."

Jon's walk back to his camp was shorter than his walk from it. It was still barely midnight. The moon had yet to reach its apex, but the world seemed brighter than it had all night.

Coyle sat on the same log as when Jon had left him. Jon rolled his eyes and said, "Rest. Tomorrow's the day."

Coyle clasped his heart. "Farmer's honor, Lord Jon Carrow, I'll dream of little lambs."

Jon lay down on his blankets, which were cool and soft from the mud underneath. It smelled earthy and clean like somewhere far away where no mortal foot had trod. He lifted his pillow to catch a glimpse of his sword. The sapphire hilt that Payton wrapped peeked back out at him. He covered it.

For once, sleep came easy.

Three tethers strapped across his nipples, belly, and knees. So tight. Can't
move.

Fraternizer.

Conspirator.

Traitor.

Ghost.

The cords yanked him deeper into his mattress and ripped him from sleep.
All hope for escape or even for movement vanished like smoke through his fingers.
The cords bit into Jon's flesh. One across the nipples, one over the belly, one for the
knees.

Something was swinging in the dark.

A sack filled with stones fell blunt and heavy to crack ribs and bruise legs.
Jon *screamed.*

Fraternizer, the Mehsanics chanted.

The second volley came, and it contained sharper rocks to slice the skin.
Jon *could hear his own screams rattle the entire castle.*

Conspirator, the torturers continued.

A clammy hand clamped over Jon's mouth.

Traitor, they claimed.

The blunt stones and the sharp stones waltzed together and soon he lost
feeling, so that it was happening to someone else and Jon was outside looking down
at some poor soul strapped to his mattress.

Ghost, they sneered.

Then it stopped. The voices vanished, the rocks dropped, the cords lifted,
but he still couldn't move. Couldn't breathe.

The Mehsanic torturers left his room, but they'd return time and again.

Jon woke with a gasp. Tears streaming down from his face, he pounded the ground. Again and again and again. It never ended. He never knew
when they were coming and didn't know why at first. The Mehsanics of Sumara suspected his treason from early on, but he couldn't simply stop, not
after they'd cast him out. Then the heron tattoo on his forearm had to go, so

26

he could prove to the South that he loved them and not the North, but only three lines could cut off its head, wing, and legs before the pain stopped him. Too, too much.

Oh sleep, why choose to be so late in your coming?

3

A Thin Scythe

Mmm, mmm, look at that moon. A beauty hanging up there and sparkling. An earring of his mother's resembled that moon, a thin scythe set in velvet. Mmm, mmm. A thin scythe set in velvet like her hair. Just like her hair.

"Always wondered why the songs are about the sun," Jon pondered aloud. Coyle was leaning against the logs Jon had been sitting on around his now dead fire and drinking water. What a miracle was that. "Ever notice that about the songs?"

Coyle shrugged. "Maybe. Sun's prettier."

Jon replied, "No. She's a beauty if there ever was," with a finger to the moon. "I mean, why'd Faedelin choose the sun? The moon I could get behind."

"Aren't you fighting for the sun? M'lord." Even Coyle, the most loyal, tacked on the honorific as an afterthought.

"You know what I mean," Jon said.

Jon pinched a charred twig from the fire pit. It held together briefly between his thumb and index finger before silt rained away in dark droplets until the thing disintegrated and left his fingerprints blushing black. So the fire had died eating life as it did. Jon wiped the stains off on his chest somewhere between the purple-and-white worms.

"I guess Faedelin just chose the Sunburst. Don't hear any stories about moon runners, do you? Only sun runners." He licked his thumb to remove the stain. The black fingerprints left a burned taste on his tongue. "Fools on an island."

"Aren't we all? Aren't we all?" Coyle mused. He was of course waxing poetic now that the drink was wearing off.

Jon recalled hearing the legend of the sun runners once. Perhaps in Trowbridge from his mother, though more likely the tale had been told by Alaryn once the old man adopted him. The tale came from a far away land. You see, Alaryn (or Jon's mother) said, the sun runners were once great adventurers who braved the high seas and fought many horrors. One of the sun runners was famous for killing a giant who was rumored to have a single, unblinking eye. During their travels, the sun runners were shipwrecked on an island and entranced by the nymph who lived there. Then, the nymph dared them to chase the sun, for if one caught it, immortality would be his prize. The runners fell into barbarity. They slayed each other in an attempt to grasp the unattainable sun while the nymph watched and dared them to run, run, run again. Only one sun runner, it is said, escaped the thrall of this goddess and related the ordeal to his wife once he returned. Jon remembered his adoptive father's tale.

Now here they were, a horde of sun runners enchanted by the Light and chasing it until they died. Though Jon would much prefer the moon and to run for it. A coy beauty that altered her image from a full round face like his mother's to the scythe earring of hers that nestled in velvety hair. Now that would be a chase.

How did the chase begin and end at the sun's feet? Why neglect the fine elegant sheen of the moon who must do battle in the endless infinity of the nighttime? The sun domineers a weak, blue kingdom. No poetry in that.

Not like the moon, like her earring. The moon conquered an unyielding realm as dark and magical as her hair. It welcomed him into that unconquerable conquered space as her boy.

To the depths with your boy, Selene, Tomathy told Jon's mother shortly before the sale.

Tomathy, enough, his mother said through clenched teeth.

No, to the depths, Tomathy replied.

I'll strike you again if you say more about Jon, Selene stated.

To the depths.

Jon wedged his ear into the thin strip between the door and its frame to listen to their words, which were words that would quake the earth with a new hero on the horizon to build Tomathy Carrow his bridge.

The boy'll make Carrow a mighty name, he claimed.

He's only nine. Show empathy, Selene retorted. And you care about making Tomathy a great name, not Carrow.

This isn't about me, Tomathy lied. Our country is bleeding, Selene. I'll not stand by.

Jon is our boy.

We have another.

Jon is our firstborn; you know the sacrilege you're doing.

Robert will suit us just fine, he remarked.

Robert snored behind Jon as Jon pushed his ear deeper into the partition of door and frame. While he uncovered the slog ahead of him along the road toward becoming a ghost, his baby brother got to lie lost in dreams that would continue to fill his nights beneath the moon and the sky and her earring and her hair because his snoring kept him deaf to the sale at work.

Jon saw Selene through the partition. She was a beauty as regal as a queen in her gown with plump breasts under her moon scythe earrings and her dark velvet hair and her eyes like frozen ponds that were so close to his own. Such a beauty.

"You're right, she's a beaut," Coyle concurred, regarding the moon overhead. "I'd give anything to make love under her."

That's it, Selene. The deal is struck, Jon's father declared.

He's my boy.

To the depths with your boy, Tomathy snarled.

"My boy loves the moon," the giant remarked in the unclear, unwanted present.

A pox on your head, Tomathy Carrow, Selene said.

Jon felt his father's hand as if it had cracked his face.

I swear I'll cut your throat if you touch Robert or me again, she stated, holding her cheekbone.

They're my boys, too; make no mistake.

Tomathy, I swear I'll take him to the top of the tower and then you'll find yourself alone.

Don't be a bitch, Selene.

"That's right. My boy loves that moon," Coyle said.

My boy; you're my boy, Jon told Dinian some twenty years after his mother had said the same.

But you're not my dad, replied Dinian, a boy of only eight.

That doesn't matter. You're a Carrow boy now. So even though I'm not your father, you're my boy, Jon said. A Carrow boy, and Carrow boys are brave boys, Dinian.

You promise? the boy asked.

Of course. We have each other and your grandfather.

But Alaryn isn't your father.

Well, no, but I am his boy.

Why? Dinian wondered.

So we won't ever be alone again, Din.

Have you been alone?

A long, long time, Jon answered.

Were you sad?

I was a very sad man, Din, and, uh, I was all alone, but then Alaryn called me his boy, and then I wasn't alone anymore. It felt nice. So, um, I found you, and I figured I could call you a Carrow boy and I wouldn't be alone anymore.

Thanks, Jon.

Call me, uh, call me dad if you want.

Okay.

Ever gazed at the stars?

No.

Come on.

Okay.

See the serpent around the apple up there?

Um.

We call that a smiling moon.

It looks like a hook.

Oh, yeah. I see that, I guess, Jon humored him.

Okay.

Look there. Do you mind if I point with your hand?

Okay, Jon.

Dad.

Huh?

Call me Dad.

Okay, the boy replied.

The boy took eight years to finally call Jon Dad. He had little more than a year to enjoy the sound of the title from Dinian's lips before he had to flee Sumara and the South. And the boy. A few hundred days during that year, a couple of times each day. Jon must've heard the word "Dad" from Dinian more than a thousand times. Not as much as he would've liked to have heard, but more than some people may hear throughout their entire life.

Imagine that. Jon left the boy in Sumara when he was the same age as Jon had been when he left his own father at Trowbridge. However, Tomathy never deserved to hear someone call him Dad. Not the way Jon deserved it, and Jon received only a year of hearing the sweet word.

Dad, he said to Tomathy before leaving the University at Trowbridge.

What?

Will I see you and mom again? Jon asked him.

Faedelin's balls, boy, enough with your mother, Tomathy snapped.

But Robert gets to stay.

Because he's not a hero, Jon, not like you, the mighty bridge-builder who I'm so proud of.

Did Jon ever realize it then? Did it occur to him he'd never see his father or mother or brother again? He'd never know now. It was remembering how it felt then that was the hard part since now he knew what had happened, but at the time Jon's nine-year-old mind never picked up on it. Like how Jon couldn't have realized then that Tomathy never looked at his son from behind those bespectacled eyes because he couldn't bear the sight of his son's eyes.

Leave your mother out of this, Tomathy demanded.

Why?

Enough, boy.

Don't call me that.

What?

Don't call me boy.

That's what you are, isn't it, boy?

Don't call me that!

Look, now you've woken your mother, he said, sighing. Selene, why don't you handle this mess?

There, there, my sweet boy, Selene sang. A satin sheet rippled behind her as she glided through the candlelit chamber toward Jon, whose shoulders hunched in his father's shadow.

Mom.

Jon.

You're wearing your earrings.

Yes. Do you remember making them for me?

I'll never forget them.

Come to bed.

Selene led Jon with his long finger in the circle of her fist. She drew him into calmness in her bed, and as he lay there resting on her roughened nipple Jon played with her earring like the scythe of the moon, which made the lavender seep from her hair.

34

There, there, my little lord, I'll see you soon, Selene purred.

Those earrings mingled with her hair like dolphin fins submerging and emerging from black waves. They dangled to kiss his face and pour lavender into his nostrils.

"I'll say, if I ever get back home I'll kiss her harder than ever," Coyle promised. The man could muse to himself all night. "What about you, Lord Jon Carrow? You got a sweetheart back home?"

"Back home?" Jon asked.

"Yeah, how 'bout it?"

"Need a home first to have a back home." His head was hurting.

Coyle's eyebrow arched. "What you call Trowbridge?"

"A rock in a lake."

"Same. Never liked the capitol, not after the farm. If only my boy could hear, wouldn't have had to go." He slurped water. And while Coyle took a reprieve from his incessant ale, Jon mused that the breweries from Calidum down south to the Far Ice up north would shut down if not for the insatiable thirst of Edric Coyle. "Had to go though," he continued despite the watery trough held at an angle from his lips. "Couldn't hear, so had to teach him." He mopped the ghost of the trough's remains from his chin.

Ghost. Five letters never knew such power, one syllable never such a cruel device, except for that friendly syllable followed by the stab of ice: Lanair. After the Sumarans stripped him of his Northern name in the South, they dubbed him the Ghost. Ghost, Ghost, Ghost. Every time he heard the word, how could he not recall the incessant torture? All that: the word, the name, they led a trail back to the other name he hated. Lanair. "Lah" seemed like such a friendly sound, but then the suffix "nair" sent a stab of ice into Jon's heart.

"Looking sick, m'lord," Coyle stated.

"Nerves."

"Jon Carrow has nerves? Call the bards, gather the poets."

"Not fond of bards. Tend to get everything fucked up."

Coyle whistled. "What a charmer."

Jon heard hurrying feet beyond his campsite. The footfalls were accompanied by a huffing old man, who nearly fell headlong into the dead fire gathered at Jon's feet. Despite the dark, his russet cheeks leaped out at Jon. A wonder that the threads of snow holding fast to his scalp hadn't melted away after the six decades the huffing old man seen. Hard years through harsh times. The man doubled over.

"Sir Badric. What's the story?" Jon asked.

The old knight raised his index finger. Meanwhile, Jon pinched another twig from the fire pit, and it refused to flake away between his thumb and finger. Badric's pointer finger scanned the heavens. Jon waited. He'd seen Badric in Wellfleet before Payton led her flight under the sewers to the tower of the Tallharts and liberated the city. The old man cut down six Mehsanic knights that day. It was one thing to kill a Sumaran, a common scab, but another story to cut down their pious killers donning the Red Hook in Mehsani's honor. Mehsanics die loudly. They screamed as Badric carved them up. That's a fighter, make no mistake. Beneath a snowy crown he cut down a Mehsanic for each decade.

"It's Lady Tallhart, my lord," he heaved. "She's been gravely wounded."

Jon's eyes snapped into contact with Badric's. "What? By whom?"

"No one knows, but reports suggest her courier, Piper. She pursued an unknown assailant through the city. Ended up at a tavern, where she was knocked unconscious out back. Alanna is with her now," he explained. As he did, Jon rolled the twig along the length of his thumb.

"Is she going to be okay?" Coyle asked.

Badric glared at him. "Look who shows a glimmer of humanity."

Coyle threw up his hands in feigned incredulity. "Never claimed to be an animal!"

"Only an animal could cut down a boy. You should've been hanged after what you did in Wellfleet," the huffing man said.

"I don't weep for lost sheep," Coyle stated. "They've got no right to don a shepherd's skin. If given the opportunity, I'd do it—"

"Where is she now?" Jon interjected. No need to have two fools quarreling over the past.

Swallowing a retort, Badric turned back to Jon. "In the tavern she was injured behind. I'll take you." Jon nodded. He flicked the twig at Coyle, who jumped when it bounced off his cheek.

"Let's go, Coyle. Got to see what Tallhart got herself into."

Badric led them through the city, deep into the heart of the camp of the Northerners, which sat on the eastern bank of the river. Everyone was awake. Must be those ghosts Father Gaebriel had mentioned. Ghost, ghost, just a fucking ghost. Spooking all his men when they needed a good night's sleep. Not a fox, not a shepherd, not a heron, just a fucking—

Enough.

"What?" Coyle asked.

"Hmm?"

"You just said, 'Enough.'"

"Did I?"

"Clear as my piss on a sober morning," Coyle replied.

"Nothing. Forget it. Slipped out."

"As you say."

Weary soldiers thronged the entrance to the tavern Badric brought them to. "Lord Carrow!" some exclaimed. Others barely held back the ball of spit they'd have loved to hurl his way. Jon knew to a man who cried his name and who dammed a reservoir of saliva, though he didn't care either way. Tomorrow both sides would bleed.

The common hall of the tavern was cleared out. The barkeep wore a glum face as he probably dreamed of the coin he was losing because of Payton's adventures. Jon stopped midway on the squealing wood floor to fish in his pocket and pull out a gold coin. He whistled at the barkeep, underhanded the coin to him, and winked. "Go home. Get rest for tomorrow."

Oddly, the man frowned and slammed the coin onto the bar, and then stormed out of his makeshift establishment. Coyle raised his eyebrow, but Jon shrugged. "Fuck it. Keep guard out here while I talk to Tallhart."

Coyle plopped his rear on the bar and swung his legs around. "Look at all these beauties just for me," he said, rubbing the casks. "I'll be good right here, Jon. I'll let you handle the tough stuff for once."

Jon followed Badric into the congested back room of the tavern where Payton Tallhart lay on a thin cot sagging beneath her, nearly scraping the rotten boards. A bruise colored her cheek purple. Alanna sat in a rocking chair holding her hand. Her moving lips uttered a prayer to Faedelin. Hope that he hears it. That plum ripening beneath Payton's eye will need the grace of Faedelin to shrink.

Alanna cut her prayer short at the sight of Jon, but he motioned for her to continue. "Don't stop talking to him on my account. He never gave me much mind anyhow."

"What do you want?" she scowled.

"Come to pay my respects."

"She's not dying."

"No need for prayers then," he replied. "Wait out front with Badric and Coyle. I'll stay until she wakes up."

"What a sight upon awakening."

Jon peered into a window to his right and caught his reflection. "Hair's receding a bit, but I still have those baby blues, don't I? Not altogether a bad sight."

"Don't joke," she suggested. "Comes out queer as a Mehsanic singing Faedelin's praises."

"A fitting analogy."

Alanna pressed a kiss to Payton's forehead, and for a fleeting moment, her blonde hair mingled with Payton's ruddy curls. On her way out, she shouldered past Jon, who watched her scarred face vanish in his periphery. Badric followed quietly in her wake. Here he was alone with Payton Tallhart, the Red Hart, the liberator of Wellfleet, but not of the capitol. That was him, that was Jon Carrow, the holder of the reins. They chafed in his grasp.

He lifted the rocking chair and placed it next to the window. After opening it, he produced a pipe from his pocket and stuffed it with tobacco. What he'd give for a pinch of something stronger. He blew the stale smoke out

38

the window, where it ascended in tendrils toward the moon sliding from her zenith but still crowning the partition of roofs in a narrow strip of sky.

Payton began to stir. He watched her idle hands run through her matted orange curls and avoid the ripe plum marring her freckly face. Those freckles coming off a boat in midsummer had sparked an urge in a long dead fool.

Jon stroked the curved arm of the rocking chair. Selene used to rock him to sleep in a chair like this while he played with the earring. As his hands came down, brushing her breast, she smiled at him. The real beauty was the five words that followed. Kissing him when he was hers and she was his and the lavender filled his nostrils. I love you, Jon Carrow.

I loved you, Selene Carrow.

Payton grunted, and her eyes drunkenly flickered open. Suddenly, she bolted upright on the mattress and clutched her stomach as if to retch. She held the startled position, holding her stomach. Then, apparently satisfied that she was okay, Payton eased herself onto her side. Upon seeing Jon, her eyes widened.

"My, my, Payton Tallhart, you've had one busy night," Jon said. She groaned.

While Payton repositioned on the bed and struggled upright, he stared out of the window and looked up at the thin scythe set in velvet, musing how pretty it was and how very much it resembled an earring swimming in her hair.

4

The Spook

Payton held up her hand. The man shut his mouth.

She'd lost track of how long the man had been rambling about some spook wearing a scarlet scarf. He'd been visited, he said. Visited by some apparition in a red scarf; truly, the spook was a vision from Faedelin. Who was he to rebuff a vision sent from Faedelin himself? Any vision, any sign, any word sent from the Lord Faedelin must be followed posthaste, lest the heavenly spirit smite the disobedient follower.

Fatigue seeped into her marrow each time a petty lawbreaker invoked the name of Faedelin. Now this lawbreaker, who was kneeling in front of Payton on the floor of her pavilion, claims a vision was sent from Faedelin himself. On and on and on the rambling went, but in the end, this man spilled the blood of a courier. Simple. The law was broken, Faedelin or not.

If she knew Faedelin—and following years of her father's invocations, how could she not—Payton knew that Faedelin would never send a vision, he would not endorse a scarf the color of his traitorous brother, and he would never order the death of a courier. How much of what she knew was worth less than a dull penny. Payton would never convince the lawbreaker, whimpering now in the pavilion she'd been stationed in this week, that he'd violated the law. Once a man has the blessing of Faedelin, no following action can be judged by the laws of mortals.

Her guards, who filled the periphery of Payton's pavilion, rocked back and forth on the balls of their feet. She saw Alanna, whose hand rested on the butt of her blade's handle. Badric's arms were folded as his eyes glared at the man kneeling in front of Payton. The afternoon was a far cry from dusk, when shadows stretched far, but the shadows of her guards swallowed the crying man. He bobbed on his knees. Alanna coughed. The man jumped.

He had a freckly face, not unlike Payton's, but his was a bony visage protruding beneath waxy and sallow skin. It begged her for mercy. Prophetic, he called the spook in the scarf. The Book of Laws be damned, the man had a mission, set forth by a forerunner of Faedelin himself.

"I've already passed my judgment," Payton stated. "If you have any final prayers or thoughts before I take you to the block, speak now."

"It was the vision in the scarf! Please, Lady Red Hart!"

Payton winced. How she despised that nameless nickname; not only did it strip her of Payton, her given name, and Tallhart, her House's name, but it evoked a figure whose imaginary, legendary void she could never seek to fill. Nor did she care to fill it.

"I killed the Sumaran courier only because the man in the scarf told me to!" the lawbreaker whimpered. "The man's voice was so assured. He told me he was saving me from the devil inside. Said I could stay the power of Mehsani if I killed one of the couriers. I swear it!"

Someone would have to clear up the slobber from her pavilion. Payton wished she could say few had been so pathetic, and yet the city was littered with them. Maybe the days had gotten to her. Six days. Six days she had sat the stool in between the singing metal and the crying people, and six days that riverbank had grown soggy. At first, it had held her feet with a little give. Now her legs plunged into the rotten earth up to her shins. What a waste. Nothing

42

would ever grow there now. Not with so much rotten earth beneath their feet and slobber everywhere.

"The man in the red scarf showed me the Sumaran courier," the law-breaker explained. "The courier was a Mehsanic, one with the Red Hook emblem. The man in the scarf promised that his death would be my salvation! How can you strip me of that?"

"Quiet," she said. "I don't need to hear about these spooks. Not today. Regardless of who spoke with you, your hand spilled the blood of a courier. The Book of Laws clearly states that the murder of an emissary calls for execution. 'Let emissaries know we shall hold our blades, so that they might hold their lifeblood,'" she quoted. "Faedelin's words are clear."

That might as well be a quote, too. How many times her father had shoved her nose in Faedelin's book, the Way, reiterating the clarity with which the man had spoken, she could not say.

Snot popped out of his nose. "Please, Lady Tallhart. He told me to do it. Said every Mehsanic deserves a metal kiss."

"Silence. You'll speak when I give you space," Payton declared.

She leaned forward on her stool. A breeze wafted up from the river below, where the cobbled road met a muddy mess. The day was still hot, a blanket of clouds like gray cotton brewing overhead and threatening rain that would not come. Payton sat on a roughly hewn stool, the solitary seat in her pavilion, which was filled with twelve guards whom she called the Harts.

Payton got off the stool and walked to the edge of her rounded pavilion, a tongue of rock that dropped sheer in the river below, growing ever noisier as the clog of bodies broke away. Across the river was the Sumaran camp. Jem was there. He hadn't emerged to see her, nor had he sent a letter. Payton couldn't expect him to. Not anymore.

She gazed at the jagged mess of Alaveren. The Holy City. It loomed over the valley, a solitary thumb in the Narrows reaching toward the heavens, but it was as empty as the promise of a Mehsanic priest. A Faed priest, too. Both of them buzzed around Alaveren like flies around a horse with a broken leg who was slow and unquiet in its dying.

"It all began with the dying, Payton," Kala warned, some nine years ago. Payton recalled the conversation like this morning's routine.

"I know that," she replied.

"Don't let it end in dying."

Kala gazed at Payton, brushing her cheeks with palms dotted by domes of calluses. The woman had ruled Calidum, the great Southern continent that baked beneath perpetual sunlight, for twenty years by the time Payton had arrived. The queen of the country took Payton in as her father begged for soldiers.

"Leon Tallhart will die eventually, and with another war brewing for your country, you'll stand a heartbeat from the throne of Braeland. They're calling this war the Reaving."

"Hard to gain anything without the death, either," Payton reflected.

"Yes." The old woman pursed her lips, which were chapped like the caked clay beneath their feet. "Hard, but not impossible. Eyes ahead, Payton. Maybe you'll see a way that no one else can. Then you'll earn the title they'll give you."

Payton blushed, ignorant to just how soon Leon Tallhart would die thereafter and how quickly she'd have to earn the title that fell onto her.

"My lady," Alanna said, breaking Payton's reverie. "Would you like the lawbreaker taken to the river?"

"P-p-please!" the lawbreaker cried.

"Yes, take him down to the river now," she told Alanna. The woman, who bore a beautiful patchwork of scars beneath trimmed blonde hair, yanked the lawbreaker by the collar. His feet jumped each time they dragged over the next cobblestone.

"P-please, Lady Tallhart! What was I supposed to do? He possessed me, I swear it. The man in the red scarf. If only you knew..." His voice trailed off as Alanna marched out of Payton's pavilion onto the road through the camp, around the bend, and out of sight.

"Clean the block, Badric. I'll be down in a moment."

The old knight, one of two captains in the Harts, along with Alanna, bowed his head and waved for Caelia, Elaine, and Hector, the youngest of the Harts, to follow. Seven others—Tam, Thanet, Gawaen, Bors, Gwenaever, Tristam, and Morgaese—remained with her, forming a half circle near the mouth of the pavilion.

On her desk rested the blade. Running a finger along the edge, she beckoned over her shoulder to Tam, the Hart with the white scar beneath his eye. He came to stand by her side. "Payton," he said quietly.

"Any sightings of this man?"

"The one with the red scarf? No," he said, a fleck of amusement in his tone. "Sounds like a spook to me. Many of our people have claimed to see things in the night. Little pans out to truth."

"You're sure?"

Tam smiled, a jaundiced quarter moon. "Look at who you're talking to, Payton. Not even your father coaxed me into a cathedral. Small chance I'd believe in a spirit filled with spite for Mehsanics. But even so, I searched. A few said they might've spotted someone. Nothing definitive."

She nodded. "Okay. Let's go."

"Just a matter of curiosity, Payton: if there had been a man or spirit sent from Faedelin, would you still complete this punishment?"

"Yes," she answered. "Why?"

"I'm not sure Leon Tallhart would have. Good thing that's yours now." He nodded at the blade. "After you, my lady."

Payton lifted the blade, sheathed it at her side. She led her men and women to the block down by the bank.

Doom doom. Doomdoom. From across the river, the Mehsanic drums shook loose the boyish grin with mischief at the corners below a tussle of nightingale hair. *Doom doom.* The great storm drums scored every Mehsanic prayer in the afternoon. There was a time Payton believed them only a fairy tale. *Doomdoom.* Then her eyes saw the truth.

Many years ago, a young man named Saewyn asked, from behind his boyish grin, "Have you seen the drums?" Saewyn was a Sumaran, born and raised under his uncle, Lanair Mavogar. Though he'd never rule over Sumara and its holdings, he'd gain a strong position at court.

"The ones Mehsani built himself?" Payton asked him. "I thought they were only legend."

"No, no," Saewyn replied. "They're as real as Mehsani's Light. I'll show you." He had led her deep into the depths of Sumara during her stay, several years ago. She'd never heard something so profound.

Doom doom. Doomdoom.

Payton's procession continued toward the riverbank. It rested down a slope, where the shadows from her pavilion above fell. *Doom doom.* Everyone began to walk with quicker steps once the drums began.

"Again?" moaned Thanet, whose fiery hair closely matched his spirit. "Dirty fucking scabs ought to show us some respect. Show our eardrums some, anyway."

"Ought to pop all those drums," Gwenaever replied. "Fix the problem real quick."

"Throw the damn drummer in a cell while you're at it," Gawaen suggested.

Tam whistled. "So it'll go."

They were coming down on the riverbank where Father Gaebriel hovered over the petty lawbreaker, who was writhing beneath the priest's touch. The river drifted nearby the kneeling lawbreaker. Badric stood aside while Alanna held the man over a block. Beneath her boots, the river lapped upward, waiting to cleanse what the man had done.

The priest smiled at her. "Lady Tallhart. How are you today?"

"I'm okay. Spooks abound this afternoon. You seem cheerful, Father Gaebriel."

"No reason for tears at Faedelin's Light. You and I share the honor of absolving our brother of his transgressions," he pointed out.

The priest clutched the Way in his palms, a child sticking to a parent's guiding leg. In the leather-bound volume, the works of Faedelin and Mehsani waited, the Book of Testaments through the Books of Laws and Ideals, concluding with the Books of Dreams and Nightmares. Father Gaebriel bowed his head in reverence. Had the sun emerged, his bald pate would've blinded her. Few were so pious any longer to keep to Faedelin's first rite.

"Nothing gives me more pleasure," she replied.

She couldn't help but grin. Pleasure. She and Jem used to buzz around the university's sloping roads and laugh about pleasure. The Mehsanics in Sumara were open to pleasure. The Faeds in the University at Trowbridge had other opinions. What else would the case be?

"If there's one thing Faedelinity loves, it's pleasure." Jem rolled his eyes even as he said it.

"No one'll know. Even if your father finds out, you shouldn't care," Payton replied. "Don't listen to this stuff about perversions. The king's toy is an open secret anyway."

"That's the king, Payt. I'm some boy from Calidum."

She frowned. "Fine. If you don't fuck him, I will."

Jem laughed.

"No, I will. Don't you doubt me, Jem Nalda. I'll have him studying my ceiling before you can say, 'Faedelin,' five times fast."

"You think Faedelin cried out his own name during sex?"

"Heard he called out Mehsani's name."

Jem doubled over laughing.

"Fine, I accept your challenge, Payt. Light, I wish I'd been holding the pen when they wrote the Way."

"Oh, there weren't any pens! It floated out of the sky!" Payton snickered. His arm was around her as they sat at the trunk of a tree. The Yard of Kings smelled of wine and fresh grass. Ants crawled all over her legs, which were blanketed in orange fuzz.

"Leon still hasn't taken a razor to you," Jem noticed.

"Tried to. Been wearing pants more often recently, so it's sort of slipped his mind."

Jem squeezed Payton tight. "Gotta be more like you, Payt. If the king has his toy, I'll have mine."

"There you go. I acquiesce. He's all yours."

"Gee, thanks, Payt," Jem said with a laugh.

"It's yours now, Lady Tallhart." Father Gaebriel's voice made her refocus. "Lady Tallhart?"

"What?"

"I said the ceremony is yours now. I've read the Faedelist rite."

"'Faedelin smiles on you,'" she quoted.

"And he shines upon you, Lady Tallhart." Father Gaebriel stepped aside to where Badric stood.

The Harts milling about behind her, Payton planted the tip of the sword in the fringes of the lapping river. Suddenly, the man became subdued, his eyes transfixed on Payton's sword. In accord with the frozen lawbreaker, the Harts silently took their places.

Payton mouthed the words to some verse her tongue had a vague recollection of. The preliminary prayer. When her lips pressed together, the priest beamed at her.

"Do you have a final statement?" she asked the lawbreaker. "If so, let it be heard by Faedelin and the Light."

"Please," he breathed.

"Very well."

She began to kneel, but his body's spontaneous rigidity startled her. His chest flattened atop the block that Alanna held him on. Alanna's jaw popped open, and she doubled back two steps. Gazing straight at the ground, the man released a deep, monotonous voice. "You are killing the hand that stayed the power of Mehsani. Go on and make your sacrilege. Faedelin shall judge you."

The liturgy cut off. His body sagged on the block, head dangling over the edge. No one else seemed to hear his words.

Gradually, Payton kneeled. She mouthed the words of verses in the Book of Laws. What went through her mind as her lips idly flapped, she couldn't remember in the next moment when she pushed herself up.

"Before the eyes of Faedelin and the Light, let this judgment pass," she intoned.

She swung the sword over her head and slashed it downward. His head dribbled down the bank into the river. A crimson torrent pulsed from the stump of his neck, rushing toward the waters, the final absolution of his sins.

"Faedelin forgives him," Father Gaebriel said.

A flash of red caught Payton's eye. The hue matched the bloodstain on the bank; it ran red into the threads of the scarf. There he was. Face obscured by the river's breadth, the spook in the scarf observed Payton's justice. He lingered to study her while he tightened the thing round his throat. Though she couldn't see his eyes, she felt them, knew that they were there and that they blazed incisively at the sacrilege she had committed.

5

Far Away Places

Doom doom. Doomdoom. Doom doom. Payton held her head in the bowl of her palms. The drumbeats were low and ominous across the river, where Mehsanics struck Mehsanic drums in the shadow of Faedelin's city. *Doomdoom.* The midday prayer was underway.

Payton hissed out a long sigh. Her men began jeering near the riverbank and tossed slurs across the water. Fools. Couldn't they see the drums were drowning their voices?

Doom doom. The drums drew her back.

"Would you like to see the caves?" he asked behind the boyish grin.

"Where are they?" Payton wondered. Sumara came back to her.

"Just below the Stone Drum, but I know a secret way," Saewyn replied.

Doomdoom.

"It's this way, Payton," Saewyn told her, his youthful smile conspicuous in the torchlight. His future land holdings prevented anything she might share with Saewyn, the nephew of Braeland's most formidable lord, though Payton reckoned she had time to spare for a few adventures. While she and her father stayed in Sumara, she yearned for contact with someone her age.

"We have to be quick."

"Okay."

Saewyn had escaped adolescence, maybe at twenty-three then, but several pimples scarred his olive face. His nightingale curls bunched up around his forehead and slanted over one eye, while his hair was smooth like the mane of a stallion on the sides. Payton thought his shoulders looked funny, the way they slanted down from his neck instead of flanking outward in a firm mantle.

"How have you liked Sumara so far?" he asked, taking her hand as stepped down the stairs, warm even in the night.

"I like it. It's not as hot as Calidum, but way hotter than Trowbridge. It's winter up in the capitol anyway, so I'm glad we got to come down here."

Saewyn laughed. "You might be. My uncle is furious. The famous Leon Tallhart gets to babysit him for the king now."

"It's just to help rebuild."

"Come on, Payton. You don't have to lie when I already know the secret."

She stayed speechless because she knew the secret, too, and wasn't skilled enough yet at making new lies to keep it covered. If you're going to say something stupid, don't say anything. Payton just followed him in the night.

The fortress called the Stone Drum loomed up all around them. It was a labyrinth of rock and clay, but it looked like one piece, as though Mehsani had found a great rock and meticulously chiseled each hallway and doorway and staircase out of it to shelter his people from the storm. Each ceiling soared away from them, obscured in its own shadow.

Leon Tallhart had taken this palace in the Reaving a year earlier. The only man to have ever breached its walls. Now he came back a year later, and the ravens were all around.

Saewyn took Payton to the lord's hall, where his uncle ruled over Sumara. Lanair had gone to sleep by then. Bars of moonlight stabbed through the columnar windows along the hall's length. She took her hand from his, and, confused, he led her to the simple throne that Mehsani had sat upon three hundred years ago. The seat, whose armrests curled at the ends like the hook of a shepherd, would've fit better in a dining hall than in a castle. It was said Mehsani had carved it from a dappled whitewood, one of the few trees strong enough to survive in the harsh lands around the city.

"No one knows about this, so I'm trusting you to keep my secret," he said provocatively.

"Okay." Her heart was thumping. His eyes held Payton motionless for a few beats.

"The moon makes your hair look like a sunrise."

"What're you, some lovestruck poet?" she quipped.

A nervous hybrid of gasp and laugh escaped him. "Come on."

He pressed the wall softly behind the throne, and it popped open. A rush of humid air whooshed forward and tussled her orange curls.

She followed him down the passage. It wound down and down and down until it came to a great balcony overlooking the drum caves. Below, pairs of faceless naked bodies sat interlocked and swaying to the *doom doom* of the Mehsanic drum. The great drum, forty paces away on the lower level, camped in the torchlight. The bare cavern was a fluid mingling of shadows and firelight. Two pairs of drummers ran to the drum and swung a stick the length of arm. *Doomdoom. Doom doom.*

Saewyn took her hand. "Amazing, isn't it?"

She swallowed. So forbidden and so wrong. "Yes. I've heard stories about the storm drums. They're more enormous than I imagined."

"Nothing can capture it truly. Only the eyes."

"Yeah."

"Would you like to pray?"

Payton glanced at him. The humid cavern had frizzled her curls, and she could feel the sticky beads of sweat scrawling down her back, her armpits, her neck. The perspiration was salty on her lip.

"I'll give it a shot," Payton answered. "Not a word to my father."

Grinning, he replied, "Sumaran's honor."

Saewyn tucked his arms into his shirt, then his head, and then tossed it on the ground. He began untying his breeches.

"You know why we pray like this?" he asked. "Mehsani taught us that we all sin, so we should help sinners redeem themselves. The cleansed one sits on the outside, while the sinner sits between his or her legs. The drums help us lose ourselves and forget the mortal world. It's only then that the good spirit of the cleansed can flow through the sinner and drive out the evils."

His pants hit the floor. His penis hung limp between his thighs. She slid her shirt over her head, and it got caught in her mane of fiery curls. For a moment she thought about her scar and how it must be glistening with sweat. Then she stepped out of her pants. His eyes never left hers. He didn't even look at her scar. He didn't seem to mind.

"Mehsani had this balcony made so he could worship among, but above, his people. He liked to monitor his flock." He stepped closer and took her wrist in his palm, which was covered in a film of sweat. "Have you sinned, Payton?"

"Yes. I touched myself in my chambers after my father fell asleep the other night." She had the sin ready to say, for at Trowbridge it was an easy enough sin to admit to the priests.

Saewyn snorted. "You Faeds have queer sins. I tug at myself every day but I never come down here for it." He must've seen her gritting her teeth because he quickly added, "Look, that's fine. That's fine. Let's pray."

Payton sat in between his legs. They began swaying back and forth to the rhythm of the drum. It wasn't long before she was gone, lost in the ecstasy, the mastery of the drum, the heat of the cavern, the sweaty skin rubbing on salty flesh. The drum reached into her soul, and she could feel it all leaving. No more worries or demons or spite. The drum drew out the weight of sin, as if it had encumbered her breast under the weight of lead and weakened it with the bite of poison, and the drum took her to a far away place.

Then she could feel him growing against her back. Her own thighs were wet and slick, and then she reached behind and grabbed it. He moaned and she whipped around, shoved him onto his back, and climbed on top.

Doom doom. Doomdoom. She loved the way their skin rubbed together and how the smell of their bodies filled the balcony.

Later that night, to the sound of the drum, Leon Tallhart went off, tearing apart his study as he berated her and swore to have the boy put down, for he had the blood of the Usurper in him, and any progeny between them would be tossed from the walls of the university to join the rest of the animals in the wild.

"'If a child is born of a lusty encounter, let that child be thrown from the walls of the city, for it is an animal,'" he quoted like a parrot. "He says it clearly in Laws. Carrow's boy, that abomination you've taken to, doesn't deserve the time of your day, either, Payton."

"Who cares, Father? It happened. The moment doesn't own me. Clearly, you're not as strong."

Leon spat. "Faedelinity is *it*, girl."

"Faedelinity is old. Faedelinity is tired."

The stinging in her cheek didn't leave for days. Payton had never seen rage boil in someone's eyes like it had in his; the brown irises had suddenly become red. She didn't speak with him for days afterward.

Dinian was no animal; she'd never allow him that. Despite the size of his ears, he was barely seven. They would've made better butterfly wings than ears. And his top teeth draped over the bottoms. But he was a good boy. Jon loved him. The only time Payton had ever seen the man smile was around Dinian.

Months later in Sumara, days after her twenty-fourth, Jon propositioned her. He thought she'd be a great mother for Dinian. And him seven years her senior, talking to her by the sea even as her father told him to stay away. Leon was a jealous dog, always biting at visitors who got too close to its owner even if the owner had welcomed the visitor. Leon had pinned Jon against the wall as he approached her chambers one night. His livid whispers she could barely hear, but when he stormed back into the room he tossed a night flower out of the window. Jon never spoke to her again. Not until after the Sumarans cut Leon's throat. Not until the night in the screaming cells, where Jon stalked around like a caged cat, and the flight north when the shepherds hounded them. Right around where she'd left Jem after Calidum, four years before moving to Sumara.

Calidum. It was hot. As though the sun had dropped to earth to bake it into a distant memory of earth. Far away down south, where the coolest nights were the hottest days in Trowbridge.

Leon collapsed as soon as he and his daughter stepped off the ship. It had been a long voyage from the southern shores of Braeland, a month's sail across the boiling basin. Hands clutching at his chest, veins bulging in his forehead like worms about to pop. He drew her near to kiss her forehead. A few curls were pasted to her flesh in the film of sweat. That was love. In the moment that might be your last, drawing a hot sweaty forehead near to kiss it with quivering lips.

Kala's men swooped in to take him away. They led Payton to the Queen of Calidum, who lounged in her palace of baking clay. Kala opened her arms wide to her even before she told Kala her name. Her naked breasts pressed flat against Payton's, and her sweat tried to take her shirt with it when she leaned away.

"Daughter, he will persevere. Today is not the praeco's day."

"I'm sorry?"

"Come here, Daughter," she said, drawing her back in. Only then did Payton cry, but she hoped the queen was right.

"You know the common language well."

Kala laughed, the deep laugh of a happy fat man. "I do." She cupped Payton's cheeks. "Did you expect a hoard of mutes who clacked at one another with their tongues?"

Payton's mouth hung open.

"Laugh, girl. The oceans and seas and rivers and streams were forged with the tears of the Mother. Now is the time for laughter."

And she laughed, and Leon lived. Kala took them in and taught Payton during the brief pauses of her talks with Leon, who called for her aid; the Reaving was coming. Jem was with them. He saw Ogari first and challenged Payton. She won.

Ogari's arms were muscular like a farmer's, not at all like a prince's. And his hands were callused like hers.

"You don't mind?" she asked.

"No," he replied, leaning in as if to kiss but never quite doing so. "All women should have calluses. A woman or a man or a child with no calluses has not done enough in life."

He took Payton's hands and ran his tongue along the patches of hardened flesh and rubbed the backs of her hands with his. It tickled at first.

Kala called Payton in later that day. "I see you've noticed my son."

"I'm sorry?"

"Ogari has eyes for you, too. And both of you are eighteen. You're adults in Calidum." Kala's skin blended with the shadows of her cool chamber. Payton thought she was so beautiful. Thin and strong, her face was a spider web of lines. She hoped she would look like Kala in old age.

"I don't think—I mean, I didn't mean to…"

Kala held up her hand, and Payton shut her mouth.

"Words and words lead to only more words. You do not need to keep explaining everything away to the wind."

"Okay."

"Come walk with me."

Kala took her out to the sea where the breeze gave no relief from the sun overhead. It merely blew hot air laced with salt into one's face. Kala clasped her hand with a ring of calluses that made Payton's feel like newborn skin. Her breasts flapped against her chest with every step.

"Payton, why do you still wear your shirt?"

Payton blushed. "I couldn't take that off. Not in public. The things Father would say…"

"Leon Tallhart is a brave man. He is a strong man. He is an aged man. But brave and strong and old do not mean wisdom. And Leon Tallhart is not a wise man."

"It's good to hear someone else say that. Though he knows more about Faedelinity than anyone I know."

"Is it wisdom to chirp the words in a book? Is it wise to echo the mantra of a nymph? No, no. You would be no better than a sun runner if you did." She sniffed as the tide scraped along the shore. "Besides, Faedelinity is an erroneous name. Mehsani wrote the books in the Way. Has your father ever told you that?"

"I knew that was the case, though he never mentions it."

"Let's stop for a moment, Payton."

Kala's left hand guided Payton's from the top and ran in circles. Then the queen bent over to clasp a handful of sand with her right hand. With her left, Kala peeled open Payton's fingers. A thin rain of sand poured into Payton's open palm from Kala's fistful. Some flecks of brown bounced off and were lost to the beach.

"The earth is an ambivalent host. We're like little gnats that buzz around her ears, so she tries to slap us or squish us against her neck. So why should we help her and swat at one another, too?"

All of the sand had fallen from Kala's right hand and now made a little hill in Payton's. Kala placed her left hand below the sand hill, then with the other hand turned Payton's to the side so that the sand began pouring back into her clutches. A few beads vanished to the beach.

"Sometimes, we forget how ambivalent the Mother is to us. Every day she questions our birth. So a few of us fall off. Storms, wild animals, earthquakes; she sends reminders to us that she does not sit well under our feet. But we are deaf and do not hear her warnings. We are blind and do not see the signs."

When the sand was finished returning to her and a few pebbles were lost below, her left hand floated above Payton's palm, tilted sideways, and rained the sand back to it.

"Since we are blind and deaf, we do not realize that the Mother is taking some of us back because we did not deserve the birth she gave us in the first place. Then we disagree about the birth. So we start turning on one another and helping the Mother take us back."

Her hand full of sand glided away from Payton's so that only half of the dwindling stream fell into her palm below. The rest was lost.

"Spats, disputes, battles, wars. They accumulate."

Kala drew whatever remained in Payton's hand back to her own palm. The sand was mostly reclaimed to the beach below them, for the cycle continued without pause for the grains it was throwing overboard.

"Then one day, we find ourselves a ghost of what we once were, bitter and defeated, small and insignificant. Then the Mother will take back her house."

She flipped Payton's hand over, and the sand fell.

"And so, Payton Tallhart, we must remain vigilant. It does not suffice to chase after the sun, killing one another for its glory because we've adopted verses that tell us to do so—saying that we've killed other sun runners because the sun commands it."

"My father says there's a special providence in the fall of a fox."

"Mmm. Do you agree?"

"No."

"Why?"

"He thinks Faedelin's own hand might as well have spilled Sumara's blood. That if House Mavogar falls, it falls because of Faedelin's own intentions. I think it's just a ruse to swing a knife."

Kala nodded solemnly. "A fair point, young lady. You've heard of the island of Laecuna, I assume?"

"The island of the sun runners."

"Yes. I once met a man who was a sun runner. He escaped Laecuna and told me the secrets of that place."

Jem was running up to the women on the beach. Kala smiled at Payton and kissed her forehead.

"Go, Payton. I've rambled on too long. Old people do that. I'm sure your father would agree. We'll resume this tomorrow." Smiling, she walked back across the beach to where they'd come down from the palace.

"Payt!" Jem shouted to her, breathless. "I've been looking everywhere for you."

"Hi, Jem."

"Ogari was looking for you, too." Jem always had such a wicked grin. Like his eyes held a secret while his smile told you something else. They were obscured by a crop of hair reminiscent of Saewyn's.

"I'll see him later, I guess. I don't want my father angry."

Jem sighed. "Oh, Payton. Just fuck him and be done with it. Either that or I'm going to beat you to it."

She laughed. "Is this a response to my challenge at the university?"

"You bet your ass it is. Let me tell you, you're lucky to get so much time with him." Jem shrugged as he mopped sweat from his brow. "Well, maybe he's the lucky one. He would've had some chapped lips after I was through with him."

"That all you think about, Jem?"

"Not all. I was talking to him last night about Calidumi folklore. It's fascinating! Way better than what the crones at the university ramble on about. Wish I'd gotten to stay here longer before moving north." He unclipped a sack of water hanging on his belt, took a sip, and handed it to her. "Have you ever heard of Meraxes's box? It's an old Calidumi tale. It's called 'The Golden Box and the Farm Girl,' but most people up in Braeland call it 'The Box of Meraxes.' It's a good one. They had this other one, too. It was called the praeco. Well, not a story really. It's a more of a legend."

The water felt good on her lips, somehow still cold in this heat. They started walking back toward Kala's mighty clay palace. Rising from the hot flats of the seaside, the palace rested on a great bay of near bathwater. On the hottest days, steam wafted up from the basin and shimmered the palace behind it to incoming sailors. The palace climbed to a flat peak some hundred feet in the unrelenting sky. Left and right of the plain peak stretched terraced halls that wrapped around the boiling basin. Payton thought it resembled a lion whose paws encircled a puddle and whose head was oddly geometric. Thousands of years old, Kala's palace was a bulwark of sharp angles and pragmatism.

Jem continued: "They call the raven a praeco. It means 'herald of night.' They think that ravens are birds of life. Can you believe that? They're supposed to usher the soul across the night waters into the next life or something."

"I haven't heard that one. I'm surprised Father is asking them for help."

"Why?"

"The night waters and the praeco? I've never read that verse in the Way."

They went back to the palace, which was cool after the long walk on the beach. After dinner, Ogari and Payton were talking, and then it came to fumbling around with each other, and him lapping at her calluses again, and his fingers going between her legs, and her moaning, and him. The whole affair felt forbidden, and even then the word "vagina" felt queer inside of her head, as if even the thought of vagina would bring wrath upon her.

Kala's voice, muffled slightly in the next room, woke Payton the next morning. "Love is love, Lord Tallhart. Let them rest."

"You will never tell me what to do, Kala."

"*Lord* Tallhart is what I call you. It's an unnecessary formality I follow. I would ask you to reciprocate."

The sound of Leon's footfalls sounded like a lion pacing before it took down its prey. Air hissed out of his nose.

"Let me take my daughter back to her own chamber to sleep. Enough has been defiled already tonight."

"If Faedelin were a man of love, then he would embrace the sex of Payton and Ogari. A man who suppresses love is no man of love at all," she intoned.

A foot slammed the ground. "Do not defile my daughter with those words. She's already been defiled by that sunburned..." Leon seemed to catch himself, but too late.

"Out of my house, Leon. Now. Get out and let them rest. They rolled around. Nothing to be concerned of."

"How you do it beyond civilization does not concern me."

The sound of hand hitting flesh made Payton jump and Ogari wake. Leon made no sound, and neither did the queen. Then:

"Calidum was a civilization long before the two brothers carved out a kingdom of children in the North. It shall be civilized long after as well. We do not cast around terms like 'sunburned' and mean them as slurs. We would not cast out a young boy because he loves other boys."

"I took Jem in and called him my own. I opened my house."

"Within which you cast words like perversion."

Silence.

"Do not forget, Leon, about the men and women you came to ask me for. Already whispers dance on the tongues of the North. The Reaving, they're calling this one," Kala reminded him.

"I know. I've heard."

"Then you know you'll need my help."

A long pause.

"Keep it far, far away," Leon warned.

Kala sighed. "It's not my capitol that'll face destruction."

"Trowbridge shall be fine."

Then Leon burst in, collected Payton from the chambers, and they were speeding north and north and north. Miles east of Sumara, Jem left them for the libraries at Wilbraema. She never saw or heard from either Kala or Ogari again; it was as though the weeks they spent there had been a passing dream, a fugue period. Upon return, no time had passed. Though an ache in Payton told her that some time had elapsed, a certainty that she was missing a portion of herself. It was a paradox she could not reconcile.

"Lord Nalda has sent a letter," someone said. She was dreaming, gazing over the river.

Jem's face had receded away and away until six days ago. Payton broke from her reverie. A courier hunched in front of her on the plush rug of her pavilion where the murderer had knelt only minutes before. His back was almost as curved as the Red Hook stitched onto his tabard. A scar crossed his face from his left temple to the bottom of his right ear. Payton grimaced.

"Lord Nalda has called, Lady Tallhart," he repeated. His voice was like sandpaper scraping against a rock. "Here is his ledger." He handed her a note sealed with wax, drawn out while still hot to make a spider's silhouette. The paper was wrinkled as if it had been submerged in water.

"Thank you, sir."

"Not a knight, my lady."

Payton ignored the response and flipped open the note.

Dear Lady Payton Tallhart,

I hope this ledger finds you well. I don't know if my other notes have failed to reach your hand or if you have had no time to return them. Lanair hopes to meet with you and Lord Carrow to find terms to end this conflict if Lord Carrow consents. Not a patch, like the last Reaving, but a solution to end our conflict and to forge peace. Lanair hopes to avoid any spats like those we've seen the past six days. I look forward to seeing your face again.

Warm regards,
Lord Jaremy Nalda

What formality. Lady Payton Tallhart. So he no longer saw her as Payt, who once played king and queen with him and stole glances at older boys with him at the university. He had loved the dark-haired boys who brooded beneath their black curtains. How had eight years wiped all that clean?

Jem and Payton's kingdom had been a peaceful one. No two brothers or Alaveren or the Narrows. They lived in a fertile valley that still grew night flowers and lilies of the valley. The Spider King and the Fire Queen.

"My lady," the courier said.

She glanced down at the hunchback. Payton stood just five-and-a-half feet from the ground, though his ailment capped him lower still.

"Sir, how did you get that scar?" As she asked, she found herself drawing a line beneath her navel.

"No one's ever asked me that before." His shoulders relaxed, but that only gave him the appearance of hunching further. "My older brother gave it to me. When my father died, he left me his horse. I was the favorite." That last word sounded bitter; she could practically taste what it left on his tongue. "After my father passed, my brother cut my face open, stole the horse, and vanished." He stared at the ground. "Never saw him again."

"I'm sorry that happened to you." She stood and placed a hand on the man's shoulder. She stood two heads above him.

His head craned up to look at her. "Thank you, Lady Tallhart."

After sharing a short glance with the man, she walked to her desk. Dipping her pen in ink, she began writing *Dear Lord Nalda,* but crossed it out and crumpled the paper. On a new piece, she simply wrote: *The broken bridge by the market. Your side. Midnight.*

Payton folded it up and handed it to the courier. Those eyes must have never left her back.

"You're a very unusual person, my lady."

"How do you mean?"

A nonchalant shrug accompanied his reply: "You just are."

Payton smiled. "No, I'm really not. Make sure that gets to Lord Nalda as soon as possible."

The hunchback bowed. How that motion didn't topple him, no one would ever know. He shuffled toward the flaps that bordered her tent.

"Sir?"

"Yes?"

"Tell Lord Nalda I said, 'Hart's asleep, mischief's deep.' Can you re-member that?"

The man's mouth scrunched up in thought. Then he nodded. "I can, my lady."

"Thank you."

The courier embarked on his journey. She was grinning again. Hart's asleep, mischief's deep.

She remembered.

"Let's go, Payt," Jem whined, impatient to start their nighttime journey. She always waited several minutes longer than necessary to start. Mustn't be too quick. You'd get caught that way.

Payton would slip the note under Jem's door in the tower facing hers across the university courtyard. He would meet her by midnight. The gray castle of the University at Trowbridge loomed overhead.

Hart's asleep, mischief's deep; when Leon Tallhart fell asleep, possibilities abounded.

"Where tonight, Payton?" Jem asked once they met.

"Another kingdom."

"What?" His eyes bulged in the moonlight that bent around the columned towers of the university.

"This isn't Braeland anymore. We're not in the university." Payton hopped up on a bench, marched end to end, and puffed up her chest, still flat as week-old ale. "This is the Kingdom of the Spider King and the Fire Queen. Our city is called Laughingvale. Most famous in our city is the Hall of the One Thousand Hearths, which could fend off even the most bitter winter winds and where all of our subjects eat in peace. But beware!" She leaped off the bench and tackled Jem to the ground. Payton felt enormous in those cavernous halls. "The Nefarious Iceman lurks in the Snowy Mountains to the North. And it is his mission in life to blow out the last of the One Thousand Hearths."

Her breath smelled awful because she hadn't brushed that night, but Jem never complained, even as she pounced on him and breathed into his face. He gazed up at her. He held her sides. He still had both hands back then. His eyes were swimming in thought, lost in the Kingdom of the Spider King and the Fire Queen.

"Well," he replied, "I guess we'll just have to stop that Nefarious Iceman."

"To the Hall!" she shouted.

Laughing, she ran through the darkened University. With sticks they fended off the Iceman before Payton blasted fire out of her hair to destroy him once and for all. Jem overturned a wash bin they found and stood defiantly over the melted Iceman.

"I guess he couldn't handle the heat," she said, and Jem doubled over in laughter.

No one, not even the Nefarious Iceman, could destroy their kingdom. They'd ruled peacefully, an eight-year-old queen with her nine-year-old king.

"Hart's asleep, mischief's deep," Payton murmured.

"I'm sorry, Lady Tallhart?"

Payton glanced up to find Badric standing in front of her. Her confused stare was enough of an answer.

"You said something about hearts and mischief."

"Oh. Nothing, Badric. What is it?"

"I wanted to let you know that Tam and Thanet found no sign of this man in the red scarf from earlier." He waited for a response.

Payton pressed her eyelids together. Had she merely imagined the spook after striking off the murderer's head? "Tell them I thank them for their efforts."

Badric bowed his head and walked off.

"Fuck," Payton said. She turned to peer across the river. The dusk would be gathering within the hour, and midnight not far behind it. She hoped Jem would read her message soon.

Something caught her eye. Floating in circles, far above the camp of Sumarans, was a black speck. It resembled a raven, at least from this far. Among her other talks with Kala, there was one that stood out. She told Payton about the allegory of the praeco and the raven. When Mehsani settled the South, he set to killing the ravens that swarmed their camps, since they represented death to his congregation. The leader of Calidum at that time nearly raised her armies; the murder of a raven was sacrilege in her old society. In Calidum, ravens were called praeco.

"We came that close to blood, huh?" Payton asked.

"'Close' is a kind term," the queen admitted. "Luckily, Braeland and Calidum have never faced open warfare."

"How did it stop?"

"After your people were killing scores of the praeco, Mehsani laid down his weapons when my ancestor explained to him the significance of the praeco to our people." Kala was with Payton on the sands once more, late in the night before Leon stole her away. "He realized the mistake in killing praeco and made peace. No sense in tearing apart another culture, he figured, if it meant losing his own. If he hadn't, Calidum and Braeland could've destroyed each other."

"A good thing we're not on Laecuna. They wouldn't have stopped."

The queen laughed. "Now you sound like me! Yes, yes, a good thing. Those foolish sun runners can't see past their own shadows in the sun they love so dearly. You see, a sun runner can't stop because of the sun's promise for supremacy. If only he can catch it, he can be the hero who won eternity for his tribe. A tantalizing prize to give up in the name of not killing."

"Leads back to special providence," Payton pointed out. "Do you agree? There was no special providence in the fall of a fox?"

"Yes. Yes, yes, yes. Of course!" Kala's enthusiasm faded suddenly as she crouched and scooped a handful of sand. Her eyes withdrew to regard only the sand; Payton felt as if she had somehow vanished from the queen's mind. "There is no special providence in the fall of anything," Kala murmured.

Boots crunched on the soil behind Payton in her pavilion. She spun around and met the gaze of a man who stood at the doorway of the linen. His eyes were in an icy world far, far away.

6

Stories

Like sapphires stripped of their sheen. Two gems burnished decades ago that were left out in the weather to fade and scuff.

"Payton. Hope I'm not intruding."

Like the sky when it fades from blue enamel to gray chalk. Two heavens marred by earthly pain and mortality.

"Payton?"

Payton hadn't seen Jon in nearly two days, not since the Southerners flanked them from within the city. Jon's army had lost nearly a hundred soldiers. Gray half-moons hung beneath those faded sapphires. Was there a soul peering out from behind them, or did they just drink everything into a sleepless pond? She couldn't decide what his eyes were: sapphires, skies, or ponds.

"Hi, Jon. Take a seat."

"I'll stand. You kept the Harlot up." He nodded to her flapping banners outside the tent. The red silhouette of a women glanced over her shoulder at the world.

Payton paused before returning to her stool. Jon clasped his hands behind his back and stepped into her pavilion. His wide shoulders were wings that flanked his neck. He combed back the blond hair that once fell to his eyes, perhaps a result of its receding line. But Jon's jaw still sat firmly. A slab of rock that went untouched even as the moss and plants above it began to wither.

"I did. Fuck the priests."

"Fuck the priests," he echoed, raising an imaginary toast.

"I'm glad you've come. I want to discuss tomorrow." Payton sat. "The Sumarans want to meet."

"Yes, I agree. We should broker a pact sooner than later. Lot of death for six days."

She skipped a beat. No one could've predicted such a speedy accord from Jon Carrow. She spoke warily.

"How about the last bridge? It's symbolic and safe. It's a good, open spot."

"It's a bad spot."

"I'm sorry?"

"Bad spot. Too open, too public." His eyes dropped to his boots. Flecks of soil dotted the toes of malleable leather, and he frowned as he brushed them away with the other foot. Then he glanced back at Payton. "The broken tower is more fitting."

Payton snorted. "Unlikely, Jon. Just the suggestion would be an insult to the entire Sumaran army."

He shrugged those broad wings. "Rather fitting, I think. Mehsani's last stand, Faedelin's ascension, the penning of the Way. It all fits, doesn't it?"

She mopped sweat off her eyebrow. "Jon, you'd kill any chance of reconciliation before we even spoke to them. Asking them to go where Mehsani died is nothing short of saying, 'Fuck you.'"

He smirked. "Been no shortage of saying that over the years."

"Faedelin's balls, Jon. Grow up."

He strode toward her desk where she'd written the letter to Jem and kept his hands clasped at the foot of his spine, tapping his inner hand with his outer. With his head turned from her, he gazed out of her pavilion toward the rubble all around them. He tapped on and on and on.

"The apple tree was supposed to be just over there," he said with a nod of the head. "Before all this. They say Faedelin saw it first. 'Are you not my brother?'" he quoted.

"Jon, 'Apples Without Worms' was only an editorial addition to the Way. It came from a Calidumi folktale, and some scribe named the brothers Faedelin and Mehsani." Payton scanned the ruins through her linen curtains rippling in the afternoon. "Might've never happened."

"I'd heard that somewhere."

Payton saw that beyond the spot where the apple tree supposedly grew, the broken tower spiraled skyward in the gathering dusk. Parts of its western wall had crumbled. Its walls looked like crooked teeth and its floors like gnarled fingers. The broken tower defied the Mother's pull and reached for Faedelin.

Being a Tallhart, Payton knew much, perhaps too much, about Faedelin and the man's legacy. It was said her family descended from Faedelin himself, her ancestor Julien a cousin to the founding father. She often wanted more distance between Faedelin and her surname. Though he cofounded Braeland with his brother Mehsani, Faedelin basked alone in legend.

Payton stood to pour herself ale. Flat. She couldn't remember the last time she had ale that foamed at the head and bubbled on her tongue as she swigged it down. The university, probably. After the night climbing over the walls and Jon sailing in under the fog of the night. She swirled the ale in her cheek's pocket for a few seconds, then spat it over the edge of her pavilion.

"Want something to drink?" she asked Jon.

Jon shook his head. "No. Too many ghosts."

Payton winced. She recalled how the word "ghost" twisted into a haunting moniker that the Sumarans hurled at Jon. For years, he never heard his own name. Saewyn had first told her what they called Jon in Sumara.

"There's the Ghost," Saewyn said, pointing at Jon, who was a distance from the two of them.

"Ghost? Why Ghost?" she asked.

71

"Just look at him," he replied.

In Sumara's main square, Saewyn nodded toward where Jon was walking toward the Stone Drum. The great fortress doused them in shadow as they huddled behind a wagon wheel. Jon glided along with his fingers woven at the foot of his spine.

"He's so, so pale," Saewyn said. "I hear he burns even in the winter. Isn't that strange?"

Payton shrugged and felt a stab of empathy for Jon. "I'm paler than him."

Saewyn's mouth hung open for a moment. "No, no, not like that. It's just—look at him! He glides around silently, as though his feet never touch the stones. No one ever hears him coming, no one sees him going. He's just a ghost, Payton. Just a fucking ghost."

Jon had vanished into the Drum.

"The tower is the place," Jon stated back in Alaveren, here in the present.

"Look, I understand why you want cover, but I'm not bringing my people into the broken tower," she stated. "It's too crowded. It would be a butcher's den if anything went awry."

"A controlled den."

"Jon, this must be a peace negotiation."

He shrugged. "Never can tell with those scabs."

Scabs. It sounded so foreign and queer on his tongue. A word manufactured to build face.

"I've lost too many men and women to this fight: the king, my father."

"I've lost fathers, too," he snapped, whipping around to face her. His lips twitched, but his eyes were nearly empty save for the shadow of a glint of pain.

The same glint filled his eyes when he entered the screaming cells below Sumara. When he'd materialized from the stairs above, obscured by the darkness, the swinging lantern illuminated his every other step as he slowly, methodically, steadily approached, covered in splashes of red, breathing heavily, eyes wide, but hands steady. He stared at the lead turnkey, the one whose hands were not on Payton, as he stepped forward.

"Ghost," the turnkey shouted. "What the fuck are you doing here? They've taken Tallhart. They're going to hang him."

He hadn't known Jon was involved in the plot to poison Lanair. Fuck, he'd created the plot. They thought it was just Payton and her father. Jon stepped closer.

"Get out of here, Ghost! Lord Lanair will need you!"

Jon stopped beneath the swinging lantern. Calmly, his hand reached upward to stop it from swaying, and when the halo of light caught his hand, streaks of red leaped off it, rivulets of blood crying over his knuckles and palms. It matted his hair and beard and lips. A life had been snuffed out of those beautiful blue sapphires, and a ghost gazed out at the world.

The turnkey recoiled. "What in the name of Mehsa—"

His sword took the turnkey's head off in a blur. Then the four others rushed at him in the narrow corridor. Jon pinned the first to the wall, parried the second, ruined the third's throat, tripped the second into the fourth's sword, ripped open the first's belly, pounced on the fourth, stabbed again and again and again. In the end the fourth's face was gone.

Payton shrunk back in her cell. She watched Jon stretch his neck as if waking from a long sleep. He unlatched the satchel strapped to his back. After fishing around for a moment, his hand produced a flask of water. He tossed it to her. Then he pulled the wooden stool closer to him, sat on it, crossed his leg, lay the blade along it, and began to wipe it clean.

His voice croaked, "Go. There's a tunnel further down. I'll follow."

Payton peered away from the stairs where he'd emerged. He was death embodied. The corridor descended into obscurity, and a cool breeze seemed to come from it.

"My father is dead," she remarked casually, as if assessing the rain.

He didn't look at her or answer her. The lantern turned the red on him to a blackish maroon.

The breeze came again. She followed it. As Payton took the first step down the stairs leading into oblivion, a high whistle filled the stony catacombs

73

hugging her tight on all sides. When she turned around, she saw Jon sitting on a stool, corpses piled all around his feet, whistling to each stroke that mopped the blood from the metal. And though two years had elapsed since that night, Jon remained a tense, caged cat craving the kill.

"Payton."

Jon's voice broke her memory. He continued staring at the broken tower, at its pinnacle.

"Yes?"

"Piper's here."

Payton turned to see her courier, Marc Piper, standing awkwardly behind Jon. The man was like a boy compared to him. Piper bowed his head, but his eyes seemed glued to Jon.

"Lady Tallhart, I have a parcel from the capitol. More ration cards for the men and women."

"Thank you." Piper's hazel eyes kept darting toward Jon at their corners. Jon still gazed at the broken tower. Piper motioned to leave.

"Hold on," Payton commanded.

"My lady?"

"I received a letter today from someone who mentioned several others he'd written. Did you misplace anything meant for me, Marc?"

"No."

An answer given so quickly must've been well prepared.

"Pick your brain a bit, Marc. Nothing?" she said.

"No."

"Must not be much to pick up there." A laugh twitched on his face, jiggling his fleshy neck. "You're dismissed."

"Right. Sorry. Good day," he said with a bow.

As Payton unwrapped the parcel, which contained thousands of stacked ration cards, she noticed Jon's hands were no longer clasped. His left fingers stroked the blue cloth on his sword that she had wrapped for him in the Mire two months earlier, after he'd fallen into the bog and that strange water dissolved the old cloth away, and he'd come out raving about some orb of light beneath the earth. She thought she saw a smile on the man's face.

"Jon."

"Hmm?"

"We'll meet in the broken tower, but only under my conditions."

"What are those?"

"I have total control over the army. I should anyway, seeing as how I'll be in charge following your interim rule. You get two personal guards to enter the throne room with you. Any other legions stay in the field. No one enters or exits the tower until the meeting has concluded. The Harts will surround the entrances to the tower. And I lead the meetings."

Jon clacked his tongue. "Agreed to all, save the last."

"Why?"

"Lanair and I are the leaders of these factions. I took Trowbridge, so I'm in charge for now. It would be improper for you to negotiate when you have no legal authority to do so. Secondly, you're too close with Jem."

"Excuse me? I took back the capitol with you, Jon. The men and women faithful to me outnumber those to you. House Tallhart was always stronger than House Carrow, and closer to the throne."

He smirked, as if amused by her argument. "Fine. You're right, the Red Hart will be queen after this, I suppose."

She cringed; that nickname had emerged from her string of victories, and suddenly Payton Tallhart was replaced in the discourse with this mythic Red Hart.

He continued, "You're still too close with Jem."

"My friendship with Jem might as well have ended eight years ago when my father and I left him near Sumara. I haven't seen him since."

"You sure you don't consider him family?" The ultimate word emanated from his tongue like acid.

"Yes."

Jon frowned. "I have met you on every term but one. I think you have room to compromise."

She reached for the rest of the stale ale and downed it. Tasted like sour water.

He sighed. "Station your retinue outside the throne room. Guard the foyer and the courtyard. Make sure no one enters or exits. Put the Harts at the entrances around the grounds, for all I care. Really, if you'd like to see everyone else keep to this pact, you'd fare better outside the meeting than inside."

"Don't repeat your mistakes from Wellfleet. The scalpel won, not the sledgehammer."

He hissed. "Don't stand here and sling Royce's words at me."

"Your plan would've killed us all."

"Good thing I listened to you."

"You had no choice, Jon. You didn't allow me to follow my plan. You would've knelt, or you would've been knelt."

"Faedelin's left nut, Payton, it's a peace negotiation. No scalpels or sledgehammers necessary, right?"

"'If there were a time for nuance, a time for strength, it is the time of peace, not the time of war,'" she quoted from the Book of Ideals.

Jon snorted. "Leon brought up his little parrot well."

She backhanded him across the face. The slab of rock hardly moved. He swallowed as he stared down his crooked nose at her.

"After all you did to my family, after you threw him to the foxes, you will not speak of my father."

He continued to stare down his nose. Sometimes when a boulder is in a person's way, that person would like to wear it down. The rain hasn't washed it away grain by grain fast enough, so it's tempting to take a great ax to it and chop it away chunk by chunk. Then that person could outlast the boulder. Jon's face was the same way. Sit out in the rain and the wind and the sun with him and another person might just wither away while he drinks it in and translates it into one more line on his face.

"Look, Payton," he said, sighing, "I know more than anyone how stories…metastasize. A golden box becomes a chest of nightmares."

"Meraxes."

He winced. "Meraxes. The necklace of squirrels."

"Jon…"

"I want this to end properly. An ending with finality."

76

Payton's jaw tensed. How to read those eyes like sapphires stripped of their sheen. "Ask anyone here, Jon, they'd say the same. Even Lanair Mavogar. In fact, I received a ledger from Jem stating that they'd like to draw up an accord—a new one—that will end this."

"A letter from Jem, huh?" he said, more suspicious statement than question.

"A short one. It's on my desk if you want to read it. We'll meet tomorrow. But for the treaty they design."

His shoulders slackened. His eyelids slid over his eyes until they met and gently pressed tight.

"Jon, I'm trusting you to handle this meeting. My father once said, 'The world rests at the nadir of a long breath.' That was before he took Sumara in the Reaving, before he stormed the Stone Drum. It's no different now."

"I'm aware. I'll be careful, Payton."

She nodded. "Sign the parchment, go home. Simple as that. Jon, you could be on the verge of proving you're not cloaked in the blood of better men."

He shrugged. "It's not the worst I've heard. Ghost, the Ghost Knight, the Ward Lord, the Bloody Heron; I've got a long list of undesirable titles."

"You had one good one, though. That's all we need."

The beginnings of a grin curled at the edges of his lips. He bowed his head to her and turned to leave. When he reached the flap at the entrance to her pavilion, he dragged his feet to a halt and he observed the ground.

"I contemplate Meraxes and the moment on the bridge. How did she know? Facing down that sea of invaders. Nothing to shield her but four old men and a wooden box. How did she know that they would believe her?" He looked her in the eyes. "All this time I've thought the moment on the bridge showed the power of belief through the invaders' reverence. I was wrong. Meraxes conveyed it. To stand there with four old men and a wooden box. To let the world finish the sentence you've started. That's faith."

Payton nodded at him. "She was a powerful leader."

"And only a farm girl in the end."

With that, he spun around and vanished beyond the flap.

Meraxes. That had always been her favorite story growing up. She loved when Leon would plop her on his knee and read it to her. Meraxes was unlike any other heroine. Not like Princess Ezora, who waited for Prince Talthus to find a way past the firedrake guarding her tower. Not like Serabella, who was Rahhal's sidekick and comic relief. Meraxes reigned. Her word was absolute. She waited on no one to act.

Somewhere in her chest lay buried *Old Braelandish Folklore*, a compilation of the country's oldest folktales. Payton dug through her armor in the chest to find it. She had carried it with her ever since her father had given it to her when she was a girl.

A little brown leather book was tangled in chain mail. She brushed off the cover and flipped it over. Inside, Leon's inscription was fading from the flaking parchment: *To my dearest Payton*, his elegant script read. *Braver than Meraxes, stronger than Serabella, and more beautiful than Ezora. Love, Father.*

She carefully turned the pages to where a corner was folded over. The title read: "The Golden Box and the Farm Girl, or the Box of Meraxes." She lay down on her cot and began to read.

7

The Box of Meraxes

Long ago, there was a farm girl who carried a golden box on the pommel of her saddle so it caught the sun's light as she approached. Men could see the glistening gold in her palms from miles away, and when she reached their gates, the armored guards had already swung open the doors to their city. When she passed between the men flanking her, their heads were hung in humility, but they had seen how beautiful her face was.

Armed soldiers bordered the winding road to the palace, which sat atop three hills. Its columned towers soared to scrape the blue enamel sky and threw long shadow fingers across the plains. When the girl passed under those shadows, she heard the four men riding with her shiver.

At the palace, a fat man stood in front of closed doors. A scraggly beard draped over his round belly. The girl thought that he must wear it so long as to cover his collection of chins. She passed into a pocket of light in the courtyard. The fat man recoiled as the box awakened with a rush of sunlight.

"I am Meraxes," the girl proclaimed, "and I would have a hearing with your king."

Hand protecting his eyes, the fat man spoke. "My king will not hear words from a poor farm girl. And he will not deal with witches."

"I am no witch. I come from a farm miles north, and though it is part of this domain, the king has neglected us for years."

"If you are no witch, how did a poor farm girl come across a golden box like that?"

The men gathered in the shadows that fringed the courtyard tensed up and shuffled a few steps away from the girl. She did not look at these frightened men, but kept her gaze level with that of the fat man, who had to look up at her in the saddle. Meraxes held the box above her head.

"A river spirit gave this box to me," she shouted so all the men in the courtyard and beyond could hear. "She said to me, 'Your king is wicked, and so I will pour all his wickedness and his hate into a box, and within that box they will become plagues and nightmares. If you open the box, these plagues will pour forth, and they will kill the king and any man who remains loyal to him.'"

A great quiet fell across the city, and not even the wind dared to break it.

"This box would give me what I desire," Meraxes declared.

"And what do you desire, Lady Meraxes?"

"The lands of your king, which he has malnourished with neglect. The throne of your despot, which he has defiled with wickedness. The crown of your tyrant, which he has blighted with evil thoughts."

The fat man tightened his mouth and planted his hands on his hips. "A river spirit would not usurp our mighty king. Show me this box."

The girl flipped the golden latch. Before she opened the lid, the men in the courtyard began crying and prostrated themselves on the stones of the ground and begged her not to open her golden box. Soldiers threw down their spears and swords at her feet. An old man limped out of the gathering crowd and rested his papery hand on her horse's neck.

"Girl," he said in a voice like a whisper, "I am old, but look around you. There are many men here and many children and women who have not seen all the moons that the great river spirit has promised them. Take your hands off the box. Let us speak with this king, and we might find a way to save the lives of these innocents."

The girl nodded and flicked the latch closed. With the old man's hand on the neck of her horse, she trotted into the palace, past the fat man, who had fallen on his face.

At the far end of the great hall sat the king, an aged man in poor health. Many guards who had their spears leveled toward Meraxes surrounded him. The great crowd flooded into the hall after the girl and her four attendants. The thousands of eyes in that room never left the golden box on her pommel.

"King, I have come to have an attendance with you," Meraxes announced. "I come from a river town north of here that remains on the maps in this kingdom, but has been stricken from its memories. We starve, we thirst, we die, but we wish to live, dream of drink, hunger for food. A great river spirit that has kept us alive awoke one night and came to me." Meraxes recounted the river spirit's omen.

The king rubbed his chin, a firm milky knob blanketed in gray hair. His dull eyes panned up from the box to meet the girl's eyes. Then he cleared his throat.

"We have no river spirits here in my city. I have not seen a one since I was a boy and playing in my village."

"They are alive where the world has forgotten."

The king coughed. "I will not be supplanted by a poor farm girl, for my soul is not strong enough to bear the burden of that shame. Leave now, and I will not dress my city with your head."

Meraxes lifted the box higher toward the emeralds and rubies dotting the vaulted ceiling. "Look here, King. This box is a chalice of your own wickedness, and if I open it those plagues will strike dead every man who follows you."

"Enough of this!" the king shouted. He snapped his fingers. A soldier hurled a spear at her, but it missed and struck a pillar behind her.

"King, look at your terrors!" Meraxes opened the latch again, but at that moment, the king cried out as he clutched his chest. The crowd gasped, and his soldiers backed away. He stumbled down the dais from his throne and fell on his face, still grabbing at his heart.

A soldier knelt beside the king and placed a hand on his neck. He stood and proclaimed to the great hall, "Our king has died. His heart has failed under the burden of his evils. Bow to the Queen Meraxes, who has saved us from his great wickedness!"

One by one, the men in the hall dropped to their knees and bowed in front of the queen. "Hail the queen, bow to Meraxes!" the soldier shouted. He walked to her and lifted up his sword. "It is yours, my queen."

The four attendants helped Meraxes down from her horse and guided her to the throne. She stepped over the dead king who clutched his failed heart. The queen looked over her new kingdom, and everyone in the hall remained kneeling.

"Stand, for I am not wicked like your king, and I will not malnourish you like he did. I will be a just queen, for that is why the river spirit came to me that night in the north. Stand."

And they stood.

The queen ruled for thirty years, and there was peace in the kingdom. She gave birth to three sons and three daughters, but her favorite was Tomas, who was her youngest. And although he was her youngest, she wanted him to rule when she died.

When Tomas was nine years old, a great invasion came to his mother's doorstep. The army was greatly numbered and dwarfed the queen's forces. He looked out at the field before his mother's city, where a great sea of spears had followed the tide to the city's doors.

Atop the city gates, Tomas watched his mother ride out with four aging attendants. The great host of her army remained hidden within the city. She led the men to the middle of the bridge that connected her city to the land beyond, and in her hands something caught the sunlight.

"Infidels!" she shouted so that men could hear her from far away. "Behold the Golden Box!"

His mother thrust a small box cast in ornate gold toward the sky. Its glittering light forced Tomas to hide his eyes. He had never seen the box or something so bright.

"You have come on my lands, burned my crops, killed my people, and threatened my family. You have no right to this place. I was given this city by a great spirit, who forged this box from beyond this world and flooded it with the evils that drive your army now! Should I open this box, horrible plagues would rush forth and exterminate every man who holds a sword in your name.

"Back away now, and return to the forsaken lands you hail from, and I, too, shall return to my home and store away the Golden Box. For many men of your army have not seen all the moons that the great river spirit has promised them, and I would not steal those moons away. Tempt me, and I will unleash the plagues and nightmares from the Golden Box and you will bleed out your eyes and vomit out your souls and melt like wax beneath the sun."

The commander of the usurpers curiously eyed the box. He rubbed his chin and waved his guards back. Then he walked forward to Meraxes.

"Queen," he said, "why have you not brought this box forth before, when I ravaged your shores and pillaged your fields?"

"The river spirit cannot stop every evil deed. Men die and villages burn. The retreating tide steals grains of sand from the shore and drowns them beneath the sea. Not I, not the great river spirit, not anyone can stop every tragic thing from passing. But the river spirit can stop some evil. I shall not die, and my city shall not burn."

Tomas peered over the precipice of the city wall once more. His mother's voice carried far over the field and high into the sky. It was at once warm and cold, reassuring and commanding. She looked small surrounded by four aging attendants and a sea of invaders.

"Back away now, commander. You have no battle with the river spirit. Your power is no power in the face of hers."

The man broke into a charge toward Meraxes as she lifted the latch to the Golden Box. Just as she reached to fling the box open, a soldier in the commander's army fired an arrow into his commander's throat so he could speak no more, and the commander fell on his face at the queen's feet, for this man in the army was wise and feared Queen Meraxes.

The great army dispersed before the queen. Soon the fields were cleared out, and the whispering grain stretched for the setting sun to catch a final breath before the long night.

That night, Tomas snuck into his mother's room as she was changing. Her dress was up over her face so that she could not see him, but he saw a long scar across her stomach that sagged down and was wrinkled and purple like a worm. Her breasts were worn and flattened. Then her dress fell and revealed her beautiful face, which was shocked.

"Tomas!" she said. "Come here now."

The boy came to her and sat in her lap. She told the boy never to walk in on a woman while she was changing, for that would steal all her secrets from her without giving her a fair chance to keep them. He promised her would never do it again.

"Mother, where did you get that box of nightmares?"

Meraxes sighed. "Son, one day you will be king, and you must know how this kingdom was built. That box came from our ancestors long ago, and it holds secrets that not even the strongest people know of. One day you will hold this box, and you will defend our kingdom with it." She kissed her boy on the forehead. "Never open it. It would unravel our kingdom."

The queen moved her boy onto her mattress beside her, and she lay down and closed her eyes.

Long after his mother had fallen asleep, the boy slid out of bed and crept over to the great desk where his mother sat during the day. Deep within the drawers he found the Golden Box that his mother had used to defeat the great army. Curious, he thumbed the golden latch, which shimmered in the bar of moonlight that fell across the room.

Tomas flicked up the latch and flung open the lid. The box was empty.

8

Arm's Length

Jon thought it was a good rule for all men to follow, since it cut down on the hurt, it shed the pain, and it kept them there out of reach. Don't let them in. Don't let anyone in: not Dinian, not Payton, not Lanair. They all weaseled in. Now he's alone. His only friend is that rope. Keep them all out, all away, keep them there at arm's length.

He kept Iayn Darrion, the Hero Knight of the North, at arm's length as he prowled after Jon in Alaveren. It was during the War in the Narrows, which raged all around like a tempest. But that tempest was only the down-draft before a maelstrom. The War in the Narrows was nothing next to the Reaving, when Jon wore the Red Hook on his breast, but his heart was back with the North after the torture the South put him through. Only he found it was too late. No one saw him as the heron of House Carrow, but as the bloody heron, the Ghost, the Ghost Knight. All titles cloaked in the blood of better men like Iayn Darrion, who came at Jon with chaos eyes.

Those chaos eyes yanked Jon back, back, back. He couldn't stop it. He shouldn't have gone to talk with Payton. He should've known she'd exhume these bothersome cadavers and then he'd spend the oncoming dusk in their presence rather than focusing on the thing that must be done tomorrow with that fool Jasin who'd be the key in his plan. But those things melted.

The city was nowhere, though it was everywhere. Jon skulked through it away from Payton's pavilion. Those chaos eyes yanked him backbackback to the same city entrenched in a different dispute over the same book some fifteen years ago.

Darrion came at him but his eyes didn't look at Jon. They burned at him. Jon couldn't be sure if those embers wanted to incinerate him or drag him to the depths of their wells to drown him.

Jon stopped and cupped his head in his palms, and passersby paused to observe their enigmatic uncertain leader once he looked up. He hurried onward.

The blade whirled around Jon and cut through the air, blowing kisses to his shoulders. How could an old man move so fast? It was the rush of the moment, the spirit of his followers.

He really shouldn't let these things come back. Jon strived so hard and so long to keep it buried. But chaos eyes were nuisances. They did not like to stay dead.

The soil was soft in the Holy City since it had soaked up too much blood. How much blood, he wondered, for more than three hundred years, blood after blood after blood and all because one brother didn't pick another brother up after he fell from the apple tree. Then that blood circled that tree and choked it to death with a coppery taste.

"Stop, stop, stop!" he shouted. More soldiers edged away from him as he shouted at the empty air.

Darrion came at Jon, a boy of eighteen with fuzz on his chin and no purple worms crawling on his chest yet. But those scars would come, even though he had killed Darrion.

Jon made it back to his campsite. Coyle wasn't there. Jon stepped down to the riverside. The water lapped lazily over the hump of his boots. Mimicking the water over the boot, Jon's memories flooded over him.

Darrion came at him, a boy of eighteen with fuzz on his chin, and he was petrified.

Boy, he said to Jon. What have we come to?

The Hero Knight whom Jon killed had earned his title in the deep winter forty years ago, when he smuggled food into a besieged city to feed its common folk while a Sumaran army licked its lips at the city's gates, but that didn't stop him. Then he snuck into the commander's tent and slit his throat and lit the two torches that alerted the cavalry. The horses stampeded the invaders, liberated the city, and King Willem the Strong named him Sir Iayn Darrion, the Hero Knight of the North. A true hero, not like Prince Talthus or Rahhal or Mossan of the stories. He was a good man. A good hero.

Jon killed Iayn Darrion, the Hero Knight of the North.

But not at first he didn't. He lured Darrion away from the furor, from the madness, from the ashes of the bridge that Jon was supposed to build. Jon led him away from the ashes up a hill, where the cobbles met the mud, into the shadows of the city. Darrion followed Jon into a narrow alley where both of them turned to the side because they were so broad, and those embers in his chaos eyes were dying now, quashed by the waters in their wells.

He stopped lunging at Jon with the sword. He stopped edging along the narrow alley to catch his breath. He mopped the gray strands of his hair, his sword at the ready, but he wouldn't swing at Jon. He backed along, drawing Darrion deeper into the shadows like the black heron stamped on his forearm, ready for some shadow feeding. Jon held his sword at arm's length. Not yet. Jon was luring him away.

Jon, how did we come to this? the Hero Knight asked. Jon, my boy, how and why and why and why? the knight cried.

Darrion didn't look at Jon, as if once the embers in his chaos eyes died they had no strength to meet another pair. He put a hand on the side of the alley.

I thought this was supposed to end, he breathed. I hoped you going south would be the end, but I guess hope is a fool's errand. Isn't that what Minaerva Royce is always droning on about?

Darrion panted like a dog after a jog along the beach. He said, Sometimes I wonder about us, Jon. I wonder why we do this to ourselves. You know, I heard Mehsani once said the world turns to fling us off, so why should we drive each other away? A brother should lend a hand to a brother, a sister to a sister.

There was clatter at the end of the alley like a drunken orchestra banging on pans with knives. And yet for some reason, Jon led Darrion at arm's length toward the end, toward the drunken orchestra of the knives.

You know, I wonder what I would've thought of Mehsani if I looked him in the eyes, Darrion wondered. They say he brewed the first fire ale. You know I love that drink. Nothing warms you quite like it on a cold night in the capitol. I wonder what I would've thought of Mehsani if I could've looked him in his eyes.

The knives grew louder, drew closer, voices cried out for Mehsani. They were near.

What would the Mehsanics think? They would see a hero and a ghost conspiring in the alley.

For fuck's sake, I might've loved the man, Darrion admitted.

Jon drew him out of the alley with his back to the rush of sunlight, and the Mehsanics were gathered there in the street like lions over conquered prey. Then Iayn Darrion, the Hero Knight of the North, followed Jon out where the sun blinded him, so his hands went up to cover his eyes, and Jon lunged forward. The blade took him through the heart. Jon could feel the last feeble pumps that pulsed on the cold metal as the knight slumped to his back with his hands still hiding his eyes like dead embers at the bottom of a well.

Back in the real, here in the present, Jon dropped to his knees. They plopped into the flow of the river. Tears slid off his cheeks and joined the fresh water below.

The Mehsanic shepherds loved the young Jon for a moment in the rush of Darrion's fall when Northern blood stained the rocks of Alaveren, for it was a moment of catharsis, of triumph, of parading over the corpses of dead Northern sons. The Northern sons Jon was supposed to help. That's what Tomathy Carrow said. The North needs a hero, Jon, the North needs you to reconnect the North and the South, and Carrow boys are brave boys, Jon. Then he snatched the surname Carrow from Jon, and his father kicked him out of the house of the heron and stripped Jon of its name so he could enter the house of the fox. House Mavogar. But Jon was never a fox, as Lord Mavogar proved, so he could never truly settle into House Mavogar. And he was never a shepherd, so he could never truly settle into Sumara or the South. And he was never a heron, so he couldn't return to House Carrow or the North. He was just a fucking ghost who wandered through his days floating outside of himself, watching a stranger glide through the world, incapable to stick down his feet. Despite wrestling with Lanair, riding with Lanair, laughing with Lanair, Jon could never stand side by side with Lanair. Then the necklace of squirrels ignited a glint of contempt, which livened Lanair's glare like when a match is put to a pipe. It was that first spark of hate that burns so bright, then malignantly eats away at the tobacco. It spread just like that word "ghost" on everyone's tongue when they took the name Jon from him, so he was no longer Jon or Carrow, he was just a fucking ghost. Why didn't they just kill him? Why did they lock him in the dark room and strap him down and mutilate him? Easier to just kill but they wouldn't, and then he killed Iayn Darrion, the Hero Knight of the North, and they loved him. The shepherds of Mehsani and foxes of Mavogar gathered around Jon to clap him on the back and to say, "Good job."

It was a far cry from the night before the War in the Narrows started, and Lanair came into Jon's chambers with a mind clouded by the confusion of squirrels and foxes.

Lanair snarled at Jon, When we ride north to the Narrows and Leon Tallhart and Tomathy Carrow swoop in to kill us, who will tell heron from heron in the madness? Who can say which bird will get its wings clipped? Lanair taunted.

Had it already been five years since the day of the squirrels and the fox? That was the day Lanair never looked at Jon the same way again. He wished that anyone could strip the heron tattoo on his forearm away. The young man prayed every night to Mehsani just to prove that he was a good shepherd, that he was a fox who belonged with the Mavogars and the ink on his arm was a mistake and it was the squirrels that the fox had been after, not Jon, because he was a fox and a shepherd.

But Lanair continued:

My father says that Carrow men are burning our crops, trying to starve us out, and the orders come from Tomathy. Tsk, tsk. Who will tell heron from heron?

He had Jon's forearm in his grasp so his nails bit into the inky bird. It was then Jon wished he could fade away like a genuine ghost through the walls or beneath the floor. He wanted to vanish. Why had it been so important to prove it was a fox's pelt wrapped around his heart not the feathers of a heron?

Then the War in the Narrows ended, but it didn't end. It merely scabbed over. So the North called them all filthy fucking scabs because the South kept picking at the North's wounds so the wounds couldn't heal, so the scabs broke them open. Seven years later, the spat became the Reaving. Jon turned twenty-five the night it began, when Leon wandered too far down the Narrows, fired the wrong arrow, ignited the Reaving. All the fight left him. Jon couldn't spill blood in the name of Mehsani anymore because of how far the Southerners had driven him from the realms of sanity. Yet the land was falling apart, so who would notice the Ghost Knight as he snuck around scheming?

The Radiant Knight, Alaryn corrected Jon shortly after the War in the Narrows.

What?

That's right, they call you the Radiant Knight, his true father explained.

Why? Jon asked.

Because you're a hero. You cut down Sir Darrion when he could've slain countless Southern sons.

His eyes were blinded. He couldn't even see, Jon admitted.

My son, they call you the Radiant Knight, Alaryn repeated.

But Lanair hates me. I see it burning in his eyes all the time. They all call me the Ghost.

I don't, Alaryn pointed out.

Only you, Dad.

The old man sighed. Jon, have you ever heard of Meraxes?

Yes. Well, only a bit.

She was a genius. She knew faith and the power of it to make men kneel. You know what was in her box, right?

Nothing.

No, it was everything, he retorted.

What do you mean?

Men had to see only the exterior gold before they filled the simple wooden interior with their hearts and souls and minds. Meraxes had them in an inescapable snare after that because they believed in the river spirit and they believed in the nightmares, so they believed in the Golden Box. It didn't matter that nothing was inside because they had already put everything inside.

The Radiant Knight, Jon echoed.

You like it, don't you?

Yes, the young man admitted.

Those are the three words on the tip of every common tongue. So Lanair won't dare kill you or have you killed because inside your golden box shines a knight so radiant he could blot out the sun.

The Radiant Knight.

I love you, son, Alaryn said.

I love you, Dad.

Alaryn's hand on Jon's shoulder was warmer than any hug Tomathy had donated to him and warmer than any smile Lanair had given him before the squirrels and the fox.

Alaryn Tanogar was a man of the sea. A man who hated land because it stayed the same no matter the myriad of years that had passed after you'd seen it last. Damn it, a rock is a rock is a rock, but the sea moves. It's easier to hide, to get lost, to get free.

He was a man who never had a child because the waves make poor mothers, so he took Jon in. The boy who was a bastard orphan in the house of Mehsani. An adopted burden on the hands of Mavogar, who stared down his nose at Jon and frowned even as he tried to be welcoming. But not Alaryn, who was warmer than anyone and gave Jon the warmest words but for his last word.

Arm's length.

Fourteen years following, Jon scooped up a pebble from the riverbank. Oh, how he'd love to wrap these memories like parcels in a basket and send them afloat in the river so they would drift away. Maybe before the basket of memory parcels vanished, he would light an arrow to set the basket alight and give his memories an unalterable finale. Instead, he flicked the pebble into the flow. Like the pebble, he, too, sank under the flow.

A year after Alaryn comforted Jon, there was poisoned wine that killed Lord Mavogar in a few days, though he was a strong man. His muscles began bowing to the earth but held their general shape. Then he was gone, snuffed out by wine, and every eye pinned to Jon.

The Ghost.

The Northern son.

The infidel.

Who knew ghosts bleed? the Sumarans taunted. Within hours of Lord Mavogar's death, the shepherds of Mehsani had arrested him and threw him in the dungeons.

They joked at Jon as he hung in chains. They lacerated his chest and shaved away a nipple. The purple-and-white worms appeared in the soil of his chest and his stomach and his back. All places you couldn't see beneath the armor of the Radiant Knight.

The whips crisscrossed Jon's body everywhere, then they grabbed his cock and balls and pressed a rusty sword to them until he pissed and shat everywhere. Jon was covered in his own piss and shit, and they were laughing above him.

Who knew ghosts bleed?

The dark room was the worst. After a day of hanging in chains naked so they could whip him everywhere then take him down just to fold Jon up in a room as small as a fucking cupboard at night. The hot sweltering baking humid fucking hot as fuck night with his head stuffed in his knees cramps swelling in his neck his back his hips everywhere cramping everywhere sweating couldn't breathe couldn't think. He just couldn't.

The dark room always crept back.

When Lanair found Jon in the dark room, he feigned horror. Stop, you fools, I never said to do this! he cried.

But my lord, he poisoned your father, they replied.

No, it was a rebel. He's innocent by Mehsani's Light. Clean him up. Jon, I'm so sorry. I never meant this. Can you hear me? I'm sorry. You will be cleaned up, the liar promised.

Where were you? a ghost moaned.

He returned no words. He got up and left as they dragged Jon back out of the dungeon. Jon didn't think he'd ever walk again. Piss still dribbled down his carved-up legs.

He'd go back to the dark room at the recollection of that name, La-nair. That's why Jon thought of the name as a brief uplifting syllable and a dangerous suffix. You could be friends with "Lah," but then that menacing suffix "nair" that stabs ice into your heart and forces your head between your knees and locks the dark room and leaves you to sweat to cramp to suffocate.

Lanair was a friendly syllable followed by a stab of ice.

There would be a special providence in the heron's fall from the sky, and its name would be Lanair.

Jon followed the sky the way north with Payton at his side keeping them going. It was after he had to flee Sumara. The promise to Leon Tallhart the need to keep her safe he had to keep her safe. He would've given anything to just

d

r

o

p

and he could feel the tangible, vertical plummet in his belly and he could see himself falling and he knew he couldn't stop the drop. But he had to stay strong and keep his eye leveled on the horizon. Outpace the shepherds. Outpace the foxes. Outpace everything, everyone, let them see how hard it was to kill a ghost.

Payton stayed by Jon's side. She had no idea where to run and no idea which way was north south up down. Jon had to see her through, had to get her back. She'd die without him, and he couldn't bear the loss of another friend. He stayed strong. He saw her through.

Jon camped with her in hidden groves and back-country ruins. Glaring beyond the fire, she hissed like the smoke coming off the logs.

You're just a knight cloaked in the blood of better men, she declared. You're nothing like my father, nothing like Sir Darrion.

How thirteen years had melted away since Jon killed Darrion he still couldn't say. Once, he was eighteen and the Radiant Knight, then he was nineteen and locked in the dark room. Then he was thirty and whipped in his sleep with rocks and then he was thirty-one, racing away from the closest thing to home and a father he'd come to know.

No, I'm nothing like those men. I'm just a fucking ghost, Jon moaned.

Shut up. I didn't ask you to speak, Payton said. I didn't give you the permission to have a fucking pity party for yourself. My father's dead, my house in shambles.

I'll take you back, he promised.

She rounded the flame to press a knife to his throat's apple.

I'm taking us back, not you. You've done enough, she snarled.

Jon loved those orange curls. Not love like he felt for Dinian his boy, not the love for Alaryn his father, or for dancing with his sword, or for hunting with Lanair when they used to wrestle by the sea. Jon's love for her was a comforting love. The love from a brother to a sister.

She went to bed, but he couldn't go to bed easily anymore because the cords might tether him and he never could tell when they'd come. He didn't want to sleep because he couldn't bear to hear them chant, "Fraternizer, conspirator, traitor, ghost," and if he did sleep, he'd have no control over whether or not they'd come. Then the dark room was too fucking small, too fucking tight, for fuck's sake the room would swallow him up again if he wasn't careful. So he left.

The cold was better. Jon liked the outdoors where there were no cords, no whips, just him and the night that stretched endlessly upward into a velvety blanket at once infinite and intimate.

As he looked up at those stars, breath puffing into the night beneath the pale glow of lanterns in whatever town they were in at that point, Jon thought about those stars. The great fish and the sparkling fairy and the pouncing lion. Lanair was probably looking at those same stars far away in the South, where they were the Red Hook and the Calidumi rogue and the sleeping bear. But they were the same fucking stars. The same fucking stars, no matter a fish, a hook, a rogue, a fairy, a bear, or a lion. The same fucking stars.

Night after night, fire after fire, he trudged on with Payton. Why though? There was not even a promise of redemption since he slew Northern sons and his title was cloaked in the blood of better men. That was Jon's price. To serve in Sumara and dismantle the regime to prevent another Reaving, but here they were in yet another fucking Reaving.

Payton, Jon said.

Yes? she replied.

I'm sorry I couldn't help your father.

She let a brutal silence take hold.

Payton, you know I couldn't do anything, he pleaded, my hands were tied. Mehsani's ass, what the fuck do you want me to say?

Payton snapped, I want you to stop saying "Mehsani" before you get both of us beheaded. We're not in Sumara anymore, fool. You say that in the university, your head'll look out over the lake.

Your father was a good man.

I know, she said.

I'm sorry.

Her gaze pierced him worse than that sword at her side could.

What happened? she interrogated him.

It was the boy, Jon admitted. He found a letter I wrote to your father. He told Alaryn. He was frightened.

Oh, Dinian.

He's fine.

What do you know of it? The way you spoke to that boy like a wooden figurine. Oh, um, ah, yes, um, stumbling over your words like a schoolboy over Royce. What kind of father were you?

I saved that boy's life! Jon cried.

What a life you gave him.

Fine! I wasn't your fucking father! I wasn't Leon fucking Tallhart. But I saved him.

A short spell let a few breezes flatten the fire.

I was the fool, he said eventually, I shouldn't have trusted the boy with the letter, and it was my fault. I shouldn't have trusted the boy.

Her hand knocked Jon off the log. She towered over him like a column of alabaster, immovable and immensely strong, steady, steadfast, crowned in a halo of fire.

Dinian. Not the boy, she said.

Payton sat just across the fire from him, but she was good right there where the fires staved off the hurt. She was good right there where she couldn't see the hurt.

Arm's fucking length.

9

Grains

Rocks last. They're built that way. They sit under the sun and rain and wind, but years later there they are still braving the outdoors. If a little sheen fades, that's fine. Rocks are still solid beneath their weathered faces. But if you find the right spot, the right grain, the hardest rocks fracture.

Jon studied the pebble, tossing it up and down, up and down. It was gray and rough and plain. He clacked his teeth and flung it in a high arc over the river and turned around to find Marc Piper shuffling his feet up the slope near where Jon wanted more than anything to fall down and take a nap before the night came on. The pebble plopped once it hit the river.

"My lord," Piper began.

"Do you have Nalda's letter?"

The courier's jaw tensed. "She nearly saw, my lord. I took it yesterday, and I still can't look her in the eyes. I don't want to keep doing this."

Jon frowned. "Don't act like you've done your duty and want out after a job well done. Nalda managed to get a letter to her earlier today. Piss-poor work, Piper."

As Jon walked up the hill Piper shuffled a few steps behind. Jon ignored him. Some men took to him. Coyle did. Once Jon saved him from Payton's executioner that had been it for Coyle. Others backed away from him because they took him as a shepherd, a fox, or both.

Piper's muddy, dirty boots bordered the blanket that Jon had laid out earlier so he could fall down and pray, just pray, that sleep would take him. He thrust a finger at Piper's feet. "That's where I sleep, Piper. Mind your step."

"I'm sorry, my lord. Look, I can't do this anymore."

"Okay. I'll just have to tell Lady Tallhart about what you did after she took Wellfleet. She's a woman. She won't take kindly to what you did. Our contract ends tomorrow. Then you're off the hook."

Swallowing a retort, Piper extended a hand holding a letter. Jon took it. Then he snapped his fingers. "Run along."

Stuffing another retort down his froggish throat, Piper whisked himself away to the north along the river where Jon had visited Payton.

Fingering the letter's edge, Jon reflected that too many of these people concealed retorts they'd love to fling his way. Though that had played out in his favor three nights ago when Jasin caught his glance across a crowded tavern. Something before Jasin's retort intoxicated Jon. His bold and dangerous lashes were conspicuous even in the dim tavern air. An effortless beauty as if inborn like shivering in the cold.

Jon told Coyle to wait by the door. He took the stool next to the man with malachite irises. The man shifted at Jon's arrival.

"How would you like to be of service to your lord?" Jon began.

"The fuck are you?" mumbled the man who was Jasin. It came off of breath worse than Coyle's. What a waste of physique.

"I'm Jon Carrow."

"And I'm Faedelin's left nut." Jasin added a flatulent flap of his tongue.

"You don't believe me?"

Jasin sized Jon up. "If you are, you're nothin' but a turncoat scab."

Jon observed Jasin's malachite eyes ringed by handsome lashes. The man tried to ignore his lord, who stared intensely in his periphery. Finally, he slammed the counter.

"You lookin' for this?" Jasin grabbed his nethers. "Go across the river. Hear Mavogar's a regular fairy."

Jon laughed. "Clearly you misunderstand your situation. I hear you've shown great bravery. Eleven Mehsanics in the river by your hand. Hard to defeat just one."

Jasin lifted a toast. "I piss on Mehsani and his degenerate spawn." Cheers emanated from eavesdroppers.

"Here, here," Jon said, tapping the bar. "You're just the man, Jasin."

"For wha?"

"To be our sentinel."

"Wha?"

"I need a man, a brave one like yourself, to play a part at the right moment," Jon explained. He orbited his thumbs around each other as he spoke. "I think I'm about to find the grain to crack Mehsani's rock."

"Huh? You're drunker than me, man."

Jon laughed again. Refreshing to laugh, even during bitter days. "It's okay, Jasin. You don't need to comprehend it right now. Be ready when I call for you. Oh, and make that armor shine for all to see."

An eyebrow arched. "Why should I make it shine?"

"Make it shine, make it shine," Jon answered. He slid off his stool and towered over Jasin.

"Why?"

"Make the damn thing shine so the hosts of Braeland, the defenders of our country, can see your bravery," he commanded.

"Why me?" Jasin questioned him.

"Because the North needs a hero, Jasin," he insisted, "and you're just the man." Those malachite eyes would be the germ of many songs. "Make it shine and be gone. Yes?"

"Yes."

"Excuse me?"

"Yes, my lord," Jasin added reluctantly.

Jon whisked himself from the crowded counter before Jasin's confounded expression could materialize into questions. He nodded to Coyle, who followed him into the cold of night and back to his campsite, where he began a fire.

Now three nights hence, the fire was beginning to die. Jon sat down to poke at it with his sword, holding it tight where the blue-sapphire cloth that Payton had wrapped around it streaked between his fingers. A second rush aroused the flames. Jon wondered how long he could stare at them before he would go blind. Not long. Especially with sight so poor to begin with. My lord. He could barely see across the camp.

Thumbing the red wax, which was drawn out like a spider's legs, Jon ran his tongue along his lips. His trimmed nail cut the wax and popped the letter open.

To Payton,

> *I'm not sure if my letters are reaching you. I'm beginning to wonder about this courier you've been sending. He's a wreck of nerves. If this letter receives no response by midday, I'll send another by a different runner.*
>
> *Lanair wants to end this dispute and send us all home. He's grown tired of it. He can't stand to hear the reverence on everyone's tongue this side of the river, that he's the last drop of Mehsani's blood, and on and on. He wants it over. So do I.*
>
> *I know we have fought this week, this year, and in many ways, forever. I know it's strange to be on that side of the river while I stand on this side. So much has grown strange. But you are my family, Payt. That will never change.*
>
> *With love,*
> *Jem*

Mm, mm, my, my. There's the grain. That'll be the grain that irrevocably shatters Mehsani's rock. So Lanair truly was the last drop of blood that kept this silly fight going. That'd harden the resolve of Jon's freshly minted followers and frame his own plans a few shades more brightly for those who might scorn him otherwise. He'd have to thank Jem for this fortuitous letter and for the trust he'd wasted on Payton's courier.

Funny how a letter had opened his golden box, too. Showed the people that their Radiant Knight was just a fucking ghost.

Jon realized he'd been crumpling the edges of the letter before his eyes had made it to Jem's salutation. The man had called Payton family in the letter. He'd had a feeling he shouldn't have trusted them.

Family. A word so queer it might as well belong to Old Calidumi and its harsh consonants. A word so insidious it held up a mirror and focused on the void around Jon's shoulder where a tender hand should rest. A word so illuminating it finally dawned on him that he and she were too close, too secret, too dangerous. His thumb kept rubbing the word over and over and over until the ink smudged so it streaked across the page like a black comet. His fist balled up and crunched the letter. When it hit the flames, it did so with a pop.

Frowning, Jon thought about Jasin. His frown began to wane. Maybe right now Jasin would be drinking and celebrating and fornicating and not thinking about tomorrow. Good. He shouldn't. Jon preferred them ignorant. Only he knew what was going to happen, what had to happen.

The death of a hero. In the beginning, it was; in the end, it shall be.

And this man Jon had found would be the perfect hero. His malachite eyes, his pretty face and stunning jaw—these were the morsels that amounted to a hero. His memory shall inspire so many. And I found him, Jon reflected.

He grabbed a stick from the ground, turned his eyes to the fire, and stoked the flames. The fire had been softly dying underneath the whisper of the wind. His eyes emptied into the spears of fire, licking up and up and up. He prodded the logs. Fire lashed out at his knuckles. Jon recoiled silently. Not even the licking flames could melt the frown off his face.

Hidden within the flames was the letter, crumpled and blackened like a squashed spider on its back that had shriveled up to die. First, the edges charred, then the body. It made a popping sound as it burned. The letter and the word folded into themselves and vanished into the fire like a dying spider.

10

The Point Between the Pines

I remember our first night behind the four posts and carmine curtains. When Lanair came in after the gates at Wilbraema were down, I was still in the library stacks handing out food to the people hiding there. They'd been so scared of the Northern soldiers at our doors. Thought they were really wolves underneath. I knew better. I know about wolves. Following the battle at Wilbraema, beyond our walls were the snapped backs of banners from the North: hart for Tallhart, heron for Carrow, fist for Greyford. Then there was the Red Fox of Mavogar. Just under the fox sagged the Red Hook. It burned the same. Then Lanair came in, his first victory since calling for Leon Tallhart's head, an expression so hopelessly tired and exuberant. I'd come to know that duality and catch the hairsbreadth separating them; so intent on conquering him they were indistinguishable at times. That night in Wilbraema the exuberance took a stand. Mavogar toppled Greyford, Carrow, and Tallhart. Of course, no one by those names was there, save for Lanair. Payton and Jon were still on their dogged flight north, as I'd find out, while King Gareth huddled in the

University at Trowbridge. Lanair alone stood. So he's stood these past six days. He and I still spend our nights behind the posts and curtains, the wood and thread, the hue of Mehsani's Hook. Every night since has been as our first: fingers snaked together, him on top of me, and Lanair's toes dancing their happy horizontal dance beneath me in the red shroud.

There's a place within the shroud I call the point between the pines. Old Gran mentioned it once to me, when I was young and growing up on Calidum; then it was Minaerva on the island in the teardrop. Within all forests, shrouds, posts, a point exists. The place is where you get stranded and mired in endless refrain, like circling the shore of a deep sea island. "What's a forest but an island without a tide?" as Minaerva would ask. When you can't see beyond the trunks, thick and endless, so that nothing except for their cool shade and the twigs snapping under your feet remain. The point between my pines was cheek-deep in rough, sweaty pillows, my mind stripped of the doldrums beyond the opaque curtains.

Not all refrains require lamentation.

Beyond the curtains the eyes go to my gnarled stump. I forget it's there until someone else's stare feigns a startled deer. The looks never stop. Fuck the wolf. Hope he choked on one of my fingers. I wish the stares would stop. Then it hit me one morning; maybe they're looking at me, just me, coming out from the room. Like I'm some wicked imp out of Old Gran's storybooks.

I haven't thought about Old Gran in quite a while. She's the one who gave me my name. Well, she gave me Jem. Father gave me Jaremy. But no one calls me that anymore.

"Now what did I tell you, Jaremy Nalda? You keep playing swords like that, folks will talk," she told me sternly, wagging a fat sausage of a finger in my face.

"Oh, Gran, no one cares about that. And if they do," I said, drawing a paper sword, "I'll beat an apology out of them!" I used to wave that sword (in my right hand, when I still had it) at everything. The best was the Nefarious Iceman. Payt always had such an imagination.

But Gran sighed and said, "What a gem you turned out to be."

In the old stories, names were everything. Take Faedelin. When he changed his name, he knew it would have to be something that generations looked back upon and remembered him for. He could've chosen something that just means "leader," but he picked the word for "faithful one." Payt and I used to joke that he was high when he wrote the Way. Not many people know they had laughingroot three hundred years ago, but they did. I've heard Faedelin smoked bushels of it.

"What are you thinking about?" Lanair's voice severs my train of thought.

"Hm?"

"What are you thinking about? Your eyes are darting around like drunk compasses."

Lanair strokes my chest. We lounge beneath a cherry tree a mile west of the camp in Alaveren. If we were standing on the other side of this hill, where our guards were eating, we could see the Holy City reaching for Mehsani and Faedelin in their cloudy realm with myriad broken and sharp towers. The Narrows rise up all around us, gray misty mountains sloping up on our east and west. As I look at Lanair, the mist circling a mountain far off looks like the afterimage of a crown around his head.

"Nothing. Just about stuff," I reply.

"A trained scholar of the university, a favorite student of none other than Minaerva Royce, and he thinks about 'stuff.'" Lanair tries to hold it back, but a smile bursts forth on his face, peeling up over the whitest teeth. His fingers twirl in the hair on my chest.

"I think about other things, too."

"Things other than stuff?"

I open my mouth, but he slips a finger between my lips, stifling the words. He always does that. It's our little joke, his way of saying I've already outfoxed you, so anything else you say will just dig a deeper hole. Playfully, I take a nibble out of that finger. He laughs.

"You were already the favorite student, anyway. You beat me to Royce's good graces."

He pats my chest. "She liked you okay. You were always prettier than me."

"Your modesty is suffocating."

Just then, a cherry plops on the ground between us. His eyes widens as he picks it up. He pretends to stutter.

"D-do you t-think; I m-mean, c-could it be? A s-sign f-from on high? The tree has spoken; we're doomed!"

"Oh, shut up." I snatch the cherry from him and rip the pit loose from it. The fruit's bitter. Honestly, I'm not sure how anything still grows in the Narrows. "There once was a day you lived by the words of priests."

"Jem, I know you love stories, but there comes a day when we put childish things aside." He sits up and leans against the tree trunk. "I once took every word of the Mehsanic temples as incontrovertible. Then one day during the War in the Narrows, a priest was giving last rites to a fallen soldier. An errant arrow caught him in the throat. He was just a man."

Minaerva Royce said the same thing about herself when I was her student at the university. The smartest woman in the world, but still just a man. Then she laughed.

"If one were to say I was the smartest man in the world, one would imply I am the smartest person in the world. Yet if one says I am the smartest woman in the world, one would imply that there are men whose intellect exceeds my own."

I loved how the old woman's hands were covered in skin translucent as wet paper. She had a deliberate way of speaking; to her, every word was a universe you added to our existence, so you had to be careful not to clutter up the space. If everyone thought that way, there'd be a lot less clutter.

Royce was a great scholar, but sometimes not the greatest teacher. I'd leave her lessons with a brain of uncooked batter more often than not, trying to grasp at her lessons with the same success you'd wrangle minnows with your toes. Maybe that was more because of my failure as a scholar than hers as a teacher.

She never called me Jem. To her, I was always Nalda. She once said, "If you were a gem, every jeweler in Braeland would go bankrupt." Probably wasn't wrong.

Certainly wasn't any gem in the library. They took me in at Wilbraema, a sprawling labyrinth upheld by men whose hands had a faster rate of decay than the pages they tended. Almost kicked me out after a few years. Then came King Gareth Greyford's haughty fist and the leaderless harts and herons. Two months into the siege, I took to the walls and staved off defeat until Lanair arrived, liberated his port city, and moved the fight north. That'd be the day this Jem became, as they say, precious.

I knew it the moment he clutched my hand. The steam was coming off the baths set into the floors. The soapy water turned maroon from the dirt and blood coming off my legs; the water hid him as he submerged. He came up inches from me as I came up, too. Ever since I was little, I figured I'd end up with a Sumaran. The Lord of Sumara? Now there's a surprise. You could say we Calidumi have remained enamored with Sumara since Mehsani spared the praeco.

Royce always said her favorite story was the allegory of the praeco and the raven. I learned it down on Calidum, when Payt and her father took me. It was the first time I'd been back since I was maybe five, before my days of remembering. Royce left me with that story before I went south to take up life in the stacks, lost at the point between the pines.

"The praeco and the raven is a beautiful story, Jem," she said. "One is a bird of everlasting life, while the other is of ominous omens, often death. But the praeco never killed the raven, nor did the raven turn its talons on the praeco. That's a beautiful thing."

To her, lessons were a bittersweet thing. Too often she found students left her pavilion with the lessons fleeing their memories in a trail of smoke as from a fire. Hours of speech and dialogue for a head full of dreams. The smokescreen was a sign of the refrain turning. Round and round and round it turns, flinging off the lessons as if they were excess cargo.

And, I believe, her greatest fears were realized once Lanair sacked Trowbridge a few months ago. Her greatest student, Lanair, received an acidic earful from Royce following the taking of the capitol. He'd overlooked her words in the turning of the refrain. Then he sacked the city. Angrily, she lamented his memory.

"They're drunk again," Lanair comments.

"Hm?"

"You're a thoughtful one today, aren't you?"

"Just thinking about refrains. How to end them."

"Write a new song."

I stroke his back gently. "What are you, Royce's parrot?"

Feet crunch the soil on the other side of the tree. Lanair slides the blanket over us. I reach for my shirt, but he stops me.

"Lord Lanair," a voice shouts. "I have a letter for Lord Nalda."

"Come over."

Darek stumbles over the hill's crest, places a hand on the tree to support himself. His hunched back gives the impression that he's looming over us, peering in. He mops the sweat from his brow.

"My lord, here is Lady Tallhart's response," he huffs.

"Thank you," I say, accepting the letter from his hands like knobby tree roots. I peel it open. It says, *The broken bridge by the market. Your side. Midnight.* Nothing more. "Is this all Lady Tallhart replied?"

"Yes." Darek clears his throat. "Um, one other thing. She said, 'My heart is asleep, so, um, mischief runs deep.' I believe."

I stifle a laugh. Like a schoolboy stumbling over Royce's *Fires of War*. "Thank you, Darek."

"My lords." The hunchback bows his head and vanishes beyond the tree.

"What does that mean?" Lanair asks.

"What?"

"Hearts and mischief deep."

"Oh, that's an old rhyme Payt and I used to say to each other if we wanted to sneak around the castle late at night. It's actually 'Hart's asleep, mischief's deep.' He had it close enough, though."

Lanair grimaces. "I don't mean to wince. I knew her only in context of her father."

"Tough to get beyond the shadow of Leon Tallhart. I remember when we were kids she'd do anything to push against him. Still is, I guess. It's been a long while. Look at yourself. How have the reins your father handed you chafed?"

"Thoroughly."

"No different with Payt, I'd wager."

"Don't call her that, Jem. She's Lady Tallhart until we draw up and sign this accord."

"As you say, Lord Mavogar."

Lanair hisses out a long sigh. "I was always fascinated by how peaceful it is, this side of the hill. Like stepping into another world by stepping past a tree. That's how Mossan did it, in *Through the Magic Forest*. I always loved that one. One step and you're in some faraway country all laid out in green."

Lanair's eyes pan the hilly fields swooping in and out of one another until they clash with the grayish mountains miles west. Huddled in a tight group beneath the mountains is the Copse of Last Trees. All around them, dead branches and rotting stumps poke out of the field. But the Copse stands. They say that Mehsani spent his final hours within the Copse. He peered into a lake, pondering his impending fate. His followers named it the Mirror of Mehsani. When he met with his brother in the broken tower, they met no deal, and Mehsani hung from the parapets.

When Wilbraem the Wise was king, he consecrated the spot in honor of the dead. A short decade of peace followed until Faed fanatics stabbed him to death. So fell one of the five great kings. No one's entered the Copse since Wilbraem's rule. More than two hundred and sixty years. They say the Mirror of Mehsani still exists in there. Some say it's why Mehsani left footprints of steam wherever he walked in Alaveren. As if he awoke the very spirit of the earth.

My fingers skate along Lanair's back. A breeze rolls over us in the swelling dusk, and we shiver together. He reaches out for my hand. When I take his, he says, "I ought to find that damn wolf who made me choose between a back rub and holding your hand."

I flex my phantom fingers. Fifteen years later and I still feel them, as if I should look down and see a balled-up fist rather than a scarred stump.

He must be reading my thoughts, or just noticed the compasses swirling drunkenly again, because he brushes my matted black hair away from my forehead. When he spreads out on his back beside me, a rush of lavender follows him. He's always chewing it. Says it relaxes him.

"But it's okay." He holds up my left hand, spreads the fingers wide beneath the night. "I like this hand just fine." He strokes each individual finger, rubs every knuckle, and kneads the palm gently. Then he plants a kiss on my lips. "I love you, Jem."

"I love you."

I'm looking at his olive face, inches from mine, but in my periphery I can see his feet rubbing together, his toes wiggling happily in the grass as they once did at the place between the four posts and the carmine curtains.

11

Shepherd

Lanair glides along a boulevard of prostrated men and women stretching their fingertips to brush his feet as he passes. "Blood of Mehsani," the whispers go. Few glances dare flick up from the dirt to see him. To capture a fleeting stroke of the soles of his boots satisfies them. His pace hastens toward the rookery. Lanair avoids the fingertips, not because he wants to avoid crushing them, but because of his cousin's words to him before we fled the North: Build so high and who will pick up the pieces when you fall? "Blood of Mehsani," they murmur. Their fingertips retract around my feet.

So he came to me deep in the stacks of starving Southerners. They turned their mouths from the hardened bread. Outward on the floors they splayed themselves, murmuring those three fuddled words, over and over and over, until the greeting matured into liturgy, fluent on the tongues south of the Narrows. Nothing stopped it after that. Then came his cousin Alaryn's warning, and his pace quickened, dodging the reaching fingertips that'd be unable to pick up the great fall.

His shock of raven hair, the way it capped his steadfast face and piercing hazel gaze, drank me in. Barring the lines of worry crawling from his eyes, his visage suggests a man far younger than his thirty-three years. Olive skin smooth, no scars, a fine tapestry around two saucers of hazel ice.

The hazel ice brightened into a verdant flame once he rounded up the prisoners at Wilbraema. Stripped of their siege devices, they knelt beneath the blame. Without Greyford, Tallhart, or Carrow, these nameless savages answered for all three. Beneath his gaze they melted.

"You have assaulted the priceless minds within Wilbraema, threatened the holdings of Sumara, and spilled the blood of Mehsani," he announced.

"Blood of Mehsani," the whispers behind him chirped.

"You deserve no trial. Your crimes belie any excuses you could give."

They cried out, but Lanair clapped his hands, animating the Mehsanic knights with their trusted Red Hooks emblazoned on their chests. In minutes, the hall went quiet. Lanair led us out to the parapets where he ordered them ornamented with the heads. A few priests begged him to take them to the waters, but the Lord of Sumara offered no redemption for these traitors. Their blood was mopped, thrown away. It never reached the waters; their souls couldn't get to Faedelin.

When he walked up to me, a flash of surprise widened his gaze. Few Calidumi had ever worked at Wilbraema. When I told him about studying under Minaerva Royce, a smile broke on his face.

"How is the old crone?" he laughed. When he'd studied with her, it had been months before the War in the Narrows, but then he had to rush south to stop the tide of Faeds. That was when a young boy named Jon Carrow emerged from the old alliance and cut down Sir Iayn Darrion, the hero of the long winter.

I'd spoken to Sir Iayn when I was eleven, a few weeks before he met his end in an alley with his nephew. Midway through his sixtieth decade, Sir Iayn could outpace me in a footrace. He told me, during a tea session at Royce's pavilion, to not let fallen apples roll beneath my feet. He said, "An apple handed to your enemy is tenfold an apple underfoot."

Then Sir Iayn went south, hero that he was, and never came back.

Lanair claims that when his father, Lord Mavogar, knighted Carrow, the boy's face was as solemn as a priest at Faedelin's funeral. The whole stake of his knighthood rested on the blood of his uncle. What monster cuts down his uncle?

Bloodline mattered little to him. Carrow snuck around for years after that, even tried to poison Lanair with Leon Tallhart's help. A little night leaf goes a long way in the veins. Tried to commit treason over a little questioning. Lanair said Carrow was bloodthirsty after they questioned him and plotted every day against the Mavogar family.

The Blood of Mehsani would persevere. A little night leaf dashed on the rocks of the bay, and Lanair set fire to a passing ship from the University at Trowbridge. When word came that three scholars of the capitol aboard died, King Gareth ignited the Reaving again and laid waste to Wilbraema. Weeks evaporated before Lanair routed the siege, lined the parapets with heads, and invaded the Narrows. By that time, the Blood of Mehsani passed from mouth to mouth, until all lands south of the Narrows shimmered with the liturgy.

From then to now, their fingertips have stretched out, yearning for a stroke of his muddy boots. Up he built the empire. The fingertips would be too weak to glue it back together. In his wake, as my feet follow, they fall away, too feeble to graze another's boots.

The night has come to the Narrows. In the dark, banners with the Red Hook hang limp in the stagnant air. No wind takes the smell of the dead and dying away.

Across the river, the camp of Payt and Carrow dots the cadaverous city of Alaveren. How many days had we gone back and forth across the river, flanking in and out of the city, sparring on the bridge, sailing under the cover of night? Six. Six long days that saw no end.

The rookery nestles in a sloping crossroads that paves east toward the last bridge and west to the Copse of Last Trees beyond the ridge. Lanair nods to the guards, who've dropped to a knee and clutched the Red Hook over their hearts. At the parting of his lips, they'd open their veins. He hurries inside.

He chose the old rookery because of the letters it sent and received from all over Braeland and beyond. To and from, the words reached the distant chills of Wintervale or the hot flats of Calidum. It lingers in the long shadow we've cast in the Narrows.

Inside, Tehsan welcomes us. "My lords, how was your walk?"

"Relaxing," Lanair replies.

"You should take your boy over the hill tomorrow, Tehsan," I tell her. The woman keeps her face so clean she looks thirteen. "It's very romantic."

She offers half a grin. "I'm sure my lords enjoyed themselves." She stands erect behind a table with maps and letters and books scattered in an erratic papery mountain range. A tallow candle droops to its last drops atop the papery mountains. "Lord Lanair, I've been drawing up our accord for tomorrow," Tehsan says, beaming.

I feel Lanair's shoulders tense. So tightens the room. He has that power about him, to change an entire building with a clicking tongue, a balling fist, or a tensing shoulder. The air and the men breathing it adhere to Lanair's grasp. His softest step seizes the attention of armies. He hisses out a hot breath as he leans onto the table beneath the papery mountains.

"Good. We received a word from Tallhart. She's meeting Jem tonight. He can feel out where she stands."

"Oh?" Tehsan questions, her pride dimmed like the sun behind a cloud. "A private meeting with him and her?"

I clear my throat as I slide my tunic overhead. "If Payt sent the message, then we have no reason to worry. She'd never pull anything."

"Excuse me, Lord Nalda, but I believe that after she retook Wellfleet, we must consider her capable of everything," she replies, cheeks blushing as she wonders if she's crossed the line. "And it's not her pulling anything I'm concerned about."

"You think I would. I haven't seen her in eight years." I mop the black curls away from my forehead. "Besides, what was she supposed to do at Wellfleet? Carrow's line was breaking. Her force was late coming in from the north. Should she have lain down to die?"

Lanair holds up a hand. "Look, we're just talking broken bones now." He rubs his chin as he observes the map of the Narrows, partially illuminated by the candle's faint orb. The thin valley snaked north and south, bordered by jagged gray mountains on each shoulder. "I agree with Jem."

Tehsan clears her throat. "Pardon my transgressions. I don't think we should trust her so willingly, my lord, even though Lord Nalda has had extensive contact with her in the past. They were once playmates. Nalda's said as much."

"Payt..." I take a breath to reword the sentence. "Lady Payton is an honorable person. Once, when I was fourteen and she thirteen, three boys attacked me in the halls of the university. They took me into the lavatories, and they tried to hurt me." I know Lanair's eyes are studying me as the words leap off my lips, heralding news he's never heard before. "But they didn't. Lady Payton broke into the lavatory and beat them down. They fled. I would've been seriously wounded if not for her."

Lanair is staring at me. He studies people as one reads a book, even me, whom he has kissed and made love to and known for two years. He draws the words in long breaths so he can store them deep, deep within his mind and never let them go. Not as grudges. Just as memories. Lanair is staring at me. His olive skin, shades lighter than my own, glistens in the candlelight. His hazel eyes glisten with hurt.

"You never told me that."

"I saw no reason to." I walk to my bedside table and gulp wine. "Old stones, broken bones."

A spell passes inside the rookery. I look around. Its charred ruins smell smoky. Bird shit still stains the counters and walls. Centuries pass, kingdoms fall, bones break, but bird shit remains. They say that before Mehsani hung from the top of the tower, he scrawled a hook into the throne. He pricked his thumb and filled the groove with his blood. The Red Hook. It's the stains that last.

"Once Jem feels out the stance of the Faeds, we'll determine a place to meet," Lanair tells Tehsan. "For now, we need a treaty."

Lanair massages his chin. His ruminative expression says he's flipping through the words filed away in his mind, a myriad of books stacked on the shelves of Wilbraema from the distant reaches of Calidum and Wintervale and Telmar, Old Braeland, and beyond. He's filed them all away to never forget, to always remember the words that have been said, blocks that began the primordial towers and shape the preliminary discourses that pave the paths to today.

"I'm loath to trust this woman," he admits. "I spent the better part of two years under her father's grip, and it was his death that sparked this mess." He leans back against the desk and stares at me. "You know we can't win this on numbers alone."

"We never could," Tehsan responds. "Pardon me again, my lord, but Mehsani always has had a fraction of the followers of Faedelin. It is our piety and Mehsani's Light that has sustained us for three centuries. Faeds, they mumble words and call themselves devout. What has the soft North taught Faeds but fiction?"

Lanair's eyes focus on the void at his feet. His head nods so slowly you could be forgiven for thinking it were immobile. The words were finding places on the shelves of his mind.

"It's Carrow," he says finally. "Even two years ago, I knew it was Leon Tallhart and Carrow, never Payton. She was never our problem. She'd even fallen in love with my nephew Saewyn, I think." He glances at me. "Who rules the North? The hart or the heron?"

"I can feel it out," I answer. "I doubt Payt would kneel to that man, regardless the situation. She took Wellfleet back for herself, she eliminated our forces from the Mire, she planned the retaking of the university."

"I don't know if that's a vote of confidence for her or against."

I shrug. "She saw men slaughtering her people. What was the woman supposed to do? If she had sent swords to Wilbraema or Sumara, I'd fight them. I did."

"Fine. Meet with her tonight. Give her our word that our people will adhere to the terms. Take Tehsan with you, but keep it secret otherwise." Lanair turns to regard the maps. "Tehsan, can you contain yourself?"

The woman's lips tighten. "Yes, Lord Lanair."

"Okay."

Thud. The bottle of wine on the table topples over and sends a purple wave over the map of the Narrows. Lanair lunges and catches it only a second late, saving most of the papers. "Ah!" he shouts.

A small, dark shape crawls out from under the map table, rubbing its head. Dinian rises to his feet uneasily. His hand clutches the table for support in his rising. The boy bites his lip as he attempts to hold back tears.

"Dinian," Lanair breathes. "Mehsani's Grace, you scared the light out of me."

"Sorry," the boy mumbles. Barely eleven now, the boy's ears still look too large for his narrow, mousy face. I remember meeting him hours before the four posts and the curtains, after Lanair liberated the city a year and a half ago. His eyes darted around nervously at everything. Lanair said that started after he'd been abandoned the night Leon Tallhart died and Jon Carrow vanished. It got better after Lanair adopted him. Couldn't throw him beyond the walls. Mehsani's words were clear. The bloodline of a family runs strong, whether born in or brought in. Besides, the boy saved Lanair's life, after a fashion, by disclosing Carrow's plot to poison him. Short an heir, Lanair welcomed the boy as his own. Brought him along for some toughening.

Dinian loves stories. I've a special affinity for storytelling, what with studying Mehsanism and Faedelinity my whole life. Whenever he can't sleep, I'll tell him an old one. "Serabella's Ship," one of Mossan's journeys past the Magic Forest, or even chapters from Royce's *The Fires of War* or *The Way of Kings*. If you'd read me Royce when I was eleven, the words would've been through one ear and out the other. As a twenty-seven-year-old, I can hardly read her. Not Dinian. The boy's a bright one, although timid.

"Sorry," he mumbles again. "I just wanted to hear what you were doing tomorrow."

Lanair ruffles the boy's hair. "That's okay, Dinian. I told you not to sneak around like this, though."

"Sorry," the mumble repeats.

Tehsan clears her throat. "Excuse me, my lords, but I think I'll take my leave before tonight."

"That's fine, Tehsan, rest up."

She bows her head and exits the rookery.

Still rubbing his head, Dinian ducks into the back room where our beds are and jumps onto my cot. I follow. He kicks the wool blankets to the foot of the mattress and stretches arms and legs out as a cat roosts atop a chair. He lets out a long yawn.

"Jem, can you tell me a story before I go to bed?"

I walk over to sit at the foot of the cot. "How about the time I slew the Sand King of Calidum?"

The boy's eyes go wide. "Okay, now sit back and listen as we fly south to the windswept sands of Calidum where the air blows hot and suffocating in your face.

"Ten years ago, a rebel lord in the Northern cities of Calidum seized a major port called Cindara. It wasn't long before this rebel was calling himself the Sand King. The Sand King took over several more ports through Calidum before he came to Queen Kala's city.

"Now, Queen Kala was a wise woman and despised the spilling of blood in war. So she elected one judge of the city to go forth and redeem all of Calidum. That judge was me.

"I arrived at the Sand King's pavilion at dusk. I announced that I came to discuss a peace treaty on behalf of the queen, and the fat king welcomed me into his tent. Once I had won his trust, the fat man beckoned his servants to leave so we could negotiate on his terms. When I had the Sand King alone, I drew my dagger, which he did not notice, since it was on my right hip and not the left. The blade got stuck in his fat, so I left it there for all to see. Then I snuck out the back of his pavilion.

"When I returned to Kala, the queen announced the death of the Sand King before anyone in the rebels army had learned of it. Once they found their leader lying dead in a pile of his own excrement, they knew that Queen Kala was the true leader of Calidum and knelt in her name."

When I finish, Dinian is rapt. He bites his lower lip as he does when his mind is racing, racing, racing like Lanair's. "Is that true?" he asks at last.

Lanair smirks. "Of course. Jem is an honorary lord in Calidum. Even today the Calidumi sing odes to the One-Handed Knight."

"Amazing," Dinian breathes. "I can't wait to tell Grandpa when he gets back."

The smile vanishes from Lanair's face. We exchange a glance, and then he shakes his head. We've decided not to tell Dinian about the death of Alaryn, his adoptive grandfather, until we're safely in Sumara, when all this is behind us.

The boy's eyes are filled with that unknowing beauty, to not know spilled blood and to exist several paces back in time, an unmarred, departed reality in the unreal present.

"When can we go back home?" Dinian asks.

"Soon," Lanair replies. I know he regrets taking the boy with us. He'd hoped the experience abroad would help Dinian mature, but here we sit paraphrasing ancient tales. "Soon. Tomorrow we're going to talk with Lady Payton and Lord Carrow about new settlements in this valley. Sumara will have more homes, closer to where Mehsanism began." Dinian shifted; I can feel the squirming on the mattress. "We're making a new Braeland, Dinian."

A spell passes. Lanair examines the treaty Tehsan left as he moves pieces around the concise re-creation of the Narrows on the map. Something's in Dinian's eyes. A fear. His squirming grows less pronounced, but he's not sitting still.

I get up to speak with Lanair. I stroke his back, and he closes his eyes, suddenly lost in a metaphysical dreamscape far away from the shit-stained rookery.

"The precipice is so sharp," he mumbles.

"I know." I can feel the knots in his neck and upper back. He stays up too late. "Mehsani wasn't careful enough. We will be."

He nestles his head against my chest. "I like her plan. Raze Alaveren, partition the Narrows. Bold. Our people have fought long enough to have half the Narrows." His breathing takes a slow, meditative pace. "I wonder if those scribes hadn't taken that tale from Calidum, would we be here?"

"One way or another. It's natural for *us* to look at *them*."

"It was them looking at us."

"Isn't that the problem? Circles and circles. It was all of us imagining a higher tower, looking down at the same us, imagining a lower one."

"Will you tell it to me?"

"What, 'Apples Without Worms?'"

"Yeah. I need a break." He sighs deeply. "Let my mind wander."

"Okay. I haven't told it in a while. Might be rusty."

Lanair nestles deeper into my chest. Slowly, I begin the story, but it's like stretching your fingers after a long walk in the cold. It takes a few minutes to get the motions back, the right dexterity and feeling. Then it dawns on me.

Carrow. That had been the word. The moment Lanair said that name the boy started squirming. I glance over at him, his eyes still wide and gazing at nothing. They look as if he's just seen a ghost.

12

Apples Without Worms

There was famine in the land, and it touched all of the families in the great valley. Everywhere the two brothers looked, they could not find any food, and their mother had grown ill in her old age.

While searching the barren valley one night, the eldest brother saw an apple tree atop a hill. When the eldest brother told the younger, the younger wished to keep moving, for he believed they could find better spoils than apples. Since the eldest was a wise man, he knew the apples could help their ailing mother, so he marched up the hill.

The tree had bloomed in full with many apples on its branches, though most of them were filled with worms. The eldest collected them all as he climbed, but soon held so many that he lost his balance. When he fell, he spilled the apples all around the base of the tree.

Now, when the younger heard the force of his brother's fall, he rushed to the hilltop. But instead of picking up his brother, he picked up an apple. Ripe and wormless as it was, he took a bite.

"Are you not my brother?" the elder asked.

"What do you mean?" the younger replied.

"If you were my brother, would you not pick me up rather than an apple?"

"You can pick yourself up, brother," the younger replied. But what the younger could not see was that the eldest had twisted his ankle in the fall and had trouble standing. The younger divided the apples in half and gave them to his elder. When the eldest looked into the basket the younger had given him, he saw that all the apples had worms and that the younger had kept the fresh apples for himself.

But their mother was wise. When the two brothers returned home, she asked the younger the same question the eldest had asked. "Is this man not your brother? Who are you that you should have the apples he discovered and not help him to his feet?"

Ashamed, the younger prostrated himself on the ground and begged forgiveness from their sage mother. She took the fresh apples from him and gave them to the eldest, so that he and his brood might eat the fruit without the worms. To the younger she gave the tainted apples, for his was a tainted soul.

For many generations, the eldest brother's sons enjoyed the freshest fruit from the tree, while the sons of the younger had to eat tainted apples. Only after the great famine had ended could the sons of the younger enjoy apples without worms.

13

The Great Refrain

She's changed. The way her shoulders don't hunch forward, the level plane her chin keeps that makes you look down at her rather than looking up at you, the hardened quality of her eyes that go unblinking even in a gust of wind. Men huddle around her the way a halo surrounds a candle, as a faint periphery. But the candle is the light. The candle is the heat. Her hair hasn't lost its luster. She was ever the sunset that made eyes go blind longing after it. That hasn't changed.

No, no. I have to catch myself when slinging around terms like candles and sunsets. Following a life in the stacks you'd think I know better. Yet the knowing of words and the trusting of old muscles aren't two things that coexist. Eight years later the muscles fall back on candles and sunsets, dumb as I am to the true words I should use.

Lady Payton Tallhart. The Red Hart. Those are the words that strike the true nature of who stands in front of me.

Payton has rowed across the river to my side, her rowboat lapping at the shore in the dark of the broken bridge's jagged fang. Several faceless guards wait on the eastern bank, accompanied by a man with wisps of snow on his head, her nervous courier teetering on the balls of his feet, and a woman with scars on her face. Everyone focuses on Payton, who's looking at me.

A streak of dirt smudged across those freckles brings a smile to my face, as do the two words that considered washing the streak. What a rage those two words sparked. A vein or two might've popped in the forehead of her father. "Fuck that," she'd say.

As I leave Tehsan up by the mouth of the broken bridge, I see Payton's eyes wide in the midnight dark below. Her eyes were wide when we first met at the university. She'd never seen someone with skin like mine. I explained to her that my mother had come from Calidum.

"Hart's asleep, mischief's deep," I say with a laugh.

She smiles. "I wanted you to know whom you were meeting after all these years. After that formal letter you sent me, I was a little nervous about whom I was meeting."

"Only my last was formal. I'm assuming my other ones never made it to you."

"Other letters?"

"You never got them?"

"No."

I frown. Messengers can be fickle. "They must've gotten lost in the fray. Your courier's always got his head in the clouds."

Payton shrugs. "He does. May be in the market for a new one. I'm glad to see you again, Jem."

"How long has it been?" A sigh comes from me in a huge gust, and I can feel the stress leaving my shoulders. For all the changes to her face, Lady Tallhart has maintained the old Payt. A sudden urge sparks in me to go back to the Kingdom of the Spider King and the Fire Queen and battle the Nefarious Iceman. That point on the loop has passed. We're mired in the kingdom of the two brothers, a broken Braeland that surrounds us all with its gnarled bones and tired stones.

"At least eight years. You left for Wilbraema just after you turned nineteen."

"That's right. Just a few months after Calidum." My face screws up with a grimace. "Your father happy to see me go?"

"He loved you, Jem, in his own way."

"What a funny way it was."

Her feet shift in the mud. A cloak the color of mud drapes over her shoulders. "You know the North doesn't accept that as much, Jem. Believe me, if he hadn't loved you like his own son, he would've killed you after he saw those boys sneaking through our tower."

"I guess we can call that love." I glance back up at Tehsan, an obelisk always ready to swing her sword. Across the river, Payton's retinue looks on. "Want to take a walk?"

"Yes." Payton waved off her attendants across the river while I shout to Tehsan to remain there. She frowns. Despite any misgivings she might have, the woman remains silent and nods back at me, her gaze locked on me and Payton. The woman is probably running through verses of the Book of Testaments right now, wondering how they'd assess her lord walking off with her enemy commander, how they'd justify her taking off Payton's head.

As we begin walking along the river, away from our camps upstream, I wonder about us. Since we parted ways her face has been a receding loop in my mind, turning away farther up the path from where she and I shared our final hug. The receding loop takes her farther away with each revolution, and I can no longer see her freckly face with any clarity beyond what flawed memory can serve. Then I go to Wilbraema and the great library within, failing to send letters and receiving none from her, lost in the rush of personal and trivial things. Then a great torpor forces us to a halt. As I settled into the refrain, her face lingers farther and farther away along the receding loop of our last moment together. The loop turns her into some queer cast of an enemy. The cycle frames the fight the same as it has its countless ancestors. Then I wonder: Can she and I speak like once before? Can we form an ellipse on the myriad of ephemeral moments in between then and now? Can we pretend like myriad ephemeral moments have no say in the blink between her turning her back on the dirt road and her rowing across the darkened river? I wonder about us.

For several paces, we say nothing. It's enough to let our boots squelch in the moistened riverbank. Soon Tehsan and Payton's attendants will have been swallowed by the shadow of midnight somewhere north along the river, the heart vein that strikes at the core of this refrain. Perhaps she is thinking the same.

"You're second-in-command now, huh?" she asks. "How'd that happen?"

"Saved Wilbraema from your generals. Fell in love with a fox. And you're the Red Hart, famed across Braeland."

"I suppose. What does that even mean, the Red Hart? Could be anyone. Could be my father."

"Payt."

"Yes."

"I need to know, since I know Lanair will ask. Did you give the charge six days ago or did he?"

She lets a long pause linger, as if the silence is a more chilling indictment than any word her tongue could flick into existence. The water laps at the mud, unseen fires lick at wood, and the weeds shiver all around. Then she tacks on, "Him."

I frown. "I assumed. But Lanair would ask."

"He gave quite a rousing speech about your lot profaning the Holy City. Got them nice and primed for some killing."

"Should've camped outside the city's walls," I admit, "but Lanair didn't think Carrow would give such an order, especially after we handed you back the university. Then your soldiers come thundering south as if Faedelin himself had rode an army out of the clouds."

"I know, I know, I know."

"Sorry."

"No, it's fine, Jem. I've spent the past two years with the man. If a piece of rock lined with ice can be called a man."

Our boots crunch for a while. The city recedes behind us; I can see the velvet fields rolling south into the maw of the night.

"There are times I want to just hug the man," Payton says. "Others I'd like to strangle him."

I stop for a moment. The buildings here have that drooping quality old people have when they've been walking too long, bent but not broken. Moss blankets their bottom halves. An echo of an echo of what could've been.

"Like at Wellfleet. He stood by me then," she continues, pondering up ahead. "After all the priests scowled at me like prudish boys who weren't asked to the ball."

I smirk. Faeds were always introverted, pubescent disasters with clammy hands and awkward tongues. Payton and I joked that if men could get laid with the ease with which they dreamed, the priesthood would go extinct.

She saw how easily we settle into the point between the pines and lunge after the complete and utter mastery of it. The lunging traps us in the pines. As such, they master us. Even so, we convince ourselves, while mired in refrain, to run for the sun under the flawed notion that its imprisonment equals our liberation. We break our backs reaching for it, unattainable in its high seat. Words on a page that mirror desires of the mind are a fine consolation for broken backs. Unable to clutch the sun with hands and fingers, we content ourselves with ruling it with songs that trick us into chasing it over and over and over again.

"Jon was okay then. But after we fled from Sumara, he changed. Faedelin's balls, already two years ago." She crouches near the river and begins to pick up pebbles and skip them on the tranquilly gurgling surface. "I found him with a rope one night. Maybe I should've made him use it."

"How'd you see him after the university?"

She nods. "I knew he'd broken. Something his father said in dying. Not Tomathy. Lord Tanogar. More harm than good, I suppose. Perhaps there was a moment floating out there unseen," she ruminates, casting her fingers over the water. "That was the moment he should've died, or he should've been killed. Then we missed it, and he lived. Here we are."

The first words of Jon Carrow's disappearance were the shadow of Leon Tallhart's death in Sumara. My father who was not my father, an image of him remains with me holding his heart on a chilled platter. Another boy was on his knees in my room. I don't even remember his name. My true father came in and went off like a powder keg kissed by a firedrake. He damn near strangled the boy, still in nothing but his skin. I pounded that thick flesh, left a poppy bruise on Lord Bryce Nalda's temple. He tried to take me farther north where he'd reform me. Said the Southern sluts and whores turned me.

Payton filled the doorframe when he came after me, and I cowered behind her. Even he seemed cowed by her, though he stood heads above her. Shadows never bothered her.

"Go back to that hole in the North you crawled out of. Never speak to Jem again. Never think of him."

"You have no say," Nalda said, scowling.

"Why? 'For women are fair, and they should remain in their chamber until men return?' Fuck Faedelin. Go back to the hole where they mutter that shit every day."

He wagged a bony finger at her. "You're nothing but a sluttish heretic. Your father would cry if he heard you defiling Faedelin's words."

She moved closer to him. I think he might've stepped backward. "So you're telling me you didn't defile Faedelin's words when you blew your load into some Calidumi woman? Or the sunburned savages, as I've heard you refer to them. But even Faedelin forgot himself in the warmth between a woman's legs, didn't he?"

I thought his eyes were going to erupt from his skull. I'd heard him refer to my mother's people like that at times. Never in front of her, though. Eventually, she left for home with sourness on her tongue that tasted like Faedelin. Eventually, he left me to my perversions and my sluttish heretic.

That wasn't the first time she'd been my vindicator. The year before was when the boys cornered me, dragged me into a lavatory, and held my jaw at the ready. I was reeling from the beating and couldn't move.

"Shouldn't be a problem for you," the boy sneered.

128

"Back away." Her voice cut the room, ripped it apart, made all the more pronounced by the palpable silence that followed. They cleared like clouds to reveal the sun. She produced a knife in her palm, scaring off one of the boys. A second came at her, but she swiped at his wrist, which blushed in a spray. He fell down to stem the tide. The one who'd spoken rushed at her; she leaped sideways, tripping him, his pants slumping to his ankles. Before he could stand, she began stomping. The screams came at first, but soon he fell asleep. It was a red worm dripping red juice. At that moment, I realized that at the heart of every fire burns a deep, deep dark.

A dark, which, I can only assume, burns darker since Lanair called for Leon Tallhart's head two years gone. The Reaving wasn't slow in reopening after that. Wilbraema was surrounded within a month. I left the library to defend the walls after Lord Eamon fell. I'd grown tired of life in books anyway. If there's one thing I learned from those innumerable pages lining the walls of Wilbraema, it was what a scatterbrained calamity we are. Words come from old words. We all share them, orbiting the same thoughts over and over and over. All is derivative claiming to be novel.

Lanair liberated the great port a month later. I slunk back to the great library, and that's when he came to visit the person who had held the Southern stronghold. His eyes studied me as soon as I went up to shake his hand. Politely, he extended his left.

"So you're the man who saved Wilbraema," he said to me.

"I am, my lord."

"A one-handed knight."

"*The* one-handed knight, according to the Calidumi, my lord."

A grin broke on his face, and then his eyes widened as if in shock that he'd smiled. "You've been there, I imagine?"

"Lived there for my first five years. Spent a year with Queen Kala a while back."

"A lovely person, and brilliant."

"You know her?"

"Calidumi are no strangers to the Mehsanic peoples, as I'm sure you're aware. Most of Mehsani's words come Calidumi folklore," he acknowledged.

"'The world revolves to jettison us, little gnats to her great ears, so why should we wake to slaughter one another like sheep?'" I quoted to him. "'We are all the sheep, and all of us the shepherd. Let us build a flock together, brother and brother, sister and sister.'"

"I should've known a bookish boy like you could chirp Mehsani."

"I studied Mehsanism under Minaerva Royce."

His eyebrows went up at that. "Minaerva. Tell me, how is the old crone?"

He told me about his days studying with Royce. He shared her distaste for bloodshed while under her wing. Regardless, he ornamented the parapets of Wilbraema without a whisper of a trial. He stood by taking Leon Tallhart's head.

I never could stand by Royce's utter disregard for execution when so many others had complete neglect for life. The others wouldn't stop because you never began.

Soon Lanair and I were alone in his chambers. He invited me to wash away the battle in his personal bathhouse. As I lounged in the water, bars of moonlight cutting the top of the darkness out of the room, he walked in, standing above the bath sunk into the oak floor. The steam rose all around us. He dipped into the water and floated toward me. Then his hand was already down there, familiar in its stroking. His lips were soft on mine.

He led me back to his bed, a four-post island lurking in carmine curtains. He rested me down, ran his tongue along my hardened shaft. I buried my head cheek-deep in rough, sweaty pillows. While within the pillows and his mouth working wonders, the finery beyond our little island evaporated.

As he lay next to me, he began telling me about his plans to raze Alaveren, split the Narrows in two, and forge a new Braeland. He explained that once a sword shatters, you can weld the disparate pieces back together, but it won't ever be as strong. It'll always be weaker at the fissures. Better to melt it down, destroy it utterly, and create it anew.

The tone clinging to Payton's name on his lips belied his intentions. I hope it's the light of her father molding his perception of her. She's crouching still by the river. Quiet, this whole time. Only the faint whisper of the breeze, which is like a faint echo of a faint whisper of a breeze.

"What're you thinking about?" I ask to end the quiet.

"Wellfleet. The dash though the sewers."

"I want you to know, I don't blame you for what you did."

She shrugs. "What if you did? What could I do?" She stands. "Part of me wanted to see you tonight, to see my friend again. But now, I don't know."

"What?"

"I hope Lanair's ideas work tomorrow." Payton looks at me, expressionless. "Jon seems open to your terms, but he wants to meet at the broken tower."

I pinch my nose. "They'll never accept."

"I said as much. It's my task to convince you."

"Convince me all you want. It's them that'll turn up their noses."

"That's the only place he'll meet, Jem, and since he had command of the force taking the university, he has the final word."

"We might as well have handed you that city back. He didn't take it. It's not his word."

"I don't like this, either. Let's meet there, old symbols be damned, sign the parchment, and leave this fucking city forever." She skips a stone into the river. Before the third hop, the current sucks it down. "Let it rot."

Beyond the dense curtains, or if there'd been no curtains in the first place, the broken tower could be a place to meet. Superstition sloughs away. Without its verses to encourage the slicing of skin, it grows mute and ends its grip on our souls. Yet those poor souls in the Southern and Northern camps huddle within the grip of superstition and change the name from the Tower of the Light to the broken tower. They sink deep into the curtains' shadows.

Some refrains do require lamentation.

"We should head back," she states.

"Okay."

The way back is long and quiet. There is a layer of ice, thick and impenetrable, that has frozen over us and holds our tongues in stasis even as they struggle to form words for each other. But they mold merely the vague shapes of words, which fizzle to nothing in silence. A layer of ice that has frozen what was to show us what could never be once more. I long for the days when she was Payt and I was Jem. We've passed long beyond the horizon, ever proceeding from the far side of a receding loop.

"Lanair, you, and a third party will enter tomorrow," she finally says. Tehsan's silhouette emerges on the bank up ahead. "Jon and two of his will do the same. I'll hold the courtyard with my men and women until the agreement has been signed."

"So Carrow will accept."

"I hope. If you accept the tower, he should accept the treaty." She frowns. "He seems open to anything if he gets the tower."

Tehsan's silhouette becomes a fine outline a hundred yards ahead. She bows her head to me. I bow mine.

We reach Payton's rowboat, bobbing at the bank in concert with the water beneath it. She turns to face me.

"I'm glad I saw you, Jem. You look well." Then she turns away.

"Payt."

"Yes?"

"He's not evil, despite what he's done."

She peers into her boat. "I'd have killed Leon Tallhart, too. Better not to dwell on broken bones or old stones."

I nod. "Okay, Payt."

"Get some rest."

Someone has taken that candle I thought she was and lined the wick with a glob of spit. Try to hold a match to it; it'll drown that spark. The wick is ruined, because, of course, she's no candle after all. Unfair of me to expect so.

She rows away from me, receding into the dark as she shrank along the loop in my memory. The loop leaps from the kingdom of us to the remains of the two brothers, indifferent to the queen and king it pulls apart. It strands those young rulers across a bloody river with only a petty rowboat to visit for a breath. Reminds us that here and there are disparate things.

I stand on the west of this river, she on the east. I live in the south of this country, she in the north. One brother went north and the other south, and because they did not remain in love, we can never be in love, separated by names on a page but torn apart by generations of hearsay and imagination. The turning, turning, turning of the incessant wheel. Centuries later, the world, for all its invention, mires itself in this great refrain. For years and years and years, it molds the hapless generation in a grim echo of its predecessors with the ideas of two brothers flying north and south, spoken in disparate words, written in mismatched letters. So confident in our words and letters, we cut ourselves down over the difference. Impervious to erasure, they hold her on the eastern bank, trap me on the western.

14

The Red Hart

Payton kept her father's tower on her left shoulder as she sprinted toward the sewer gate. The arrows of shepherds thrummed the air all around her. The burning of Wellfleet pulsed unseen in the night. By turns, the fires breathed in and out. The night responded, black and orange. Clouds of soot poured into the breathing, pulsing night.

The lord's tower loomed on her left shoulder. This road was clear. The Sumarans were across the bridge, though, and would be quick in the assault against Jon, who struggled to hold the city to the south and east.

"Badric, take out the map," Payton ordered.

The old knight slung the sack off his back and unfurled the tattered parchment, squinting at it in the dim light. He shook his head.

"Wrong turn, my lady. The sewer's that way."

Alanna and Coyle beside him swore. He pointed behind Payton, to the bridge that was blocks away where the Sumarans poured over legion after legion after legion.

"There's no way around?" she asked.

"No, Lady Tallhart."

Coyle cracked his neck beside her and dug his feet into the cobbles, a bull ready to charge. "Get back to Carrow. What the fuck are us four going to do against an army of scabs?"

"Shut it, Coyle. We have to get to the sewers. If we can make it to the tower, it'll split them."

"Why bother? Carrow can handle it."

She shoved past Badric, nearly knocking the poor man off his feet. "Coyle, there are hundreds of Sumarans still passing the bridge. Carrow's failed. If we don't get to the sewers, the Sumarans are going to press us out of Wellfleet or smash us within its walls."

He pointed to each of them in turn. "This is a group suicide. I got no part. I'm going out alone."

"Coyle, you answer to me." Strange that he once answered to her, before Jon adopted him as his own. "You're coming with us."

"Two women and an old fuck," he snorted, nodding his head at her. "The three of you going to take down the army of Lanair fucking Mavogar?"

"The four of us."

His jaw tensed inches from her face. The sweltering night frizzed her orange curls, plastered them to her back, made her want to scream. She had to look him in the eyes. Ignore the heat.

"Coyle," Payton began, softer than before. The fires swirled skyward and with them the clatter of swords. "When they write about this night, do you want the name Coyle to appear in the footnotes? Or just Tallhart?"

She had him. It was the way his eyes suddenly flicked to her after wandering to the space at her edges.

"Good."

She spun around to Badric, who was examining the map. He bit his lip and looked up.

"My lady, we can cut through this building here." He pointed to an inn a block north. Dozens of blocks more away, the lord's tower was a solitary thumb erect in the black-and-orange sky. "It'll take us through the bulk of the

136

Sumaran van, but it's the fastest way to the sewers. It shares several small alleys with a butcher's shop, an apothecary, and a chapel."

"Fine, let's take that way. Follow me," Payton commanded. She was commanding, as queer as it was. Only a year ago she had scurried in the shadows with Jon sipping and looking at the rope, dragging down their pace. But she didn't know where to go or whom to trust. Payton kept him alive as much as he did her.

The inn's door was missing. Payton leaped across the threshold into the dank common room where plush chairs were overturned, a lonely hearth breathed cold air, and a bar stood dry. Vaguely she wondered if Leon had ever entered here when Tallhart held the proud city. Wellfleet. Now shattered. Old stones, broken bones.

At the far end of the inn, she peered out of a window with no pane, up the westward alley toward columns of marching Sumaran soldiers, the Red Hook flapping proudly overhead. They marched forty paces away. The smoke blurred the alley.

"Move!" Coyle hissed.

"If I have to cut out your tongue, Coyle, I won't blink twice."

Silence.

Nimbly, she swung her legs over the sill, and Payton landed on the soil of the alley. The butcher's shop shot out of the ground three paces away. The columns marched along. With a calm breath, she sprang across the alley, a cat diving for the safety of home from a rabid dog.

Inside the butcher's den, a lifeless air hung over her, the odor of animals cleaved apart and the sweat of the fat men cleaving them. Coyle and Alanna appeared through the window. Coyle covered his nose. Then Badric clambered over the sill, kicking loose a shard of glass as he fell to the floor.

Voices went up in the street.

"Down! Behind the counter!" Payton commanded in a whisper.

The four of them huddled behind the counter as a door erupted at the front of the shop. Two Sumaran soldiers rushed in. Spears led the way. Through a crack in the counter she saw the Hook curled on their chest. Mehsanics. True shepherds.

They paused, dogs ready to pounce but waiting for their prey to reappear. Their beady eyes panned the shop. Their knees bent slightly; they could leap paces at a moment's notice. Spears swayed back and forth, paced to their panning eyes.

"You sure you heard someone?"

"Glass. It broke."

"You sure?"

"Yeah, I'm sure."

"Okay. Look quick before the captain calls us back."

As the first soldier who spoke remained stationary, the second soldier who had heard the glass inched forward. His dragging feet left imperfect trails through the dormant dust that settled in a blanket on the floor. He took two steps toward the counter, and then turned right toward the window that Payton's group had climbed through a moment earlier. Alanna pushed further behind the counter. The second soldier's scuffing feet stopped. She couldn't see him through the crack in the counter. Only the first soldier, still panning his eyes. Then the sound of glass briefly scraping the floor. Her hand tensed on her blade's hilt. He was holding it. The soldier was holding the piece of broken glass. She glanced at Badric, who was clutching his leg as a thin snake of blood crawled down his calf. The blood. The soldier saw the wet, fresh blood smeared across the broken glass. She closed her eyes. A thin sheet of air cut through her taut lips. She funneled her strength to her legs.

A scream. *"Get down!"* A crash. The butcher's shop trembled.

Payton opened her eyes. She found herself on her rear behind the counter. The dust coating the shop shook loose.

"Let's go!" the first soldier screamed. Another crash. The shop trembled. The world, the whole world shook. "The Faeds are coming!"

"It's bloody," the second soldier murmured, barely audible above the chaos. "The thing is bloody."

"Fuck the blood, the Ghost is hitting us head on!" Another crash forced the first soldier to clutch the doorway. "Come on!"

Payton edged her head above the countertop. The first soldier vanished into the street and took off to the south, toward Jon and his flailing army. The second soldier lingered. He turned his back and thumbed the bloody glass. His head craned up, as if deep in thought.

Coyle reached under the counter. When his hand emerged, it was clutching a rusted knife. Payton shook her head. He raised his middle finger at her, crouched, and moved away.

The soldier kept thumbing the glass. His eyes seemed to scan the trail of ghostly feet left in the dust on the floor. The freshly settled dust covered the trails in a faint veneer.

Coyle crept toward him. He brought the knife up.

The soldier took a step into the doorway.

Payton lunged out, wrapped Coyle's throat in the crux of her elbow, dragged him back silently.

The soldier left the shop.

Coyle whipped around. His fist found her nose before she could blink, and then he stood up, dousing her in his shadow.

"You crazy fucking bitch. I could've had him."

"The point of this is not to draw attention to ourselves." Blood streaming into her mouth, she pinched the bridge of her nose. She felt tears boil up on her eyes. An ache seeped from her nostrils to her cheeks up through her eyes until it pulsed throughout her skull. "You could've brought a legion into this place. Then it would've been a real butcher's den."

"Hilarious. Your wit is killing me. You were about to a moment earlier. I saw you."

"Yeah, so he didn't tell the other about the blood."

Coyle threw up his hands. "Fuck this," he hissed. "Do it your way then."

"Fuck off, Coyle."

Alanna helped her to her feet. "You okay, Lady Payton?"

"I'm fine. I've broken my nose before."

"Playing sticks with Nalda?" Coyle sneered.

"He's tenfold the man you are."

"Fake men play sticks. Real men play swords."

She laughed. "Boys play sticks. Men play swords."

139

It was dark, but she knew he blushed.

"We have to keep going," Alanna interjected. "Carrow won't distract them forever."

"Go," she ordered.

Alanna, hunched over, made her way to the window on the far side of the shop. She went over with a lunge. Coyle followed. Badric clambered up, limping on his wounded leg. Payton eased him on, a gentle hand pressed against his back. Slowly, deliberately, painfully, he threw himself into the second alley. She reached for the sill.

"Faed bitch."

Payton dropped to the floor as the blade lodged itself in the sill. An open palm took out the man's knee. With a whelp he dropped to the floor beside her. She ripped the sword from the sill. The soldier rolled out of its reach.

"Lady Tallhart!" Badric shouted.

"Go on!"

She charged the Sumaran, bloody glass poking out of his grip. He dodged the whooshing sword, pivoting on the balls of his feet to stay just out of arm's reach, even with the length of the sword at the end of her outstretched arm. He licked his lips. The bloody glass glistened in the darkened shop as it pointed at her, at her heart.

"You know what we do to Faed women after a victory?"

He was drawing nearer with every pivot. Her arms were so tired.

"We take them out to the stables and—"

As he pivoted, she lunged headlong into his belly. A rush of air left him and the smell of unclean man flooded over Payton, like how it flooded over her every night at the Crossroads when Jon snored away, puffing away, and filling up the small attic with the stench. The Sumaran coughed when her shoulder drove him into the floor. The glass came cleanly out of his palm and into hers. His eyes bulged, but no words came from him before she plunged the bloody glass into his throat. A geyser of blood was unleashed. He clutched at it with muddy hands, but the blood wouldn't go back in no matter how tightly the man pressed it. Moments later his eyes gazed at the ceiling they would never see again.

She dashed to the window as shouts thundered outside. Payton jumped through as an arrow thudded the wall of the butcher's shop and boots trampled the dust within. The three of them were already through the apothecary and on their way into the chapel. No. Not three. Two. Coyle. Where was Coyle?

Abandoning the battle up the street, a handful of Sumarans stormed the apothecary. Three in total, more to come. The first swiped sideways to remove her head. She ducked, took him in the belly, winced as a pile of red, rubbery snakes splashed to the floor. The second grabbed her orange curls, but as he began whispering some foolish taunt, she reached up, opened his wrist, spun around, and took off the head so alarmed by her agility. The third stared at her.

"They're flanking us!" he screamed, backing out into the street. "The fucking Faeds are flanking, turn back!"

Fuck. Sprinting to the next alley, she was stopped by the unmistakable sound of glass clanking together and the shuffling steps of drunken boots. Coyle stumbled out of the back of the apothecary's shop, a bottle in hand. His half-moon eyes stared death at her.

Without a word, Payt climbed into the final alley, into the chapel, sprinted across its pews. She heard myriad boots stomping the street outside and running parallel to her in the chapel. The lord's tower loomed up ahead, faithfully on her left shoulder. She didn't care if Coyle had escaped the apothecary. The doors of the chapel broke down in front of a squad of Sumaran soldiers, devout Mehsanics with the Red Hook emblazoned on their tabards, all of who leveled crossbows at her. Three steps away. Countless clicks, then *whoosh* as the arrows hurtled forward. Two steps. She dove through the glass. *Thud thudthud. Thud thudthud. Thud.* Some of the bolts poked through the wall. She spun around and sprinted down the northeast alley away from the street with the Sumarans, toward the end where Alanna waited at the gated mouth of the sewers.

"Go!" she screamed.

Then Coyle appeared at the end of the alley. The bastard took a fucking short cut. He shoved Alanna into the black, open mouth of the sewer. She pushed him ahead, the boots drawing ever near at her heels down the alley. She swung the gate closed behind her as Coyle started down the tunnel. She stretched though the gate's metal lattice for the key lodged in the hole.

"Leave it, Tallhart! Faedelin's cock, they're nearly on us!" Coyle cried.

She tore the key loose of its hole, but it slipped and clattered on the cobbles. Her fingertips grazed the rusted key. They were coming. Coyle swore, yanked her back into the tunnel, and reached through. He tossed the key to her a moment later and sprinted north and east into the dark toward the sewer. As arrows dinged the metallic gate, she sprinted down into the tunnel after him.

Alanna and Badric had already plunged into the underground river, a stagnant tube of water that smelled of month-old shit. They trudged through the cylindrical swamp toward the port beneath the lord's tower. Payton slid into the shit behind them. A hundred paces. That was all.

As Coyle clambered in ahead of her, his voice echoed unnaturally loud in the tunnel. "So what happens if we get to your dad's tower and it's still filled with scabs? Ever think of that one?"

"It won't be. They don't have enough men to spare in the field to keep in the tower."

"A lot's riding on that assumption."

"Sometimes, I wonder if you want us to lose, Coyle."

A column of light stabbed into the tunnel up ahead. The port from the tower. Just a few paces more.

"We could be walking into a slaughter," Coyle moaned.

"We've been walking between a slaughter, around a slaughter, and now under a slaughter," Alanna shot back. "I guess into and over a slaughter are the last on our list."

Payton couldn't help but smile.

Badric was the first under the cylinder of light. Together, Payton and Alanna hoisted him up so he could reach the grate covering the drain, and with a little help, he punched it open and pulled himself into the tower's basement. He reached down to help Alanna, then Payton, and finally Coyle out of the sewer. Before the grate had closed, the tunnel filled with the clang of metal. They'd gotten through.

"Hurry, up the stairs. Who knows how many there are," Payton said with barely enough air to breathe.

She knew the corridors well. These hallways had been her kingdom before she went to the university and founded the Kingdom of the Spider King and the Fire Queen. The Hook was scrawled all over the walls where her father and mother used to dine together, where they had invited lords and ladies and even King Gareth to share their food. The Hook stained it all, but the corridors were the same. They couldn't change them.

She led them up a spiraling staircase that peered out into a great atrium, one that left the heart of the lord's tower empty and cold. As she neared the top, blurry figures dotted the foyer below.

"Bar the doors," she ordered Badric. "They have to see the banner." She'd reached the top, the balcony where Leon Tallhart once surveyed the mighty city of Wellfleet and the lush lands reaching far away on all sides. She cut through her parents' bedroom, tapestries torn and defiled, defenders' corpses rotting on the floor. "They must see the power of Tallhart has returned."

Payton moved to the balcony, and then she saw it. The city her father had built burning away, logs for a campfire. Old stones, broken bones. Tears stinging at her eyes, she took it out of the sack. The banner with the red woman, a thin silhouette glancing over her shoulder at Payton, the one she'd found with Jon. He'd handed it to her that night outside the Crossroads. The only blanket either of them had, and he gave it to her. That night had been cold. Tears tickling her cheeks, Payton reached up to the Hook banner flapping outside her parents' bedchamber and tore it aside. She let the wind take it far, far away from that balcony. Then she hoisted up the Red Lady. As the moon emerged from behind the clouds, Payton lit the arrow Coyle had brought, fired it up into the sky, prayed they saw it.

Perhaps it was the moonlight's aura crashing upon her, or the burning arrow that had streaked overhead, but the army of shepherds had split. Half the sea turned back to storm the tower. It was working. Moments later, the fractured force that had remained began to falter, drowning beneath the waves of Payton Tallhart and Jon Carrow's army. The screams swelled in the night. The half of the army that had turned to the tower then split, half returned to help the failing legions, half continuing toward the lying tower. Only minutes later, the small fragment at the base of the tower remained alone. Perhaps in realization of Payton's trick, they rushed away from the vacant tower, but in disarray, were overrun by Jon.

"It worked!" she cried, laughing as tears poured across her face.

Badric joined to watch the surrender of the army's surviving sliver. He kissed her on the side of her head. He began to tell Payton how proud Leon Tallhart would be and—

The door to the chamber burst open. Coyle was waiting in the middle of the room. Only two Mehsanics, young ones, had made it up. The rest had fled. Coyle strode forward.

"Run, run, little scabs," he hissed. He was waving his sword through the air slowly, a lazy conductor at a drunken tavern. "Run, run."

One of the Mehsanics stumbled backward before taking off down the staircase and out of sight. The other one, a boy with no acne scars, dropped to his knees. He released his sword and began crying. A spreading stain darkened his pants, seeping toward his folded knees. His weeping filled the chamber.

"I'm sorry," the Sumaran whimpered. "I'm so, so sorry. I never even loved Mehsani."

"Then why are you wearing his stupid little hook?" Coyle growled, flicking the boy's tabard. "You're all shepherds until you meet the sword. Then you're just lost sheep."

He rounded the kneeling boy, waving his sword like a conductor's wand. Coyle planted his feet directly behind him and stared at Payton. He *glared* at her. Smirking, he cocked his head to the side, a child wordlessly asking if he's about to get into trouble.

"Coyle," she began, stepping slowly out of the moonlight.

He sucked in a long breath. "Do harts cry for lost sheep?"

"Coyle!"

The sword cleaved the boy's head like a melon.

In a flash she was on him. She knocked the sword from his grasp and took him to the floor. It was on his breath as he struggled to keep her hands from his throat. Her grasp tightened. In seconds his face turned purple. Too slow. She slid the knife he had taken from the butcher's out of his belt. She pressed it to his throat.

Coyle stopped thrashing and, for the first time all night, he was serene. His eyes examined her apathetically.

"Do it, cunt."

Payton pressed the knife deeper, let it linger until it broke flesh, but then she lifted it away. She knew that was strength. Not the ease of driving the sword down, but the burden of lifting it up.

Payt climbed off of him and threw the butcher's knife aside. She stared at the dead boy. Let the image of his halved head sink into her memory. Then she stumbled back to the balcony to let the breeze cool her off, the breeze that danced with the Red Lady, a sinuous, impressionist piece of artwork who crowned the greatest city in the world.

Jon made it to the top of the tower an hour later. Payton was hunched on her post on the balcony beneath the coy gaze of the Red Lady. Jon eyed her as he leaned next to Payton.

"Payton, uh, you okay?" he asked.

She nodded.

"I can't thank you enough, Payton. I don't know how much longer we would've held them." She could feel him sizing her up, wondering what was wrong. He cleared his throat. "Someone in your unit's been saying you came at him?"

"He killed a boy."

"I know. He says you went mad after he slew a Sumaran who broke into the chamber. Said you almost slit his throat for it."

She sighed. "You know, Jon, I might be younger than you, but at least I know that sometimes, stories are full of shit."

"Not all of them. Think of Meraxes. She isn't full of shit. She just won us this battle."

"We won this battle, Jon."

"Think about it. The tower is the box, you were Meraxes, the Suma-rans the invading army. All the same principles. If they hadn't thought your Northern retainers had arrived and taken the tower, we might still be fight-ing."

"You hate stories in the stars, Jon," she pointed out. "Why do you always invoke Meraxes?"

Jon's mouth opened, closed. He shrugged. "It's the truest of them."

"Let's just rest, yeah?"

They let a spell pass at the top of the city. The breeze was cool on her cheeks. Rain misted down. It was cooling Wellfleet, putting out its fires. Jon stood there awkwardly beyond an arm's reach.

"You're not taking it down?" he asked suddenly, gesturing to the Red Lady banner.

"No. Why?"

"Priests. They talk."

She grimaced. "All they're good for, I reckon. The Red Lady. I think I'll keep her."

"The Red Lady," he repeated. "That's what the inn was called anyway. The curve of her little breast told the priests she was the Red Harlot."

Payton shrugged. "So she is."

"So she is." He looked at her a long spell. He had inched closer, so that if her arms were outstretched they might kiss the tips of his fingers. The lines around his eyes broke the ice that been frozen there for months, since they fled Sumara and he left Dinian. The smile widened. "The Red Harlot. Others are saying a different name. Close, but better. The Red Hart."

Jon reached out as if to take her hand but grabbed the stone balcony just beside it instead. He closed a fist atop it before turning to leave. "I'll talk to this Coyle. He just killed the guy without pause? Huh." He turned his back and walked through her parents' chambers. "Might be grounds for imprison-ment," he said over his shoulder.

The Red Hart. Maybe she could live with that.

15

On Guilt

Marc Piper was missing.

"Said he was feeling ill. Nerves the night before," Alanna explained when Payton reached the eastern bank of the river. Her retinue had hardly budged since she'd left with Jem for their walk to the South. Even old Badric stood erect.

"Okay. Let's move on back. Thank you for waiting." Payton led the Harts down the road through the sloppy mud, which caked her boots in a thick crust. They mounted the band of horses tethered to the dead husk of a tree. Following her, they headed north to her pavilion.

"He seemed fine earlier," Payton said.

Alanna shrugged. "Said he might throw up. Then he left. How did the meeting go, if you don't mind my asking?"

Payton frowned. "Fine. I wanted to pick his brain a bit, see where they stood going into tomorrow."

"And?" Tam asked, trotting to the head of the column.

"I don't know. They want to split the Narrows, raze Alaveren, and form a new Braeland."

Tam whistled. "Ambitious." He ran his fingers through his salty hair, smiling in spite of himself.

"Mmm."

"You think Carrow will bite?"

"He rarely does. Especially when Lanair is the bait."

"How do you know Jem Nalda? Childhood?" Alanna asked.

Payton nodded. "My father adopted him when we were younger." She wished she had said more to Jem, whom she had had trouble calling Jem. His shoulders back, chin up, he had been the image of his father minus a hand. Guilt welled up now as it had then. When they were young teens, she faced the woe of Jem's expression after he'd awoken from a comatose week to find a bloody stump instead of his hand. The infection had spread too quickly by the time Payton had led him out of the woods and back to her father's castle. She blamed herself. It had been that wolf, though. Leaped out of the brush when their adventures took them too close to its den, threatened its children. What a sour taste. She blamed herself.

Jem had held such hope in his eyes when she first saw him across the river. So much had flurried in her chest. It was as if the seeing of it in his eyes dashed it from her. Seeing his smooth, dark skin; his tuft of curls hanging in a slant across his forehead; his missing hand; his smile. They reminded her of what she'd lost. She'd wanted to see her friend again.

She hoped she hadn't hurt him, for after the dashing of it from her chest, every word had been cold and indifferent flying from her tongue. Staring into the river, reliving her sprint through the sewers of her city, she hadn't seen it vanishing from his eyes. She'd let his hopes dash against her turned back.

There she was again. Blaming herself so quickly for every disappointment, whether she was the catalyst or a far-flung periphery with no inkling of control over the situation. Like on the flight north with Jon, blaming herself for her father's fall. That had been him, not her. That was them, the guilty. Not her.

Even when she was young, Payton always thought it was her. She pricked herself with blame. The blame came from imagined minds long lost to the recession of nights, but she held fast to it and stuck it to herself. But that was them, the guilty. Not her.

Payton made sure the door was locked every time. She put out the candles so not even she could see herself. Then she lay back in bed. The first orange strands were sprouting there, already wet when she slid her fingers down. Payton gasped as they plunged in. Too fast. It was sticky and smelled like something she hadn't before and shouldn't ever again. Payton massaged the outside, and that was enough for then. The wet seeped below her bottom into the mattress. Every second stopping to check if someone had picked the lock.

The next morning she scrubbed her hands until the smell had gone. Panicking, Payton doused the mattress with wine to mask the stain and drown the scent. She kept peering out every window. Could anyone have seen? Then she laughed; how could they peek into a tower on high?

But if they had heard?

Payton waited hours before leaving the room, and when she did, she dodged every "Good morning" and "How are you, Payton?" with awkward half grins and restless eyes. Everyone from her father to the cooks seemed to know. She couldn't meet their eyes. They would know. The guilt was a boulder tying her down by the shoulders.

Even as a young girl, the guilt was oppressive. Payton found a way to blame herself for what happened in the room that night and applied a reason for why she had sinned. Every eye pierced her. Guilt was a seed planted and harvested by the unseen eyes that scrutinized and the scrutinizing eyes that hadn't seen.

At least a year, maybe more, vanished before Payton could do it again. Only after countless days, drowning in prayer to wash the thoughts away. She kept the congruous gap on the pew between herself and others, the breadth that Faedelin had ordered to prevent sins from metastasizing. Payton embraced the Light. She let the oppressive, smoking thurible choke her as the priests hung it in her face, dangling right in front of her mouth, as they peered down their stomachs at her on her knees. When she left the church, the thought beating in her mind was oh, oh, oh, and when could she slide her fingers down her vagina again and feel wonderful. Payton hurried back inside.

"And now you know the price of sacrilege," Leon scolded her.

It was barely hours after they'd sewn her back up after the fruitless endeavor. It hurt. It still did. What hurt even more was the secrecy Leon forced upon the ordeal. No one knew, save for them two and the midwife, who he sent away to the villages of the north.

"Eternal loss. That's the price." She would've screamed at him, but her stomach felt like it would burst. "If only you'd listened to me, stayed away from that prince, this shame wouldn't rest upon our name. I knew those sunburned monkeys shouldn't have been trusted."

"Kala was going to help you," she whispered, incapable of more than that.

"She gave me two fruitless gifts. Remind me never to ask a Calidumi for help again."

Fruitless, barren, desolate. A wasteland of wounding words.

Four years more, as Payton prepared to go south once again, this time to Sumara. The Reaving was taking a breath, and she was able to face the world again, and she could look at herself, touch herself once again. She divorced herself from that wasteland. Its shame sickened her. Put a sour taste on her tongue.

"Good evening, Lady Tallhart." The men bowed their heads to her. All around, bowing to her as she marched away from the river in Alaveren.

One night she locked the door again. Payton blew out the candle, but then she lit the wick again so she could see it. Then, out of some wicked flash of adventure, she unlocked the door. Shivers ran over her naked body. The flickering candle accenting her body, she peered into the mirror. She ran her hand over her body: her mane of orange, her orange curls above her vagina, her white scar beneath the left eye, her small breasts, one slightly larger than the other, that she could cup and conceal in callused palms, her scars and her scar at the navel. Her callused palms traced them all in the light. This was Payton Tallhart.

She knew that if Kala had been there, she would've accepted it long ago, rather than after ages of guilt and shame receding endlessly beneath the nights but never vanishing. She had taken Payton in one night.

Kala asked her if she'd ever looked at herself naked. Payton said no. The queen shed her gown.

Her breasts hung long and flat, areolas withered from many children. At the base of her belly, skin bunched up as if in honor of her children's gestation. Her arms were thin at her sides. They hung strangely low, nearly to her knees. Strange, dark freckles dotted her chest.

"Look," she commanded softly, seeing that Payton had looked away. "It is just a body. Look at yourself, Payton. There is not a speck of flesh on you that you should be ashamed of." She bent to the floor and slid her gown back on. "Have you ever noticed that Faedelinity turns women into trees?"

"Trees?"

"Yes. Faedelinity has turned us into trees. Men are willing to climb our branches, use our shade, and pluck our fruits. But they will not listen to us. How can you listen to a tree? Could you take a tree's philosophy seriously? Even I might think a tree is crazy for asserting some misplaced sense of agency. So even as I discuss this philosophy with you, I am asking myself, 'Have you gone mad with a runaway notion of autonomy?'

"Since we are trees, we forget that we are the ones who drink of the earth and breath back into it. We are the mothers of the earth who are the daughters of the Mother. Why should we feel guilty for it? Let us embrace what we are.

"Do not fear transgression, Payton. It is not transgression to orgasm, but transcendence." She cradled Payton's cheek. "Embrace yourself, Payton," Kala told her. "There is too much in the world that is frightening to run scared of ourselves."

Payton shook the memories loose. They were clouding her focus when, here at the fulcrum of the night, she required as much focus as she could muster. Seemingly hundreds of Northerners thronged the streets.

"I swear it, Carrow stopped the thing in the dead of night," some men were saying in Payton's earshot. One, who she believed was called Eames, scratched his belly fat. He milled about with a small band of sleepless soldiers. They congregated along a crowded bazaar where men and women flocked for midnight sustenance.

"You're lying," another man said.

"No!" Eames exclaimed. "The horse charged at Lord Carrow, all wild and savage. Then he started murmuring this incantation by the river, and before we knew it, this wild horse was eating out of his palm. Then he says a calm voice does it. Calm voice, my ass. The man's got some dark magic lurking in him."

The men around Eames muttered in accord. One replied, "Everyone knows they teach sorcery in Sumara. Every boy learns it."

Fools, Payton thought.

"Do you think this treaty could work?" Tam asked. He was beside her on his horse. "Three hundred years, and no one has made one work."

"Yes. It could happen," she answered.

"You think so?"

"Of course," Payton responded. Eames and the men who had been talking sorcery and about Jon's wild horse vanished around the last corner somewhere in the bazaar. Fools. She dismissed the Harts after she noticed Badric was beginning to fall asleep in his saddle. Tam waited for a moment.

"Of course, I think so," Payton continued. "Do you?"

The man shrugged. "I wonder about Carrow. Going into that tower alone. Wonder if he's frightened."

"It's not Carrow I fear for."

"What do you fear? I see the worry in your face."

Payton locked eyes with Tam. "Transgression."

"Sorry?"

"Nothing. You're dismissed, Tam. I can ride the rest of the way myself."

"It's just around the corner; I don't mind."

"No, I need some time with my thoughts."

"Need someone to talk those out with again?"

She caressed the man's cheek. "Tomorrow night."

"Very well," he replied, pressing his face tenderly into her palm. "Good night, Payton."

He directed his horse toward the nearest tavern and tied it up outside. Then Tam strolled inside. When Tam had gone, Payton headed toward her riverside pavilion where the Red Lady hung limp in the windless night.

The thoughts of guilt bounced around her head. Reels of shame revolved in her mind. Just a tree imagining it could walk.

Fuck, vagina, masturbation, penis, cum. All forbidden like chocolate before supper, but what are they except a random vomit of letters?

Payton froze. She'd found Marc Piper.

16

The Chase

The lone candle burning within Payton's pavilion illuminated the man's shiny face as he rummaged through the paper tomes on her desk. If not for his thick neck, he would look like a squirrel—dark, beady, caffeinated eyeballs darting around. He had no place in her pavilion.

Payton slipped off her horse. The shadows slanting off adjacent buildings concealed her in a dark embrace. Her pavilion, resting between two eddies of the river, stood beyond the reach of a tiny canyon. From here, she could observe in secrecy.

The man rifled through her papers, tossing maps and insignificant leaflets aside after a quick glance. He mopped away the sweat glistening on his cheekbones. After examining several more sheets, he slammed the table.

A spark went up inside her. This was her pavilion, her papers and maps. His hands were all over her things, his eyes reading words that belonged to her. And for what?

Years and years and years later, she still couldn't escape that intrusion. Not in her chamber in Wellfleet as a young woman, now not in Alaveren as an adult. Always the eyes of men peering into Payton.

She lingered in the shadows for ten more heartbeats. As she waited, Piper's motions grew quicker, his glances more caffeinated. She knelt, wrapped a stone in her palm, and tossed it across the small canyon. It hit the desk beside him. Like a deer suddenly aware of someone approaching, he froze, his head suspended in a tense gaze beyond the light of the candle. For a moment, his eyes lingered on her. They soon flicked away, however, since Payton was obscured in darkness.

Licking his lips, Piper straightened several papers. It made little reparation for his mess. Then he rushed out of her pavilion.

Payton quickly followed in his wake. The faint murmur of drinking soldiers resonated throughout the city's darkness, permeated by a mutual and unanimous sense of restlessness. She squinted to keep sight of Piper, who sped beyond her pavilion and down the road.

Late at night, the men and women of her army still wandered the roads of the Holy City. Piper rushed through the crowds. He was barely visible in the light of flickering torches. Payton strained to keep sight of him.

She remained several paces behind him. Conscious of her fiery curls, she donned the hood of her cloak. Hopefully, he would take no heed of a hooded figure; the sky, growing cloudier throughout the night, threatened rain. The world around her seemed to grumble with thunder deep in its belly. Where would it crack? She tucked a stray curl under the hood.

The dead city loomed ominously in the night. Its shattered buildings, black teeth in a black sky, felt closer than in the daylight. The space between them narrowed in the illusory dark. She shivered.

Piper weaved through the crowd. His shoulders hunched up high, he looked like a great vulture gliding awkwardly through the nervous soldiers around him. They were looking at her, curious at the hooded figure trailing the vulture up ahead. Again she fingered her orange curls. The sweat kept them tucked away. The night had grown hot again after a brief chill as thick clouds rolled out upon the sky, thickened the air with water. It cast a haze. She squinted to keep sight of Piper.

He was coming up on a building that was mostly intact. A shattered pile of rocks was a jewel in this place, a dead city in a barren valley. A sign hung from the apex. The Naughty Friar, it read. She recalled a brothel named the same back in the university. So business followed them the miles south to the Narrows, to Alaveren, and to Piper.

He waited out front. Soldiers, some shirtless, some sleeping, some drinking, sat clustered beneath the balcony of the second floor. Their dull murmur, like a handful of inebriated bees, dulled their words to the vague sounds. They eyed him. Even in a drunken, tired hour, they recalled their training, remained wary of interlopers abroad. He darted inside.

Payton sighed. She backed out of the street, disinterested in conversing with her men, fairly hopeful to remain unnoticed. The shadows of Alaveren sucked her in.

She withdrew into a building, a medical clinic that had been set up, she remembered. Jon had had that limp while fleeing north. These men and women, lying asleep upon cots in the foyer, were missing legs. Others lacked arms. And though his wounds hadn't compared with these, he had been a burden nagging her during the chase.

Payton peered out of the window, careful not to wake the men and women sleeping off their pain. And she remembered. The past coalesced in her mind. And in remembering, she went back.

✿ ✿ ✿

Jon Carrow was hurt. Saewyn had cut his leg, she knew. And Saewyn was dead. She knew that, too. Payton knew many things now. Leon Tallhart, her father, was carved up like a pig. The Reaving reopened. But she kept her eyes ahead, to the North, to home.

157

"Get up, Jon," she snapped. The man lay beside the dying fire, his eyes emptying into the flames as it flickered out of existence. The man would go blind soon, staring pointlessly at the brightness. "Let's go."

"You go."

"Jon, no one likes a man hollowed by self-pity."

"Can't. I can't. I just can't. Please, let me go."

Payton commanded him, "Get up. Drink some water."

He took the flask of water and pathetically sipped it.

"The Crossroads are a mile away. We can get there by sundown; the Sumarans shouldn't catch us before then." The hillsides wrapped around them, a transient reprieve from the shepherds dogging them to the south. East, west, and south, the Reaving was breaking open. Braeland burned once again.

Jon dropped the flask. As she picked it up, she inspected him from head to toe. His blond hair, flowing and beautiful just days ago, was matted to his head in a dirty, sweaty rug that she could smell from here. Pimples dotted his face. A beard had begun, but it was the scraggly, unkempt, unwashed beard of a pauper, not the robust beard of royalty. And somehow, more light had faded from his milky skin.

"I should leave you," she threatened.

His eyes flicked away from the fire at her.

"You killed my father. Lord Leon Tallhart is dead because of you."

His expression was stone.

"Saewyn is dead because of you. What the fuck happened?"

Silence. The fire whispered itself away.

"What happened?"

Jon sighed. "It was the boy. He found a letter I wrote to your father. He told Alaryn. He was frightened."

"Oh, Dinian."

"He's fine."

"What do you know of it?" She snorted. "The way you spoke to that boy like a wooden figurine, 'Oh, um, ah, yes, um,' stumbling over your words like a schoolboy over Royce. What kind of father were you?"

"I saved that boy's life!"

"What a life you gave him in return."

Jon sprang upright to his knees. She towered over him. "Fine! I wasn't your fucking father! I wasn't Leon fucking Tallhart. But I saved him."

A short silence flattened the fire.

"I was the fool." He rested back on his haunches. "I shouldn't have trusted the boy with the letter, and it was my fault. I shouldn't have trusted the boy."

She smacked him so hard he fell over the log behind him. She leered overhead.

"Dinian. Not 'the boy.'"

Payton sat back down across the fire from Jon. Drawing in a long breath, she realized she felt better this side of the fire. She didn't want him to see the hurt her father's death had caused. He couldn't have that power over her. She owned him now. She was good right there. Right there, beyond arm's reach, where she couldn't see his pitiful blue eyes asking the world to feel sorry for them.

❂ ❂ ❂

A scream went up in Alaveren. Payton jumped, knocked her head on the wooden frame of the window. The wounded woman closest to her stirred in her sleep, but after turning over, the soldier sunk deeply back into her cot. Seeing this, Payton turned her eyes back to The Naughty Friar.

Another scream. Half of the soldiers out front hurried inside, while the sound of shattering glass sounded high and sharp in the night. Following the breaking glass, Payton darted back into the street.

"Fire!" somebody yelled from the upstairs window. "Evacuate the building!"

Payton broke into a run. As men and women bustled outside, she charged into the brothel. Burning wood seared her nostrils. She drew her sword.

Terrified men streamed past her, ignored her as she waded toward the roaring flame that Piper inarguably set. She hadn't seen him flee. He must be lying in wait.

The fire ascended quickly up the staircase and took to the tapestries lining the walls. Payton held cloth over her mouth. Coughing would begin in moments. She'd find Piper, lest his body crisp up in his handiwork. It'd devour the building in minutes at this rate.

A shape appeared on the opposite threshold. Though she imagined her courier coming forward, the shoulders were spread too broadly, back straightened too rigidly. The man, whose face was hid under a hood, floated calmly into the maelstrom toward Payton, who was on a knee to duck the smoke. He drew closer, ostensibly unperturbed by the hell set in the common room. Then, as if flicking a fly, his fingers loosened the red scarf around his throat.

Payton leaped to her feet. The man in the red scarf lunged forward, his blade singing through the smoky air. She deflected it. They swapped stances, her landing on the common room's far threshold and him blocking the only exit she knew of. Pitch clouds choked the ceiling. Hunched, Payton beat the man back. He met her blows with seeming ease and confidence. So perfect and timely were his movements, she felt as though she were striking at a mirror. A cocktail of fear and frustration quickened her strikes. She hacked his forearm. Pain erupted inches above her wrist, though no blow had fallen there. Screaming, she fell to her knees.

Cowed only briefly by the wound, the man pounced toward Payton. She rolled over and sprung toward the escape. His footsteps hounded her. Payton whipped around, took out his knee with a fist. Suddenly her legs buckled, and they collapsed in a heap together. She recoiled. So did he. In rising, she was stunned that they had rotated again so that she stood opposite the only exit with him in the way.

That fire wouldn't delay. She knew she must be quick. Payton stepped back. Perhaps the smoke tricked her eyes, but the man seemed to edge toward the door. She retreated to the far threshold and glanced back. His form had dropped behind layers of smoke. She raced backward into the hallway and toward a rear door that opened to an alley.

Trailed by, or rather pummeled by, a wave of hot air, the rear door swung open when Payton barreled into it. The ground was cool on her cheek. Coming out of the stumble, she whipped around. Her sword, steam emanating from the metal, pointed at the man's chest as he approached. He approached her with assurance. The wood, its joints cracking at every seam, squealed as the maelstrom peaked and ate the building alive. The ceiling whined, moaned, screamed. Beneath it, the man raised his sword as if to throw it. Before he could, the ceiling knelt to the fire and doused him in a blanket of flame and timber.

Payton covered her face. The collapse swept the back alley with another wall of burning air. Following the ceiling's fall, the night went quiet again, letting the fire crack its joints peacefully. For a moment, she observed the wreckage. It ate the wood so peacefully. Snapped beams and boards evoked the twisted masts of shipwrecks. One might be forgiven for thinking it just a bonfire, perhaps for Faedelin. How did a thing so transient and apathetic burst with such dominion and passion?

The alley behind the brothel was all black. Though the man had been swallowed in the collapse, Payton gripped her blade. Someone had smashed the lantern mounted to the wall of the alley. Piper, probably. She tiptoed through the patch of shards. Smoke, translucent as mist, curled up from the candle, which had fallen with the glass.

Restless Northerners flocked to the scene. They'd look for anything to take their minds off of the meeting the next morning. It was ostensibly a peacemaking effort, but they were smart enough to know they were packing fireworks in a volcano. They were frightened.

Payton benefitted from the distraction. They considered her with half a glance and indifference. Her mind kept turning, turning, turning. What had Piper been searching for in her private notes? Where was he going? Who was he going to?

And why did the spook in the scarf from this afternoon return to make an end? No matter. He made his own end.

Ever since that night in Sumara when, unbeknownst to her, those around her had been fashioning a noose for the Tallharts, she ignored no mischief. First, it had been Saewyn, who hadn't minded her scar; then Dinian with his toothy grin; then Jon's tender, if awkward, disposition. That night they vanished. Ignorant drunks barged into Saewyn's chambers and as he listened to their words, he wiped her saliva off his mouth and his eyes filled up with hate.

She clenched the sword round its rouge, cloth handle. Come for anyone, come for Faedelin himself with nothing but his skin to save him, you'd carry off the Light embodied like a babe. It was only while riding Shadowblight, wielding his great sword, that Faedelin triumphed over Mehsani and the usurpers of the South. Take away the steed, take away the sword, what was Faedelin but the remnant of a legend?

Yet they clung to him. Payton often wondered if there would be a Braeland without Faedelin. He had given the hilly, windswept country its name, written its founding document, given it the Way, the book that brought all the others beneath a single title. She often failed to find where the one ended and the other began.

Of course, of course. But what don't the priests in the church reveal? If Braeland evaporated without Faedelin, the country vanished lacking Mehsani.

Beyond the alley, a prayer group encircled a small altar next to a makeshift barracks. Atop the altar, a priest read verses of the Way from the Book of Ideals. Her father's favorite. She spotted Piper, nestled deep within the crowd. The man was toying with her, trying to shake the chase by appearing as mundane as any other soldier within her army.

When she was young, Payton had studied insects trapped beneath a jar at the university. Innocently, she thought nothing of it. When she'd grown and first touched herself, she found herself within the jar held down by the palms of others, who peered down at her with their scrutinizing eyes. Then she pitied those bugs.

Now she held the jar. She could reveal herself to these men. They'd fall to their knees for her, tear Piper to shreds if she asked it. Something within her wanted to know the deeper powers at work here. So she held the jar. Let him be the helpless little bug.

❂ ❂ ❂

"No, no…no no no not the room," Jon muttered. His breath was hot with the stink of sleep. Payton slept barely an arm's length from Jon, passed out on his cot in the attic of an inn at the Crossroads. The man rarely slept, she noticed, but when he did, a chorus of tormented mumblings narrated his slumber. Annoyed, she couldn't sleep when he did. She watched Jon as he begged an unseen tormentor not to put him back into the room. "Please, not again. No no no."

Payton kicked off the blankets, stood, and nearly bumped her head on the slanting eaves. She'd asked for the smallest room in the inn. The women at the bar had shrugged and led them to the attic, more of a closet than a room. Other than their cots, a bedside table sat opposite the door. She pushed the door open.

Five flights later, she entered the common room, empty save a few slumbering guests whose drink had prohibited the long walk upstairs. A shy hearth cracked and spat across from the bar, where a woman leaned on the grainy wood and peered into a pint with no head.

"It'll go flat without the foam," Payton said as she took a stool.

The woman shrugged. "I like it better that way."

"Flat?"

The barkeep shrugged again. "Habit."

"I'll have one, please."

The blonde barkeep filled a pint and slid it across the coarse countertop to Payton, who caught it awkwardly. The foamy head plopped onto her hand. The woman laughed at her.

"You don't frequent bars much."

"Guess not."

"It's okay. Couldn't catch a sliding mug worth a damn my first time."

Payton eyed the woman. "What's your name?"

163

The barkeep smiled. "I'm Alanna." She scratched one of several scars on her face.

"How'd you become an innkeeper in the Crossroads? Lucrative business."

"Veteran's benefits," Alanna answered. "After your two years in Faedelin's Guard, they give you a pretty penny. Prettier if those two years turn into ten, like mine did." She pointed to her scarred face. "One for every year."

"So that's why you prefer flat beer."

"Yep. Good luck finding fresh ale miles away from the nearest village and five months deep into a campaign." She swished the flat beer. "Reminds me of younger days."

"What campaign did you serve in?"

"Plenty. The Winter War. The War in the Narrows. The Reaving, for a time. I fought for Gareth's succession after Willem's heirs died. I helped the Incorporation in Calidum. Too many to count." Alanna sipped the beer. "What about you?"

"Huh?"

"You've seen fighting. I noticed the sword, noticed your wariness. What you running from?"

Payton filled her mouth with ale.

"Don't worry. I left the Guard long ago. Tired of it."

"We're not running," Payton insisted.

"No? A high-born woman takes an attic under a fake name as the Reaving reopens? Reminds me of all those shitty fantasy tales. The bumbling heroes always escape even as the dark lord sends an army to slay them."

Payton took another swallow.

"Look, I spent ten years doing this. Forgive me if I've overstepped my place."

"No, no, it's fine." Payton thought for a moment. Since Sumara, she'd kept her curls hidden, used fake names, and paid gold for nooks in the attics of every inn. Too close to Sumara for tongues to utter "Tallhart" or "Carrow." But the Crossroads was farther north. A motley stew of Braeland, the Crossroads offered a lukewarm welcome to every traveler.

"We're coming from Sumara," she said finally. "Refugees from the purge that just happened."

Alanna whistled. "I heard about that. Nasty stuff. Lord Tallhart lost his head for it, they say. Didn't believe it at first. I mean, *the* Leon Tallhart. No way he's dead."

Payton swallowed. "He's gone."

"King Gareth was fucking furious. Especially after Mavogar fired on the ship from the university. Besieged Wilbraema as a response not five days later. Word has it Lord Lanair is marching on the city as we speak. Probably will have it free, if his leadership is what I hear," Alanna explained.

"So an old book grows its body count," Payton said, sighing.

Instead of replying, Alanna frowned and finished the rest of her ale. The women let the silence linger a few minutes. Revelers outside got into a heated discussion. Something about the Narrows. The closer the proximity to that valley, the touchier the conversations grew. Payton recalled her father describing the Crossroads to her as a child. He had called it a bowl of mud boxed in by four mud heaps and led by muddy men and women. They spoke with razor tongues, slicing their way back to that holy valley. The Narrows. Reveling inevitably sank to confrontation. Payton shook her head, finished her ale.

"I fought with Lord Tallhart once," Alanna said suddenly. She stared into the bottom of her empty glass as she spoke. "It was during the Reaving. I was with him when we took Sumara during the last stages."

When Payton realized Alanna intended to say no more, she touched the barkeep's wrist. "Please, continue."

"I was in the van with Tallhart. Never seen a man so brave as him, though sometimes I think it was piety that drove him, not bravery. If you think on it, piety's a bit selfish. You're willing to lay down your life for Faedelin, but only so the Twelve Sentinels accept you into the Light. That's selfish. Killing the infidels so when you get killed, you get your prize. Sometimes I wonder if that's what drove him.

"There was a boy dying in the hall of the Stone Drum. Was in charge of holding the gate. I found him with his throat slashed. He kept waving at me to come closer, and at first, I avoided his gaze. But before he faded, I leaned in to see if I could hear anything. His throat was ruined, but I could kind of make out a word."

The silence irked Payton. "What?" she demanded, a tad hastily.

Alanna flicked a glance at her. "Ghost."

The door slammed open behind them. Payton whipped around. Ten Sumaran soldiers sauntered into the inn, blades drawn.

✪ ✪ ✪

Piper was sliding away. Nudging his way through the prayer, but not as to disturb the others or to draw attention to himself. Payton pushed gingerly through the crowd. Couldn't lose him.

The parishioners weren't moving to let her through. She pushed a few men to make a path, eliciting tired grumbles. In the crowd, she lost sight of Piper. She pushed faster. Her disturbance awakened the dormant restlessness in the crowd. The next man she nudged smacked her back.

Payton fell forward onto the cobbles. Through the legs of those around her, she saw Piper take off at a sprint. She was so focused on him, she didn't notice her hood had come off in the fall, unleashing her fiery mane. They gasped.

"It's her!"

"The Red Hart!"

"What in Faedelin's name!"

"My lady, I apologize, I'm so, so sorry."

"Move!" she cried.

Stumbling over the men as they fell to their knees, she broke off at a run, chasing the thief as he vanished into the shadows.

✪ ✪ ✪

Payton's hand went to her hood instantly. Busy surveying the sleepy common room, the Sumarans took little heed of her impulsive reaction. They spread out in a line and blocked the door. Nervously, she tucked the strands of her orange hair away. Then she noticed Alanna noticing her.

"You the innkeeper?" a soldier asked. Tall for a Sumaran, he stood a head over Payton, who kept her face averted at a slight angle. A fresh wound slanted across his face.

"Yes," Alanna replied. "This is a private establishment, and on the north side of town, I might add. What business you got here?"

Clearing his throat, the man slapped a paper on the counter. In her periphery, Payton saw a rough etching of her likeness. The artist had even colored her hair. "Looking for this woman. Seen her?"

"No."

"Quick answer. You sure?"

Alanna narrowed her eyes. "Who is she?"

"What does the name matter?"

"Well, I'm not blind, boy, so I haven't seen her. Maybe I've heard her name, though. Lots of folks pass through my inn, and as the liquor flows so do loose words from their tongues."

The soldier cleared his throat again. "This woman is Payton Tallhart, daughter of Lord Leon Tallhart, who recently planned the assassination and overthrow of Lord Lanair Mavogar in Sumara. She's a traitor."

Alanna's eyebrow arched. "Technically speaking, by both Faedelin's and Mehsani's words, treason would be taking the life of the king. Lanair Mavogar's no king."

The soldiers rustled. The man beside Payton tensed after Alanna had spoken; his palms creaked the counter as he clenched its edge. She could hear him choke down a swallow.

"Not yet."

"Mmm. See, those words sound more treasonous than anything Lady Tallhart has done." Alanna spread her palms on the counter, rasping loudly as they adopted a wide, confident stance for the woman. "In fact, it sounds like she hasn't done anything. You've already killed her father. Leave it at that."

The man whistled. "Talk about loose words flowing from tongues."

She grinned. "I've got a very loose tongue."

That took the soldier aback. Then he laughed. "Maybe you can show me one day."

"I take boys from only north of the Narrows to bed."

"A shame." He folded the paper up, tucked it away, and began to depart. Payton remained tensed as he did. She waited for the door to open, but it never did. Then a lock clicked.

Alanna put her hand under the counter. "If you're not drinking, you're leaving."

"I'll leave," the man's voice came, "but a word of advice before I go. Cut your hair or dye it, Tallhart. There's no good way to hide a sunset when it lights up the whole sky."

Alanna whipped a blade out from under the bar and turned to Payton. Expressionless, she said, "Run."

Payton imagined her orange hair flowing behind her like the torch's trail in a runner's grasp.

Piper had ducked around the nearest corner, which led to the heart of the eastern camp. That was where all of the soldiers were, the lines of makeshift shops and taverns. The bazaar, as it were, was fairly busy. She would lose him quickly if she didn't hurry.

She thought about calling out his name, but her sprint had drawn enough attention as it was. She would have to catch him on foot. And there he was, darting into a tavern.

She hurried in after him. Immediately, the fazed patrons were whispering, "Is that her?," and other confused questions. Payton heard a door slam in the rear of the bar. She bounded toward it.

When she hurtled into the alley, Piper was already swinging a sword at her head.

The clatter of blades erupted in the common room. Payton blasted through the door to the kitchen. No thoughts churned in her mind. Only pure need. A knife, a pot, a fork—she'd take anything. That poor woman wouldn't last long against ten trained soldiers. And then they'd be after her.

She heard the door swing open behind her. Two soldiers, including the one who'd spoken, appeared in the doorway. They darted after her.

Payton ducked into the freezer. Great cow carcasses hung in rows and columns that she slipped in between to shake their trail. In the cold, her breath came out in misty clouds. They were close.

At the far end of the meat locker, she found a table of cleavers. She grabbed one and fell to a crouch where she could peer beneath the dangling carcasses and watch their feet. They had slowed down, stepping carefully around the cows several rows away.

Payton crept toward the nearest Sumaran. The tile floor absorbed the sound of her padded feet. To soften her presence even more, she breathed through pursed lips.

The one she hunted turned suddenly. He was moving too far away to pursue; the other one could flank her too easily. So she turned toward the second Sumaran. She crouched beside the man, one cow separating them. "You see her?" he whispered.

"No," the first replied.

"Maybe she's gone."

"Maybe."

She swung the cleaver. It sank into his calf with a sickening crunch. His legs swung up after the assault. Payton leaped out from behind the cow carcass and glared at his bulging eyes.

"You!"

Before he could finish, she ripped out the cleaver from his leg and planted it in his face. The second soldier appeared at the end of the row, broke into a sprint after a heartbeat. Then Payton took off at a dash, holding the cleaver tightly in her grasp as she fled.

✿ ✿ ✿

Piper's blade grazed the cap of Payton's head. She rolled away. As she came up to her feet, he rushed forth. In a single motion, she drew her blade and blocked his, barely an inch from her heart. He foamed at the mouth like a rabid dog. His weight had thrown her against the wall opposite the inn. Gathering her strength and using the wall to push off, she tossed him back.

"What are you doing, Marc?"

"It had to be done!" he cried.

"What did?"

"He saw me doing it and said what you'd do and so I had to do it."

"Do what?"

"I couldn't go on. He owned me after that," he whimpered. "You should see him when he's angry, Lady Tallhart. The power his voice holds. I had to take them because he saw me doing it."

"Take what?"

Piper raised his sword above his head and came at her with all his fury.

✿ ✿ ✿

The Sumaran chased her inside. The common room was a mess, and her breath was heavy, and so was the bloody cleaver in her hand. Yet she held it high as she sprinted through the kitchen, out of the inn, dashed across the alley and into the stables, where she hid in a stall.

The Sumaran was close behind, his feet crunching on the hay. His pace slowed. He said, "Come here, Payton," but she kept silent, despite the smell of dung.

Payton crept toward a horse as he said, "I don't care for you since you're a Faed girl. All I want is my salary and to go home. I won't touch you. I won't even look at you if you don't want me to. All I want is my salary."

And as he said that, she gingerly and athletically climbed on the horse, as her ancestors rode the harts of the North woods and mastered the craft of riding the deer, fleet and nimble. So unique was the talent held by her earliest ancestors they named themselves the Tallharts. The horse barely made a peep.

The man continued, "You read those stories about mercenaries trailing the bounty, and then it's all rape and violence, but not me, Payton, not me. All I want is my salary and to go home. Sometimes that's just what it is." She whispered in the horse's ear while he finished with, "Just money."

The horse erupted from its stall with a kick, and its hoof took the man's jaw clean off. For a moment, the man stood in complete shock. He gazed at his ruined jaw on the ground. The horse came down on it, shattered the curved bone into pieces. His gaze shifted upward to Payton. His eyes seemed to say, "What in the name of Mehsani?" Then they rolled back, and he slumped to the ground.

✪ ✪ ✪

Piper had wasted his breath. So had Payton. She thought he seemed to be hunching over and moved in to strike. It was a ploy. He drew her in, stepped back, threw her off balance, and swung the butt of his sword into her cheekbone.

The force of the blow sent the ground rushing up. The soil sucked her in. The sky seemed to flee from her, abandoning her to the inexorable pull of the earth.

As her vision blackened, she watched Piper scamper away, turn south, and disappear.

✪ ✪ ✪

Alanna's eyes were wide when she came out to the stables. She whistled when she saw the Sumaran's head missing its jawbone. The tongue hung limply as a dog's hangs when its thirsty.

"How'd you get out?" Payton asked.

"The man you're with," she replied. "He appeared out of nowhere, took out two of the Sumarans before any of us even knew he was there. Like an apparition."

"Where is he now?"

"Packing your things. Where will you go?"

Payton patted the horse. "North. My father's castellan, Sir Badric, holds the city of Wellfleet thirty miles from here. We'll go to him."

"You'll need a hand."

"Will I?"

Alanna knelt. "In a strange way, tonight has reinvigorated my sense of purpose. Let me fight for you."

She frowned. "More bodies'll attract notice. We need to make it past the disputed grounds to friendly territory with few footprints."

"I'll be an extra body, but also an extra blade. Besides, they'll have my head for the mess inside after this."

Payton nodded. "Fine. But you'll have to pack now."

Alanna sped off.

When Payton got to the attic, Jon closed the flap to his bag and handed Payton's to her. Wordlessly, he brushed passed her down the stairs.

Before Payton turned away, she saw the rope swaying from the rafters.

✪ ✪ ✪

Payton didn't know how long she'd been out, for when her eyes fluttered open. After a beat, she recalled the force of the blow, the pain in her fall. She shot upright. Her hand went to her stomach in fear. A few seconds passed before she was content that everything was safe.

The smell of booze filled her nose. She realized she was probably in a tavern her people had set up for the week. She rolled onto her side.

"My, my, Payton Tallhart, you've had one busy night."

Beside her, rocking in a chair by the open window and blowing rings of smoke over its sill, was Jon Carrow.

17

Old Stones

"What are you doing here?" she asked after struggling upright.

Her vision was blurry, but she could make out the man in an unvarnished rocking chair, thumbing down a ball of tobacco in a pipe. Chatter from a nearby room buzzed from the half-open doorway, through which fell a dim scalene of twitching torchlight. The wooden walls of the room were stained with smoke, and with soot, and with time.

"Word got to me that you'd been running around like you'd lost your mind," he replied. "Some said you were chasing the spirit of Mehsani through the streets, him fleeing before your flame."

She snorted. Sitting upright made her nauseous, so Payton rested against the wall. It had a slight give under her weight.

"So was it him? Mehsani reborn?" Jon jested.

"Marc Piper."

Jon nodded knowingly. "What were you chasing him for?"

173

"After I," she began before stopping. Better to not mention meeting Jem, not when under the lens of Jon's calculating, indifferent stare. "I found him rummaging through my things. Had said he felt ill to Alanna and Badric before sneaking off."

Jon extended the pipe to Payton, but she shook her head. Then he lit it and took a drag.

"I wouldn't dwell on it, Payton. I always thought Piper was a strange man. You're sure it was him?"

"Undoubtedly."

"You did get hit on the head," he pointed out.

"Yes. By him."

Jon eyed her as smoke came out of his nostrils in twin spindles. He tapped the long, curving pipe on his knee to the beat of some unheard song. After the spindles had emptied from his nostrils, they pooled around his lap and rose, in clouds, obscuring his face momentarily.

"Don't dwell on it. What we have tomorrow. Or later today, I suppose," he realized.

"My courier spies on me, runs from me, and tries to kill me, and you think I should just let it go? You, Jon, who can't let anything go?" she pointed out.

"I let everything go, Payton, but everything keeps coming back."

"The night before the most important meeting in years, with Mehsanics and Faeds at the other's throat and a murderous man loose in our ranks, and you want to let it go."

"I'll put out a ransom on him. Feel better?"

Payton clenched her jaw. Arguing with Jon Carrow was like debating with a wall. Push all day, try to move it, it'll be where it stood that morning and you'll be panting for breath.

"I'll put out the ransom," she replied. "He's my courier."

Jon's hands went up in mock defeat. "I surrender." He hissed out another pair of spindles, this time out the open window. Then he displayed a rare grin. "Love that moon."

The paint was chipping off most of the walls in the backroom. She assumed that this had been and was once again a bar, given the bitter scent of beer and buzzing murmur of people in the next room. Old Braelandish bars often had rooms like these. Either the proprietors lived in the bar or they took naps during nightlong shifts.

She thought that this was the sort of place Leon Tallhart would never set foot in. Sometimes she thought the man's resolve against liquor had come from some unspoken addiction from before she was born. Her mother having died of fever when Payton was a newborn, she never had a source to corroborate her theory.

"No one's sleeping tonight," Jon observed, peering out of the window as his tiptoes held the chair fixed at a reclined position. From there, he might see up the alley into the street. "They're drinking and praying their way to dawn."

"You couldn't sleep?"

"No. After I visited you this afternoon, I saw a boy dying by the river. A stake had gone through his throat." He clicked his tongue. "Never had a chance. I slept a little after that, but you know me. Sleep never lasts long.

"I was walking north, toward the bridge. I figured you'd be back at your pavilion. Then this horse comes out of nowhere. Thing was wild with spirits; none of the men could calm her down. I did eventually, but she might've hurt herself if I hadn't."

"The men said you used some Mehsanic magic to soothe her."

"I'm sure they did. One foot in the South, one foot in the North, as they say."

"Why are you really here, Jon?"

His head snapped to meet her gaze. She couldn't tell if he was shocked or hurt by her suspicion.

"I couldn't sleep after the horse, and then Badric told me you'd been running around. Forgive me for caring."

"Don't be passive, Jon." Payton massaged the lump on her face. "Tonight has been strange."

"You'll be the leader of Braeland, Payton. Everyone respects you. You can't be running through Alaveren like a little girl."

"I'll be the leader of Braeland, Jon. I can do what I want."

He smirked. "Talbot the Tyrant probably said something similar before they deposed him."

"It's strange how this night feels," she spoke over him. "While I was tailing Piper, I felt as if I was two years back, running north with you from Sumara. Then I could've sworn I saw—ah, I'm not sure. A spook from this afternoon."

"It is similar to then. But now we hunt."

Ignoring him, she continued. "I felt like I was back there again. Especially our time in the Crossroads."

She sensed a spark of tension in Jon. The man's rocking adopted a quickened pace, shedding the leisure he'd displayed when she awoke.

"The men Alaryn sent to kill us. You remember them."

Through grinding teeth, he answered, "Yes."

"That why you tied the rope?"

Jon inhaled for an inhuman span before blowing the smoke into the room. Again it settled beneath her line of vision and, again, it floated up, obscuring the image of Jon. She heard the pipe tap the wooden sill.

"I thought you don't like old stones or broken bones," he finally said.

"Some are worth reconciling."

"Not these."

"But we never talked about it."

"Because there's no need," he muttered behind gritted teeth. "I didn't use the rope, Payton. We didn't die, and we're not going to. We hold the city, we have the numbers, and we will have the Reaving."

"What were you thinking when you stormed this place?" she demanded, letting her voice rise abruptly. "Our plan was to broker a ceasefire from the start. Then I hear about you flanking the city, toppling Lanair's legions. Faedelin's cock, Jon, you stoked the flames like a hurricane of hot breath."

His boots slammed flat on the floor. "I come to check on you and you dredge up these grievances. Why?"

"They bring me back to my question. Why do you want me to forget about Piper so dearly? You pardoned Coyle, you told me to forget about hanging those men after the university, and then you acted unilaterally to fuck this situation. So why should I trust you now?"

Jon shrugged with an air of irritation. "They're different situations entirely."

"They share one commonality: you exist in that troubled head of yours without allowing anyone to shine a light inside. You feign the limping horse so no one takes a second glimpse at you. Then you ride a bloody wave through the Holy City." It was only after she'd finished that she realized she'd been thumping the bed with a fist.

The silence lingered between them for a few minutes. He kept tapping the pipe on the sill, scoring his unknown unheard tune, and staring out of the window. Payton watched his eyes orbit in agitated circles.

"They named this city after their father," Jon said.

"I know. Alamon, they called him."

"Know what it meant?"

Payton nodded. "Beneath two flags."

"Beneath two flags," he repeated, still staring out the window. "Division from inception." He fished in his pocket. A moment later he produced a bag of tobacco. "We ask ourselves, where did we go wrong, where did we lose our way, and when did we become such monsters? So we flock back to the same moment over and over and over, beguiling ourselves into thinking we'll find a different answer. Time and again, we're disappointed. We're disappointed because we forget. Each time we exhume the moment, we expect to reclaim some golden age, a sanitized vision of then to purify the stained visage of now, but all we're doing is digging up a pale monster that lurks in the part of our mind that can't remember. He's a savage built in the mirror of us. Like children, we go to sleep, dreaming of that sanitized vision, and, like children, we're terrified each time our dream translates into nightmare. And like all nightmares, the pale monster waits at the end."

A chilly breeze spilled over the sill. Jon didn't shiver when the cold air washed over him, but Payton saw the hairs along his forearms standing alert, a semitransparent patch of yellow grass. He kept rocking the chair.

"You know why the monster's pale?"

She shook her head.

"We've buried him so far underneath our feet that no ray of sun can touch him. He withers deep down in the soil while worms and rocks eat away at his skin. So the skin turns pale. Paler than me, paler than you; an otherworldly color like parchment diffusing in milk.

"It's asinine, if you think about it. We push the monster deeper and deeper and deeper with a twisted sense of victory, as if the farther beneath our feet he sleeps, the less he can harm us."

Jon emptied his pipe out on the sill. Frowning, he finished packing the bowl with tobacco. He placed a match over the bunched-up material until it sparked, the color a torch makes pulsing far off in the night. Clouds puffed out of his mouth.

"I've struggled with that, Payton. I've tried to bury the pale monster at the center of the earth, hoping he'd never come back, or wishing I'd find a sanitized vision if I dared to look back. It's all buried. And you know what?"

"What, Jon?"

"The pale monster is always waiting for me at the end."

The pipe leaked translucent tendrils toward the ceiling of the room. Jon's fingers mingled with the smoke. Together they danced in sinuous lines. Ebbing around his fingers, the smoke never touched them, but kept a paper-thin gap away.

"But for many of us, I'd say the pale monster isn't so frightening because he's there or not. He's terrifying because he tricks us into arguing over the symmetry of things rather than about their purposes. So when I do things out of, say, vengeance, and you say out of some other motive, we forget we're going for the same ends." He nodded to himself. "Reminds me of an old paradox."

"Which one?"

"'The Steel Ship,' it's known by some." He smirked. "That's a foolish name, and not really to the point, either. 'Ships of Symmetry.' That's its name."

She repeated the name. "I've never heard it."

"Love that moon," he murmured, as if not hearing Payton at all. "My mother had an earring just like it." His gaze seemed to track how far the moon had traveled. "We've got a minute or two. Want to hear the story?"

Payton shrugged, nodded.

"Okay." He gathered himself with another drag of the pipe. "Maybe afterward, you'll understand me a bit more."

18

Ships of Symmetry

A builder named Therian was asked to design a new ship by his king, what with a fresh war brewing across the sea. Therian had extensive experience on warships, so his expertise was valued. A patient man, the king waited several months for his builder's invention.

The shipbuilder unveiled his innovation to a large assembly in the king's port. Its sleek design, thirty yards by ten and low to the water, impressed the king. He noted the foreboding steel bowsprit in particular.

"It is so she may ram any enemy and doom her men," Therian explained.

Though expensive, the king commissioned the ship. He sent it into the warring sea to test her might. Therian proudly captained her and set sail.

Therian's masterpiece sank seven ships within the month. His steel bowsprit sliced through any obstacle, a cleaver to warm cheese. Before two months had gone, the ship of Therian had gained fame across the kingdom.

Because of its rugged task, the ship needed repairs: a plank here, a beam there, and eventually the famous metal tooth.

More than a year after the king's hasty commission, Therian took his ship again to war. He felt the grains of the wheel rasping in his palms, and it occurred to him that this fresh circle of wood was the final replacement to his creation. Not one of the virgin planks remained.

Therian steered the vessel toward its next victim, pondering whether this was still the ship he had loved so dearly.

❂ ❂ ❂

Jon stood up from the rocking chair. Apparently done with the story, he tapped out the tobacco and pocketed his pipe. His boots clunked the floorboards on his way to the door.

Payton cleared her throat. He turned around.

"What happened in the end?" she asked.

He shrugged. "That is the end, so far as the university's cabal of philosophers is concerned. Not much in terms of closure, I admit." He slipped his hands into their pockets, and suddenly he resembled an awkward professor. "Therian wonders if it's the same ship. 'Course they're the same ship; they're both thirty by ten capped with a steel spike. But of course, they're different, too; it has not one of its initial bolts or planks. But neither of these points matter. Same or opposite, Therian's ship cleaved vessels apart and drowned their men in the depths."

His face tensed when he said "depths." It was the wince of someone in a cold wind's way. Then Jon continued. "Before, during, and after the transition, the ship served the same gruesome ends. While great thinkers debate ships of symmetry, people drown in icy graves."

19

Broken Bones

Tehsan pivots in the soil, lunges at Lanair. He dodges the blow of the wooden stick, leaping to the side, floating through the air, and landing with prowess on his toes. An exemplary swordsman myself, I've struggled to beat Lanair. He moves as a river around the rocks in its way.

Sleep has abandoned us all. No luck on the eastern side either, not with countless torches like red stars fallen to earth. Earlier, some Faed men were yelling at us from across the river. They were drinking and fighting, too. The drums score the tension of bloodlines between the two brothers. Now it's all quiet and restless.

Tension winds up in Lanair's neck, and though he fights here to relieve it, his shoulders coil higher, tighter. Within his mind, the words "Carrow" and "tomorrow" tie knots.

Tehsan, a proven fighter despite her youth, keeps up with Lanair. She grazes his arms a few times, but for the most part, Lanair evades everything

Tehsan throws at him. He wears the woman down slowly. Then without warning, he moves in, strikes her chest, and knocks her to the ground.

"You'll get me next time, Tehsan," he says, offering a hand.

"Thank you, my lord."

Sweat glistens on both of them. Lanair walks over to a bench by the edge of the portico. The columned porch stands imposingly opposite the river, but the temple behind it has fallen. Tossing a flask to Tehsan, Lanair nods at me. "Hop in, Jem," he says.

"You sure you can take me after that?" I ask.

"The One-Handed Knight is fodder for the Lord of Sumara."

"In more ways than one," I reply.

Tehsan hands me her practice blade. I stretch for a moment while Lanair drinks. His back is turned. Loosening my arm in a windmill motion, I say, "Payton's worried, Lanair."

"Aren't we all?" he responds. "What else?"

"Carrow is taking two men into negotiations," I say. "You're to do the same. She'll hold the courtyard and the field while the armies wait outside. That part I trust."

"Courtyard?" Lanair questions.

"I had to agree to meeting in the tower."

Tehsan spits out a gulp of water. "What? That's an insult to every man and woman this side of the river!"

"I said the same. Even Payton said the same," I add.

"Bah! Carrow plays the tyrant yet again!" she cries.

"He is castellan of the capitol," I concede.

She flings the flask against the nearest column. "We demand a change of place. That's our only option."

"She's already sent word to prepare the tower, clear the debris," I tell her.

"Prepare a trap, you mean," Tehsan snaps. "I know you grew up with her, Lord Nalda, but you're not children at the university any longer. She's the enemy's general."

"Payton would never put me in harm's way."

"Wake up, Lord Nalda! Carrow pulls the strings, not Tallhart."

"End it." Lanair's words cut between Tehsan and I, invisible as the wind and sharp as its kiss.

"I'm done," I say.

Tehsan screws up her nose, but sighs. "Done."

Lanair spins around. "Good. I don't like the place, but I'm done arguing with Carrow. We could prolong this meeting another few days, wear him down, and convince him to change the place. But then we'd find out he'd been planning some other slight to us all along. It's useless. I don't want to see the men's faces when they hear, though. I mean, the spot where they hung Mehsani. Not a graceful way to spit on us, not even for Carrow."

"I guess it's for reparations," I explain. "A poetic statement, if you will. Here's where we divided; here's where we unite."

Lanair shakes his head. "No matter the way you look at an apple with worms, it's tainted fruit." He frowns. "No, there's no use arguing with Carrow. His mind is set on it. Meraxes," he wonders at last.

"Meraxes?"

"Nothing. It's just, I recall Carrow's obsession with that story. I guess it fits here. He thinks he's seen the emptiness inside our power, and now he believes he can set any term," Lanair answers. "He lived by that story in Sumara. At least we'll have space on our side. If either side lashes out in such a boxed area, both sides will fall apart."

He wraps a new bandage around his palms before we spar. He stares at the soil scattered across the stone portico, a good place to practice. Secluded and shaded in the day, it's been our private space since we arrived here weeks ago. "I learned long ago that picking that man's mind is useless; not even he can. We can still have the upper hand. The space cuts off their numbers, while we've dictated the terms of the negotiations. I like our predicament."

While I wait, I grip the gnarled stump at the end of my right arm. I often forget what it's like to have a hand there. I roll the stump over in my palm. You become awful fond of something after losing it. I can't tell you what I'd give to grip a pen between my fingers, nice and snug.

Lanair is that to me. Before I know it, he's gone. He's swimming in his own mind, perhaps even oblivious to me sitting next to him. He can't go into tomorrow like that. He needs to have his mind focused. There's no margin for mishap. No margin to lose yourself in the point between the pines.

"Let's go," I tell him.

He nods and picks up the wooden stick. He steps toward me, somewhat lazily. I strike at him suddenly, and it catches him unaware. Lanair has to stumble backward a few steps before regaining his balance, an uneasy footing at best. I don't stop. My stick whizzes over his head a second after he ducks, which forces him into a roll. The soil crunches underneath him. I press the attack so he can't find his footing. Even so, I can't touch him.

"Come on!" I shout. "Faster!"

Lanair's eyes bulge. Above them, the brows and creases in his forehead are dotted with pebbles of sweat. Lines of pain streak outward from his eyes, too. Every leap is an effort for him.

"Faster!"

He parries me, and then drops back. Light, he's quick. Even before I can chase him, he's found the balance he needs and obtained the footing I wanted him to fight for. Now he's in control. In lightning bounds, he storms toward me, barely making a sound on the portico's soil. He attacks my right arm. To block it, I throw myself off balance. In a blur, he pivots, launches himself into a spin, and cracks the stick on my exposed shoulder.

"Fast enough?" he pants.

"We've fought too many times," I respond once enough air comes back to me. "No one would've been able to pull that off in the field."

Lanair shrugs. "Maybe not. But I won."

I wave at Tehsan for her to toss me the flask. She plucks it from where it fell and lobs it to me. The stuff is bathwater.

Tehsan clears her throat. "If I may, my lord." Lanair bows his head. "They broke Mehsani's neck at that very spot. They scoured the fields of Sumaran men and women and purged the Narrows of them after Faedelin won. Going to the broken tower plays into his hands. Shows Carrow that he does hold the box."

"But he does, Tehsan," Lanair says, sighing. Her name accentuates his irritation. "There's no use pretending not. It'll only distract us."

"The Faeds can*not* be trusted, Lord Lanair."

"No one can!" His voice rushes upward, silences the chatter beyond the reaches of the portico. He runs his tongue atop his bottom lip to regain himself. "We're just talking broken bones here, Tehsan. I've had enough of it. If I have to put my neck near the noose to send everyone home, I will."

"I'm sure Mehsani said the same three hundred years ago, my lord."

"Then I'm proud to say it tonight!"

Tehsan tightens her lips, as if to shoot back a retort at Lanair, but the tension relaxes in her face and she rolls her shoulder back. She'd never overstep her boundaries with Lord Lanair Mavogar. She'll come close, sniff at the air across the line, and then drop back like a nervous puppy.

"Apologies, Lord Lanair. I just can't look a Faed in the eyes without bile burning in my throat."

"Clearly," Lanair replies curtly. He walks toward the edge of the portico to finish the water from the flask. Leaning against a column, he stares at the torches flickering across the river.

I sit next to Tehsan on the steps leading to the spot where the temple once stood. They built it for Sylvaea, the mother of Faedelin and Mehsani. You can tell by the snakes spiraling down each column and the wolf altar in front of the temple. It's said that the Light visited Sylvaea in the form of a snake and impregnated her while she slept. After she died in childbirth, a farmer found them. The man, Alamon, adopted them as his own.

"He's tense," Tehsan whispers.

"Aren't you?"

"I just want to see the Faeds brought to their knees for once. How many generations have we answered to their words?"

I watch Lanair. He could be part of the temple for all his stillness. A likeness of Mehsani himself.

"The boy is all over the place," the woman continues. "Never seen him so restless, and this is Dinian we're talking about. Caught him hiding at the top of an old watchtower down the river while you were with Lady Tallhart."

"Really?"

"Said he was spying on the Ghost."

Carrow. His specter stretches as far as a shadow at dusk in the boy's mind. On our way to Alaveren Dinian told me about the night Carrow fled Sumara. The boy said more than ten soldiers attacked him, but Carrow cut them all down. Only one managed to cut his thigh. Otherwise, the man had slaughtered them mercilessly in front of Dinian.

I suddenly notice something around Lanair. It's like a plume of smoke, or rather steam, which encircles him slowly but inexorably. I stand up, and so does Tehsan. Sharing a confused look, we edge toward Lanair. He doesn't hear us coming.

I take hold of his shoulder. No response.

"Lanair," I say, but his closed eyes don't open. The steam grows thicker. The thin wisps flatten into sheets, low and flat as fog. He still doesn't wake from his reverie.

"It's a ghost!" a voice squeaks behind us.

I look up at Dinian atop the fragmented wall behind the portico. He's pointing at us, eyes wide in fear. "It's him!"

"Careful up there!" I shout back.

Dinian tries to move away, but he loses his balance. We watch him tumble backward and out of sight.

"Get him," I tell Tehsan. She darts away toward the temple's interior, into which Dinian fell. When she emerges, she cradles the boy, who nurses a purple forearm. I brush past Lanair to help.

Dinian cries out when I touch the bruised bone. "Lucky it wasn't your neck!" I chide him. "What were you thinking, climbing up there?"

"I wanted to watch," he says, wincing. "Did you see it? Did you see him?"

"Who?"

"The ghost."

"Quiet down, Dinian, and stop moving." I place a hand on Tehsan's shoulder. "Will you take him to an infirmary? A doctor needs to see that bone."

Tehsan nods.

"Quickly!" I nudge her gently. "Dinian, don't leave Tehsan's sight, understood?" The boy nods, squinting in agony.

Tehsan stands, but then she nods past me toward where Lanair stands. When I look, the steam has vanished to reveal Lanair, who's rubbing his head in his hands.

"Go. I'll see to him."

Tehsan turns and runs with the boy.

I slowly approach Lanair. He rubs his eyes as if waking from a deep slumber during the day. No steam remains from the billows moments ago. He moans.

"Lanair."

He glances at me, surprised by my presence. "Oh, Jem."

"Are you okay?"

"Why wouldn't I be?"

I rest my hand on his shoulder. "Do you know what just happened?"

His lips flatline. "Did Tehsan get offended? I'm sorry; I just feel so thinly spread. I can go find her."

"No," I say, perhaps too sternly. I draw him in for a hug. "We should go for a walk."

He nestles his scruffy chin into my neck. "How about to the fields?"

"Okay. Whatever you want."

Then an old adage shatters my serenity. It sends chills down my spine. They used to whisper it in the streets of Sumara, when the legend of their founder was proliferating. With awed voices, they'd say, "When Mehsani walked through Alaveren, steam rose from the ground where his feet left prints, as if the touch of his feet had awakened the spirit of the earth."

20

A Crown of Feathers

I massage Lanair's neck as we walk the path beyond the west camp and toward the tree atop the hill. I've never felt him so tense. Knots knotted by tomorrow and Carrow. And though he's tense, beneath the tension I sense a strange sense of weightlessness, as if a boulder were pressing on a cloud.

The fields and the Copse of Last Trees beyond lie a minute up the road. As we near it, I think of Mossan and his story "A Far Green Country." Not many know about Mossan, but the man's stories were fascinating. He's one of the few historical figures who became a character in his own lore. His most famous is *Through the Magic Wood*. In it, he stumbles through a copse of trees and into a faraway field of green. Paradise. Lanair fancies the Copse of Last Trees his magic forest, the field before it his far green country.

When we reach the tree from this afternoon, Lanair slumps down at its roots. I cringe; gnarled roots offer little cushion. When I look at him, however, the roots seem to have caught him, made him a throne.

191

"Want to talk?" I ask. He presses his eyes closed. "I know Tehsan must've pissed you off."

He shrugs. "She's got the spark of the Shepherd in her, to quote Alaryn. She'd be a good leader one day, if she sets aside these brash impulses. I mean, if I could strike the other side of this river with my spear and end it, don't you think I would?" Lanair laughs bitterly. "Bah. She's all sledgehammer and no scalpel."

"Sometimes that's not so bad." I sit next to him. His beard has come in since yesterday morning. "Sometimes you need the brashness."

He shakes his head. "She's dangerous. I've tamed her, but I can feel her tugging the leash. She wants me to let go of it."

"Have you thought of that?"

Lanair snorts. "I'm wondering if it's a mistake bringing her tomorrow at all. Though maybe not. Two level heads and one fiery one. Not a bad mixture."

"What I mean is, have you thought about letting go of that leash? For one moment. For one man."

Lanair frowns. "I'd not put that omen on my head, Jem Nalda. Not for any man."

"Any story you read, remove the villain and it's happy forever thereafter."

"Jon's no villain. Might have no good left in him, but mostly he's just broken." Lanair taps a root. "And if he is a villain, I made him."

For a while, we stay quiet. The bulk of the time Lanair and I have been together has been in silence. He's such an intense thinker, always delving through the annals of his own mind, that sometimes it's hard to get a word in. I don't mind. Often I wish I could squash the jumbled thoughts in my own head. But to no avail.

"You confident in our plan for tomorrow?" I ask.

"Just wondering why Jon wanted to meet now. Why not a week ago before stoking a new fight?" I feel him tense up again. "I'm hurting, Jem. I don't want to keep sending men and women into the river. That's all I feel I've been doing. In the name of some man who lived three hundred years ago."

192

"You're saying nothing novel, Lanair. Better men have worried the same thing as you. Did Prince Talthus really want to spend all those lives to win Ezora back from the firedrake? No, but he did. Every story has the dejected general. Don't be that type."

He smiles. "There's only one thing I should say, then."

"What's that?"

"That I'm happy. Right now." He spans his hand over the field before us, purple beneath the cloudless night. "In our far, green country." He takes my hand suddenly, straightens my chin so I look him dead in the eyes. "Listen. The truth is, I've resigned to accept tomorrow as the end of the line. The cries for Mehsani are growing hoarser."

"I don't like to hear you say things like that."

"There's nothing to be scared of, Jem. I'm saying that the world has grown tired of us stomping over her, digging into her because more of us have fallen. There'll come a time, and maybe it's not tomorrow, but there'll come a time where even we're tired of it. Blood won't taste so fine on our lips anymore. Blades will lose their edge. So will our zealots.

"I think that every belief has its half-life. Nothing can last forever. Tonight, I've realized that this one might be nearing the end of its life. Braeland is tired. Aren't you?"

I reply, "Sure, I'm exhausted. There's only one problem, Lanair." I turn his chin so that his eyes scan the field. "Here's where your zealots lose their edge. Through the magic forest."

He laughs finally, swats my hand away. He stands up and peels off his shirt. Then he cocks an eyebrow up.

"Again?" I question.

"How did a scholar like you graduate but still maintain such a filthy mind?" Lanair asks.

"Failed scholar," I remind him, finger raised.

"Semantics. Come keep the Balance with me."

"I'd rather just watch you."

"Suit yourself."

Lanair steps away from the tree to where the grass of the field meets the brown patch ringing the roots. He removes his boots, wriggles his toes in the grass. Padding the ground with his feet, Lanair makes a solid balancing point.

Mehsani taught the Balance when his people faced open war with Faedelin. The Shepherd thought that it would center the mind with the soul before battle and, if you died, you died a unified being. The practice also aimed to prevent death through improving agility and strength.

Lanair stretches his shins, his calves, his thighs, deeply breathing in and out. Then he raises his right foot, places it on his left knee. His right knee points outward, away from his body.

I feel something warm beneath me. I notice that the ground is steaming. It's a faint wisp, almost like the white smoke a dead fire emits. The steam is warm to the touch. It also emanates from the ground under Lanair. Whereas beneath me the steam is faint, it billows up slowly in a great cloud around him. I notice his leg wobbling slightly; he must be fatigued. Regardless, Lanair holds the Balance better than anyone I've seen.

Lanair keeps the Balance as the steam inches up around him. He doesn't notice it's happening. The steam is coming from the grass, inexplicably breathed from the soil, exhaled from the earth beneath him. It forms a silent, amorphous halo around Lanair as he continues to hold the Balance.

He rests on the ball of one foot. I can see the sweat dripping in globs off his arms through the steam. The beads begin to vanish. It's the steam that's swallowing them. Soon he's clean, no sweat on his body.

His shoulders go up a few inches, his trembling leg goes steady, and his chin levels out. As the stress fades out of him, the steam billows beneath. He holds the Balance.

I hear a caw overhead. My eyes find a circling black shape in the sky directly above Lanair. With ominous certainty, the thing spirals downward. Slowly, unhurriedly. It barks out at each revolution. Despite the noise, Lanair never looks up. He's holding the Balance.

I call out to him, and either because of the steam or his concentration, he can't hear me. Above him, the thing comes into view. It's a raven. A huge one, bigger than any I've ever seen. It continues to descend leisurely, a predator serenading its prey. I scream out to him, but he doesn't hear me. He holds the Balance.

The raven descends into the grasps of the rising, rising, rising steam. Lanair's body hunches, lost to the accumulating mist. I try to move, but something unseen holds me to the roots beneath me. I squint to try to see through the haze. I can't see him. I can't see the raven. They've been swallowed in mist.

There. The water vapor thins out. The ball of fog spreads out into tendrils, into fibers, into nothing. Lanair rises from a crouched position. The raven has gone, but its feathers continue to orbit his head. They fall mutely from the space around his head. One by one they weave into his black locks. The hair wraps around them in welcome. The feathers stand at attention.

Suddenly, Lanair lowers his leg to the ground. When he turns toward me, his eyes are glazed with a black lacquer. They match the feathers, which form a crown upon his head, a crown of feathers fallen from the sky.

21

The Mirror of Mehsani

Lanair's eyes take no notice of my hand when it waves in front of them. The black orbs stare blankly ahead at me, but past me, through me. I snap my fingers an inch away from them. Nothing.

"Lanair."

I thought I saw some flicker of recognition from him, but he remains statuesque. For a beat, I contemplate going to fetch Tehsan; she might know how to handle him. But then he blinks.

"Come," he tells me, his voice octaves deeper than usual. He turns around and begins to walk toward the Copse of Last Trees, some miles down the hill near the mountains. I call after him. When he doesn't respond, I resign to follow him toward the copse.

When we near the copse, the chilly night suddenly feels warmer than it did during the daytime. Not hot, simply warm and comforting. The trees loom overhead in the dark, a shy band of a dying race, hanging fast to the last of the hospitable soil. The warmth emanates from them.

Lanair steps past the field dotted with rotting trunks and rotten branches into the shadows of the copse. I hesitate for a moment. They say the Mirror of Mehsani lies within this place. The lake he stared into moments before meeting his brother in the Holy City, hours before he hanged from the parapets. At this place, they say, his soul ascended into the Light.

What shred of truth lies in that tale? No one has ventured beyond where I stand in two hundred and sixty years, when Wilbraem the Wise consecrated it. No one until Lanair just marched across the boundary.

Drawing a deep breath, I step into the Copse of Last Trees.

The sounds of the night vanish. Though the night contains few sounds, you frequently hear the chatter of drunks on the wind, the rustle of trees, and the crickets. Within the trees, the noises perish. It's not the padded softness you find exiting a tavern from the muffled joviality within. The sounds cease to exist. I am Mossan, carried beyond the forest into a faraway country.

My first footfall pulses outward; the farthest tree in this wood can sense it as if my foot had stomped on its root. I know it. I can feel it feeling me.

The woods glow with a faint dark light. It's not the impenetrable black of a starless night, but it's not the liquefied onyx of a darkened sea. Some unseen source breathes the glow into the space between the trees. The mist rising from the ground shines with the strange, purplish hue.

My next steps reverberate throughout the woods. Even the purple mist brightens in response to my footsteps. All around, the copse answers to its intruders.

Its lead intruder, Lanair, marches onward. He's obscured by the purple mist, but with slightly squinting eyes I can make out his shape several paces away. Despite looking straight ahead, he doesn't trip on the spider web of gnarled roots and rocks beneath our feet. His march is steady. Not even the raven crown trembles as his steps shoot waves of energy throughout the copse. Everything holds the Balance.

Lanair leads us up a slope and, before I glimpse it, I know what lies beyond the crest. The steam has been filling up the wood from this place. The heat radiates from this sacred spot. Even the purple light must originate from here.

The Mirror of Mehsani fills the bowl of the valley below us. A wall of steam covers the water below, which must be as still as a looking glass. It flows off the invisible lake and over the roots snaking down to drink. Through the blanket of steam poke several arching roots like grizzled knuckles. The steam laps its way up the bowl valley to our toes, where it thins out in a fine sheet.

"It's true. The mirror is real, Lanair. Mehsani really did stare into this lake before he died." A trickle of steam dances its way up to my face. I swirl my fingers in it. "They said the mist was a primordial energy that he awoke with his final prayers. I never believed any of it."

Lanair doesn't move from his perch beside me. The black, lacquered eyes peer toward the invisible lake pouring steam into the Copse of Last Trees. The feathers maintain their militant stance in his hair.

"Lanair," I breathe into his ear.

"Come," his ocean-deep voice commands.

He takes us deeper into the bowl. Immediately, the steam fattens into clouds around our ankles, then our calves, our knees, our waists. It wraps my belly in a tingly embrace. Suddenly, rising as if with the steam, numbness takes my feet away from me, I lose feeling in my abdomen, and my head swims with dizziness.

"Lanair."

I drop to a knee. The steam parts around me, and I notice that among the myriad roots are dandelions that have bloomed. The white balls flake away in the gusto of my fall.

Lanair hasn't noticed my inebriation. He steps closer to the edge of the immobile water, steam peeling away before his path. The steam, which closes back up behind him, blurs Lanair into an indistinct shape. He wades into the water.

No, he's walking atop it.

I try to call out, but my tongue forms inaudible mumbles. My body goes limp. A bed of dandelions braces my fall and puffs white seeds into the air. They float away in a rush. My mind drifts off in their wake, riding the wind.

22

Catching Shadows

Payton felt her way out of the tavern's darkened rear by gliding her palm along the raspy stone of the hallway. Her head throbbed every time her foot took another step. The welt was blooming on her cheek.

"…not really sure yet," Jon was saying in the barroom. "She says it was that courier fellow. I'd say a Sumaran spy."

The floor tilted like a seesaw. She downed a long draft of the stale tavern air. It did nothing to help steady the oscillating floor. She wished the throbbing would vanish.

"And he tried to take Lady Tallhart's life?" Alanna asked.

"Not exactly. Just knocked her out."

Payton closed her eyes. She recalled a trick that Kala had taught her eight years earlier to concentrate. Imagining a waterfall, full-bodied in its foamy fall, Payton went to one foot. The rapid rush of the water lagged in rhythm with her breathing. She soaked in the murmuring roar of the fall until it softened to little more than a breath of mist. The fall froze. She wobbled on her foot, but the water had stopped. She'd mastered the power of the water, of the inexorable pull of the ground. Dropping her foot, she opened her eyes.

"Who was it? Do we know for sure?"

"Unidentified," Jon replied. "Probably Sumaran, like I said."

"Seems strange," Alanna said. "How'd he get that deep in the camp? Why not kill her?"

Payton stood in the doorway. Alanna stared down Jon in the open space of the floor. Badric leaned against the wall beside the front door. Outside, two women stood guard: the Harts Gwenaever and Caelia, by the looks of them. Coyle was there, too. He drummed his fingers on the bar to Payton's right as he sipped an amber body beneath a cap of foam. The patrons who'd been there when Payton stormed through had been cleared.

"It was Piper."

Her husky voice drew all of their eyes. Alanna rushed over to her, offering an arm for support. When the woman was in arm's reach, she grimaced. "Your face, my lady."

"It's fine." Payton stepped toward a stool. She propped herself up on the oak bar, roughened throughout the years. The sheen of the faded polish glimmered in dappled splotches.

"Piper," she repeated. "It was him."

"*Marc* Piper?" Badric asked. The old knight had recommended Piper to Payton before the Reaving reopened. She nodded. Badric cradled his wrinkled forehead in his hands.

"Spotted him in my pavilion after meeting Jem."

"You met with Jem?" Jon's teeth were clenched together.

"Yes."

"Without telling me."

"You're in charge of the North, Jon, not of me."

"I am until tomorrow, Payton. I captured the capitol."

Ignoring him, she said, "We've got to find Piper before tomorrow morning."

"What do you want to do?" Alanna asked, massaging Payton's neck.

"Rally the Harts."

Coyle snorted. "Got a war to end, and you want to play chase."

"We're not stopping until we've found him, Coyle."

He held up his hands in acquiescence.

"Good. Rally the Harts," she told Alanna. The woman nodded and left.

Payton had assembled the twelve men and women on the way to take the capitol back when Jon was busy planning his brazen assault of the island city. Alanna and Badric were the first; then Caelia, Thanet, and Hector, the three siblings from Wellfleet; and finally Elaine, Gawaen, Bors, Gwenaever, Tristam, and Morgaese. Tam had been the last. All twelve had held a district of Wellfleet while the Sumarans, led by the extreme Mehsanic forerunners, slaughtered and pillaged her city. With only two hundred soldiers, they stood. Nearly six hundred Sumarans, with the Mehsanics leading the onslaught, pressed down on them. But they never broke.

After the battle, when she'd taken her family's tower for her own and Coyle had put down the lost sheep, Badric had relayed their bravery to her. Payton honored them with land holdings to be claimed following the Reaving and with the honorific title the Harts.

Payton would trust them until they'd sown the Reaving back up. Through innumerable battles now they never failed. They'd follow her through the hottest fire.

Jon pulled up a stool next to her. He plucked at the blond beard sprouting from his chin, brushing back his receding hair with another hand. Only thirty-three and the man faced thinning hair. He said it wasn't his fault; stress had sat heavy on his head.

"Are you sure about this?" he asked. "With the dawn so close, you want to have them running amuck?" She supposed the man had to swallow a bulk of pride about her meeting Jem, and maybe he was swallowing it, perhaps choking on it, with the day dawning in which he'd have to hand over the reins of Braeland.

"No one's sleeping anyway, Jon. The whole city's awake. Might as well call on Jem and Lanair right now. End it early."

"Think about it like this. If Piper wanted you dead, why didn't he kill you?"

Her fingers skimmed the surface of her welt. "I don't care, Jon. We're hunting him down. Can't have him loose with so much on the line tomorrow."

He shrugged. "Your choice. Better to look from all angles, though. Especially with these people. No telling what they'll do."

"That's it, Jon. I'm taking the Harts to hunt him down."

Jon stared at her with those eyes like chips of ice. The longer hers were locked with his, the more Payton thought that beneath the ice slumbered a reservoir of pain that he had tucked away before the winter had set in. Were the ice to thaw, an ocean might pour forth. And yet, they were shallow puddles beneath a thawing skin. Easy to suppose an ocean were underneath when the same depth might suggest a puddle. The ice concealed whatever it was that slumbered.

"Okay, Payton." He got up and walked over to Coyle, began whispering with the man. Every so often, Coyle flashed a glance at her. His russet farmer's face was ugly in the twilight torchlight. Look at them. Plotting and scheming and whispering. It was a different method, but it was the same deceit that Leon Tallhart had employed, though her father was all bombast and no nuance.

"These are bad, bad people, Payton, and we're going to end their scourge," Leon told her as a girl.

"Why are they so bad?" Payton questioned.

"They took everything from us. The Lord Faedelin wanted this country for *us*. They besmirched that heavenly deal."

"They took nothing, Dad."

"Everything," Leon answered. "They would kill you now if they could. They would steal you from me if they were within arm's reach."

"Why?"

Leon's jaw was a firm, motionless flag flying from his neck, a pole of stretched and tanned leather. It bobbed imperceptibly when he spoke. The words came from seemingly nowhere.

"We're going to Sumara to put an end to this once and for all. This is the moment Faedelin dreamed about. Payton, you're only twelve. I wish you could understand the gravity of tomorrow." Tears welled in Leon's eyes. "Your father is going to end the scourge of Mehsanism."

She scratched her crop of curls. "If Faedelin was the Light's warrior, why didn't he stop the spread of Mehsanism?"

Leon opened his mouth, closed it again. Then he grinned, ruffling Payton's curls. "Don't let these questions worry you, Payton. We're going to win this time. We're going to prove to the Light that it's us, the North, the sons of Faedelin, who are its chosen people."

Payton hissed out a sigh. Such lofty phrases couldn't take root in the ground beneath her feet. She thought back to her days with Jem in the gardens of the capitol, enjoying the coolness of the earth pushing between her toes and how real and true it had felt.

"The Light watched us for a long time," Leon sermonized, "even before we got here, back in Old Braeland, it looked after us. When our fathers fled persecution to follow the Light, it guided us. When the spears of Faedelin skewered the Usurper, it blessed us. Then the Light named Faedelin as its champion. He became the Light Embodied. Once he had killed Mehsani in a duel blessed by the heavens, he built a new Braeland for us. He meant this kingdom for the children of the North. The Light had even shed a teardrop to form an island for us in the North. All the signs were clear.

"When Faedelin was finished, a cloud swept around him and his body was gone. The Light had taken him back, had given a seat in the clouds to its chosen champion. And now he waits for us. Adorned in the Light. That's why we're going, Payton," Leon insisted.

Payton shook her head. "No, Dad, I meant why are those people bad? The ones alive now."

Leon's eyebrow curved; he was stumped by his young daughter.

"Not the dead people," she rephrased. "Why are the people right now so bad?"

He patted her on the shoulder and tucked her into bed. "I'll return soon, Payton. Sleep well."

When Leon had gone to Sumara fifteen years ago, then eight years ago, and then four years ago, it had been to claim the city for the Light. What did they do there? It was as Alanna had said at the Crossroads. They killed them, hares caught in a trap. Yet something had eluded the Light's chosen warriors that day. The boy whispering, "Ghost," into Alanna's ear hadn't ended it. The darkness had escaped. It crept away once the Light stormed into Sumara. But the Light had to leave eventually, like at the close of any day. And once it retreated, the shadows elongated.

"But if you shine a light, it casts innumerable shadows," Lanair said years later to Payton in Sumara.

"Not always," she claimed.

Lanair wagged a finger. "Always."

He approached her in the darkened library of Sumara. He stopped ten paces away in a column of moonlight that fell between two stacks of books. The ribs of light and dark repeated five times more between him and her.

"Shadows are a product of light," he continued. Clearing his throat, he quoted the Book of Dreams: "'And he took the Light to rid the world of its shadows. They followed him, the Lightbearer, until it shined upon the distant stretches of Braeland. And they called him Mehsani, their Lord Savior.'" Lanair clucked his tongue. "Fools, whoever wrote that verse."

He ran a finger along the edge of the nearest shelf. His eyes scanned the shelf, which reached for the second floor of the small library. Payton clutched the Way behind her back so he wouldn't see. He'd materialized from the shadows, no warning of his approach.

"You see, Lady Payton, you cannot shine a light and not cast a shadow. So do you blame the shadow for being cast? Or blame the light for casting it?"

"There's always a way, Lord Lanair. There must be a way with the Light."

"No. You see, your father thinks that because he won the Reaving and because he carries an ancient name, he can waltz into Sumara and rule us. Thinks the Light is a panacea." As he neared Payton, passing shelf after shelf, he emerged from shadow ribs that gave fragmented glimpses of his widening grin. "Shine a light, it casts a shadow. The two are inextricable. You cannot have a light without the shadows it creates; take the light to rid a world of shadows, and you'll just throw shadows farther, further. Light is tainted before it ever shines." Lanair entered the shadow she stood under, his face obscured. Payton could smell the lavender on the man's breath. "Only the dark is pure."

He reached around her back and plucked the Way from her grasp. "Good luck catching shadows, Lady Payton," he told her. Tossing the book into the gulf between the shelves, he stroked her cheek. "Better to leave stories about shadows to children."

Lanair had been right, Payton thought. Two years now casting the Light, casting its shadows. Where did one begin and the other end? Lanair had been right. Lah-nair.

"Lah-nair." Jon was whispering the man's name. "Lah-nair."

"What did you say?" Payton asked.

Jon had retaken his stool beside her, while Coyle had vanished from the tavern. Badric's head slumbered in his hands.

"Lah-nair. A friendly syllable and a stab of ice, don't you think?"

"Huh?"

"Never mind."

The welt's throbbing had calmed down since Alanna had left. Must've been about twenty minutes ago. She'd be back soon.

"Lah-nair. Must've been a spy sent by him. I can feel it."

"Jon, why are you still here?"

He looked at her as if she had spoken incoherently. "I'm going to help you. In case Piper needs killing."

Payton pinched the bridge of her nose. "Do you make every choice based on spite?"

"Hmm?"

"I've seen the glares you shoot at Piper. He cowers around you. Now you're suddenly onboard to help if it means killing him. Silencing him, one might paraphrase. Do you make every choice based on your spite?"

Jon narrowed his eyes, leaned toward her. "All of us make choices on our deep-seated emotions. If I make mine on spite, so be it. Ships of symmetry, Payton."

"You're chasing shadows, Jon."

"How do you mean?"

"Dwelling on these childhood trifles, how do you plan to catch the past? Only the past can catch, and it catches you."

His nostrils flared. "Childhood *trifles*?" He practically spat at her. "You have no idea what they put me through. Treated me like a fucking dog. Put my eyes to the candle. Locked me in the dark room."

The instant he said "room," his voice adopted a breathless quality. His cheeks blushed, and he began sweating. Jon looked at Payton with trembling eyes, as if he needed to scream for help but no words would come out. He leaped off the stool and backed away, then began pacing in circles. He tugged at his shirt to fan himself, the sweat accumulating before Payton's eyes. He panted. His whole body trembled.

"Are you okay, Jon?"

"Fine," he shot back. "Just need a breath."

He stormed outside before she could say another word. When the door slammed shut, Badric jumped up in his chair.

Another twenty minutes passed before Coyle swung the door open to tell Payton, "Harts're here."

She gave her thanks and exited with Badric. Her small, trusted retinue grouped up in an oval atop horses. The band wore black cloaks so their edges merged with the night. They bowed their heads to her.

"Thank you for coming to me on short notice. You briefed them?" she asked Alanna. The woman nodded. "Good. He was heading south last I saw."

Tam appeared at her side. "Your cheek," he breathed.

"I'm fine, Tam," she whispered back. His worried eyes studied the welt. "Honestly."

"Okay," the man nodded. He squeezed her hand tenderly, subtly, out of sight.

208

The Harts trotted southward along the road, toward where it bent into lonely silence. Led by the three siblings, the group began the hunt.

"Let's find this scab fucker," Thanet said to Caelia, who laughed. "We'll give him a good scab or two," she replied.

Tam whistled again, as he had this afternoon.

Jon turned away from her, dodging her visage. "We're with you, Payton. Lead the way." He furtively stroked the blue cloth that she had wrapped around his sword hilt.

Payton nodded and mounted the horse Alanna had brought her. We're with you, Payton. Something told her these words were as empty as his eyes in an icy world far, far away.

23

The Hart and the Ghost

Payton kept stealing glimpses of Jon as he stroked the cloth while they hunted for Piper. By the slight, slow movement of his fingers, he must've thought no one was watching. She was. She realized that that was her duty from now on. To watch.

She had found the blue-sapphire cloth wrapped around the fist of a dead Sumaran in the Mire. The dead man's face came back to her. His blood seeped into the soft side ringed around his messy knuckles, but the shiny side facing toward Payton was sky sapphire, the color that she imagined Jon's eyes once were before they froze over, bottomed out, changed utterly. She stuffed it in her pocket, wondering to herself how many of them hid within the Mire. This one, a Mehsanic youth, had died loudly. Her axe had finally taken him in the face. That made him quiet, but little else softened this light-forsaken swamp teeming with mosquitoes and snakes and shepherds. The axe didn't stop it, nor did the dead boy who whispered, "Ghost," to Alanna. She took the blue cloth from his fist. He wouldn't need it anymore.

211

After finding it, Payton looked over the Mire's reeds oscillating in the wind. They were precise columns of green, distinguishable even as they sinuously broke rank, mimicking the slithering pattern of a snake. Below them the bogs were sponges soaking up the Mire. They squelched beneath her boots.

"I hate the squelching," Jon was moaning. "It's like vomit beneath our feet, and every day we're swatting mosquitoes away before they sink their little saws into our necks. The Sumarans are up ahead in a little patch of wood. Badric's scouting them now."

She knew to watch where she stepped; pockets of the swamp were bottomless, open-mouthed to inhale careless travelers. Beneath the bogs were bodies of the old tribes, the native ones who lived here before the two brothers expunged them. Once expunged, they became sponges. So the earth turns, making puns out of them all.

The boggy cadavers were exhumed a few decades ago when Willem the Strong sat on the throne. Perfectly preserved specimens, they fascinated Payton at a young age. They lay, slightly terrifying, in the museums of the University at Trowbridge. She determined then that when she knew she was going to die, she would walk out into the sinuous reeds, march until a chasm caught her feet, and drop. By that measure, centuries later, the next queen or king would pull her out, freckles still beaming and red hair still curling, and rest her in the timeless halls nestled deep in the teardrop.

"Tell them to circle the group. I don't want a single Sumaran escaping," she instructed Jon. Her soldiers huddled around the wood patch Jon had found. Even in that patch, the ground was a sponge.

"Okay, we've got them circled. They're on the way; let's go," Jon said. "We shouldn't be too far behind."

"Okay."

"Okay."

The Mire had plenty of ways of killing, with those pockets of eternity, the diseased bugs, and the Sumarans. Perhaps that's why King Gareth sent her there: to die, to vanish, to air the room for the legend of Lord Leon Tallhart, who died in his study in the South in the name of Faedelin, as the

Light adorned him. The king took her and Jon into his halls with slanted and suspicious eyes, especially for Jon Carrow, the Ghost Knight of Sumara, the traitorous ward who killed Sir Iayn Darrion. Weeks melted away. No word of hers could convince the king that it was Jon who had opened the gates during the Reaving to let Leon take the city protected by the Light, that it was Jon who dismantled Lanair Mavogar's regime from the inside while waiting patiently for his vindication that would not come, that it was Jon who saved her from jailers and an ignominious death in the South. He seethed at Jon. Said how could he trust the son of a cheap lord ("That opportunistic cow!") who welcomed the slaughter of thousands of his kinsfolk. Turning his eyes on her, he had nothing but spite to spit out of that yellowed mouth, broken blood vessels surrounding the lips in bruised pinches. He gave Payton, reluctantly, the title Warden of the North and wished her good luck upholding Leon's legacy.

"Leon Tallhart is dead," Payton replied coldly.

The king had few words for Jon, naming him Lord Jon Carrow, no longer Sir Jon Carrow, the knight of the Narrows who killed Darrion, but now a lord of the North, a hand of Faedelin, a leader of fifty inexperienced boys who were destined for the Mire, which lay just south of Trowbridge, to cleanse it of the guerillas that dwelt there.

"They'll back down. They've got to," Jon hoped.

"Not against only your fifty men, Jon. Gareth has tolled your death knell."

"What do I do? What do I do? They don't even listen to me. Just one foot in the South, one in the North. That's all they see me as."

"Command respect, Jon. This is a challenge from him. If you can take back the Mire, maybe he'll give you more soldiers, more supplies."

"Why fight for this stinking pit?" Jon moaned. He tossed pebbles into the pools frosted green by moss at their edges.

"Why fight? Take your head out of your hands, for Faedelin's sake. Eyes ahead."

"Okay," he said wistfully. "Eyes ahead."

The words came quickly after that: Wellfleet fallen, Mehsanic flags flying high. Was it her fault? No sense wondering that. She could uphold the legacy of Leon Tallhart. She could do more than that.

"Just forget it, Jon," Payton snapped. "Eyes ahead. The task's at hand now. Win the Mire, then we'll take back my city."

"Eyes ahead, eyes ahead."

But what was he looking for in the indistinct haze up ahead? The dewy haze emanated from the sighing reeds that the Sumarans were concealing themselves within, withholding the victorious moment when both Jon's feet could stand in one place, so the eyes of everyone could stop glaring at him. But what was the victory worth?

Was it worth the reach of his arm, so frail that even if he could incinerate the Mire, it wouldn't make an end? But get up, she said, get up get up get up, barking the orders without seeing the scars.

After a month of searching, Jon caught a scant trail. A few southern-made mugs, a Mehsanic edition of the Way, a bag of stones from a table game in Sumara. Things only a person with experience in Mehsani's city would know. Jon knew. He found the remaining host of Sumarans in a drier patch at the Mire's heart.

"There they are, Payton," he cried.

"Fire!" she screamed. Arrows dotted the guerillas' camp.

"We're winning, Payton. Quick, archers, take them out. Don't let them out of sight," he shouted, conducting this business in perfect concert with her. He smiled at her, though she didn't see.

"Fire!"

"Chase them down, charge, leave none alive."

As Jon broke into a sprint, he plummeted through one of the bottomless pools the fairy tales blabbered about. They were supposed to be fake. Yet Jon sank, down down down, and the world flipped in his view.

The pool sent Jon through a tunnel, soaring into the earth while brushing him with the boggy peat on his shoulders and arms. He couldn't grasp it to stop himself. Finally, the watery tube spat him out into an underground, endless ocean.

Beneath the bogs, the world was silent and dank, smelling like sulfur. The underground ocean sank to an interminable depth, as if the ground above from where he'd fallen was the skin of the apple and he was sinking to the core. The water below Jon extended infinitely. It did not end. He squinted toward something that floated below him, a light flashing from some type of underwater lantern. Though he couldn't make it out, the light was matching his heartbeat: faster quicker erratic epileptic. He sunk in the ocean until the orb of light was in the palm of his hand, warm like the sun. He felt a grin curl on his face. Behold this trip: Jon Carrow alone in a beautiful, undiscovered ocean, clutching the sun itself.

Suddenly, the orb dived into his chest, burning *burning BURNING AHHH!* Make it stop, enough, enough, he shouted, though the water drowned his plea. Jon would drown soon. It'd all be over, but then how could it end? For the light stabbed out of his fingertips in slim poles of tangible brightness until the orb of light burning inside him felt within his control, instead of a malignant fire burning him alive. Perhaps the light was settling into him, choosing him. Perhaps. What did this orb of light signify for him? Maybe he could—

His chest jerked upward, and he shot out of the ocean.

"Light, be careful!" Payton shouted at him. Their soldiers were gathered all around, mouths uniformly agape. Payton was wiping the bog water from her forearm, shaking her head. "Could've drowned," she muttered.

It was cold outside the bog, and the burning stopped.

"Thank you, Payton," he whimpered.

"Just watch your fucking feet from now on."

"I'm sorry, Payton."

"Forget it." She nodded up ahead to the dry patch, the last stand of the Sumaran guerillas. "Look. We did it."

The men were chasing the rest of the Sumarans into a snare set within the bog, and now Payton and he had the high ground. The arrows fell. So did the Mehsanics. They screamed until the end, and then they were the bog's property like the bogmen in the city. Would they reappear in a hundred years as the centerpiece of an excited exhibit? A variety of people would come to see

not the dead Southerners but a masterpiece of nature set in a timeless cast by
the sulphuric bogs squelching under Jon's boots.

"So it's done," Jon realized while convulsing in the cold.

"Yes."

"What now?"

"I'm taking back Wellfleet."

"I'll help."

"Your hilt!" she exclaimed.

"What?"

"Your clothes! They're dissolving. Look! They're melting away!"

The damn things sizzled like eggs in a skillet, smelling like sulfur and
slick with the swamp water. The cloth burned up, evaporating before his eyes.
What did that mean after the infinite hole he'd slipped into? Was it a result of
the orb of light that sparked a conflagration in his blood? And now he stood
naked as the day they ripped him from Selene Carrow.

"What's happening to me?" he cried.

Politely, Payton averted her eyes before the last of his undergarments
burned away. "Here, take this blanket. Rest until later," she said.

Then she went around to inspect the dead, who were beyond counting thanks to the sheer number and to the hungry holes in the Mire. She
found the blue-sapphire cloth wrapped around the fist of a dead Sumaran.
The blood seeped into the dull side ringed around his messy knuckles, but the
shiny side facing toward her was sky blue, the color that she imagined Jon's
eyes once were before they froze over, bottomed out, changed utterly. Payton
stuffed it in her pocket, wondering to herself about her city in the near north-
west, burning beneath the flags of Mehsani.

When she returned to Jon, he was crouched over a small pool, dropping palm-size rocks into it. Once one plopped, he shook his head. "No bottom," he was whispering. "Is that the point: no bottom, no end?" While he
distracted himself, she lay his blade across her lap and began to wrap the blue
cloth from the dead man around the hilt, the bloodied side face down so that
he couldn't see it lying in wait.

"There it is, the tumored eyeball," she said a few weeks following. Placed on the ridged lips around the University at Trowbridge, the capitol reared out of the teardrop like a stone thumb, its nail overgrown in the gray spires of the school. With Wellfleet under her control, the Mire guerillas expunged, she set her sights on the capitol and the final wisps of Lanair's rebellion.

"A tumored eyeball," he repeated.

"Don't you see it?" she replied, pointing to the ring of water round the rock. They stood on the headwall of the valley in which Trowbridge and the teardrop were.

"I don't think that's even a word."

"What?"

"Tumored."

Jon flexed his fist as he leaned on the stern of the boat. The university loomed up ahead. The encompassing lake never looked like a teardrop. Truly, it was more of a tumored eyeball than a tear or a drop. The university loomed overhead atop its rock. Just another lie. Like the lie they'd tell later about that night, when Payton and Jon scaled the impregnable rock walls of Faedelin's city.

A supernatural fog licked the waters of the teardrop. It blanketed her as the rowboats drifted toward the city thumbing skyward. The fog followed them and obscured the port so that hundreds of boats wandered into the city unseen.

As they entered the harbor, he began nodding. "The light beneath the bogs was a sign, Payton. It means things are going to go up for me."

"You think?"

"I know," he replied. "It must've been a sign things will change for me after tonight."

He continued nodding as the boat lurched on contact with the dock of stone. "Things must change," he whispered.

Payton sprinted up the slopes of the city, stone houses intact, flowers in bloom hanging from the windows, but no one in the streets. Jon took the lower city, the barracks, and the other ports while she raced for the throne room. Where were they? Where were the forty thousand Sumarans throwing Faed priests off the roofs? The moon lit her way, an empty and unchallenged path to the palace.

Inside, a few lords huddled together tied in a circle on the floor. No Lanair. No Jem. No forty thousand Mehsanics desecrating the temples of the Light. The university had been vacated. Trowbridge had been abandoned.

Then Jon, typically cadaverous and bloody, waltzed into the throne room, and as he stepped past them, the lords and ladies of Braeland knelt to him, to the Ghost Knight of Sumara, to the man who slew Sir Iayn Darrion, to the innocuous boy sold to the South in a sign of good faith. He stepped up the dais and stood beside Payton.

"What happened, Jon?"

"Alaryn died," he breathed, and his voice resembled the echo of a whisper.

"How?"

"My father, my only father is dead, and he called me the word when I looked down at him."

Shuffling drowned out his next words, for the hall prostrated itself before her and him, to Payton Tallhart and Jon Carrow, the vagabonds on the run who had made it to grand new heights, to the stuff of storybooks and daydreams.

"What do you mean?" she asked.

"I mean that he's dead, and that's it, no more to say."

Because if Jon said more, he'd have to say it, and he couldn't say that he'd leaned in to catch the solitary word on the dying breath. Jon couldn't repeat it, no, no, don't fucking say it, not the word Alaryn said on his dying breath. He'd looked up at Jon, at his son, whom he never said it to. Don't fucking say it. So that's what I mean, that I won, no more to say, Jon thought. It'll lead to the solitary word he said on his dying breath. Alaryn breathed it up to Jon after Coyle put an arrow in the old man's back, not knowing what he meant to Jon, what he had meant to him when he was a boy, and what he still meant to Jon as Lord Carrow, as the castellan of the greatest city in the world.

That old man meant everything.

Even atop these grand new heights, that cadaver meant the world entire despite the solitary word he said on his dying breath. Jon couldn't repeat it. Yet he had questions. Why was he here when the host had left? Had he been left behind by Lanair? That must be it; he was left in charge of the final men who never would escape because Jon had trampled them on the way to the port. Not even Alaryn, who was whispering the solitary word on his dying breath, would escape. Jon wished he could let it slip away. Let that one vanish. Jon could live without that one word, especially now that it was the solitary word on the dying breath.

"Jon," Payton breathed into his ear.

He leaned in to catch

"Look at me," she whispered.

to catch the solitary word

"What?" she asked.

the solitary word on the dying breath.

"What was the word?"

"Hmm?" Jon asked.

"You said something about a solitary word."

"Did I?" he breathed.

"Yes."

"Nothing. Leave it. I can't say it, I just want this day to end." Jon skulked away, leaving Payton to bask in the adoration alone.

❂ ❂ ❂

Payton rode alone now, in the shadows of Alaveren. Jon pushed up ahead with Coyle as they searched for Piper. She watched them prowl through the Holy City's darkened streets; the way their shoulders stooped, they were vultures. Something told Payton that the scavengers hoped to find Piper's carcass somewhere in the southern neighborhoods of the extinct city. Though her image wasn't accurate. She knew they were more predators than scavengers.

She rode alone, though Tam was several paces behind her, Alanna several in front. The houses and shops and chapels and markets slumbered peacefully in this section of Alaveren. The fighting focused on the northern districts. These sank into their mossy graves, like the ones across the river she'd seen earlier tonight with Jem. It was quiet. Payton could hear the river here, since it flowed undisturbed by the mumbling, grumbling horde of Braelanders.

Alaveren was empty and quiet for the grimmest of reasons. How many throats had been cut to achieve this solitude? Payton felt like she was more in one of Mossan's parables rather than in the broken city at the center of her country. The uninhabited buildings staggered out of the ground like cubed bushes; the streets were right-angled rivers. A strange concoction, the Holy City's quiet remains recalled an unnatural ecosystem, returned to peace by centuries of blood.

The other Harts had peeled off. Caelia, Thanet, and Hector went southwest, toward the road leading to Sumara at the other end of the Narrows. Gwenaever and Gawaen doubled back north, suggesting they might have missed something in the dense neighborhoods. Tristam and Bors rode southeast. The rest, Payton couldn't recall.

She nodded off, caught herself, gulped air through her nostrils. She refocused. Then the metronome clops from her horse entranced her; she repeated the process. In the quiet of southern Alaveren, the clopping sounded far too loud and carried perhaps too far.

In the three-piece train of Alanna, her, and Tam, Payton began to feel a pair of eyes on her. They dwelled in the mist, which hid the farther sections of roads. She wondered, with a dash of mirth, if she found these eyes, would they be blue when they peered back?

"Careful," she said to Alanna. Payton didn't have to raise her voice, though Alanna was far ahead now. A whisper could carry a country mile in this quiet.

"I know," the blonde warrior replied. "I feel it, too."

"I agree," she heard Tam say behind her, "I just know there are some hobgoblins and gremlins up ahead."

Payton frowned at him.

"Sorry, you're right," Tam smirked. The moonlight glittered on his silvering hair. "Shouldn't poke jokes while folks are losing their minds."

They turned right down another boulevard, peering into shop windows and searching for any sign of a trail. They found several foot traces, though all led to dead ends. Finally, Tam said, "I would advise you to keep watch for harpies, though. They'll get you."

Payton sighed, but smiled in spite of herself.

"All fun and fine till a scab puts an arrow in you," Alanna warned.

"Sure, the *scabs*," Tam replied. "What a ridiculous slur." He clucked his tongue. Payton scanned the misty boulevard, listened to the amplified clopping hooves, and ran her finger along her hilt. "You know, Braeden the Bold was the first guy to call the Mehsanics 'scabs.' Said the North had grave wounds that wouldn't heal; it was the scabs who kept breaking open and making us bleed. He ruled for only seven years, the shortest of any of the five great kings, and yet more Mehsanics and Sumarans died during his reign than under any other king in history. Braeden was a pickled swine."

Alanna rotated her head half around to say, "You know a fair share about Braeden the Bold."

"As you can tell, I'm his biggest admirer," Tam quipped.

A flash of red caught Payton's eye. She whipped her horse to the left and darted down the alley it came from. Tam's and Alanna's shouts faded behind her. Her horse skidded to a halt at the end of the alley. The cloud of mist dissipated in the rush. She found, however, nothing but the soil beneath her and the connection to another alley.

There. The mist, ebbing and flowing in the breeze, revealed the red sash and the man wearing it. It was unmistakable. Payton would never forget the spook in the red scarf.

"It can't be him," she uttered aloud. Tam and Alanna caught up.

"Payton, what was that?" Tam exclaimed.

"Him," she answered and pointed to the man in the red scarf. He stood fifty paces away beyond the fog and the alley.

"Faedelin's nuts," Tam breathed.

"I saw him die," Payton said. The man continued to stare at them, his face blurred in the mist. Only the scarlet scarf was visible. "In that brothel fire, before I was injured, I fought him. The whole building crashed down on him and burned him alive."

"Faedelin shall judge you, Payton Tallhart," the man stated. His voice was profound and mournful as a cello string. The fog leisurely circled him. "I have told you this much."

"How did you get out?"

The fog wrapped around him, and he vanished.

Payton kicked her horse toward the end of the other alley, but here, too, she found only the soil. The man in the scarf was gone again. Fuck, how can he simply disappear? Payton wondered. Then she noticed a faint trail of prints. She jumped down from the saddle and followed them. Tam and Alanna were in her wake.

The prints led down another alley, into the boulevard, farther south, down toward the river, back up the street. She felt like a dog glued to an infinite trail. Tam and Alanna were falling behind. Their shouts grew muffled. Payton heard only her breathing and her footfalls, driven by the need to find this man.

The trail swung into a narrow street. By the measure of decay, she thought this must've been a slum. Twisted boards and unhinged doors lay in the street, as if the wake of a windstorm. Animal carcasses bordered the road in the place of curbs. She covered her nose.

She ran faster. The trails led around a pile of carcasses and into a back alley. She was close. She felt the man in the scarf near. She needed to know. She needed—

Jon's body collided into hers as she neared the alley. They held each other to keep from falling down.

"Payton!" he cried. "What's wrong?"

"Jon, what the fuck are you doing here?" she shouted.

"I found a trail. I was following it," Jon replied, indignant at her suspicion.

"Me, too," she breathed. "Where's Coyle?"

"We split up. Figured we'd have a better chance at finding Piper. Where's Tam and Alanna?"

"Fell behind," she replied. They continued to hold each other up, and she reflected that this was the first time she'd been within Jon's reach. He wasn't so tall, now that she truly saw him.

"The prints go into that alley," Jon noticed.

"I know, I..." she trailed off. Over Jon's shoulder, she saw the man. The fucker was toying with her.

She shoved Jon aside and shouted, "Stop!"

Payton dashed after the spook. Coyly, he ducked into the building at the alley's end. She heard Jon's feet rushing after her. Before she thundered through the door, Payton saw the scarlet scarf waiting for her in the common room. She was steps away. The moment she burst into the building, the floorboards whined and cracked under her feet. Payton halted, but the whining redoubled. Jon sprinted in after her before she could warn him. Their weight was too much. He reached her, though a moment later the floor splintered and swallowed them into the basement below.

24

What Waits in the Dark Room

Their bodies were tangled in the dark cellar. Payton glanced at Jon in the pitch black, his body unmoving at the back of the room they'd fallen into. It was more of a storage closet, empty save for a broom and bucket. If she were to spread her arms, she could flatten her palms on both sides of the room at once. She struggled to disentangle her legs from Jon's.

Her back pressed up against a metallic door. Payton shoved it, but it wouldn't give. She glanced around. Without having to move, she felt the four walls of the room, a lightless box in the cellar of some forgotten place. The walls climbed ten feet to the floorboards above, broken like twigs. Faint moonlight outlined the hole they'd made.

Jon remained immobile. Even as Payton pushed off him to shoulder the door, he lay motionless. Since he padded the worst of her fall, she wasn't surprised he'd been knocked out. His great frame was crumpled in the shadows. His back slumped against the back wall, and his feet brushed the metal door on the opposite end.

The boards creaked overhead. Payton looked up and saw the man in the red scarf peering down at her and Jon. His boots stood on the twig floorboards, and yet no whining came from them.

"Who are you?" she demanded.

"You know, Payton Tallhart. You know, in your gut."

With that, the man in the red scarf turned away and left her with Jon in the cellar closet.

"Come back!" she screamed. She pounded her fists against the walls of the closet. Panic stoked her heartbeat. How the fuck would anyone find her and Jon?

She lunged again at the door. Either some long-dead tenant had bolted it shut or something on the other side blocked any chance of it swinging open. On the tenth try, she slightly split her shoulder.

Payton screamed for Tam, for Alanna, even for Coyle, though she had no idea how far south her chase of the man in the scarf had taken her. They could be miles away, with hundreds of unexplored streets and hundreds more buildings between them. She was alone.

"The dark room," she heard.

Payton faced Jon. In the faint moonlight, she saw his bulging eyes, rigid as the rest of his body. He'd been alert this whole time, she realized.

"You going to just stare at me all night?" she snapped.

"It's back," he breathed. "The dark room."

"What? Jon, help me. I can't budge this door. Must be bolted shut." Her fingers searched for a lock in the darkness. Nothing. "Fuck. We've got to find a way out. Everyone'll pack and go home before they find us here."

She glanced at him. Jon still hadn't moved, his eyes still ballooned from their sockets. She snapped her fingers. He seemed departed, as if though their bodies were entwined, they dwelt in different worlds.

Payton remembered the nights they spent at the Crossroads in Alanna's tavern. He'd been reluctant to take the tiny attic room, staring at it from the hallway for a minute before crossing the threshold. Jon insisted that the candle stay lit. Later he claimed he simply didn't like closed spaces.

Faedelin's balls, wasn't this a brilliant situation she'd been handed. No way out of a closet with a man petrified by the dark and tight spaces.

"I can't help you if you don't speak," Payton told him. Jon didn't respond. She crouched against the relentless door. His stare went right through her. "Jon." She flicked his boot. "Wake up. Tell me what you're thinking."

"The dark room. It's back."

"What's the dark room? You've mentioned that before." No answer. "At least we've got a little moonlight," she said, followed quickly by a sigh. Payton picked up the bucket, though it fell apart along trails of termite teeth.

Abruptly, his hand went to the walls. "It's just like I remember," he whispered. His palms rasped on the earthen walls. Overhead, a breeze spilled some dirt on them from outside. It sounded like somebody whistling. Jon's body trembled.

"They're coming," he whimpered.

"Who, Jon?" she asked. His trembling worsened. His feet kicked at her. "Careful!"

"They're coming," he repeated. The wind whistled again. "They're almost here. They always whistle before they open the door."

"Jon, nobody's coming."

He condensed into a fleshy ball. Muttering came from between his knees, where his head cowered, so Payton couldn't make out his words. She moved closer and patted his shoulder. As her hand lifted, she felt that it was filmed in sweat. Squinting, Payton noticed that the man was drenched in perspiration.

"You're burning up," she said. "Come on, lift your arms."

Payton stretched Jon's arms over his head to slide off his coat and black shirt. It clung to his back. Once she'd yanked the shirt loose, she tossed it aside. It splatted against the door. Then Payton pulled his legs long and slid his torso into the dim moonlight so the breeze fell directly onto him. She swore when his body came into focus.

Innumerable scars covered Jon. She'd never seen so many scars in her life, forget on one body. Purple, white, black—they came in variety. A swath of purple blushed across his breast, where the nipple had been flayed. On his

227

other breast, a shepherd's hook was branded, a strange clash with the heron tattoo on his forearm. It stood out from the blade marks. The marks covered him like messy brush strokes and left little virgin flesh behind. Jon's body was some grisly canvas completed by a sadistic painter.

Payton crouched over him. So this is what they made of him, she thought. This is what they did to the Ghost. She traced a few of the scars. Some were still grooved; they'd gone so deep and wide, the flesh couldn't fill back in completely.

Since his shirt came off, Jon's hyperventilating subsided. He returned gradually to stillness, staring blankly at the moonlight. It made a faint aura, since the alleyway outdoors blocked the moon itself. He touched her wrist. Their eyes met. Then his closed, and he fell asleep.

Payton stood. If she extended her legs, she could push herself up to the first floor with her back against the opposite wall. She and Jem used to climb all over the university in a similar way, in the small nooks that the adults overlooked. It'd been a decade since she tried it last.

She planted one foot, then the other, on the wall near the floor. Her tailbone wedged tightly against the opposite wall. Payton pushed her back up, then her feet, and again her body. Her muscles ached. They were slow to recall old habits. In two minutes, she was within reach of the floorboards.

The first one she grabbed flaked off and fell near Jon's feet. She pushed herself sideways toward the firmer boards, which ran parallel to the hole rather than hanging out over it. She edged her elbows onto the floor above. Payton pushed, but the pressure from her elbows pulled away from her feet, and she slipped. Her left hand grabbed the floor, but her body swung round and slammed the wall. She tasted blood from her nose. But she held the floor.

Payton pulled herself back onto the floor. She balanced over the beam beneath the boards, where she knew the floor would be strongest. Following that beam, Payton stepped away from the hole and out into the alleyway.

She knew she'd have maybe a few minutes before Jon awoke, and if he found himself alone in the dark closet, he might lose himself in terror. Payton hurried to the street. Here, beneath the crescent moon's direct light, she could see clearly. There were pieces of debris scattered everywhere. Doors, boots, mugs, carriage wheels, shattered glass. The wreckage lay there in memoriam, and perhaps always would.

Payton dug through piles of the mess. Most was useless to her. She'd need a rope to fashion some sort of pulley. Quickly, she realized she'd find nothing useful, for the closest items she saw to a rope were frayed tethers barely a foot long. To pull Jon from the cellar, the rope would need to be at least twenty feet.

Payton sighed and crouched in the center of the ruined boulevard. There seemed to be no one around her, not even the spook in the scarf. It was her and the moonlight, which fell beautifully from its crescent seat in the sky.

Something caught her eye in the nearest pile of wreckage, a simple wooden stick that thumbed out. Payton stepped out of her crouch and moved closer. When she grabbed it, its bottom half remained stuck in the mess. On the second pull, Payton overcompensated and jerked back with her whole weight. She landed on her back, but stared up at a thick hammerhead. She could use it to demolish the lock on the other side of the door and release Jon that way.

Payton returned to the building. Across the ruined floor, a door remained closed beside the bar. She supposed that door would lead to the basement. Starting with the tip of her toe, Payton balanced on the joist running parallel to the hole and paused to peer down at Jon, who slumbered. Hammer in hand, she tiptoed along the beam to the rear of the common room. She swung the cellar door open, and the stairs sinking into the ground confirmed her guess.

The stairs, chiseled into the bedrock under the building, held beneath her weight. Payton descended two at a time. The bottom of the stairwell swung left into a broad hallway with several doorways spaced along its length. She saw only one was filled by a metal door; Jon waited beyond its rusted lock.

Writing on the opposite wall gave Payton pause. She could make out the words on the wall because of the box of moonlight stabbing through the door's edges. They were deep maroon, made deeper by the dark. The message blended into the drab rock it was scribed on: *scab whores*. Her eyes panned down. A pile of skeletons littered the opposite end of the hallway. They'd been in dresses and simple shirts when they died. Hatchets and cleavers remained lodged in the skulls of some, while others displayed the fatal blow in the breaks in their bones. Payton shook her head.

She proceeded slowly as an usher at a funeral. She pondered how many years ago these Mehsanic women had died and which Faeds had killed them. Had they been murdered during the Reaving, during the War in the Narrows, the Southern Marches, any one of Braeden the Bold's wars? Payton scanned the heap of bones. Despite their decomposition, the bones were piled halfway up the wall.

She reached the metal door. It was five or six strides away from the dead women. Payton reflected for a moment, her palm wrapped around the rust of the lock, on the scene before her. The Mehsanics slaughtered by her kinsmen to the left, the Faed man butchered by her foes beyond the door. Quite the legacy you left, Faedelin.

Payton raised the hammer, swung it down. The lock shattered on contact. She had to wedge the hammer head between the door and the frame to pry open the way. When it gave, it did so suddenly that she was flung back into the hallway.

Jon's feet slid a few inches into the hall. His toes limply fanned outward, no longer supported by the door. She picked up his shirt, sopping despite the time off his back, and draped it over her shoulder. Then Payton pulled Jon to his feet, ducking her head under his armpit and holding his waist upright.

"C'mon, Jon, wake up."

"Hmm," he mumbled.

She stumbled out of the closet with him, his feet dragging behind them. Every few steps, Payton stopped to reposition Jon's limp body, and then, before he slipped again, she'd dash another three or four paces. At the foot of the stairs, she sat him down, and his head lolled sideways. Payton climbed behind him and took him upstairs by his arms. She did not look back at the message or the women.

Once she managed to get him to the top of the stairs, Payton sat down and gasped for breath. "Faedelin's balls, you're heavy," she told him. He seemed to be coming to.

"Payton?" he groaned.

"Yeah."

"We're out?"

"We are."

"You took us out?"

"I did."

Jon held his head. Looking down, he noticed his shirtless torso and flattened his hands over the patch of scars and the shepherd's hook brand. Wordlessly, Payton handed back his soaked shirt. He stuffed his arms and head through its holes.

"How do we get out of here?" he asked her.

Payton nodded behind her. "There's a support beam that seems to be holding. That's how I got to the stairwell. Should hold us, but you've got to have your balance back."

"I do."

"No, Jon. You need your balance back. Wait a minute."

They did. As they waited, the wind whistled through the front door again, and Jon perked up, freezing for the length of the breeze. When it died, his body relaxed again.

"Okay, let's go," Jon said.

"Okay. You fall, you're on your own," she replied.

"Haven't I always been." It came out as a declaration of fact, not a question.

Payton took the first steps across the floor. Jon's footfalls came close behind, though their pattern was sloppy and loud. Whining sounded from beneath them. She sped up, made it across.

Jon was soon behind her. The brief walk had drained him. Barely out of the alleyway, Jon collapsed and propped himself up against the first building in the boulevard. Payton studied him for a moment; his panting spiked rapidly. He held up a hand, mouthing, "I'm fine." She sat down beside him.

"You never told me that Lanair's people did that you," she said. "I had some ideas, but never that."

Jon frowned. "Trust is more precious than gold, and should be spent accordingly."

"You don't trust me?"

"No one." His breathing normalized.

"Why?"

He looked at her. "You saw what just happened to me. That's because I put too much trust in the South and its people, and they put me in the dark room."

"What's the dark room, Jon?"

He sighed. "Faedelin's nuts, I could've gone a lifetime without you seeing any of that or hearing any of this."

"If you ignore it, you think it'll get better?"

He looked away.

"Jon."

"No. I know it won't." Jon rubbed his thighs, as if easing out a cramp. "They locked me in a cupboard, if you've got to know."

"A cupboard?"

"Well, no. I don't know what to call it. It was a room built only for agony. It was so small and narrow I couldn't sit, stand, or lie down. I kind of crouched and hunched for hours. Days, sometimes. They took me out only to cut me up."

Payton winced. "That sounds awful."

A long pause preluded: "It was."

"Why did they do it?"

"They thought I killed Lanair's father. This was a year after the War in the Narrows, when I was nineteen. He was poisoned by some rebel who thought Lanair's father was spineless in defeat at the Narrows. Thought he should've fought until King Gareth or Leon Tallhart killed every last Sumaran." Jon turned his massaging to his calves. "Lanair thought it was me and had me thrown in the dark room."

"Lanair ordered this?"

"He acted like he didn't, but I knew. The Ghost always knew."

"That's why you wanted the meeting tomorrow."

Jon shrugged. "Not entirely, no. I do want to see this thing through. I think I've been put through enough to earn a place at the end of all things."

Payton nodded. "I suppose that's a fair argument. Still, I never knew how personal this was for you." The breeze hummed by them.

"You never asked," he said.

"No, I did not," she said. "You let them shape you, though, Jon."

He grimaced. "More than that. They molded me. You saw their hand-iwork." He signaled his chest. "How'd you do wearing one nipple and conflict-ing sigils on your body?"

Payton couldn't think of a response.

"I know everyone hates me. I understand. But I have hatred, too. I have desires and feelings and wishes." Jon rested against the building's façade. "How about you, Payton? You don't think you've been shaped?"

"Huh?"

"Leon's little parrot. Chirp, chirp, chirp."

"I'm no parrot, Jon. Words have no domain over me."

"Whether you say them with passion or say them with pathos, you say them, Payton." He began sketching gibberish in the soil next to his buttocks. "Ever think about just changing the songs written by the dead?"

"What do you think I'm doing, Jon?" she asked.

He shrugged.

"Jon, you're not the first to bleed, and you won't be the last. But if you work with me, we can avoid as much blood as possible," she suggested.

Her words incensed him. "Fuck the others. I don't give a fuck about the others. Until you've been carved up, don't talk to me about some nameless, faceless others. Fuck the others."

"You're missing my point. You've been strapped to the table and faced the questions and endured the knives. And here you stand. Help me silence the questions. Help me blunt the knives."

He shook his head. "You just don't understand. No one ever under-stands. It wasn't an interview. It was a massacre."

"I know," she said.

"You do not know!" he shouted. "You're just like that nymph Royce rambles on about. You trap everyone on your little island and make them play blood sports and chase the sun."

She drew back. "I am no nymph."

"Don't speak to me again about what happened to me until you cease those verses. You're no more than that nymph. You've got all these mindless idiots doing your bidding." He barked a laugh. "Who are you, anyway? The Red Hart? The fuck does that mean?"

"Shit, Jon, calm down," Payton said.

"You're some girl playing a nymph disguised as a hero." Jon frowned. "I've never sung those songs and never claimed to. I've written my own verses. I've never sung those songs."

Payton sighed. "You're the singer and the sung." She stood up and took a few steps away from him. "We're just talking past each other."

"Ships of symmetry, remember? Don't forget that we're heading toward the same goal. You and I, Payton, we're going for the same ends."

"In such very different ways."

"You just have to trust me. I know what I'm doing."

"You're just signing the treaty, Jon."

He paused. "I know."

Their exchange ended there. She'd give him a few minutes more to work out any cramps in his legs and regain his strength before returning to the camp. They'd be back soon enough. In the meantime, Payton folded her arms and watched Jon. The man lounged against the building and gazed up at the crescent moon. A warm, genuine smile curved on his face. That smile gave no clue he'd suffered a fall and a panic attack within the last half hour. He was content.

Jon's hand went to his earlobe, and he began thumbing it as one thumbs an earring. She felt herself fade from his consciousness. There seemed to be only him and the invisible earring, as he happily hummed to himself, "Mmm, mmm, look at that moon. Love that moon."

Payton looked up at the moon, too, and recalled how Leon used to say the crescent was Faedelin smiling down at them. Coupled with that thought was the suspicion that Jon would fade back into himself following their moment under the moon. Payton determined that the task was hers to complete

234

once the sun rose, for the nearest thing she had to a partner was trapped waiting for the torturers to come for him in a darkened cellar.

25

The Mote of a Soul

"Wake, Jaremy Nalda," a voice says to me.

Steam pours up my nostrils when I draw my waking breath. The voice comes at me from everywhere in the Copse of Last Trees at once. I can't pin it to a source. The voice is as ubiquitous and inexplicable as the purple light shining between the trees.

I'm standing, though I don't remember getting up. My head feels heavy like after an overlong nap. Somehow, Lanair hovers above the Mirror of Mehsani. His body hangs suspended, arms out, straight as arrows.

"Calm yourself," an omniscient, unseen voice assures me.

The voice is a woman's. I wonder where it's coming from. So much about the Copse of Last Trees reminds me about the stories I used to read with Payton when we were little. I've never seen anything like this place. The whole forest is connected, one side knowing the feelings of the other. A perfect balance. Maybe nothing needs a source, like the woman's voice, since the forest itself is the epicenter for everything within it.

There's a story about a swamp that eats anyone who enters. The swamp's name was Oro. Men went there looking for treasures swallowed by the growth, but they found themselves eaten alive by the monstrosities that gave life to Oro. Parents would threaten naughty children, saying, "We'll send you to Oro if you don't listen." Perhaps the Copse of Last Trees is a foil to Oro. Life permeates every morsel of air here, whereas death holds domain there. If the copse is real, can Oro be, too?

"You are frightened," the voice states.

Her voice comforts me. She knows my thoughts. I can feel her skimming through my mind as you'd sense a voyeur nearby. I want to reach Lanair, but I'm afraid I'd sink into the mirror, though I know he'd been walking on it.

"You want answers. All of you do. Come to the mirror," the voice says.

"Why?" I ask her.

"To attempt to find the answer," she replies.

"To what?"

"Everything. Or nothing, perhaps."

Unsure, I stay where I am. Lanair continues to float in stasis, raven crown pointing skyward.

"Come. The hour draws near for you to go to the tower."

"Do you know what will happen tomorrow?"

"I do not. Though I can predict."

"How?"

"Couldn't you?" For the first time, her voice has a fleck of amusement to it. "Come to the mirror, Jaremy Nalda, and you will see the answer. The answer to why she is held on the eastern bank and you are trapped on the western."

Were these trees pine, I might faint. Though they stretch not three miles across, the trees draw me in like the infinite pines of my imagination. She knows what hides there. The thoughts, the dreams, the anger. Not one seems safe from her, whoever she might be. Wherever she might be.

Taking half strides, I approach the slumbering lake. It draws me toward it, like how the ground sucks you down when regarded from a high vantage.

"Drink," the voice instructs.

"What will it do?"

"Give you an answer."

"What is it? Water?" I question.

"The essence of what I am. My nectar, some used to say."

I kneel down and take a sip. It has no taste, no texture. Suddenly, I feel my body tense up. The lake in front of me vanishes in glowing sparks, innumerable embers flying madly out. All goes black.

✹ ✹ ✹

Ambrose wanted to turn back.

The monsoon had drowned several horses when the river lurched over its banks and surged eastward. The waters dragged some of their followers, too. He saw them get taken, legs cut out from under them as if they were flower stems in the way of a kicking boot. Under they went, away they soared. Their legs poked back up, then submerged, bobbing in the river like crooked flags raised at half-mast.

After the river shrank, they found most of their supplies scattered for miles. They were implanted in the muddy bank. Two months of food wasted by the end. That end was coming. Ambrose felt it. Time to turn back.

Marosia refused. She called him weak, faithless. Storms, murderous rivers, spoiled food; these were merely tests in the chosen land. Damned if she gave up before she passed the tests. Conquer the river or go back to chains. She refused.

"But the natives know these hills better than any of us," he insisted. "It's got to stop." He punctuated each word. Got. To. Stop.

"They'll have the upper hand for now. We'll handle them after we escape the empire." Marosia always found a way to sound so sure.

"They don't even recognize us, Marosia. The general routs us. We never should have fled."

Marosia grabbed her brother's blond mane of hair. "When we said, 'To the end,' did you mean it? Or did you merely want to act out some poem you'd written?"

He grimaced. She then took his hand and led him to the hill overlooking their camp. "Look." Sun-bleached tents forested the valley. Around its edges, guards in crude armor hunched over where they stood, posts they'd taken near dawn. "We go back, all of them die. You want that on your head before they take it?"

Ambrose sighed. "Fine. Onward."

She'd been right so far. The sun blessed them with three captured captains from the general's ranks. Marosia knelt them on a rock for everyone to watch. They spat up at her, but the comets of spit crashed on her thighs. One, two, three. Marosia sent their heads back north as those in the valley fell to their knees, begged to touch her feet. At the name of Marosia, every knee should bend. So went the whispers.

The riders sped north with her message. Ambrose knew she had the minds of the valley in her hand the moment she cut those three off.

Confidently, she turned to her brother and promised, "Our voice will quake them yet."

✪ ✪ ✪

I lurch backward from the lake. The steam holds me up with metaphysical hands, protecting me from the roots below.

"Have you seen?" the female voice inquires.

"Yes."

"You have watched, but have you seen?"

"Who are you?" I wonder.

"Jaremy Nalda, have you seen what has been shown? The world gives us only one chance to see that which we must see above anything else, so that you can make the proper choice. Then your chance evaporates."

I rub my head; slowly it begins to feel drowsy and numb once more. No one should dwell in this place long. Can't quite be part of the mortal world.

"Tell me what you have seen," she demands.

"Uh, two people. They were scared."

"Uh. Do not say, 'Uh.'" Only one person has told me that before.

"Royce? Can that be you, Minaerva?" The omniscient voice doesn't quite sound like Minaerva's, though she was the only person to correct me on my stuttering before.

"What else did you see?" the voice asks, ignoring my query.

"I, um." But then I catch myself. "These folk were fleeing a general. The woman killed three of his captains. The man was more uncertain. Wanted to retreat."

"Why?"

"They didn't say."

"Didn't you know?"

I had, in a way. I had been everywhere and nowhere, like this voice and the purple glow. I had known their thoughts, their motivations, and their past.

"They preached against the emperor's rule."

"Stirred the pot. Sparked a flame. Beware the gestation of a heated thought."

"Who are you? Can it be you, Minaerva?"

"Drink," she commands.

Lanair's body dangles above Mehsani's mirror. She must be the force holding him there. Resigned to fate, I drink. Again, the lake diffuses in a cloud of glowing spores.

❂ ❂ ❂

A quiet came from the North. Marosia took the chance to answer the native question. The natives came at her during the night, belying the trust she and her brother had put in the rocky braes that had sheltered them thus far.

Scouts said they hailed from Calidum, a hot continent to the south. There they should've stayed. So they would go, or fall under her swords in the great Northern quiet.

The ambush took six men. Marosia was among the wounded after an arrow lodged in her shoulder. It hadn't slowed her down. Four natives died at her feet, either side of the injury.

She allowed a day for recovery. Marosia left Ambrose to his writing and called for a tracking mission through the endless stretches of bog that hugged their southern camp.

They stank of sulfur. One man went down, never came up. When she peered into the pool through which he'd slipped, a faint light, as if from within a lantern, pulsed at her. Marosia felt drunk. She couldn't help but plunge into the pool.

Marosia plummeted through a narrow tunnel in the peat, sinking rapidly as if a boulder were tied to her ankle. Her hands slid off the sides of the peaty tube, so she couldn't stop, while the stink of the water whizzed past her. Moments later, the woman was spat out of the tube into an endless ocean beneath the bogs.

With her body submerged, she saw the endless void hanging beneath the spongy surface. She couldn't discern a boundary to this underground ocean. Yet there was a light, floating far beneath. The light came up, up, up. Marosia screamed when the burning started. It permeated her every fiber, eviscerated each vein. She felt as if the sun were burning her alive.

Her body was yanked upward. Her men pulled her out a beat later, but the burning lingered long after she'd dried off and abandoned the pool.

"I saw a light," she told them, a tremble in her inflection. She related her ordeal, which held them rapt.

The burning, an incessant flame between throat and heart, persisted, despite plenty of water, until they hunted the natives to a narrow valley whose mouth seemed closed to the passerby. The general at their tail, the savages at their head. Her body ached. Onward was the only way.

"We're at the point of consolidation," Marosia told the men gathered around her like a halo. "That narrow valley holds the key to our survival, our supremacy. It was promised. We need walls before the Northern quiet ends. Those are our walls," she said, pointing to the closed mouth. "But someone has stolen them from us. Let's take it back! Our people must find the valley vacant. It's ours."

They nodded solemnly. Marosia embarked for the valley once night came. Faithfully, the hunters ran with her into the narrows to polish the rocks.

✪ ✪ ✪

The voice repeats her question, barely before I've stopped swaying from the vision. "What have you seen?"

"Marosia scourged the Narrows."

"What else?"

"Said her brother was a writer, stayed away from the menial stuff while she cleared them a path. That—that light beneath the bog. What was that? I felt the burning as Marosia once felt it." It had felt like bathing in a bath of hot oil.

"A force unknown to us, though we call it by many names in stories. The force may enter any careless buffoon unlucky enough to sink into its void," she answers.

"What was the force, though?"

"A resource, like your lumber or your water or your jewels. Rare, but only a thing." She pauses, and the trees rustle. "Marosia may have called this thing the Light because of its peculiarity. But remember, Jaremy Nalda, it is only a resource."

"So why did it enter her?"

As if shrugging metaphysically, she replies, "For she fell. So it did."

"So it went into her only because she fell."

"Yes. Only because she lost her footing," she says.

I move on to another topic. "Marosia lied about the natives. Said they stole the valley. Used it to justify their killing, as if some special providence fueled their blades."

243

"The Mother turns the earth to spin us off. Our words can hold us to the ground as we reach for the sky."

My memory jogs suddenly, flinging me far past Royce and the university, to a land of hot baked clay.

"Queen Kala, is that you?"

Again ignoring me, the female voice asks, "Why are you seeing what you see?"

"For the answer. My queen, where are you?" I scan the far bank of the steaming lake.

"What is the answer?"

"I don't know."

"What is the mote of a soul?" she asks obscurely.

"I don't know. Can you tell me?"

"No, Jaremy Nalda. You have to see."

The world bursts in a flurry of sparks.

○ ○ ○

The natives had scattered like a handful of sand cast into the wind when they saw her. She polished the rocks on the long road south, where the narrows emptied onto a sweltering plain stretching far beyond the horizon's limit. The valley vacant, she ushered her battered followers to safety.

Though something strange had accompanied this victory. As if in answer to the murder of the natives, the light from beneath the bogs returned. It shone from her orifices, blinding the men and women who'd been around her at the time. The light could be seen from miles away. When it vanished, the men and women around Marosia were gone, vanished by the light, and a brilliant scorch glimmered on the soil around her feet.

She felt empty following the light's return, though if anything it minted her followers forever. Not only did they see her power, they wished to serve her well enough to be consumed by the light. They salivated for the honor.

Weeks later, Marosia lashed her lieutenant for not holding the southern mouth. The savages flooded back. Before she could muster a response, they'd returned to myriad caves and began to pick away at her people from the tunnels snaking below her feet. Each tunnel led into another cave. Whereas they had scattered at her first coming, they dispersed in orderly fashion at her second, scurrying down dank networks into the unknown. She lost more men to the tunnels and the unknown than to any savage's sword. Traps waited patiently in the deep.

Word wandered its way to common tongues, as it was wont to do. Once there, it twisted the whispers from bending the knee to Marosia into her bending the knee to them. She tasted mutiny.

While she considered its flavor, with a twitch of her nose, Marosia rolled the letter along the frowning curve of her thumb. First they lacked the disposition to repel the general, now they reneged on the Light's promise. Sunburned specters stole it. Yet they held on to the belief that the narrows and the stony braes belonged to the thieves. The situation painted the back of her tongue in bile.

The old priest who called himself Alamon cleared his throat to end her solitude. He'd appeared in the doorway. Through it Marosia watched as the last row of stone was set atop their walls. A modest beginning, those walls would slow the general's advance nonetheless. The stone ringed an orchard they'd claimed. An old tree, its roots a gnarled network sinking into the soil, stretched its branches behind Alamon's head, apple earrings conspicuous in the leaves.

"My lady, your brother requests a word." Since he was among Marosia's most ardent followers, he kept the crown of his scalp bare, naked for the sun to see, frying his wicked thoughts in its light. She'd taught this lesson in her first sermon.

"Okay. Another story of his?"

"You'll enjoy this one, Lady Marosia. I promise."

"Mmm. I need a good story today. The others have been sour." She handed him the letter. When he unrolled it, Alamon mopped away the sweat glistening on his forehead.

"'A Letter to Ignore,'" he said, wincing at the title. "This isn't good."

"No. 'Silence, woman. Your ink is a waste of parchment. Send another, we'll return the might of the empire.' So hastily written they didn't even sign."

Alamon frowned. "Perhaps Ambrose can help. You should go see him."

"Writing all day does no one any fucking good."

"Your power is together. Don't hold him away." He motioned for her to lead him.

Marosia crumpled the parchment, stuffed it in the oven. She marched past the priest, who'd abandoned the Twelve Gods in admiration of her words. He stepped quickly in her wake. Marosia passed through the small town, lugubrious in twilight. The newly minted walls were superfluous when compared with the sod huts they hid. Her people loved those huts. The first roofs they'd had since sailing to Braeland, they were a gift from the Light itself. Any respite from rain was revered.

Reverence tilted the heads throughout the town at an angle. A blacksmith paused his hammering, a baker offered an old loaf, patrolmen clutched their breasts. "Lady Marosia," they mumbled. Two empty words with no feet. The patrolmen passed, the baker bit the loaf, the blacksmith's hammer sang *ting. ting. ting.* Beyond the hammering, her city wallowed mutely in the blanket of its superfluous walls.

Ambrose waited beyond those walls in a tent that welcomed the wind through light cloth. His hair was a bird's nest, straw brushed with soil. Her brother hunched over a makeshift table of one splintered plank horizontal over four logs. Parchment littered the plank. A tallow candle splayed outward, trickled downward. Its wax congealed in a leprous cylinder. Ambrose's half-open eyes fixated on it. He didn't look up when she entered. The priest waited outside.

"How's your writing?" she asked.

His shoulders peaked and dipped indifferently.

"Father Alamon tells me it's your best work yet."

"Guess you could say that."

"Not your favorite?"

He gestured to the parchment. "Could hover over this until it became nothing." Instead of the papers, Ambrose lowered his fingers to touch the flame. The underside of his hand glowed. He spread his fingers, then the orange dome dissipated.

"Thought you told Alamon I should come speak with you."

"Yes. About the native question. You were saying yesterday how the people don't want to kill them anymore."

"They think we're stealing their land," she said.

"And?"

Marosia glared at him. "Retreat isn't an option, Ambrose."

He shrugged and handed her a parchment from the mess.

"The Book of Testaments," she read. "What's this?"

"The first book. Read it," Ambrose instructed.

She did. Throughout its forty brief chapters, she learned how the Light had placed these savages in their valley as a test. They hid in caves where the Light could not touch. It was the people's job to take the Light there, to spread the domain in which it could shine. Were they to give up on spreading the Light, then it would surrender its guidance. The shadows would swallow them up. The native test led to deliverance or to ruin. And they would find deliverance if they adhered to the guidance of the two siblings.

"Excellent. Really good stuff, Ambrose," she said an hour later. "You think this'll be enough?"

"That, and the two others. The Books of Laws and Ideals. Have your priest start preaching." He filled a kettle and placed it over a tiny fire.

"Okay. Alamon," she called.

The priest ducked his head in.

"Have your scribes start producing these. I want every family to have one by month's end."

Alamon nodded, took the Book of Testaments.

"Have these, too." Ambrose passed along two more tomes, titled Laws and Ideals. "That'll suffice for now."

The priest departed.

247

"So the native thing will be answered. What about the question of old ghosts?" she asked as the water boiled for tea.

"Why don't we submit as a colony? The offer stands."

"We'd never earn a place as equals if we submit to colonialism. We'd be servants."

"Those stories can fuel our people, but the empire won't bat an eyelash at them." His eyes, a green mirror of hers, fell back upon the candle. "We need another spark."

"How do you mean?"

"We once tapped into their hearts. The long trip here dulled that control. We need another spark. That'll get us back into control, and luckily the smallest mote of their spirits will suffice."

Marosia drummed her fingers. "A spark for the savages, a spark for the ghosts. One's a moral quandary, the other a dilemma of fear. So for the latter we need a figure who can eliminate their fright."

He thrust a finger at her. "You're not?"

"The empire doesn't recognize me. Even their letters teem with apathy, almost amusement, at our claim." The kettle began to simmer then, so Marosia moved to pour it.

"It has to be you, Marosia. You're our face. Always have been."

Marosia regarded her brother, who remained entranced by the leprous candle. With her hair wrapped, as it often was, a bundle of straw brushed with dirt, the two siblings could be twins. Only the white scar under her lips designated Marosia from Ambrose.

He let out a long sigh that threatened the flame, but it held on to its wick. Ambrose turned the candle sideways. Its resurging flame lit a parchment and quickly leaped to two neighbors.

"What if I let it linger? Might burn down the town, though I want only these three parchments to vanish."

Marosia took the water, which had just come to a boil, and doused the table. The fire had been poised to devour the rest of the tent. The water hissed in its stead.

"Not worth the work we put in," she replied. He was inanimate.

"To Marosia they don't reply. To some other name they might."

"Yours?"

"No." Thoughtfully, he looked up at her. "What was that old thing they used to call you? Before we had to run."

A smile curved on her face. "They called me 'my Faedelin.' Means 'faithful one,' roughly."

Ambrose closed his eyes and rocked on his stool.

"Faedelin. Now there's a name. Use that."

She did. Marosia fashioned a response with new demands for the general to vacate their country. Ambrose reviewed it, inserted some flowery syntax. Then she signed it Faedelin. Something about the loneliness of the word bothered her, so she affixed two more that made her new name pop. A title so compelling the empire would listen. The Lord Faedelin.

❂ ❂ ❂

"What is the answer?" the voice asks.

"I don't know."

"What is the mote of a soul?" she repeats from before, as if the enigma should make more sense the second time.

"What do you mean by that?"

"What is the sum of the sparks?" the woman's voice questions.

"I...I don't know."

"I thought the Spider King would know everything about his domain," she jests, her cadence slightly amused.

"Wait. I—I can't think. Payt? Is that you?" Only Payton knew my alias, the Spider King.

"What is the mote of a soul?" the voice repeats.

"I don't know!"

"Watch. See."

Flaking embers erase the image of the lake. They fly out, ripping the earth's seams. The embers explode, and the world vanishes.

26

Apples Underfoot

Marosia lost herself in the thumb of rock. For hours the woman stared at it from the lip of the valley, a mile up the grassy slope swooping toward the lake. It gave her hope. A teardrop. She never thought a teardrop would be a fine sign, not after so many real tears had been shed, but here it was, her precious teardrop.

Once the general had knelt to her at the Mire, where the Light had chosen her as its Lord Faedelin, the people named her the Light Embodied. They dedicated a temple to her in the city. Its five pillars were five fingers, her fingers, that blanketed the city in their grasp. The people walked into the palm shadow, the nurturing palm of Faedelin herself.

Marosia announced her victory over the savages and the specters within a week's run of each other. She harvested the Narrows. "Plenty" be-came a modest adjective for the new country's resources. No follower of Ma-rosia would know the lurch of a starving stomach.

Five years to the day since the Lord Faedelin's victory, she and her brother decided to spread the Light's reach, so firm was it in their fertile valley. The Narrows was too small for a province as immaculate as the Light's. Opting to venture north, in the event of the empire's return, Marosia instructed Ambrose to go south, where they'd make a new kingdom to complement the Holy City. Ambrose accepted. He rode south with uncertain retainers while Marosia backtracked to settle the northern reaches.

Marosia's road led back through the Mire. The woman stopped by the place she'd fallen years before and thought she found the hole that sucked her beneath the surface. Her followers prostrated themselves around the pool. Murmurs thanked the Light for finding their deliverer. They prayed to their Faedelin. She pressed her face into the water.

Instead of the Light's vast underground abyss, her nose found a muddy bottom to the pool. The cool bottom startled her. Must be the wrong hole, she thought. Rather than dart away, Marosia calmly rose and flicked away the mud on her nose before her people looked up.

"The Light remains true," she announced firmly. "It stays with us as we spread it dutifully."

Marosia's brood came to the stony braes shortly thereafter, unchanged from the early days of hiding within them. Today she owned them. With the rocky outcrops hugging their shoulders and vibrant grass underfoot, Marosia began to feel at home once again. Planting a banner beaming with her Sunburst, Marosia named this place Wellfleet, a junction of three rivers in the braes. Julien Tallhart, a distant cousin of hers, requested the honor of building her first city. Marosia accepted, and she dubbed him Lord Julien Tallhart, the first Watchman of the Light.

Marosia led her followers west as Julien drew the foundations of the city. It'd stand for generations. The Lord Faedelin knew it in her belly; an unshakable feeling told her yes, this was the place. At the intersection of three large rivers, Wellfleet could be the grandest castle Braeland ever knew. North and west of that stronghold she searched. The westerly river brought her through a patch of woods, ancient roots, and streams mingling throughout. When the trees vanished she saw it.

Miles away at the bottom of a bowl-shaped valley a lake wrapped around an immense thumb of rock. Instantly, the woman knew the words she'd use: the Earth Mother threw her arms to the Light, thrusting the rock upward, while in response, the Light shed a single tear to shield this new haven. This place was the one they'd searched for without knowing what to look for.

After gazing at it for hours, Marosia scouted the island with one hundred of her people. The rising landmass offered bountiful gardens and lumber. A day later the settlement began. They built up the mountain toward the seat of the Lord Faedelin.

Once they'd reached the pinnacle they asked for a name. Suggestions relied largely upon a variation of her name. Others called it the New Holy City.

"No, no," she instructed. "The Holy City is our home, remains our sanctuary. This is new. We will have this be a space of tolerance, for intolerance drove us away. This rock shall teach us the ways of its flora and fauna. We shall study the lessons of the Light. This place will be called Trowbridge."

❂ ❂ ❂

Ambrose came out of the vision slowly; the herbs this far south grew more potently. He'd needed them powerful. Ever since sparing these filthy ravens, he faced bitter naysayers who insisted each wing flap was tolling their demise. The black birds flew everywhere. Not even within the vision could he stave them off. Harbingers of doom, the people called them, but killing them was off the table. So they fluttered, so the people fled, and so did Ambrose, into the disturbed peace of his visions.

They wanted to turn back. His sister had already laid the brick to two castles north of the Narrows while Father Alamon held the Holy City for them. How far had they stretched from the days squabbling with savages? Wellfleet and Trowbridge. And here he was, lingering in the haze of drug, dying in the dreaded heat.

Using his words, Marosia threw up an empire. Faedelinity was the language, the Way its alphabet. Faedelin, Faedelin, Faedelin. What a name for his little sister. It spread, and spread, and spread. Before the fifth camp failed, he caught a group whispering her name in the dark, pleading with it to deliver them from the Southern evils, to teach Ambrose how to lead. More dark wings sent cowards flying. They were losing. Losing to that confounded woman, who stole his words to fashion a throne.

Ambrose came out the vision reluctantly. The letter stared at him from the table, equidistant to his palms flattened on either side. His tired eyes regarded the salutation. Had she forgotten him? Had the distance stretched them too far? The Lord Faedelin. Who the fuck did she think she was?

The stares of his captains hastened his coming down. They circled the table, drumming their impatient fingers. Maybe later he could take another lungful of the medicine.

"Ambrose, maybe we should accept her offers. Our Faedelin seems to have a foothold," someone suggested.

"It's true. Our Faedelin is offering ten times the gold we've got left."

"That island has completely sustainable gardens. They never even have to sail ashore."

"Let's go back to the Holy City."

"Ambrose, wake up."

"I'm here," he mumbled. "Can't go back."

Sighs encircled him.

"Her words, not mine. What's the matter with you anyway? This is a place protected by the Light," Ambrose reminded them.

"Sumara, we know. You've had a knack for a name with pop, Ambrose. No one's denied that. You were never the leader, though. Let's go back. We tried."

He beat his chest lazily. "I tried. I'll still try. We'll win."

"There's nothing to win!" a man shouted. Who was that? "We already have a city in the Narrows!"

"We must spread the Light," Ambrose argued.

"Leave that to Our Faedelin."

"I invented the Light," he retorted.

"Okay then, Ambrose."

Several captains pushed away from the table and exited the tent. Ambrose vainly shouted. They let the flap fall behind them. He bolted upright, chased them out. They spun around, eyes wide at his flailing.

"You listen to me!" he screamed. "I am your fucking commander, not some advisor to shrug off."

"Ambrose, quiet down," a tall one said. "You're going to humiliate yourself."

"Shut your subordinate fucking face." The man shook his head at Ambrose. "I am building an empire, as everyone always asked me to. Then you dare to desert me? I could have your head for this."

The captain who'd told him to hush looked around. "Who'll take it for you? Certainly not these people. Fling your spit at me, man, and I'll walk unscathed."

Ambrose reached for the dagger in his belt. Laughter filled the chorus. The captain shrugged and drew his blade. "So be it," he said.

The man ran at Ambrose, who ducked the blade, but tripped over the man's ankle. He coughed in the dust he kicked up. The chorus heightened. The captain planted a sure foot on Ambrose's shoulder and shoved him to his back.

"What should I make of our great shepherd, who can't keep one light-forsaken sheep from the shadows?" The recommendations turned Ambrose's stomach. Just as the captain pointed his blade toward Ambrose's throat, an arrow took the man in his. He crumpled to the ground. Ambrose gasped and crawled away from the dead man.

The crowd parted around an archer and scores of other men behind him, their faces painted white. In those faces were sets of eyes glazed with the haze Ambrose sought. Bare-chested, the men sported a red hook in the likeness of a shepherd's.

The archer who'd saved Ambrose knelt at his feet. "We cannot stand by while those threaten our savior. You are our shepherd."

Ambrose could smell the drugs on the man's breath. "Thank you," he breathed.

The archer stood and turned to the gathering crowd. "Kneel before your protector! Bow to the Great Shepherd! This is your Mehsani!"

Warily, as if unsure of the ground beneath them, the people eased to a knee. Surrounded by these ambivalent faces, the men with the red hooks began chanting, "Lord Mehsani! Light, bless our lord! Light shine upon Lord Mehsani!"

Ambrose pushed himself to his feet. The drugs had worn off, but a spark in his belly told him he didn't need them anymore. He had found a new vision.

The captains who'd defied him within the tent refused to bend the knee. Ambrose gathered them atop the hill where men were building his masterpiece, his drum of stone. Everyone could see him. Even the metal making their neck hairs shiver didn't sway them.

"Stand down, Ambrose," one commanded.

"Call me Mehsani," he growled.

Marosia thumbed her lip as she regarded the Holy City and the smoke rising from it. Somewhere along the parapets crying red, along the line of spears like skinny, perfect trees bearing dark fruit, was Father Alamon. He'd held the city at her order. Carrion was his prize, and also to gaze from a gruesome perch at her return, weeks too late, as the city's liberator from her brother. Accompanying the speared heads were crude standards. They proclaimed the rise of the Great Shepherd, whose hook was etched in the color of the crying parapets.

The Shepherd called for every true son of the Light to come home to him, the one hero of its might. Infidels would be speared. With all those infidels, there'd be no one left to feel the Light's grace, whenever it decided to finally shine. Marosia had long felt it vanish from her. Even so, back she came in its honor. The southern ride had been for the Light, for the Light's people, for her title. Yet here they stood in the shadow of their own city. A stone obelisk built to the sky, the Tower of the Light outpaced its neighbors gradually catching up to it. A single monument for two siblings. No, no, no. It could not last. Marosia fingered her lip, looking up at the disgraced monument that would, hereafter, stand for one.

Though dusk had fallen several hours ago, the air teemed with an amber glow, pollution from the buildings turned to giant pyres in her city. She tasted the soot. A miracle that didn't black out the intrusion of the Light. In the glow she saw flies dancing in the amber.

Her brother had given her the name; she never doubted that. He'd named her in that city not seven years ago when the dark in the periphery crept toward the core. But this new name he had, the one he'd purportedly snarled before taking heads and heads and heads. The night dimmed.

A courier she'd been waiting on kicked up the dust on the road ahead. Be quick, woman, lest the arrows of shepherds cut you down. Hovering overhead were those flies dancing in the amber. Were they near her ears, she'd swat them flat.

The courier began speaking before her feet hit the ground. "Your brother has agreed to a private meeting regarding the war for the city, my Faedelin."

"Good. When?"

"An hour. We're to enter through the south gate by the river's mouth. You and only ten attendants may enter the city."

Only ten attendants. Though her eyes and ears estimated the number of shepherds within the city, a paltry squad within a large margin of error, Marosia knew the ten attendants were fodder for her brother. She patted the courier on her arm.

"Thank you, Sarah. Go set a watch on the main gate. Wait for my call."

Sarah bowed her head and dashed northeastward through the forming sphere of ten soldiers. Marosia kissed each forehead after ten kisses graced her palm. How their faces mixed interchangeably in the night. She'd known two, Ben and Timothy, since childhood. They'd come with her on the first boat to Braeland. Yet she knew history would lose their names, and they'd become the faceless band of a hero's quest, those meaningless tropes that take up space on a lazy author's page. At least posterity would recall her name.

They hurried to the southern gate where a torch designated it from the walls. They were hustled inside. The foyer within had been converted to a stable since her departure five years ago. She removed her hood.

A man stood several paces away. She walked up to her brother, his back turned from her in hushed disgust. Placing a hand on his shoulder, she felt the wooden plank under his jacket, the shoulder of a scarecrow. She tilted it round. The horizontal plank leered at her: FALSE SHEPHERD.

On the balcony around the yard, archers popped up from the shadows. Their arrowheads glistened at her. Timed to the strumming of bows, Marosia leaped to her side and dodged the projectiles. "Fire!" she cried.

Ben lit an arrowhead and sent it skyward. Before the signal had even reached its climax, Marosia heard the chorus of ten thousand hooves on the dust outside coupled with notes of "Our Faedelin! Our Faedelin!"

✲ ✲ ✲

Marosia sat at the base of an apple tree following the bloodletting. To the east, the horizon blushed. To the west, where her brother stood, the night maintained its morbidity. She hadn't noticed at first, but now, illuminated by the dawn, his glazed eyes struggled to latch on to her or any one thing. Marosia could smell it from here. It'd be pleasant to smell something other than her leg, raw and infected already. White maggots fed there. They became translucent and unassuming as earthworms in the shadow of the tree behind her. Ambrose glared, or attempted to glare, at her. The sea of her faithful hugged her every side.

"A leader stands to meet his opposition," Ambrose mumbled. He wriggled in his shackles.

"Criminals should kneel to their captors."

"Ha. You master now?"

"Take a look, Ambrose." He turned his nose up. She sighed. "Take a look. Mehsani."

258

He canted his gaze to her.

"Will you sign an accord of submission? Or does this discussion need to resume within the tower?"

"I'll not submit to you, Lord Faedelin."

"Don't call me that, Ambrose."

"Declare what's rightfully mine, Lord Faedelin. Tell them all about the words I wrote, the things I invented, the places I built. Think they'll still fall on their hands and knees for you?"

Marosia shook her head and sighed. "We built it, brother. I never claimed more than what lies north of here."

"Mmm, and how fitting that you should find that bountiful land, while I wasted away in swamps and deserts." Ambrose spat at her feet. The sea threatened to awake. "At least my shepherds know my true name."

"Who? Mehsani? A contrived persona." She snapped to her guards, "Take him to the tower. I'll wear him down when I'm ready."

Just as they motioned to take her brother, the wind snatched an apple from overhead. It rolled uphill to Ambrose's feet. Bewildered, the audience watched the uphill fruit and momentarily forgot the cadavers blanketing the city. Ambrose stared at it once it rested at his toes. Then he glared back at his sister. Methodically, sadistically, barbarically, Ambrose drove his heel through the ripened apple and squashed it into a saucer of mush.

Before the guards took him, he mused, "We made it quake."

✿ ✿ ✿

"I don't know. I don't know. I don't know," Marosia said, worried. She sat with her brother in the hall of the Tower of the Light. Sunlight fell through the window of scored glass at the rear wall of the chamber. They sat in chairs, which sat in the oval of stretching sunlight.

"What do you mean you don't know?" Ambrose asked. "Of course I have to hang." He'd been speaking about hanging himself in front of the whole city as if the notion were as simple as a trip to the market.

259

"It's not that easy anymore, Ambrose. The things we've made, the sentences we've said." She shook her head. "They're beyond my grasp. Scary what a word will do. Sometimes the words are all that matter."

"The mote of a soul," he intoned. His tethered hands rested on his lap.

"Hmm?" Marosia asked.

Ambrose sighed. "Father Alamon used to call it 'the mote of a soul.' The first spark that makes a conflagration." The glaze had faded from his eyes so that they pierced Marosia with frightening lucidity.

"Yes. That's it. The mote forms the whole," she recalled.

"Never listened during his lessons, did you?" Ambrose taunted. "Too narrow-minded for that throne you always wanted."

"I never knew my brother to be so petty."

An unfamiliar silence settled between them. Marosia thought briefly of their youth, when their parents couldn't manage to keep them quiet. Then: "Our power was together, Ambrose. That's a truth we can't ignore. Why run from it? Aren't you tired of running? It could've ended. It could've stopped."

Her brother grimaced. "No, no, no. Two motes, you and I, walked through a field of dry grass. Then it was the field's monster to tame. Nobody'll remember the two motes, you and I. Don't flatter me with your silence. Both of us know that it won't end with me alive. We can do it outside, Faedelin."

"Don't call me that."

"The question is," he resumed, "will it end after I'm dead? Silent after all this time? Let me tell you a story.

"South, where you've never been, there's an island they call Laecuna. There lives a goddess come to earth who enjoys trapping shipwrecked sailors and forcing them to chase after the sun. They never escape."

"Why are you telling me this?" Marosia asked.

"Because it's their own fault they never leave the island. It's the sun runners' own hands that the blood of their competitors are on. Know why? Because there's no damn sun, no damn goddess. Just a horde of fucking sun runners who want the light all to themselves. They run for glory and need a justification for blood spilled, an approving providence that says, 'Run, run, run.'"

"And you think I'm this goddess."

Ambrose shrugged. "Could be either of us. My, my, what are you going to do, Faedelin?"

"Enough."

"Why are you afraid of the name?"

"Just not now, please. Let it go."

"If not now, when?"

"We can fix this," she said.

"Even your voice sounds weak. Your tone gives away how little you believe that."

"Enough."

"You need to quench the fire, Faedelin," her brother said, smiling as he said her moniker.

"Stop saying that," Marosia commanded.

"Say it with me. Come on. Faedelin."

She stood from her chair, flexing her fists.

"Faedelin. Faedelin. Hello? Faedelin!"

"Enough!" Marosia bellowed. She tossed her seat aside in fury.

"Yes, enough. Enough pretending. We must recognize," he said, lucidity gleaming in his eyes, "that the smallest mote is a spark hot enough to burn down a forest. Time to put out the fire."

"Put the rope down." He'd slid it out from beneath his chair. His grip was awkward with tethered hands.

"No, it's time to talk to our people. Let's make an end." Ambrose stood to face his sister. The sunlight through the scored window danced on his dirty blond hair, and Marosia thought to herself that he was seeing the same thing on her head.

Her brother walked to the throne centered beneath the window. He produced a knife, quipping that her guards should've searched him better, and began chipping at the wall near the stone seat. She joined him under the window. Here, they were out of the sunlight. Marosia saw his crude carving, that he'd engraved the shepherd's hook that flew on his banners.

"Ambrose."

"What?" Her brother finished making his mark.

"I would've stopped it, if I'd known what the mote would become."

He offered no reply. Instead, Ambrose extended his middle finger, pricked it so that blood beaded on the tip, and dropped the knife. He retraced the hook he'd engraved into the wall with his finger. He lowered his hand and revealed the hook reddened by the blood. Then Ambrose faced his sister in the chilly shadows and smiled at her.

"Good-bye, Faedelin."

❂ ❂ ❂

"We are the Light in the dark," Marosia declared to the great audience.

She allowed her words to sink into the crowd gathered around the spot where Ambrose had submitted to her. The mood was somber, the air quiet. A gray heaven seemed to nag them overhead.

"When my brother wrote those words, he meant them for us all. We are all of us the Light in the dark. I urge us to move forward, to take the Light with us, and to hold dear the memory our brother Ambrose."

The throngs of weary Braelanders left. Several shot slanted eyes in her direction, muttering only offhandedly, "My Faedelin." She stepped through the dispersing crowd and into the shade of the apple tree. Marosia examined its branches, which had begun to die the same day as her brother.

Ben cleared his throat. "A fire's awakened in Sumara, my Faedelin," he said. "A group of rebels calling themselves Mehsanics."

She pressed her eyelids together. "Send a hundred soldiers. That should quell it for now."

"Of course, my Faedelin. Can I do anything else for you?" Ben asked.

Marosia felt a tear tumble down her cheek. She stroked the brittle bark on the tree.

"He called it the mote, the first spark." The dead tree loomed overhead. "This is the sum of those sparks."

The wind plucked an apple off the tree, its core devolved to mush. She'd watched them fall for weeks. This one cascaded down the roots and tumbled to the gap between her feet. Marosia cupped it in her palms. Out of a brownish hole near her thumb, a worm wriggled to catch a glimpse of her. Its eyeless gaze held her transfixed before it burrowed back indifferently into the rot.

27

A Period's Fall

My body sways uneasily as I come out of the vision. The sparks invert, sucked back toward the lake beneath the steam, fading as they consolidate. I stand steadily once the numbness leaves my head. It is over.

"Tell me what you have seen," the voice says.

"The moment before Mehsani's death. I saw their final conversation." I couldn't believe what I'd seen. Years ago, before I left for Calidum with Payton, I'd spoken with Royce about that exchange. She said that if Faedelin and Mehsani hadn't found any peace, it was probably because they didn't want it anymore.

"What is the mote of a soul?" the woman's voice asks me.

I massage my temple. "The smallest variable that changes the world."

"Yes. The mote is the first spark. What is the sum of the sparks?"

"The sum is the cost."

"Which is what?"

"The war."

"Not the war. Wars end."

"What then?"

"The Way," she replies.

"Which leads to the war."

"By our choosing, Spider King."

"Who are you?"

"I am nameless until given a name. I am shapeless until you mold me. What will you call me, Jaremy Nalda? How will you shape me?"

"The Mother." Only she could hold such power over a place like this.

"Yes," she says, with a sense of remembrance. "There are some who have called me that name."

"Queen Kala spoke of you. How do you know all the things you do about me?"

"Everything I know, you have projected onto me. Were anyone else to walk in here, I would know only what he or she brings. It is you who shapes me, you who gives me the power."

"Are you going to release Lanair?"

"Do you fear for him?" she asks.

"Yes."

"Why?"

"Because I don't know what you're going to do with him."

"You are so ruled by fear of the unknown," she laments.

"What are you going to do with him?"

"Nothing more. It is done."

"What is done?"

"Transcendence."

"Enough riddles!"

There's a slight pause. Lanair's body glows. Then she says, "Every seed is a new forest waiting to bloom. So it is with the mote of a soul, the spark of which is the inception of a new order. Not even the nimblest planter can predict where the forest will spread after planting the first seed. So it is with the mote, Spider King. It is the genesis, but where will the last period fall?"

266

The Mother's voice cuts out, and Lanair's body drops like a doll into the steaming lake. I rush headlong into the water. It splashes silently around my feet. The copse trembles as the Mother's voice rises, unceasing in its fury.

"You fly like little gnats around my ears. Why should I not swat you?"

I wade deeper. The water thickens as it inches up my thighs, up my waist, up my chest. It feels like pushing through pudding.

"You flatten my forests. Why should I not crush you?"

Like two unhurried shark fins, Lanair's feet circle round and round and round up ahead. I can nearly reach him.

"You pluck my fruits with savage yellow teeth! Why should I not starve you?"

I grab his nearest ankle, drag him toward me. I bob in the water, propping up Lanair's limp body.

"You destroy the houses I give you!"

Her voice thunders in my ears. My labored breathing is a whisper next to her anger. What has caused her sudden fury?

"Why should I not evict you?"

I kick our way back to the shore. The steaming gives off the stench of sulfur. It didn't smell like this on the shore. The bog smelled like this, in the vision. I yank Lanair out. I listen for a pulse, and his chest rises and falls, so slightly I can barely see it. A sigh takes the weight off my head.

"Tell me, Spider King. Why should I not evict you?" Her volume has fallen, though the anger remains.

Panting, I hold my hand up, asking to give me a moment. Could she even see me? Could she feel me?

"I've tried! You must've seen. I've tried."

"You do not deserve the longevity bestowed upon you."

"How could we earn it?"

"The mote has sparked, the genesis has passed, the forest has spread. Where will the last period fall?"

"Tomorrow."

"In one way or another, you must be right, Spider King."

267

Exhaustion creeps into my muscles. I don't think I can carry Lanair all the way back to our camp in Alaveren. I'll have to call for Tehsan.

"We are little gnats," I mutter.

"What are you going to do about it?" the Mother asks.

I wonder for a moment. My final conversation with Royce recalls itself. "Equilibrium. That's the key."

"But how, and how, and how?"

The feather crown has vanished, lost somewhere within the Mirror of Mehsani. Where the feathers stood at attention are burn scars, the ghost of a raven crown. I gently peel back his eyelids. The hazel irises have returned, the black lacquer jettisoned.

There's a restless breeze waiting to rush through the copse. The air between the trees swells with it, rushing outward in a sudden downdraft. I can feel the farthest tree rustling. The forthcoming gust hangs ominously over us.

The purple light begins to flicker. Heretofore a steadfast, unwavering glow, the illumination strobes fanatically now. The steam glowing purple thickens. The transformation obscures the woods.

"Find the balance, Spider King. Maybe then you'll not be evicted."

"How do I find it? How do I re-create it?"

"That, Spider King, is your next question. Perhaps Braeland hinges upon the words you put before the punctuation."

The lights flicker maniacally. I squint to avoid vomiting. The billowing steam forces me to choke down the thickened air in uncomfortable gulps. Beyond the lake, near the fringes of the forest, that building gust inhales.

"Wait! Tell me! How do I find the balance?"

"You tell me. What is the difference between the praeco and the raven?"

Even her voice is barely audible over the roaring wind. It explodes from the trees, awakens the mirror in a perturbed whirlwind. The purple light dies. Only the howling wind remains.

"One's a bird of life, the other death! Opposites."

"No. What is the *difference*, Spider King? Think back to Minaerva Royce."

The canopy begins to vanish. The wind is erasing it in a reckless rage. It vanishes in a cloud of flecks, like the lake before it.

"The difference..." I begin, but trail off. In the worsening storm, I go back to my last conversation with Royce. I haven't forgotten. "There is none!"

"So end the refrain, and find the balance."

The storm reaches a fever pitch. The Mother's voice cuts out. The canopy disintegrates and leaves a black pit overhead. Rushing wind eviscerates the trees. An explosion of bark, of soil, of leaves, of water soars toward us. I close my eyes.

Darkness falls.

28

The Sum of the Sparks

Wrong. Those five letters draw me out of darkness. Sticks of grass tickle my nostrils. The canopy rustles. The lake pops under an acorn's fall. Though I hear these things, I know they and I no longer share the Mother's connection. Wrong. Within the woods, something has soured.

Stepping beyond the boundaries of the red shroud and the four pine pillars sickens me. Nestled behind those thick drapes, these wrong, sour, forgotten things can die quietly without turning my stomach. That woman thrust them at me. Now they tear down the carmine curtains I cherished and reveal the way things were, the way they've become. Figments of the two brothers fill their void.

No—the two siblings. So wrong. How did everything get so wrong?

In the band of trunks, no longer purple, no longer alive, I feel at once thrust beyond their protection, naked to the sharpened imagination of the idiot, and tucked into their shroud where my feet find their footing. But I no longer like where my feet stand. The placement's wrong, according to the story of the two siblings.

The heel had gone through the apple. So a germ became a disease called Mehsanism, ever accursed because of that heel, which certainly flattened the apple. That fruit, worth tenfold had it been in Marosia's hand, depreciated to mush under Ambrose's foot. Because of that heel, Lanair and his people are left as the product of a rotten stomp.

His hands lift me up. He's regained consciousness somehow, while I start slipping away. "Easy, Jem, easy," he assures me. "I've got you." Lanair lifts my arm round his neck and props me up. "How did we get here?" he breathes.

We limp along the stark forest. Where did the Mother flee? "Jem, say something."

The limits of the trees appear ahead, the lights of the city a somber backdrop. Weakened as much as I, Lanair can't hold me long. The ground rushes up.

The wind shivers over us. The Last Trees shiver with it. They send their restless energy over the Narrows, through the old stones and over the broken bones. From that valley, they stretch across Braeland to those who are deaf to their whispers. So the wind reaches out in vain. It sinks back toward the valley. The Last Trees linger unnoticed by the world. They rustle in the gust that resigns to shiver across the stones of the city, where its gentle embrace wakes me again.

Lanair hovers over me, his worried eyes tired in a taut face. "Jem, are you okay?" The ceiling of our rookery hangs concretely overhead.

"Don't you remember?" I ask.

"Remember what?"

"The raven crown, the forest, the purple light? That voice?" It comes out as muddled as I remember it.

Lanair's eyes go narrow. "What're you talking about?"

"Lanair, we were inside the Copse of Last Trees. The energy that kept that place going was incredible."

"Jem," he says, sighing.

"You led us there!" My voice spikes. "A raven came out of nowhere. A huge one! It left a crown of feathers on your head."

"Jem, it's a forgotten batch of twigs. We must've fallen asleep after walking there. You sure I led the way? Spirits must've played with your dreams."

"It happened, Lanair. I swear it."

He leans toward me and embraces me with one arm around my neck. Then he kisses me, lingering there to keep our chapped lips together. Resting a palm on my cheek, he says, "Let's get some rest, huh? We'll talk about all this with clear minds tomorrow."

He slips under a sheet next to me. We're silent for a few minutes. There's no sense trying to convince him about it now. We'll talk tomorrow.

Lanair falls asleep in seconds after turning over. His chest rises and falls calmly next to me on our bed. I sit up, back against the wall yellowed through the years, my mind racing.

The sequence I saw in the forest begins to blur. Did it really glow with an ethereal, purple light? Were the trees linked somehow? The only thing that remains vivid in my mind is that voice.

There's a knock at our door. "Come in," I say.

Tehsan pokes her head through the cracked door. "Sorry for bothering you so late."

"No worries. Let's go outside. Don't want to bother Lanair."

The air outside is still cool; once those clouds vanished, the heat evaporated in only a few minutes. A supernatural chill, like the steam and the copse and the raven crown. Strange how hot it'd been when those clouds had rolled in, though. A sweltering, oppressive heat. Then they cleared out as suddenly as the ceiling of the forest had ripped away.

"Thought you'd like an update on Dinian. He's okay, sleeping at the infirmary right now," Tehsan informs me. "He didn't quite break it, but the bone is bruised."

"Thanks."

"He'll be there until morning. You want him brought here before we leave?"

273

"No, let him rest. We'll be leaving real early."

"Okay."

The moonlight graces her scarred face. She earned so many of those throughout this new Reaving, never minding the blood, saying it ran for Mehsani, was the color of Mehsani, was the shade of his hook. A beautiful girl whose face resembles a patchwork scarecrow, an image enhanced by the sandy hair she yanks back in a tail. Despite the scars, the skin covering her face is taut as one of Mehsani's drums. Her eyes have always peered out of that drum as if on the prowl.

"I have something to tell you, Tehsan."

"Yes, Nalda?"

"Lanair and I went into the Copse of Last Trees tonight."

She pivots away so that she's glaring at me sideways. Those narrow eyes diverge a little. Her taut forehead creases. Tehsan regards me as if I've said I'm the ghost of Faedelin herself.

"You did what?"

"Entered the copse."

"That's blasphemy!" she proclaims. "That's sacred ground. Only a man tainted by the North could've stooped this low." Disgust sharpens her tone.

She spins away. I say, "I saw it, Tehsan. The Mirror."

The young woman halts. She interlocks her fingers on the crown of her head, drops to a crouch. "That's a legend."

I regard her. "Of all Sumarans, you'd be my pick to believe a Mehsanic legend." She frowns. "Of all Sumarans, the Mehsanic sect is the most devout, but they're heretical schoolboys next to you." She shakes her head beneath her fingers. "It's real. This voice, a presence of sorts, told me to drink from the mirror. I wasn't anywhere; I simply existed in this memory. I saw the moments. The ones we allowed to shape us. I saw them, Tehsan. The two siblings, Faedelin and Mehsani."

She scoops a handful of soil, begins to rub it between her palms. It mists to the ground. The mist sounds like a quick, husky rain.

"Faedelin and Mehsani were good leaders, Tehsan. Until the end."

Tehsan leaps to her feet. "What're you talking about? Have you lost your mind?"

I hold up my hand. "I know it's strange, okay? Inexplicable, really. But it happened."

Her scarred face studies me with a cruel cast. She doesn't trust me, doesn't trust anyone who has lived north of the Narrows. "What do you mean, siblings?" she questions.

"Hmm?"

"You said, 'The two siblings, Faedelin and Mehsani.' What do you mean?"

Had I seen it right? "Faedelin was a woman, Tehsan. Named Marosia. She was the true leader in the beginning, in the end."

Tehsan shakes her head. "And this presence told you to drink."

"Yes. It was an energy that united each organism in the copse. She knew everything about me."

"She?"

"It was a woman's voice."

Tehsan barks a bitter laugh. "The energy woman showed you Faedelin and Mehsani. And one was a woman. Now you'll tell me Mehsani really was of lesser blood."

"Not of lesser blood. Of lesser logic." I knew she wouldn't believe me; I should've just let her walk away after she told me Dinian was okay. "I saw the morning Mehsani hung himself at the broken tower. The siblings had this realization. Looking back on what they'd done, Marosia thought that they couldn't control the Way after they'd started it. They wrote the words, but they had little authority over what happened next."

She smacks me. "Everyone knows that the false shepherd backed Mehsani into a corner! Any good Sumaran, any faithful Mehsanic, any trustworthy shepherd knows it; Faedelin killed Mehsani. Any decent Braelander will back that up. No word said in that tower matters. The hero died. The true hero of the Light. That's what matters. We're fighting for the true Light, Nalda. Abandoning the fight abandons the Light. No word said in that fucking tower matters at all."

I stutter, "I—I agree."

Tehsan cocks her head to the side. "What?"

"Ever since coming out of the vision I've been wondering. Praeco, ravens, apples underfoot. What if Faedelin had murdered Mehsani? What if Faedelin had been the monster? What if Mehsani had been the hero? Would it ever end, fighting on that truth? I can see now. My eyes are open. The lie that's fueled the fight made a blueprint unwinnable for anybody fighting for it. It's a blueprint for an unsound house. I bid you to find a way to solve that problem, focused on the fight for the lie.

"No. A fight for truth, a fight for a lie, neither offers an outcome of any kind. But I've been wondering, Tehsan. What if we don't think about the initial spark, but rather douse the final one? The way I look at it now, there's no other chance. Put out the final spark. I trust you follow my logic."

Her attention is rapt. She nods knowingly, fingering the lace on her sword. "It'd have to be quick. Can't put anyone else in danger. If he's the thing tethering the fight together, then we'll have the day."

"And when do we stop?" I ask her. "In the lust, you'll forget yourself. You'll hunt for more fires to douse. When do we stop?"

"When every blade of Faedelin melts away."

Tehsan paces, cracking her knuckles. Her pacing is more of a prowl, a caged sand cat that's caught the scent of easy blood. It carries the scent of Faedelin, the name that boils her blood.

"Tehsan, I know what I saw. Can't melt every blade. Maybe the one will suffice."

"I know you think you saw something, Nalda. The stories are endless about the copse. Maybe you saw some version of what occurred. It changes nothing."

"It changes everything!" I shout. "Think of what we could change, Tehsan. The siblings never intended for their spark to become a fire. We've stoked it into a conflagration! It's been us all along, damn it! Fuck Marosia, fuck Ambrose. It's been us!"

Tehsan rounds on me. "Know what happened to my little brother, Nalda? He wanted to be like his brave sister, serve for Mehsani's Light. Signed his papers on the eve of the Reaving. Fought bravely, little shepherd he was. I found him on the floor of the Stone Drum after Tallhart took my city. His throat'd been cut. They said his last word was 'ghost.'" She shakes her head. "Whether we do it or the brothers did it, everything's the same. Blood is red no matter who it falls from." Her fists crack and release, crack and release. "I'll melt the one, but I'll want the lot."

"If we're going to do it, I need your word."

After a long stare, fists shrinking small and stretching large, she sighs. "My word."

I grab her arm as she turns. "I know what I saw."

Scowling, she rips her arm free. "Keep it to yourself. They'll lock you in the sanatorium if they don't take your head first."

She marches away without uttering another breath. The night swallows her.

Back inside, Lanair slumbers on our bed. I kneel beside him, and I feel my eyes widen. A red band is drawn across his forehead, an echo of the raven crown. I brush his black hair, splitting the strands to track the brand of the feathers around his scalp. It encircles his whole head.

His lids flutter open, then sleepily sink lower, held down by the insurmountable pull of fatigue, the kind that throbs in the marrow.

"You okay?"

"Fine," I reply. I run my fingers through his hair. "Go back to sleep." I kiss him, and he rolls over. Within seconds his snores fill our little shit-stained rookery.

Tomorrow dawns with a gestated, heated thought. Tehsan's words took root in a unique moment. That day tuned her eyes onto the hunt, narrowed them in suspicion, fed them in hunger. Ready to kill. So they shipped her off, afloat on the river of Mehsanism, flanked on both sides by the banks of Faedelin.

The two siblings planted the forest hopefully, ambitiously, zealously. That seed has infected shore to windswept shore, so that now we can't even discern where the first seed fell, though we stand where they planted it. The forest has become an ugly growth, an untamed wilderness haunted by savages.

That burden rests on us. But who are we to claim a burden? So we ignore the forest, growing wilder and wilder and wilder around us. On and on and on, until this moment when I stand on the west of a bloody river staring down that darkness on the east.

29

The Gates of Linen

There, on the bottom of the eastern sky. She noticed a faint palpitation of light, as if the dawn were ambivalent that the sun should start to shine. And why should it shine? Here in this vat of silt, colored grim by the dredging of days in mire, at crossroads, there remained little recourse for the sun to rise. Yet here in her pavilion, the curtains concealed the stage where novice actors fumbled foreign names like Faedelin and Mehsani. If she drew the linens tighter, they could stop the final act of this play by a phony writer reliant on messy conclusions for his contrived narratives, which amounted to a few hours poorly spent following the drawing of the linen. They were like gates between the mind and the calluses on the feet. Those gates might spark the sun, for they cut off the soldiers, the heretics, the agitators who loved superstition. For now, though, a faint pulse would do.

She untied the curtains, which dropped, and he stretched calmly, calmer still, on her mattress as she rounded the pavilion. The playwright emptied his ink, the actors fell mute, and the vat dried up. She dropped the linen around her shoulders and joined him in the warm, quiet dark.

She ran her finger along the groove dividing his left breast from right. The hair there thinned and grayed. Maybe hers would thin and gray after this searching and failing. When the hunt turned up neither the courier nor Jon's answer, raising only a question for her, she called the thing off, sent them away for the final few hours of night. Here in the warm dark, she could realize the trivial games she'd been playing all night, all year, all her life. The gates she drew narrowed them into focus. Jon had named her the alluring nymph, but she resigned from the part. Move on, leave the stage, draw the linen. Cut short the contrived narrative. Tomorrow she'd write a new one, in her making, and then she could disown this broken valley. With so many other valleys to explore, no sense remained in bleeding over the Narrows. So many valleys. Like the graying, thinning, handsome one riding the median of Tam's chest.

The balance failed within the narrative. Yet they wrote the damned story. They wrote it, forgot it, heard it again, and bowed to it utterly. Once the story filled up the nighttime beyond the drawn linen, where the mind was sovereign, people forgot the precious calluses on the feet, which held fast to the truth hidden in the dirt. Neither Faedelin nor Mehsani could hide in the dirt; the two brothers' names were etched in the clouds. And the sky, somehow, crashed to earth, littered its dirt with words that sparked a song, rising, rising, rising again back into the crowded air, toward the sun, shining bright in flattery. When the clouds grew thick, the voices hoarse, the words crashed again, watering the earth once more in the vain song so that it could ascend into obscurity once more in the clouds. Cycles and cycles erased the inception from their memory. A self-sustaining cycle germinated. Still, though, no matter how lost the memory, how distant the inception, they wrote the fucking narrative. Prisoners to it now, they could not strike a balance.

She heard the calls that were turning the cycle. She saw it in Jon's eyes as he tried to break the cycle in his head, dredging up dark words he wouldn't hear. But she would hear them. Her father's name was a cog in the cycle now. He had died, and yet his name lingered like coffee on the breath of her men. She heard her father's name, but let it linger beyond her walls, away from her, who lay stroking Tam's chest in the realm of callus, a linen's breadth away from the kingdom of the mind.

Within that semipermeable barrier, inside the fibers of the gates, rested the power to burgeon the light. She took herself out of the play. Held it where she saw it, heard it, but took no part. The word "narrows" fled her vocabulary. The only valley remaining was his, and also hers, which enjoyed the pads of his fingers.

"Thinking about the chase?" Tam asked her.

"Yes. Of the sun, not of Piper. He's lost, whether he's here or not. I could end it, you know. I just need to find the right moment."

"Of course you could, Payton." Tam flattened his cheek on her chest and draped a leg over hers. Under the cover of his head, she became aware of her heartbeat. He cradled her stomach in his palm. "You think he was a Sumaran spy?"

"Wouldn't make sense," she replied. "Jem and Lanair wouldn't have their spy steal their own letters. There are more important villains than a courier. No, I think Jon must've been reading my ledgers. Must be why he was so eager to follow us in the hunt. But I don't care any longer."

"Maybe you should. I'm no Faed or Mehsanic, but I think you'd have a right to fear these omens. Given Carrow's past, he probably has a faint grasp on the present." Tam burrowed into her chest. "Leon once told me, back when we began the first Reaving, that the only kiss that could beat the past is a metal one."

She sighed. "Silly to claim dominance over the past, especially with metal."

"You think Carrow'll let his past with Mavogar cloud up tomorrow?"

"He could. But for once, I'm going to see that that happens before I strain myself trying to stop it. In my heart, I feel the ending tomorrow hides the truth to this story, which I'm so fucking tired of. I'm taking myself out of it. Let them play their idiotic games, and if they pick each other apart, it'll clear the way for a rapid reconstruction. I'll let him lead the meeting. If I have to repair his mess, I will. Then I'll move on."

They paused briefly. She became slightly nauseous while feeling her heartbeat under Tam's head. Then she added, "I saw what they did to his body when we fell through the floor earlier. I finally saw the proof. If they did that to his body, I can't imagine what has been done to his mind."

There was shouting outside her pavilion. Tam bounded off their mattress, and she was quickly behind him.

Alanna's silhouette on the other side of the linen leaped forward, spear drawn. Payton and Tam whipped back the curtains. Alanna had a body pinned to the ground. Payton sprinted to her side and pulled her away. Jon peered up at her.

"The fuck are you doing, Jon?" she cursed. "Could've had Alanna's knife in your neck."

"He came to me, Payton."

"Who?"

His body trembled, with neither cold nor in fright, but with elation. She pulled him to his feet. The shaking redoubled.

"Your father. Told me the secret of that light beneath the bogs. Said it was rebirth."

"Jon, what the hell are you talking about?" Tam tossed her a sheet, which she wrapped around herself. "Leon died two years before we were in the Mire."

He shook his head. "Tonight. He said it to me, Payton. I fucking swear it. Remember? That bog water burned away my clothes, and I was naked as a baby. Ruined the wrap on my hilt, too, remember? That's why you gave me the blue-sapphire cloth. So I could continue my work. He said that was an obliteration of the past. Said the Light must've chosen me. I couldn't figure it out until then, but your father's words spelled it out. That must be it. Could that be, Payton?"

Tam snorted. "You need sleep, man."

"Tam's right, Jon. Either you saw a spook like the rest of the men or you're misremembering some things." Jon's body shivered with excitement. "Jon. Jon, look at me. Look. At. Me. Clear your damn head. You need a clear one in a few hours. A clear head and a steady hand. Can't sign this accord in scribble."

"My hand will be steady."

Payton grabbed the crew of his shirt. "Do not talk past me, Jon Carrow."

He glared at her with beady eyes. "I thought you saw me, Payton." Jon shook himself loose. "I thought you saw me now."

"Listen to her, Carrow. She can guide Braeland through," Tam said, reaching out for Jon's shoulder. He shifted, almost imperceptibly, but enough so that Tam scooped a handful of air.

"That's why I suppose there'll be a place for her in the new Braeland. What's the Ghost to do?"

Tam made a fist, stepped away, turned his back.

"My hand will be steady." Jon marched away, alone, into the night while caressing the blue cloth.

Payton felt herself and Tam slipping dangerously close to the stage she insisted she'd never grace again. She told Alanna to stand guard again, perhaps not so aggressively, and returned to the warmth of the linen. When Tam dropped the curtain, Alanna vanished, but her imperfect silhouette shaded the fabric.

Imperfection would rule the discourse, as it always had. Leon Tallhart never understood that. Thought the Light was a panacea and any sentence containing it could never have a blemish. She'd break that cog in the cycle. That much was in her power. Then when the other cogs began to snap, she'd come in to remake it all.

Tam approached her and kissed her neck. She threw aside the sheet and let his fingers work. Yes, yes, yes, that's right. No more words. His thumb stroked the smile of her scar, and she found herself smiling. Payton eased backward onto the mattress as he sank to his knees, and her sighs muted the troubles, those oh, so awful troubles floating vaguely beyond the gates of linen.

30

The Unstoppable Stream

Jon lowered the wall—slightly. He'd built it to keep out the horrors, which now dwelt hungrily in the void beyond it. Something in his conversation with Leon Tallhart's apparition convinced him to lower it. He knew now his mind needed to be clear tomorrow. So he lowered the wall. If only by margins.

Behind it, an unstoppable stream churned and lashed at the wall. The man erected it meticulously, brick by brick, to bar the past from drowning him. Nonetheless, it eroded his defense and splashed over. He'd rebuild, but mortar is weaker the second time, the stream more unstoppable. The battle he waged to destroy the stream tired him out. Tired. Him. Out. Who was he to fight it? He was a trivial rube. Jon couldn't keep this dance up forever. So he lowered the wall, slightly. He must be clearheaded tomorrow.

Leon's apparition explained to Jon the underwater light in the Mire, the mystery that had burned him up. The dead man's spirit, wearing a striking scarlet scarf, told him the light had come from above. That light was *the* Light. Tomorrow hinged upon Jon's faith in it, but faith demands energy. The unstoppable stream siphoned vitality until his veins were bone dry. Jon couldn't keep this up. This man was an indistinguishable mite. He couldn't end the stream. He couldn't kill what it represented: the past.

Build the wall higher, the stream shall leap over it eventually, fueled by the angry past. It grew irate for his suppression of it. The past assaulted him with miasmic bubbles, like those rising from the bowels of a swamp. Build the wall higher; it shall fall. Each wave from the past chipped another point of fragility in Jon's wall. Eventually, the wall would fail him.

Jon knew these points of fragility well. After a life of neglect, after being kicked from homes of the Heron, the Fox, the Hart, he had only the blank halls of the Ghost left. The name of Carrow was more of an idea anyway. It was rare that he thought of himself as Jon Carrow. Truly, he was an indistinguishable, trivial mite of a rube. A sorry fucker whom only Selene with the earrings loved. When he was eighteen, Jon decided to kill all the forces fixing against him, but he began by killing Sir Iayn Darrion. I hate that moment, Jon thought. I hate it so much I call him the Hero Knight of the North, rather than Uncle Iayn. My mother's brother. Imagine if she'd lived to see her boy kill her brother. How'd she love me then? I am a quilt of vulnerability.

Divorcing himself from these weak spots on the wall, Jon severed his mind from the gravel beneath his feet. He became lost in his head. He plugged up the mortar cracks, but don't forget: that stream's unstoppable.

How does a man win against this stream? It flowed from his consciousness, bleeding into his dreams and desires, scored by chants of "Fraternizer, conspirator, traitor, ghost," pummeled by stones in his sleep, carved up in the dungeons of Sumara. The stream of his consciousness poured from the dark room, so small that he couldn't sit, stand, or lie down, and cramps twisted him insane.

Each time the past reared its ugly head, he drowned it momentarily by shoving it back beyond his wall, back into the stream. Though that method appeared to be feeding the flow; more cracks were accumulating. Water was lapping over the wall.

Jon had grown complacent. Put too much trust in these defenses. After all, the defenses were the tools of man. The unstoppable stream was extraordinary, a beast of the earth and ceaseless. It shall drown me eventually, he realized. One day, this will kill me. These miasmic bubbles sent by the past will push through my wall no matter its height. They'll survive, and then they'll kill me. I cannot stop the unstoppable stream. But I cannot be incapacitated every time I fall into a darkened room, either.

He knew what he had to do. He had to lean in, slightly, and let the stream quickly wash over him. There must be a surrender, for his mind must be made clear for the morning. Jon must remember the moments he'd flung himself over the wall and back into the stream, like Royce's chirping about the praeco and the raven two weeks ago. He would have to listen to Royce, he would have to stomach her tea-rotten breath and her cutting words. He must. For maybe the unstoppable stream waned after the levees were down, since it had nothing left to fight.

A little remembering might end the tumult. Like Royce's chirping, or Iayn Darrion's fall, or the boy's face when Jon abandoned him, or Alaryn Tanogar's last stand.

Light, not my father, Jon dreaded. Please, please, not that. I can't lean in to catch the solitary word on his dying breath. Not again. Please.

Jon was cowering in the shadows of his wall. But what if he stepped beyond the wall, or lowered it completely, to swim in nature where the unstoppable stream reigned? Could he survive the initial shock? Jon might embrace it as his champion, for otherwise, it would surely kill him after tarnishing his meticulous wall.

His hands trembled violently. Already, he felt the wall lowering. The stream would come. With it, his most suppressed horrors.

The image of Alaryn Tanogar leaped out at him. The old man's face bloodied, his body mangled. Jon leaned in to catch the solitary word on his dying breath.

He stepped back from the stream. He was resolving himself to this torture, the reliving of the old tortures. For things shoved at him by the stream never died, they got stronger and wilder, coming at him longer and longer and longer, until they couldn't be stopped. They'd cracked through the wall. Here they came. He'd hold his breath. He could not stop it; it swam over his head, through his mind. He would let the stream engulf him.

And then, maybe he would master it.

Jon leaned in to catch the solitary word on the dying breath.

say it SAY IT SAY IT.

❂ ❂ ❂

Coyle knocked his arrow as Alaryn hurried down the slope toward the docks of Trowbridge. The fires the men had set chewed the path's borders. They licked at Jon's fleeing father, who ran unknowingly in the train of Coyle's sights.

Jon tried to scream out to his killer, but the distance between them, the fires raging all around them, the howling of the nocturnal wind silenced Jon's chance. The arrow flew. Alaryn took it in his back, lurched forward, and tumbled twenty paces farther down the stone slope.

"No, no, no!" Jon screamed. He shoved his men aside as he sprinted toward his father's fallen frame. It was an anonymous heap in the shadows of Faedelin's city. He'd come so close to the docks, to his ship, to his vessel. Alaryn Tanogar, the man of the sea, who adopted an unwanted runt. His bloodied visage gazed up at Jon.

As though inebriated, Alaryn waved Jon closer while he smacked his red lips. Jon, tears hot on his face, cradled his father's head in his lap. His father kept waving, waving, waving. Jon slobbered. I don't believe it. It can't have happened. Alaryn continued his drunken wave.

Jon must have known what his father was going to say. But something told him to listen anyway. Perhaps Jon could call it love that told him to. He leaned in to catch the solitary word on the dying breath:

"G h o s t."

The lights winked out. Coyle caught up to Jon, patted him on the shoulder.

"He mean something to you?" Coyle asked.

"No, just a familiar face." Already Alaryn Tanogar was dissociating himself from Jon's mind, like how Uncle Iayn became a distant hero in his memory.

Coyle whistled. "Damn, man. Sorry if I wasn't supposed to. Can't tell scab from scab in times like these."

Jon rested his father's head softly on the stone pillow. "Forget it, Coyle. You did your job."

"Sorry, m'lord."

"I said forget it. Take him down to the teardrop."

"All of these scabs?"

"No, just this man. Lord Alaryn Tanogar. Make sure you get him to the waters, Coyle. You do that, consider your debts to Tallhart absolved."

"Where you going?"

"To meet Payton. And Royce. The old woman wanted a word."

Coyle whistled again. "Need some earplugs?"

"I just need this fucking day to end."

Jon stepped back, dropped to a crouch. If unmoved, the bodies around him would begin to molder by morning, but he didn't care. He needed to watch the procession of pallbearers. They gingerly lifted Alaryn, and as they did, Jon felt jealous of his father. Into the waters the old man went. That was it. No more pain.

Alaryn's brown boots stood mournfully on the slab of wood they used for a cot. They saluted Jon, a final gesture from father to son. Good-bye, Ghost, they said. Good-bye.

31

The Allegory of the Praeco
and the Raven

"Carrow. Come here. I want to talk."

Jon had been walking toward the courtyard where the great stone walls of the university shot up all around, lined with soldiers donning the Sunburst and holding spears, looking out over the lands belonging to Faedelin. The rumbling, rumbling, rumbling of a great beast awakening in the brisk dawn filled his ears, and he listened. It said, "I'm ready. I'm ready to die for you." And somewhere down another road the *ting. ting. ting.* of a blacksmith's hammer. It echoed in the courtyard of the university all gray and slate with its stone walls that Jon had been approaching.

Jon regarded the men down the hill where the courtyard splayed wide beyond a gate. How they were like the sheep in the Book of Testaments. That's why Faedelin could corral his usurpers, pen them up in the Holy City, and burn them away like nothing but brittle pages stuffed into an oven.

So it was here. Finally. Always running, running, running from those that pursued a finger's breadth away at his heels. Now he stood in the greatest city the world had ever seen as its castellan and peerless leader whom all the men looked to now, though a year ago few even knew his name. Then yesterday his father died and said, "Ghost," but that didn't matter now because he was here and she was here and she had wrapped the blue-sapphire cloth around the hilt and they looked to him now even if it was from the corners of slanted and suspicious eyes.

"Carrow."

"Yes, Minaerva?"

"Come here. There's something you should hear before you leave."

Minaerva Royce stood several paces behind him where the stone road crested, then dipped out of sight. Soldiers bustled on either side but were courteous of her frail presence. Her shoulders hunched. An old willow cloaked in old bark.

"Minaerva, I've really got to go. Payton is already leading a few legions south toward Wellfleet. I shouldn't be far behind." He thumbed the blue-sapphire at the hilt, which was fraying now, though only weeks old. The city bustled all around in the great deep breath before that long exhale.

The old woman extended a hand for Jon to take. He did.

"Walk with me," she said, carefully stepping in the spaces between hustling soldiers. They took several strides before the woman said anything to him. Around him his army got ready. They would go south to the Narrows, to where Lanair had taken the Holy City, and Jon would end it with his hand wrapped around the blue-sapphire hilt.

"I want to talk about that thing you did," she said, her voice the sound of arid pages of a book being scraped slowly over, bearing down inexorably on the final page.

Jon stretched his neck. "I've heard it, Minaerva. They hung. It's enough."

"Never enough, Jon. We are no housekeepers, to sweep everything beneath the carpet." She stopped at the crest of the next hill. The streets of the university rose and fell like the waves and wakes of an agitated sea margined on its shores by dense gray stone. Beyond the walls of Faedelin's school, the rest of Trowbridge stood in simpler, wooden huts and markets. The men and women of his army were a whirlpool below in the courtyard of the city.

"Look at them," she said. "Do you think they know why they're about to fight?"

"Faedelin. Apples without worms. The Great Shepherd."

She smirked. "A good answer for a priest with poor training. If I agreed with you, I would've never been asked so politely by the church to stop teaching." Royce pointed with a hand gnarled and knotted like an oak at the men and women. It was as if she were dragging some impalpable net across his army, claiming them with her grasp.

"They've forgotten why we fight, why no plants grow in the Narrows anymore, why no one has lived in Alaveren in a half century. Apples without worms." She snorted. "Maybe they fight because of that foolish tale, but their fathers and mothers of only a century ago never even heard that random amalgam of letters sharpened by the greedy thirst of one man for another's blood. You see, it was inserted into the Way from a Calidumi tale..."

Tomathy Carrow had always said learning was best done in the heart of spring. Not in the summer when the heat burns all away. Not in autumn when the cold creeps in to shrivel the world up. Not in the winter when all slithers off to die. Learning was best done in the heart of spring.

"You see, Jon, I wanted to talk with you before you left because of these random amalgams of letters. Let me tell you a story."

She led Jon onward, his head darting around to keep both eyes on his men, an ear and a half on their discourse, and the barest half of the final ear for her words, which fell like rays of sun upon dead and broken grass.

"Cerin was a boy adopted by a robust farmer on the outskirts of the Narrows. The farmer had taken him in, a boy starving and without a home in the entire world. Though the farmer had no power of great love, no ways of portraying that love to the boy, he gave him food and shelter.

"When Cerin had become a young man, and his father's back hunched in old age, he began to pilfer the family's riches. To Cerin, these were riches long deserved. He had thirsted since his childhood for the gold coins that his father had so greedily withheld in a jar beneath his bed. Cerin took them without restraint and was soon discovered by his father.

"Cerin fled his father's farm for fear of punishment. A foreign vassal, who was a fiercely pious man, hired him. Cerin had no love for the vassal's beliefs, but he desired to work for decent pay.

"Meanwhile, famine struck at his father's farm. One day, Cerin discovered his father stealing the vassal's livestock. Though the father pleaded with Cerin, conveying the hardships that had befallen their old home, Cerin shook his head.

"Quoting the laws of his vassal's religion, Cerin apologized deeply to his father, but explained that death was the punishment for stealing livestock, 'For when you take the living of another man, you might as well be taking his life.' Ignoring the pleas of his father, Cerin savagely attacked him as the image of gold coins stashed in a jar flicked through his mind."

But it was long past springtime. It had passed several months ago now. No. Several years had gone up in a breath of mist since its ending and the other ending that meant her words would fall like rays of sun on dead and broken grass.

"Have you heard that story before?"

"No. I haven't."

"Tell me what you think of it."

"I'm not your student, Minaerva."

"No, you're not my student."

Jon ground his teeth. "I don't have time for these circular lessons."

"Only time for circular actions, then?" She smirked. "Tell me what you think of it, Jon."

"I think Cerin was an insufferable swine. I think his father was a fool for stealing livestock. I think that the lot of them should've walked hand in hand into the long night."

She laughed. "Perhaps we all should walk hand in hand."

"Thank you for the story. I've got to go."

How she maintained such a grip on his arm defied reasonable logic. Might as well try to lift a boulder. She was so frail. Yet she locked him in place.

294

The staying power of those trivial and insignificant things overwhelmed him. She would outlast the mountain as it withers away a mote of dust at a year's glance. She'd endure longer than the mountain that sweats out a solitary grain with every millionth breath. Soon the world grows cluttered. Old broken things linger. The Holy City, the roads, the people, they all coalesce and ignore time as it grinds them back to meal. It all seems permanent at a point, but only she endures; all else lingers. She's steadfast. Her face was like paper; it might diffuse in water or burn up beneath the sun. Her eyes hid in the back of her papery skull like inky orbs in the maw of a cave. She would outlast them, everything tangible. The people, the roads, the Holy City, they'd fade into a memory before she shed her first fleck of decay. The highest peak, imperceptibly vanishing before our eyes, would kneel to her. For at a point, somewhere between her materialization and the inexorable collapse of her surroundings, whether over a life age or bottled into a breath, she reaches for the incorporeal and the eternal. She escapes the weapons of hate, which grow only darker and sharper as they fail to blot her out of existence. For she is not tangible clutter, but rests on the verge of the metaphysical. Only a breath's gap from him, she existed not as a piece of the palpable city, but as an imagined and accepted part of this place.

"I always find Cerin's decision selfish and ignoble. What do you think?" Royce asked.

"His father broke the law of the vassal. He had to face the punishment."

"Didn't Cerin break that law as well? Is a stolen coin any different from a stolen cow?"

Spring was long past. Years had receded it beyond the horizon into the black blight of the endless night.

"Better men have tried and failed, Jon, but silence is no option."

Funny how wisps of paper and their ink could outlast the myriad and innumerable motes of dust within a mountain.

"Look, Royce, I told you I've got to leave."

"Why?"

"What?" he asked.

"Why do you have to leave?"

"Because." Her emerald eyes glistened at him. "Because, Minaerva, Lanair sacked Wellfleet, he sacked Trowbridge, he killed the king, he stormed the Narrows, and he occupied the Holy City."

"Alaveren is a sack of heartless stones. Let him have it."

"It's words like that that had the church calling for your head."

Royce's fingers graced her cheek. "And yet here it rests."

"The Mehsanic armies have to face the punishment for betraying the rights of Faedelin's descendants. Mehsani has long been a scab on an otherwise fruitful nation under Faedelin's Light. Generations have thrown wave after wave against the North, but they've never drowned us. The Church of Faedelinity has long held the South at arm's length. We're poised to do it again. Despite his undying resistance, Lanair cannot win," Jon recited.

"A good answer for a Faed priest at the deliverance box. You're talking to Minaerva Royce, Jon. Speak truths. Jettison this animosity."

"Minaerva, I've got to—"

"Enough, Jon. When the scholars write about this day, they won't say we won or lost because Minaerva Royce distracted Jon Carrow before he paraded bravely to battle."

"Either way, I've got to go."

"What do we win? The deed to an unsound house, marred by broken windows and locked doors, haunted by spirits innumerable."

"If that's the prize, why would we keep going three hundred years later?" Jon retorted.

"Perhaps you're asking the wrong question, Jon. Instead, why can we not see that this deed to an unsound house is our prize? Why do we think it's anything more? It's not the victory that's wrong, it's our perception of it." Royce held her chin firm with effortless dignity.

With the slightest tug she pulled him aside toward a tavern with seats on the street. She waited patiently, and then he realized she was waiting for him to draw out a chair for her from the table. He picked one from which she could gaze into the bustling courtyard. Then he sat adjacent to her, his back to it.

After she waved over a woman and asked for two cups of coffee, she leaned on the table. Her breath was slow and meditative. "Think back to Cerin and the stolen cow. He perceived the killing of his law-breaking father as the fulfillment of divine law, when in reality, it was the mental image of gold coins in a jar that spilled his father's blood."

Spring had long since knelt to summer.

"He believed no more in the words of his vassal's gods than you believe in Faedelin's books. Tell me, when was the last time you picked up the Way?" Royce wondered.

"Excuse me?"

"I'd wager that the last time you did, you were perusing Mehsani's Books of Dreams and Nightmares, not any of the books associated with Faedelin."

Jon leaned in. Keeping his voice quiet was like asking a hurricane to drop to a gust. "Watch your mouth, Minaerva. It's no wonder the university barred you from teaching."

"All I'm asking, Jon, is that you don't play the part of Faedelin's golden boy when I know that at best you are a failed follower of Mehsani."

But paper could burn, he thought. Though paper transcended the physical world with the ink scrawled upon it, the paper itself could go up in a black plume. Paper could burn.

"Did you know I served in Faedelin's army?" Royce asked.

Long, long past spring for so many questions.

"It was during the Southern Marches in the year 243. After the Way, right around when we incorporated Calidum. Nearly sixty-five years ago. Light, I don't know how all that time elapses. That was two years after the first women's regiment was introduced in the North. As you know, Sumara has had women warriors since the year 14 AW. We're a little slow to the draw up north.

"We fought the rebels in the South, whom we dubbed the sand dogs. I was sickened by the way we treated them after capture. How can you sup with a rabid dog? The murder, torture, rape. It seemed all part of a great machine, all of them indispensable cogs whose removal would render the machine obsolete.

"After refusing to kill a prisoner, I was dispatched, beginning my life-long habit to be politely removed from every enterprise I joined. I left for the University at Trowbridge on my own, exploring the shores of the South. While I wanted to return to the university, I thought that a change of course might be best. Perhaps I could find some faraway country all laid out in green. A place to retire. And me only eighteen!

"I had this image in my mind of an idyllic seaside enclave where the salt rides the wind coming off the water and leaves crystals on the sand. Beyond that green hills weave in and out of one another. It would be miles and miles from another soul, where neither death nor pain could strike. A fantasy.

"I wandered for weeks without a lick to eat. Half-dead and beyond starving, I stumbled out of a copse of trees onto a beach, its sand whitened under the sun. I fainted. When I awoke, a man coming off a rowboat loomed over me. He told me of his travels after rationing off a few loaves for me. A glaze clung to his eyes.

"My vindicator, as it happened, had lost a sailor during a storm. It happened near an island. The ship nearly wrecked. He attempted for days to dock, but the island had no discernible port or beach. He rowed ashore, and his memory vanished. When his memory picked back up, it was after what seemed to him only hours, but weeks had fled. The missing sailor was with him. A lick of recollection remained with him. A goddess had held them enslaved and forced them to chase the sun. It delighted her to sup with mortals in such a way. Only after the spell had somehow broken on the sailor did she allow them to build a boat to safety."

The woman from the café returned with their coffees. Royce plopped a spoonful of sugar in it and sipped it as the steam clouded her face. Jon stirred his drink, which was still black.

Summer had come. Spring was dead.

"They chased, chased, chased that sun because of the goddess. Never caught it though, did they? But who can say whether there was a goddess, or if there was an island at all? Any of us will misremember a tragedy to lend it a sense of reason."

298

Her rasping, quiet voice amplified the softness of her sipping. Jon kept stirring.

"You know, I believe we could do a lot more for ourselves, and better yet, one another, if we resigned to admire the sun from the ground." Royce sipped her coffee. "Our plight reminds me of those poor sun runners. Imagine that. Living trapped on an island, dumb and savage, because a sadistic nymph fancies watching them tear one another apart for a promise of immortality. Same thing, really. Chasing the sun, chasing the green field, chasing the victory; they're similar prizes in that they're unattainable. We're trapping ourselves into the same fruitless chase. We're playing the nymph whilst mimicking the sun runner.

"I realized that when we marched south. Fighting over hot flats I'd never see again. Madness."

"Yes. I've studied the Southern Marches," Jon remarked.

"Have you?"

"In Sumara. As a boy," Jon added, as if that added some importance. "Lord Alaryn Tanogar sent Sumaran ships to aide King Willem's effort."

"Mmm. Did you know that, of the five great kings, only Willem the Strong never faced a Mehsanic rebellion? Better yet, he won the Marches and incorporated Calidum."

Even summer was long gone. Long dead. Autumn was on the march. And learning was best done in the heart of spring.

"Willem, the last of the greats, never faced a peep of opposition. Daeberah the Holy's preaching got him in hot water over land disputes in the Narrows. Braeden the Bold's brashness doomed any diplomacy. Wilbraem the Wise inherited a disaster from Faedelin. And of course, who can forget that original great one, who handed us the deed to an unsound house." Her eyes pierced Jon over the dancing steam of the cup hovering below her chin.

"Minaerva, there's a reason lessons have a time limit." The men would be looking for him. She would be looking for him. Looking for the end. The end with his hand wrapped around the blue-sapphire that Payton had wrapped round his sword's hilt.

299

"Why did Willem the Strong achieve what none of his predecessors could?" Royce asked.

"Sometimes I think teachers ask so many questions because they know none of the answers."

Royce let out a cackle. "You're only too close to reality to be making a joke. Of course, I know nothing. But I don't stand in a tower pointing at those on the ground saying that Faedelin put me up here and Mehsani's blood keeps you down there."

It was no longer summer. Summer was dead. What was he doing? Even the coffee was cold.

"Why did Willem succeed, Jon?"

"Expanding Mehsanic studies at the university helped."

"Of course it did. What else?"

"I don't know, Minaerva. You're the one who wrote *The Path of Kings*."

"I'm assuming you've read it?"

"Half-read, like everything else I've picked up."

Another cackle. "At least you're an honest one. Why else?"

"He never sent any soldiers near the Narrows."

"A fair point, but obvious. Why else?"

He sighed. "Willem was known for having written extensively about the Books of Dreams and Nightmares during his studies at the university. No king had ever even mentioned them by name in a document in more than a hundred and fifty years before that," he finished, slightly satisfied with himself.

"Good! Closer to the point, and a fact not many know. Why else?"

"Faedelin's balls, Minaerva! I've got to go!"

"Why else, Jon?"

"I don't know, Minaerva."

She leaned in for effect. "Willem the Strong was the first sitting king ever to have visited the city of Sumara." The coffee was now cold. "What do you think of that?"

"Maybe he should've been called Willem the Noble," Jon said sardonically.

"Maybe." Her finger skated along the rim of her cup. She eyed the men and women thronging the road over Jon's shoulders. He really should be getting ready. A long ride to the Narrows and Lanair was already profaning the Holy City. They were running scared and alone and thinking they might have won by taking Alaveren.

"You know, I often think that history will misinterpret Willem's name. Even now, the young believe he was called 'the Strong' because of how many wars the man won. He was called the Strong because of how many wars he didn't fight. Wars lined up at his door like unwelcome relatives. Like those relatives, those wars kept knocking until he was ready to go mad. Madness is hard to hold at arm's length. Willem did. He shut his door on fight after fight, refusing to plunge Braeland into bloodshed. That's strength."

Jon opened his mouth, but she quickly said, "You've got to go. I'm aware. But all this talk of Willem and meadows and stolen cows brings me to my final point." She waved the woman over and asked for a cup of tea. Then she turned back to Jon. "Have you ever heard the allegory of the praeco and the raven?"

"I don't know. Maybe once or twice in Sumara."

"Let me tell you this, and then you can decide whether or not storming south is still worth it."

"Very well."

"There was a young man who people looked to for guidance in dark times. They saw ravens fluttering at their backs. The harbingers of doom and devastation. At every turn, death and dark omens seemed to close in, riding the wind and casting shadows upon them. His land was fraught with death, so he went south to the Queen of the Hot Lands for aid.

"For days, he pleaded with her for help. His people had been an unruly group of newcomers to the region, so the queen was reluctant to extend her hand to him. Still ambivalent, she announced that it was time for the midday prayer. The young man followed her out of respect.

"When they reached the temple, the young man recoiled. Ravens swarmed the temple. He couldn't understand why these beasts would be welcomed in a holy place. The wise queen laughed and said that these were no ravens, for all their black feathers and barking. These were praeco."

The waitress returned with the tea.

"The young man asked how her praeco was different from his raven; both the praeco and the raven shared black feathers, great size, and similar noises. The queen explained that in her land, where praeco were sparse and emerged mainly at night, it was known that praeco ushered souls across the night waters of the sky to the next life. They were the boatmen of the night waters, the ushers to the other world, the herald of the next life.

"The boatmen of the night waters were more welcome to the temple than the most pious parishioner. Without them, life would vanish into nothingness. The praeco were beacons of light.

"The young man realized his mistake. He had…" But here, she trailed off.

Spring was long, long past. The cold was creeping in. Already it was filling the corners of the room and the castle and the world where the heat could hold no domain. Autumn was on the wane.

"Jon. Listen to my words."

"Minaerva, I've *got* to go."

"No. You don't. Let him have it, and he'll let you keep this."

"He would never."

"Just because we have not broken the cycle does not mean we have remained the same. Even if some palpable echo of the past resounds in the present, it does not make change a preposterous concept. Anomalies always arise. Think." She sipped her tea, then decided she was done waiting for him to think. "The same birds, are they not, Jon? One a bird of life eternal, the other a bird of imminent death, and yet the same birds. So different and much the same, a recipe for friction, but somehow, by some unearthly miracle, the praeco never killed the raven."

"Damn it, a bird is a bird is a bird." Jon finished his cold coffee.

Royce leaned in, stale tea hot on her breath. "Jon, it's your palm wrapped around the handle." The blue-sapphire hilt that Payton had wrapped.

"It's late autumn." He pushed himself away from the table. "And the frost is kissing the leaves."

❂ ❂ ❂

"Nalda. Are you listening?"

I glanced up from the scarred stump of my right arm. Minaerva Royce stared at me. She had been pacing the pavilion that overlooked the teardrop. Trowbridge huddled within the water, which toed the line between a huge lake and a small sea. An island placed in a teardrop shed by the Light itself.

"Nalda? I'm coming to my point. It takes a lifetime, I know." She continued a point I missed the introduction of. "But when Braeden the Bold stormed the Narrows, it only inflamed them more."

It never actually resembled a teardrop. From some angles, maybe, but for the most part, it's a misshapen lung. Dreams within lore built upon hopes. Makes ponds into teardrops from the sky.

"And, of course, he sparked the first war in the Narrows. After all Wilbraem had done to clean up Faedelin's mess, Braeden tore it down. A charismatic man, no doubt, but bombast has no quarter in times of dispute. 'Old stones, broken bones,' as you'll hear once you're in Calidum."

Braeden was nothing more than a lit fuse beneath a powder keg, I knew.

"That's why I always say, 'Beware the gestation of a heated thought,'" the scholar told me. "The Rift never would've happened if Faedelin and Mehsani had heeded more caution. They gestated a beast and let the leash slip."

"We always hear in lectures how it was Mehsani's transgressions that sparked the Rift," I replied to her. She guffawed.

"The church's priests tell you that?"

I nodded. She waved a hand as if swatting an annoying fly. "Bah. Old farts, the lot of them." A woman emerged from Royce's seaside estate holding a platter of tea. It was skullcap and summer mint, I knew. With a bow to Royce, she placed the platter on a table next to me. Then she vanished back inside.

"You have no great love for them, huh?" I asked.

"I have no great love, no small love, no speck of empathy for them." The scholar hobbled across the clay pavilion to sit beside me. On the pavilion was a stained likeness of Braeland, rocky shores, jagged hills, crooked bays. To the south loomed massive Calidum, across the boiling basin.

I sipped the tea. It prickled in spots across my tongue. The breeze washed over us like unseen lapping waves of the sea.

Royce dumped three teaspoons of sugar into her cup. As she stirred, she wet her lips. I'd never seen her drink it black.

"Mehsani's main transgression was claiming the city that both he and his brother had built. After Mehsani went south and Faedelin north to spread the Way's influence, the brothers saw varying challenges. Undoubtedly, Mehsani faced worse. Sumara, to this day, is a humid nightmare during the summer and a dry, endless heat in the winter. When Mehsani settled it, it was a boggy swamp offering little hospitality."

"Why stay there?"

Her eyes bulged as she shrugged. "Go where else? The boiling basin blocked them off from Calidum, which had yet to be partnered with Braeland, while mountains blocked them to the east, the sea to the west. Sumara was all he had.

"By the time Mehsani reached the South, half his followers had fallen to disease. Of course, Mehsani himself had plunged deeply into drugs. Mutiny danced on every tongue. Even if he hadn't chosen to stay where he did, he might've lost his head. Instead of pushing further, and deeply ill with the red fever, he ordered construction of the Stone Drum.

"Just as the midsummer monsoons warp and scuff the Drum's foreboding cap, the lands of the South shaped its people. Mehsani became the Great Shepherd, everyone his sheep. They loved him, though not at first. He usurped the Southern campaign from Faedelin, but without him, the whole flock might've perished. At that time, they still might. And their love for their hero grew fierce, not the passion of lovers or the respect of children for parents, but an impenetrable infatuation for their savior.

"Mehsani's baptism as leader was far more brutal than his brother's, as we know. Though it minted fewer followers, the baptism washed that handful with pious water.

"Resources were scarce, so the Sumaran people learned to go on little sustenance. They had to hide in the drum caves during the merciless storms. It was there Mehsani developed the use of the storm drums. They sparred with nature for dominance."

For a moment, Royce's eyes panned the great city of Trowbridge, which rose from the myriad towers of the university and fortresses beyond her estate by the edge of the teardrop. The city's walls hugged close to the island's margins. It was an impregnable solitude within a sacred lake. Done observing the gray mammoth, she turned back to me.

"Completely at a loss, Mehsani led his flock back into the Narrows, where the Way had begun. He found his city changed. Faedelin's version of the Way had found a strong foothold in the Holy City. The residents were little more than cold to Mehsani and his ragged flock.

"Repulsed by his lukewarm reception, Mehsani claimed Alaveren for himself. It would follow Mehsanism, which he based upon the sixteen books he had penned, the set of teachings called the Way. Faedelin wrote only one himself, though ten of the remaining twelve in the Way are attributed to him. Soon Mehsani's forces had secured the Narrows, with blood.

"But they were a starving, broken people. Faedelin answered with a crushing campaign and purged the Narrows of his brother's followers. When he arrived at the Holy City's gates, Mehsani let only his brother inside, and cataclysm ensued.

"No record exists of their discourse, but we can surmise what they said. Since Faedelin later expressed in private ledgers that he had no desire to kill his brother, we know that he probably pleaded with Mehsani to stand down. Mehsani refused. Faedelin's followers would neither look at him legitimately if Mehsani lived, nor would they rest until the usurper was dead. Faedelin had no choice but to hang Mehsani.

"Mehsani exited from the palace and gave his farewell address. He urged his followers to stand down. He had convinced his brother to shelter them back in Alaveren, albeit under his law. They say he put the noose around his own neck, proudly staring his sheep in the eyes.

"Beware the gestation of a heated thought, for it is the most pervasive germ and practices no discrimination while infecting new hosts. Faedelin wanted his brother dead no more than I you, but what could he do?"

Royce finished her tea. She poured another cup from the kettle and topped mine off. Eyes closed, she drew in a long sip.

"The death of a hero. So it began. Mehsani's followers lived restlessly at best, destructively at worst. Treaties failed. They rebuilt Sumara. Alaveren fell to disease and banditry. And seemingly, here we are." She stopped. Her eyes darted back and forth, as if reading some book of her mind, unreadable to me or anyone else.

"How do you choose either side?" I said. Another breeze burst off of the lake. Nothing like a lake draft, salt-free and pure. "Both seem too cold to be human."

"Faedelin was no saint, but Mehsani was no peach, either. Given your studies, I'm sure you're familiar with his system of law and punishment. A cutthroat system of pragmatism. But that's what they were good at! They took a sprawling horde of displaced nomads, recently persecuted twofold, and built a towering city out of the dust around them. Only a set of morals and laws could make that work.

"For all my derision of the church, of King Gareth, of the priests, of Faedelinity, I admit that without those books, there would be no Braeland." She sipped her tea as her eyes went narrow. They peered over her stone balcony to our left, out over the softly rippling great lake all around us. The wrinkles on the glassy water mirrored those on her face. Her skin was worn, the hide of a drum collapsed into a bunch. Royce had always seemed to transcend the physical. The university, and then the church, called for her head, but she kept it. She published *The Path of Kings*, *The Fires of War*, and plenty of other essays that should've had mobs hunting her. Like her pages, she endured. Somehow she evaded these deriders. Even as I looked at her then, her skin worn and wrinkly from her years, Royce appeared more youthful than I.

"We were doomed from the start," I said. "As soon as Faedelin decided to spread the Way, he placed the first brick that would build this broken house."

"Why do you say that?"

I shrugged. "Well, that's what you always say."

She laughed. "I can say that. I'm Minaerva Royce. You're barely seventeen. You have to back it up."

I took a sip of the tea. I thought for a moment. "They traveled too far. It's like stretching a wet blanket; at a certain point, the center, the core of the thing, sags under its own weight, or it tears from either end pulling too hard to keep the center up." Another sip allowed me to pause, since I was growing too eager in my words. I know I'd trip up if too hasty. Half of my mind formed the next sentence, while the other half observed her logging each word as organizing tomes on a shelf. She would tear that shelf back down.

I continued: "Once so far gone, Mehsani no longer knew Faedelin. Similarly, Faedelin had no empathy for his brother. They were living as if in different countries. Might as well have been men of a different light. Indeed, they became men of a different light. Faedelin was named the Light Embodied, the chosen savior set down from the sky, whereas Mehsani transformed into the Great Shepherd. Two clashing cathedrals under one roof.

"So we were doomed from the start. The moment the two brothers left Alaveren, the germ grew. Each step north and south only metastasized that germ until it had infected every mind either side of the Narrows. The war at the Holy City was inevitable. Doomed from the start."

Royce began to nod slowly, the motion resembling less like a nod and more the slow dip and rise of someone drifting off to sleep. Her gaze narrowed as her mouth took in tea. Her bobbing head rose and fell. Placing the tea on the table between us, she began to speak.

"A wet blanket?"

"Huh?" I ask.

"Honestly, Nalda, a first-year student could develop a better metaphor than that."

I blushed.

"Among other issues I take, the largest is that a wet blanket cannot ignite. That is the problem: the combustibility of men and their affairs. The sparks that devour forests whole."

"Okay, so not a wet blanket," I conceded, "but maybe a heavy one."

She nodded. "I do like what you've said about falling under its own weight or breaking. A nice sense of inescapable doom. You know how I love that morbid stuff. Talthus and Ezora was never my cup of tea," she added with a tap of her cup. "I always preferred *Sinsirra's Tower*. What a wonderful and excruciating fall from grace. Now. Different country and different light."

"You disagree?"

"This was and still is Braeland, correct?"

"Yes."

"And we still rest beneath Faedelinity, and the chosen son of the Light?"

"Uh, yes."

"Don't say 'uh' or 'um' or 'huh.' Flies will buzz into that gaping hole of a mouth. So how were they in a different country or under a different light?"

"I said 'like' a different country. 'Might as well have been' under a different light."

Her hands tossed up. "The evasion of a politician. Go run for mayor in some bumpkin village. It was still the same country, still very much so that same light."

"What does it matter if the reality was the same country if they saw two disparate ones?"

She leaned away from me, as if in shock. "That's the most brilliant thing you've ever asked. And its answer? Because reality does not matter any more than that worm." She pointed suddenly to an earthworm wriggling madly in the muddy groove between the cobbles of the pavilion. "Reality is worthless, because we do not act on reality."

The worm, I noticed, was stuck in the sun. It would dry up soon. "I don't care about that worm," she said, "I've never seen that worm, nor will I see it again after this discussion. I know it will die in the sunlight. I know I could save it. But it would make a poor pet, and if I expended the energy to save this miserable beast, it would soon die anyway. So why should I save this thing? It is a mite to my mountain.

"I really should save it, not because of these things I know about it, but because of the myriad of things I do not. It could be a mother to many baby worms. I could be creating numerous orphans, who will now also die because of my indifference. That worm could be the hidden witness of all our civilization, the test sent from some other ruling entity to observe us and cat- alog our progress. Maybe it, not Faedelin, is the Light's champion. It could be measuring our capacity for empathy. A poor showing I'm giving our chosen witness.

"Of course, neither of these things are probably true. So I'm leaving it in the sun. I'm not special. I'm not different than you, who didn't even notice this beast dying. I'm no different from Faedelin, who saw his brother and his brother's people wasting away at Sumara. I might as well be Mehsani, who pillaged the Calidumi settlements in Braeland. I'm no different from anyone who has lived or will live. I will let worms die and not blink.

"So the reality of one country and one light didn't matter more than that worm, which might be a mother or the chosen witness of our civilization, since they did not perceive this vision to be true, no more than I believe in this chosen witness, so they let it die, as I am going to let this die."

The breeze swelled up at the base of the cliff to my left, which dropped sheer into the lapping lake. I could hear it howling. The air on the pavilion heeded its call, rushing toward it as it balled up at the base of the cliff. The first licks of air escaped its control. Then the ball exploded in an upward plunge and rattled the tea platter to the edge of our table. I grabbed it just as it tipped over.

"Now," she continued after the breeze, "one final note I have on your soliloquy. This business about being doomed from the start. Why do you believe that?"

"Everyone knows that it was the distance and the disparity between the two brothers that caused the Rift. The Way was secure before then," I argued.

"So you think we wouldn't have faced wars had Faedelin and Mehsani not spread their religion?"

"No, I just don't think the Rift would've happened."

"What of the problem of vanity?" Royce proposed.

"Huh?"

"'Huh, uh, um, oh.' Vanity. Pride. What of them?"

My silence was enough of an answer.

"Take this for instance: Someone borrows your idea. You may have worked on it together, but he attracts far more people with the idea you perceive as your own, and people associate the idea with him, him with the idea. Conversely, consider someone takes an idea associated with you, and although fewer people associate him with this idea, those that do love him fiercely and would die for it, while your followers know your name, but love you little in truth. Which man would you be?"

"Neither," I replied.

"Exactly. Neither offers an appealing out. Neither offers a way to make yourself the truly important one, the one who becomes impervious through transcendence. Vanity compels one to act." She poured tea into her cup, but frowned when the kettle ran dry before the cup had filled. "What do you think?"

"I think I finally know why the chancellor called you a godless swine."

She cackled and clapped her hands. "One of my favorite titles. As much as I love the chancellor's charming names, I have to disagree with them. While I criticize these things, these ideas flying north and south, it is the people uttering them that are the germ. You're leaving for Calidum soon with Payton and her father. Do you remember your culture from your earlier years?"

"A little."

"Do you know what they call the raven in your homeland?"

"No," I admitted.

"A raven in Calidum is called a praeco. This word translates roughly to 'herald of night.' This black bird, an omen of death and doom in Braeland, is a tent pole of the Calidumi belief. So sparse in the hot flats of Calidum, its natives believed the praeco must possess some special power. They noticed it lurking around the elderly during their culture's infancy. Therefore they surmised that this bird was associated with death.

"Instead of fearing the praeco, they embraced it. It became the herald of the next life. Across the night waters exists the next life for the Calidumi, beyond the black ocean of the sky. The praeco's flight acts as transport through these waters, and the soul would die without its usher.

"When Mehsani first went south, he overshot current-day Sumara and settled on the boiling basin, across the great bay from Calidum. Already there were settlements there. The queen of Calidum, Ala, visited him. A tenuous accord was struck between these peoples.

"One day, Queen Ala's men discovered Mehsani hunting ravens, which had grown overpopulated in the Southern swamps. So many dark omens scared Mehsani's people. The murder of the praeco nearly sparked a war. Queen Ala and Mehsani met quickly to discuss this transgression.

"Mehsani tried to justify the killing of these birds with the dark omens they brought. The queen wouldn't hear it. She explained to Mehsani that these birds were integral to her people's worship. If too many praeco died, the Calidumi feared for their souls making it across the night waters. Effectively, every bird killed by Mehsani doomed a handful of Calidumi souls.

"Mehsani admitted this affront to Queen Ala's people. Swallowing his fears of this dark bird, he signed a decree to his people making the murder of ravens, which he called praeco in his law, illegal. Queen Ala thanked him, and from that early day to now, the Calidumi and the Mehsanic people remain close friends. In fact, do you know the name of the settlement where Mehsani declared the raven a holy bird?" she asked.

I shook my head.

"Well, you can impress them once you arrive for your scholarly endeavors," she said. "It was known by a different name then. After King Wilbraem the Wise's rule, however, it adopted a new name: Wilbraema. A center for tolerance and knowledge. It's a shame I didn't teach there, rather than here. You'll see for yourself soon enough."

I nodded, but I felt my mind slowly slipping. We'd been talking for a long while, and her words grew cluttered in my head. But I nodded and sipped my tea.

She must've noticed my fading attention, because she said, "Consider this: if I call a black bird a raven, but you call it a praeco, which of us is right?"

"Both of us?"

"Is that a question?"

"No. Both of us."

"But how can I be right if the raven is a bird of death while you are right if the praeco is a bird of life?"

"Well, you're talking ravens and I'm talking praeco."

"But they're the same black bird."

My silence was deafening.

"If it brings doom crashing upon Braelanders, does it still bring eternity to Calidumi?"

"Yes."

"How can it do these things simultaneously?"

"I don't know."

Royce sighed. "Because we have invented these purposes for these birds, so they can perform innumerable services to us. Omens of death and emblems of life are imagined by the Braelandish and the Calidumi. Because they are imagined makes them no less beautiful. I believe in the dark raven, but I think that the legend of the praeco is a gorgeous tale of faith. Like Mehsani, I'd never harm one out of respect for Calidum.

"That historical moment is my favorite. I think it's a miracle the people of the praeco never killed the murderers of the raven."

"I think I now know the heresy that forced you out of the university," an icy voice snarled.

Both Royce and I whipped around to find Lord Leon Tallhart standing in the doorway to her estate. He gazed at us with unblinking eyes, their intensity heightened by the accusatory, squinting lines that flanked them. His hand rested on the butt of his blade.

"Leon! Would you like some tea?"

312

"None from you. Jaremy, it's time to go."

"My lord, we're just finishing up a final lesson before Nalda begins his great journey," Royce explained.

Leon frowned. "Our boat is setting out for Calidum in an hour. He's spent long enough in your presence."

Royce laughed. "My presence is a benign tumor compared to the malignancy he'll face south of the Narrows. You should be embracing me, Leon, for soon Nalda will linger dangerously close to the den of true heretics."

"Heretics exist in many forms."

"This is true. But honestly, if you hope to persuade Queen Kala to provide you with soldiers for this war everyone's whispering about, you'd do good to start exercising patience *now*." She turned to me. "Nalda, if there's anything I want you to take away from this final lesson, it's this consideration of the Rift, of the Way, of Braeland. Remember the praeco and the raven. Remember how Wilbraema was founded. Remember how it all leads to this moment." She tapped the table with each word. "If Faedelin and Mehsani couldn't broker peace, I doubt they failed because they hated each other. They just didn't know how."

"Enough." Leon's voice was an icy incision slicing through Royce's resolute voice. "Let's go, Jem."

I stood, but Royce's papery hand grabbed hold of my wrist. Leon scowled and turned away. He vanished into her sprawling manor. With a gentle tug, she eased me back into my seat. Royce leaned closer and placed a warm palm on mine. "Nalda, the world is a field of dry grass, and men the embers floating through it." She added a tender squeeze to her hands. "You remember that as you go forward."

"I will."

"I know you will," she replied, smiling, her teeth slightly stained from years of tea. Skullcap with summer mint. I remember that was her favorite. I remember.

The praeco never killed the raven.

32

Ghosts

The sun was an egg yolk crowning the city's broken towers. The yolk rested just beyond the towers' reach, bleakly cut out of a gray morning sky. What were yolks but yellow dead things? Life snuffed out in its shell. Better to stay there in the shell, where no hurt can mar the soul or no sun rises in the shape of things that were but can never be again, like a pale cold reminder of the unmarred life, the crystallized perfection of all things within the yolk.

The sharpened metal dragged along his neck, making the sound of paper sheaves scraping together. Jon eyed the sun through the tent flap as he dipped the razor in a basin. The morning breeze sent prickles along the lines he'd shaved. The metal took away more hair. The next breeze shot shivers through his whole body. He glanced back up at the cold egg yolk.

Yolks were ghosts. Judgeless, cold, and peaceful, they were yellow dead medallions within the confines of a shell. If not for the claustrophobic constraints of the shell, it would be a perfect place.

315

Alaryn Tanogar had always shaved the morning of battle. A man should always look his finest when he is about to die. The man had shaved the morning Jon took the University at Trowbridge. He had looked his finest.

He taught Jon to shave when the first vestiges of manhood appeared on his chin, embodying the pale shadow of the turning of time.

Try it, son, Alaryn told him when he was fourteen.

Won't it cut me? Jon asked.

No, not if you're careful. See, just place it so it kisses your cheek, then drag it down. See? Nothing to it, my boy.

It's tingly.

Alaryn laughed and patted Jon on the back, then his finger traced the path left by the razor.

It'll do that for a little while anyway, until the hair gets darker, but you should always do it the morning of a battle. A man should always look his finest when he is about to die, Alaryn said.

The peach fuzz vanished as the hot metal swooped over Jon's adolescent face. He ran it over the last cheek, and it hit a snag. A bead of blood welled up out of nowhere.

Ow.

You're okay, my boy. Here, put that on it till it stops.

Why don't you cut yourself? Jon asked.

I've been shaving for over thirty years, Jon. You haven't been doing it for thirty seconds. Don't be hard on yourself.

Alaryn peered back in the looking glass while Jon pressed the towel to the beading blood, feeling foolish. He was just a child. The other boys had been shaving for months. Lanair's dark beard came in strong, a man in his youth, not like Jon's. His came in slow and uneven, a blond invisible echo of his brother's.

Do you know why we shave, Jon? his father asked.

No.

Because the hair grows back incessantly. Each time you shave, you're only cutting it back a little bit. It'll always come back. The hair will come back sharper and darker than before.

What if we never shaved to begin with? Jon asked. Then the problem wouldn't exist.

Jon's father leaned on the bowl and peered into the water bubbly with soap. What did he see deep in that shallow basin?

No, Jon, I think we'd have to start at some point. It's only human to come back sharper and darker, Alaryn said with a sigh.

"You're doing it again," a disturbance in the present said.

It's only human to come back sharper and darker.

"Lord Carrow," Coyle said.

"What?"

"You're doing it again." Coyle pointed at Jon's palm, which was a crisscross of scars. He was running his blade over the palm, back and forth, back and forth, slowly but incessantly. "You do that whenever you're just, well, you just get lost sometimes. Did you even know I'd come in here?"

Jon glanced around his small tent, pressing, always pressing at him like the dark room. "No. I didn't."

He observed his palm. Its pale scars resembled the scratching of a broken philosopher who couldn't secrete the truths in his head fast enough, so instead of transcendent prose, he scribed madness.

Coyle walked over to him. "At least you didn't break the skin. Eat up." He tossed a loaf of bread at Jon, who caught it.

"Thanks."

"You thinking about him?"

"About who?" Jon bit off a mouthful of bread.

"Your father. Lord Tanogar, I mean. You've been saying his name in your sleep lately. When you sleep, that is."

Jon tossed the bread onto his cot and turned to the mirror. The paper sheaves scraped once, twice more. Coyle gulped the bread down behind him.

"If I'd known the man was your father..." Coyle began.

"No. Not anymore. Just forget it, Coyle. Please."

"Okay."

The paper scraped the sand. "I left that all in Sumara. Long ago." He dropped the razor into the water. "I had to leave it there. I had no choice." He fished for the razor in the milky water to finish the job.

Coyle's mouth clacked like a cow's when it grazes while he inhaled the bread. He picked up a bottle of wine, shook it so Jon could see it in the mirror, and raised his eyebrows in question. When Jon nodded, Coyle poured a glass and downed it in one swig.

"You know," he said between wine and bread, "my father died when a horse kicked him in the face. It was on the farm I grew up on. About a hundred miles north of Trowbridge. I was ten at the time."

Jon submerged the razor in the basin and toweled his face.

Father, I feel like I can't keep going, he remembered telling Alaryn. I want to die.

Coyle burped and stuffed down another mouthful.

Never say that, Jon, his father replied. We always keep going stronger than before.

"I wondered about life back then," Coyle was saying. "Man, I'll tell you, that hoof damn near twisted his head round. I passed out."

What if the first sheep decided to drop when the first days of midsummer hit Sumara? Alaryn asked Jon. What if they never reached the Stone Drum and Mehsani hadn't built our walls? What would we be?

We would be lost.

Do you feel lost now?

I do.

Why?

Who am I? Jon cried. Everyone calls me Ghost. Everyone looks at me as if I have the fever.

"Imagine me passing out at blood. Me! A long time ago," Coyle was rambling.

I never call you Ghost, Alaryn replied.

Only you.

That's enough for now, Jon. Think of it like this. If you're riding your horse through a stretch of fog and cannot see the end of the fog, do you stop riding? Jon, don't wallow in silence.

No, we don't stop riding, Jon answered.

Of course not. We keep riding.

"But his head twisted around. I couldn't go near the horses for nearly a year," Coyle was saying. Jon pushed himself deeper into memory.

Alaryn continued, We push on through the fog because there is an end, although we can't see it.

"Are you listening, Lord Carrow?"

Fog dissipates, Jon. It always abates, his father prophesized.

Then Jon found the little newborn in the arms of a whore after visiting Saera, who took him in nearly every night from when he became a man until he was twenty-two. Every night with her plump breasts always filled with milk for the babies around the Shepherd's Hole. It was a dingy hut, but a home.

Jon, the whore whispered.

Her voice was the sun emerging from a wall of clouds on a windswept day in winter. Her fingers twirled the laces of his pants as he stared at the ceiling made of creaking boards, which whined as the bed above it squealed with pleasure. How many nights did he spend staring at those ceiling boards, counting the grains and dark spots in each one while Saera napped beside him?

Her hands went down his pants.

Are you tired tonight or something? she asked.

No, I'm, uh, I'm sorry, Saera. Just been thinking a lot.

You want my mouth?

That's okay. Let's just talk.

She stroked Jon there. Despite her gentle touch, the soft pads of her fingertips skating along it, he hung limply, lifelessly. He kept his cheek pressed to her roughened nipples.

What's on your mind? she wondered.

Meraxes.

Huh?

Meraxes. It's a story my father used to read to me when I was a boy. It's my favorite.

What's it about?

This farm girl who understands the weaknesses in men, Jon explained.

But as she rested her head on his chest, her soft fingertips kissing his penis between his thighs, he knew she wasn't listening, so he stopped talking as she kept stroking.

Then cries pierced Jon's ears from down the hall where Ariana's room was, so he slid out from under Saera, who was sleeping softly. She sighed as he rested her head on the pillow, scrunched up the blankets between her legs, but she didn't wake up.

The cries filled the hall again.

A warm light spilled into the hallway from the open door when he got to Ariana's room. She sat alone in a chair rocking a newborn back and forth, and she looked up at Jon, her eyes tired and empty.

Sir Carrow, she greeted him.

Hi, Ariana. That yours?

No, thank Mehsani, I drink my moonleaf. Some poor woman showed up in the alley out back with blood all down her legs, Ariana explained. We never got her name.

When the cries grew in pitch they hurt his ears.

Shh, Dinian, shhh.

Dinian? Jon echoed.

Yes, boy's name is Dinian, Sir Carrow. Named him m'self. He was so cute, but a sad thing about the mother. There, there, shhh. One cow, two cow, three cow, blue cow. Would you like to hold him, Sir Carrow?

No, I don't think that would be wise. You hold the boy for now.

Milk, my lord, the whore said. The boy needs milk before he starves.

There's no milk. I'll talk to the other ladies, but I'm no milk mother. Maybe one of the other girls.

That's okay; the other ladies will know what to do, he assured her.

Here, hold him, the woman said.

I shouldn't hold him. I don't think that would be wise.

Here, she insisted.

H-hi there, D-dinian. I'm J-j-jon C-carrow, he stuttered like a fool. Shhh. Uh, shhh, D-dinian; there, there.

Good. He listens to you, Sir Carrow. You sure you aren't the father?

No, I'm not, Jon stated.

Shhh, well, all that matters now is we get him to the sea. He must enter Mehsani's Light, the woman said.

Saera, Jon remembered.

Hm? she asked.

Saera will have milk. She can feed him, he said.

Jon needed a reason to keep going, and here it was. Mehsani himself must've sent it to Jon. Mehsani must've heard his vain prayers. Here was a reason to keep going.

A son.

"I miss my son, too," Coyle continued his monologue.

But wooden as Jon might've been, he gave the boy a home, and at Trowbridge, they used to throw whore children from the walls.

"He's a cute boy, but can't hear worth a damn."

"What did you say?" Jon asked, dragged from the beauty of the memory.

"I said, 'I miss my son,'" Coyle replied, face tight with indignation.

The man leaned on his knee, sitting half on the bed that Jon never slept upon. He rolled the last heel of the loaf along the backs of his fingers as he stared at Jon, little more than a reach away. How long had he been talking?

"I never knew you had a son, Ed."

Indignation tightened Coyle's features. "I've mentioned him before. But you never asked. Don't feel bad; no one ever supposes I've a family." His eyes wandered off, looking around the tent. "Imagine me cradling an infant. A lion stroking a feather."

"How old?"

"Nine. He's a bright boy, but he can't hear anything. I got a professor at the university to teach him hand talk, but the price of just an hour's lesson is criminal." He shook his head. "I enrolled to pay it off." He continued to search the tent with troubled glances. "I used to smack him around for not listening to me. Thought he was a mischievous little brat. I was too stupid to see it. Might as well stab a legless man for losing a race."

Jon shifted on the stool and rubbed his smooth face. Coyle's troubles made Jon wince. A slab of stone should shed no tears.

"I just get caught up in my anger. It's when the drink's in me. If knowing was as easy as quitting, I guess we'd have no vices."

A horrid moment bubbled up. The night when Jon had to flee Sumara and leave behind his son forever. At first, Jon tried to stop the moment. Then, he recalled the unstoppable stream, and he knew he had to relive the moment in order to finally master the stream.

I don't understand why we have to leave, the boy whimpered to Jon, nine years after he'd found him in the brothel.

Come on, Dinian.

Why, Jon?

Just stop it, stop it! Jon screamed.

There was frightening quiet from the boy. He'd found the letter already, and time was against them. They needed to fly from the South.

I'm sorry, Dinian. Just pick your head up, Jon pleaded. Come on, Dinian, let's go.

"I can't wait to see him again," Coyle continued. "I guess I'll have to learn the hand talk, too. Useless if only my boy knows it."

"I guess that's true," Jon agreed. He massaged his temples, as if the thumbs could rub away the moment he left Dinian.

Coyle bit down on a bitter laugh. "I wonder how I'll tell him bedtime stories. Can't fall asleep if he's staring at my hands."

"You'll find a way, Ed. We always do."

Jon massaged his temples and hunched over. If only his rotating fingers could grind the headache away, could stop the hurt, could stop the memories bubbling back to the surface like sulfurous miasmas lurching to the face of a swamp, carrying with them the burden of things that were, things that lay dormant at the bowels of the dank swamp, but would always bubble to the surface no matter how hard he tried. The sulfurous miasmas could not die, much like the unstoppable stream.

Like the night he left Sumara and the boy. Dinian looked at him with such a sad look, the look you give a person sick before his or her time, who lays upright in bed, and the look says, I'm sorry I can't put you back together. Or the afternoon Jon lured Sir Iayn Darrion into the shadows of the alley. All of them miasmic bubbles going *blup. blup. blup.* to the face of the swamp.

Jon turned away from Coyle and reached for a more beautiful recollection. A beautiful memory to supplant the horrid one.

Dinian, shhh, there, there, boy, Jon whispered to his infant. The wailing pierced the tranquility of the Sumaran nighttime.

That's right, Dinian, you're my boy, you're a Carrow boy now. Shhh. I'm so happy that I found you, shhh. You like stories just like me, just like I did when my father told them to me. Do you want to listen to one? That always helped me.

The baby's cries abated to whimpers.

I call this one The Ghost of Sumara, Jon began, cradling the infant in his arms. It's about a haunting in a city, but the ghost was actually a friendly spirit. But none of the people talked to him because they were afraid of ghosts because they had heard stories. But stories are just little truths wearing big lies.

The Ghost of Sumara was friends with the boy prince. Together the ghost and the prince would wrestle by the sea and they learned to hunt together, and the prince called the ghost brother, and the ghost loved the prince. He even hoped one day he would rule by the prince's side.

Then one day the ghost and the prince got lost in the woods while the dusk was coming on, so the light vanished from the trees, and the prince whimpered in fright, but the ghost ruled the dark of the night.

A great beast lunged out of the brush at the prince. Since the ghost was brave, he swooped in and protected the prince from the beast with its gnashing teeth blushing red. Its two heads snapped wildly at the ghost, but the ghost could wield his sword, unlike the prince. He slew the great beast and liberated the forest from its darkness.

Later that night, though, the prince told a different tale to his father, the king, and the king looked down his nose at the ghost saying, I'm sorry, and saying, That's that, and the priests have spoken. The beast has named you an infidel. You cannot live here anymore.

Always, always, being told to leave, the ghost grew tired. So the ghost decided to become a ghost and glide from shadow to shadow unseen by the prince's men.

Then one day, the prince became king when a little poison made its way into the king's nighttime wine and closed up his heart. The eyes of the kingdom pinned to the ghost, who had been minding his own business in the shadows, but the prince's men dragged him into the light and cut the poor ghost to pieces and locked him in a cage like an animal, taking him out only to cut him up again.

The prince pretended to be sorry, but the ghost knew a lie when he smelled it burning like shit on the tongues of others because he had heard lies his whole life.

So the ghost walked among the shepherds, but he was not a shepherd, because they cast him out of the flock for they knew he could not be herded like the other sheep. But what they forgot was that you can't see a ghost when he wants to go unseen. So the ghost started plucking off their little sheep in the shadows.

The shepherds started screaming, What is happening, where are our sheep?

But they couldn't see the ghost who floated in and out, in and out, of their circles with a scythe in hook's clothing. One by one the ghost plucked off little sheep from the flock.

As Jon spoke, the baby nestled quietly in his arms. Dinian's nose bored into his armpit for warmth. Even then as a tiny two-year-old, he felt a burden, the pressure of him on Jon's chest like a boulder. Damn that dark room. The room always came back even as he just nestled his baby boy. Just holding his son, he sank back into the claustrophobic torture room.

In the present, Jon shot to his feet. His vision began to fuzz and fade to black, the way it does after standing too quickly, and he grabbed his wash-basin to keep from falling over. Coyle reached out a hand to catch him, but Jon waved him off.

"My lord, are you okay?"

Jon nodded. "I'm fine, Coyle."

"We're supposed to be at the broken tower in just an hour. Drink coffee. Tallhart sees you like this, she'll come in with us."

"Payton," Jon mumbled.

Like a handful of sand

"My lord?"

scattered across a bowl of milk.

Jon winced.

Like a halo of sunset

"Lord Carrow!" Coyle shouted.

crowning a column of alabaster.

Payton came off the ship, a young woman of twenty-three, nearly seven years Jon's junior, but she was already so mature, waltzing across the planks into the den of the foxes where Lanair took her hand and pressed a kiss to it, biting back his distaste for her father's presence.

Payton came to Jon last, for the Ghost stood at the end of the welcoming retinue. But she smiled at him with a face like a handful of sand scattered across a bowl of milk and hair like a halo of sunset crowning a column of alabaster.

She was so beautiful and agile, like a sand cat of Calidum. But Jon never felt hard for her. He saw a woman he could talk to, who could tell him about home. Not this home, but home.

Leon Tallhart pressed Jon to the wall when he brought a flower to Payton in the dark of the night, hoping she would play mother to the boy the way he played father. But Leon saw only a heron turned into a fox hiding the shepherd underneath. So Jon took to plotting how to procure night leaf and how to sneak it into Lanair's evening tea. Then like father, like son.

Once Jon had it, he wrote the letter that Dinian found. That foolish, nosy boy. No. It was Jon's fault, like when he killed Darrion. Not the boy's fault at all. Jon left the letter out on the desk where anyone could've found it.

It didn't matter once he told Leon. Jon suggested that Dinian could be like Payton's son, but he burned him away with his cold eyes.

Don't you see, Leon, he reasoned, now we can kill Lanair. It's the only way to prevent the Reaving from reopening.

Too risky, Carrow, the fool insisted.

Come on, Leon, you've heard the whispers. Lanair won't lay down and die. He'll take back what he lost before. He won't just let the Faeds win out.

I don't listen to a scab's whispers. It's over.

I'm no scab, Leon. Wake the fuck up. Take your head out of that stupid book. If we don't kill him the Reaving is as good as reopened. You think I'd still fight for these people?

Leon burned him away with his cold eyes. Even worse than a scab is a faithless rabid dog, he declared.

So Lord Tallhart, the mighty conqueror of Sumara, ignored the little fissures all around him until they slid his head onto a pike.

Dinian was worried the nights before Jon left, sensing the fighting like a busted knee senses an oncoming storm. He comforted the boy the best he could, telling him he would teach him to shave the way Grandpa Alaryn had taught Jon to shave before battle, but not yet. Not a single thread of hair marred his boyish chin, no pimple, no frown.

It was later that evening when they came into Jon's chambers, tied him down, and whipped him with rocks over and over and over. They chanted as they whipped.

Fraternizer.

Conspirator.

Traitor.

Ghost.

326

They chanted those bitter warning words over and over and over as they took scalpels and sledgehammers to Jon, to eviscerate the last organ, carving the heart into infinitesimal slivers, unseen, unfelt, overwhelmed by the unbroken circle of primordial spite.

Beware the scalpel wielded with primordial spite.

It felt like a mountain had crashed onto him, and he couldn't move at all. Yet the boy's whimper made his head turn, and there was the boy curled into a ball beneath his desk, staring out of the shadows at Jon, who bled silently on his bed long after they had left. Dinian's eyes were shards of broken glass illuminated by the moonlight.

It wasn't soon after that Jon saw the boy reading the letter about the poison for Lanair when he entered the chamber, still limping from the rocks, still without sleep from the fear. Then Jon's golden box opened, and the boy saw the pale wooden interior. It wouldn't be long until every Sumaran and Mehsanic saw it, too.

Jon, I don't understand, he cried. What does this mean? the boy said while holding the stolen letter.

Dinian Dinian Dinian no no.

Why does Lord Tallhart need the night leaf? I thought Uncle Lanair was his friend.

No no no, Jon rambled like a fucking half-wit.

Jon, please, I don't get it.

Please, Dinian. Please, Dinian, let's just forget about this.

Jon put the letter about poison in the hearth, but it wouldn't burn the words from the boy's mind.

You have to tell Uncle Lanair, the boy worried. Lord Tallhart wants to kill him.

You don't understand, Dinian. Lord Tallhart is a good man. Can you stay here, Dinian? Can I trust you? Dinian, answer me. I'll be back before you can say Mehsani's Grace.

Okay, the boy promised.

Okay.

327

Jon flew to Leon's chambers across the castle, but he held him against the wall again, and even then Jon wondered why he didn't take Dinian with him to keep the boy within arm's length.

I thought I told you to stay out of this tower, Leon greeted him. I told you to only send letters. You were never supposed to look at my daughter again.

Leon, it's over, Jon panted. Get Payton. Dinian knows about the poison. I don't trust the boy. He read the letter about the night leaf. Once Lanair hears, the three of us are dead.

What?

He knows.

You light-cursed fool, why in Faedelin's name did you put the word night leaf in a letter to me? Leon spat. Could you have been more obvious?

What could I have done? You slink away at the sight of me. You're the one who told me to write letters!

I never curse, but you're a fucking imbecile.

Get her. Meet me down in the screaming cells. There's a tunnel built for times of siege. We can escape through there.

And what about all my men, my couriers, my squires? Leon asked.

There's no time.

As Jon sprinted off down the halls, the shepherds came to Leon's door from another corridor, blasted through the wood, and then the clatter of swords. The last stand of Lord Leon Tallhart. A single rivulet of blood wandered out into the hallway where Jon hid in the shadows of the late, late night.

Dinian was crying when Jon made it back to his chambers, still out of breath from the sprint through the shadows. The boy told him what he'd done. He told Grandpa Alaryn, who flew off in a rage, who told Lanair, who went to go kill the traitorous hart, but Lanair would know. Lanair, that friendly syllable "Lah" followed by the stab of ice "nair." He would see Jon's heart adorned in the black feathers of the heron, since he saw the fox and not the squirrels.

Jon flew as Dinian trailed close behind within the looming dark of the Stone Drum. The boy was saying, I don't understand, why do we have to leave? I don't understand, Jon. I'm scared, Jon. And Jon saying, Be quiet and shut up.

The gang of boys met them near the gate to the jail cells. They were five boys playing soldiers. They slowly rounded Jon and Dinian, led by Saewyn, whose eyes were wild.

They took Tallhart, he said.

I heard, Jon answered.

They cut off his head for everyone to see.

His voice was jeering. It was then Jon knew that Saewyn knew about the poison. Somehow he knew that the hart hadn't found the night leaf. That had been the Ghost.

And Payton? Jon asked.

She's in the screaming cells.

They had circled Jon and Dinian. Then he realized that they were wearing armor. They were boys playing men ready to kill.

Do ghosts bleed? Saewyn taunted. And then he smirked at Jon as if killing him and his boy was funny. Then he ripped the blade from its sheath.

He came at Jon first, and Jon shoved Dinian to the ground so he was below it all. He parried with Saewyn, the others around him. It was a blur. A blade caught Jon's thigh, but he took that man's throat. The next two were easy; they were cowed at their friend's opened neck. Then the fourth in the stomach. Then Saewyn.

Stop, he pleaded.

Stop, huh. Are you afraid of ghosts? Jon asked.

Stop.

Are you afraid of ghosts?

Stop.

Shut your fucking mouth.

Jon pounced on him, screaming at Saewyn's blank face, which gazed vainly at the night overhead.

Another hand touched Jon, and he whipped around in bloodlust, tackling the man to the ground, driving the sword toward the throat. But it wasn't a man, it was the boy gazing up at Jon, his eyes looking hopeless. The eyes of a lost lamb ethereal in their innocence, unmarred by the messy existence between dawn and dusk.

Never, never, never again would Dinian look at Jon the same. He could linger on pleading with the boy for tomorrow and tomorrow and tomorrow trying to make something out of the dusty heap, a cousin to the fallen bridge he was supposed to build that fell in furious death. At long last Jon Carrow had died, and this man truly was the Ghost. And what was that worth.

Go.

J-j-jon.

Just go, just go.

The boy wriggled out of his clutches and scampered away in the dark night. As he ran, Jon felt something break. He knew if he'd been staring into a mirror instead of the bloody street, a ghost would be staring back.

When Jon opened his eyes, Coyle stared down at him. The man's eyebrows pushed together above his nose as his fingers scratched his chin. Suddenly, he jumped.

"You're awake."

"I am."

"Sorry to move you, but you just sort of fell asleep." Jon then noticed that he lay on his cot.

"Hm?"

"We were talking and you stood, but then you started swaying and then..." Coyle shrugged. "You passed out."

"How long ago?"

"A few minutes. No more than five." Coyle's eyebrows were still pinched. "You sure you're okay?"

"Fine, Coyle." Jon sat up on his cot, and the darkness began to blur again. "Any sign of Piper?"

Coyle shook his head. "No. You trust him?"

"I don't need to. He fears disobedience." Jon thought for a moment. "Maybe he fled. Payton chasing him all through the city didn't help. Quite honestly, he's an idiot if he's still here."

"So what about today?"

Jon shrugged. "It's all the same for now. Our part, anyway." He hissed out a long breath. "What about Jasin?"

"Waiting outside for you." Coyle paused briefly. "I don't mean to push, Lord Carrow, but you sure you thought this through? I mean, with you passing out and all, and Tallhart chasing Piper. She clearly knows he was involved with something."

Jon pursed his lips and shot a look at Coyle. He could smell it on his breath already, but who was Jon to blame the man? He probably grew frightened when his lord passed out. "After the university, why did you join my services?"

Coyle leaned back at the question. A long spell filled the tent as his tongue ran along his lower lip and he sized Jon up. "Because you could finish the job."

"And I spared you from Tallhart, did I not?"

"Yes."

"I can still finish it."

Coyle nodded. "Okay."

"Hand me that wine."

Coyle swished the liquid his glass. "This is the last. Finish it off."

Jon felt the man watching as he downed the last mouthful of wine. Little crumbs floated at the top. Flotsam on a purple pond. Jon grimaced as they went down.

"You kept saying, 'Dinian,' over and over while you were out," Coyle mentioned.

"Did I?"

"Yes. Who's Dinian?"

Jon waited a long moment before he spoke. "He was my son. A whore's boy that I adopted while in Sumara."

"Where is he now?" Coyle wondered.

"With Lanair. Stole the boy from me, in his own way."

"We'll get 'im back, Lord Carrow."

"Mmm. Go let Jasin know it's time to have the people see their sentinel."

"You coming?"

Jon shook his head. "Not yet. I've got to clear my mind."

Coyle nodded, exited the tent.

Sometimes a man must let go of the past when it turns away from him. He had to just let go. The world had paved him a path, and he had to just let go of the boy.

Dinian had scampered away in the dark of night, full of misunderstandings and full of lies. But now it was morning. Over the river was his son. He would clear up the stories about ghosts and shepherds. Set things right. He would find the boy.

Dinian.

33

A Tall Heart

The sun was a poor artist's rendering of a crown behind the clouds. Payton stood on the edge of her pavilion staring at it, bright in the morning haze, and yet she could glare at it without blinking. The watery drops streaked the light upward from the center and stabbed sideways. At its core, the jewel burned. A poor drawing of some crown. Like every crown, the sun drawing sat atop a body of nothing, a vacuum where men said stars ornamented the Light's halls, beyond which sat Faedelin while he waited for his adherents to join him. No, no, no. There was the poor, messy crown; there was the emptiness they called the king. There was the space in the sky filled by the imaginations of stargazers.

Payton felt herself nodding off. The ledge of her pavilion rolled down a hill into the restless river, which had picked up its pace in the early morning following a quiet night. Its liveliness sounded queer. So many days had passed next to a voiceless river that even its fatigued croak sounded like a shout. Its return lulled her as she stood on the ledge.

Soil sifted over the precipice and cascaded into the river. She tried to focus on those noises, the ones that came naturally from the nudge of a foot or pull of the drop, from the calluses on the feet, so that perhaps, before the cluttered masses huddled into the broken tower, she could face the monster they'd created. Then, catching herself, Payton weakened the wall she threw up. Better not make the monster paler. And so the clatter of metal, clanking of armor, and trudging of boots harmonized barbarically with the sifting soil and croaking river.

Across that river, Lanair Mavogar and Jem Nalda would be rallying their soldiers to cross the last bridge. It wasn't long now. The meeting neared, and Jon had already paraded his watchman named Jasin through for everyone to see. Admired his shining armor with the Sunburst at its center. The Sentinel of the Light, he'd called him. They'd be coming directly, Payton knew. It'd be soon now.

The running river brought to mind her first night in Sumara three years ago. Payton wasn't used to the sound of the sea, since the lake around Trowbridge lay largely silent. After the welcoming feast, as cold in manner as its food, she stepped out to the seaside balcony. A voice startled her.

"I like the sound of it, don't you? The sound of the surf?" the man sitting on the balcony asked.

"More accustomed to quiet water," she answered.

"Fresh rather than salt, too, I'd imagine."

"That's right," Payton replied.

"I was, too. Before they sold me. Your father didn't win anyone over with that speech, by the way," he warned. He peered out at Sumara's sea. It was a frothy soup of liquid obsidian.

"What do you mean?" she asked him. During the welcoming feast, after Lanair uttered two or three greeting sentences, Leon Tallhart took to the stage and delivered a half-hour speech on Faedelin.

"You'll see, you'll see," the man on the balcony said. "My name's Sir Jon Carrow." The salt laced the air. One couldn't breathe without feeling the crystals coat his or her tongue.

She'd heard the stories about the Knight of the Narrows, the boy who'd cut down Sir Iayn Darrion. Payton never expected him to be so young, nor so drunk. Jon had been startled that afternoon when Payton kissed his hand, too, in the manner of royalty. He'd been waiting to the side of the Mavogar family and the other Sumaran royals. He seemed to expect no one to notice him.

Jon swayed his foot like a pendulum, his leg the lyre and his foot the bob, which glimmered between the columns beneath the stone railing. He peered into a goblet of red wine and smacked his mouth: "Mmmmmm." He took a bite of a heel of bread, regarded the leftovers, tossed it over the balcony into the sea. His head tilted lazily toward Payton, standing in the moonlit portico.

"You'll see, Lady Payton. A careful tongue blesses you with more days. By all measures, Leon Tallhart did not use a careful tongue. The Ghost knows these things."

"Excuse me," she replied, "but my father's fine. He once took this city."

"The exception, not the rule. Honestly, I thought if he said, 'Faedelin,' one more time, the bastard might've appeared spontaneously right in front of us! Some welcome, I tell you. Wow, wow, wow," he said with a whistle.

"Don't laugh. It's actually a fine diplomatic move. We're welcoming you back into the fold, back into a united Braeland," she pointed out.

He touched his chest. "Oh, thank you, Lady Tallhart! You're welcoming us back to Braeland!" His tongue spat flatulently. "Braeland isn't united."

"We ended the Reaving. It's over."

He shook his head. "I was a knight during the war. Know why we called it 'the Reaving'? Because we actually cracked the ground in some places with our fires and blood and bombs. We tore this place apart. Then we tried to use a bloody poultice to plug up the cracks." Some memory drew a grimace on his face. "Want to hear what Tomathy Carrow used to say about cracks? Plug up your ass all you want; the shit won't stop. That's right, that's what the old motherfucker said. Plug 'em up; shit doesn't stop."

That night, and every night since, including last night, Jon had wallowed in pain and had worn his chest as a field of scars. She never knew. What Payton saw that night in Sumara, as the rest of the world did, was a bitter man, slightly off-putting and asocial. Like her, no one asked him, why was he that way? Why did he act on petulant impulse?

Perhaps Jon possessed better insight than anyone gave him credit for. He was correct; the speech Leon gave in Sumara wasn't given with a careful tongue. There was more cheer at Faedelin's funeral than at that welcoming feast. And despite his apparent disconnect with his surroundings, Jon's perception of his followers wasn't myopic. He knew, nearly down to a person, who viewed him as an adversary, as a turncoat, or as a leader.

Boots on soil told Payton someone had come. "My lady, Lord Lanair is ready to cross," Alanna's voice told her.

"Okay."

"Should we greet them as they cross?"

"Sorry?" Payton cleared her throat.

"Should we greet Lanair and Jem once they cross the bridge?" the woman repeated.

"Yes, of course. When are they coming?" Payton eyed the last bridge in her periphery. The slate arch lasted on its foundation and unbreakable path. The others plummeted into the water, washed away in it.

"They're ready, but I told them to wait an hour."

"Thank you."

Alanna shuffled her feet. Antsy, she couldn't find a stance she preferred. She settled with her feet tightly together, knees locked. "I need to apologize for my errors last night, my lady."

"Alanna, don't worry about it."

"Please, my lady. I swore myself to you at the Crossroads; my words carry weight to me. I failed you." She went down to a knee. "I can understand if you don't want me in your services today."

Honor that rigid must be hard to swallow. "Get up, Alanna. Can't have you crawling around with important things to complete. Come on, come on, up! It happened—largely because of my own foolishness—but it happened. Accept it. Eyes ahead."

Alanna nodded stiffly.

"Make sure our hosts are ready to greet Lanair and Jem when they cross."

"Of course," she replied, but instead of leaving, she cleared her throat to stop Payton's turning. "I feel the need to say something, Lady Tallhart. If the space allows it."

Payton waved a welcoming hand.

"We played a game at the Crossroads every night. Wouldn't fall asleep without getting in an hour or two. They called it the Bishop's Parley, though it might have some other name here. I still lay awake thinking about the rounds we used to play.

"The point of the game is to settle a newly discovered island. You play the settlers, and then there are robbers and a bishop. Since it's in the middle of the sea, the island offers few resources, but you've got to use them to build a new kingdom. You spar with other settlers for supremacy while robbers chip away at your footholds.

"If you need money, arms, or advice, you pay a large sum for a parley with the bishop, a completely objective figure. Only problem is, the bishop offers the exact same commodities to anyone who parleys with him. So you leave the bishop to stake a claim, but end up facing new threats armed by the same bishop who helped you. Soon the settlers burn up their resources and arms, while pirates invariably swoop in to finish you off. The more you defeat others, the more you lose, and the game ends."

"So how do you win?"

"You don't. There's never a winner, and the pots always go back to whoever put them in."

"Why play then?"

Alanna frowned. "If only I knew. Looking back, it was a colossal waste of time."

Payton couldn't help but laugh. "Alanna, you spent every night playing an unwinnable game with a bunch of drunks? Did you think you could break the bishop somehow?"

"We all did. That's why we were addicted to it, I guess. We wanted the bishop to give us the edge, because if he did, oh my, we'd be legends. But he never gave an edge. What a waste of time."

Payton shrugged. "All of us play foolish games at one time or another, Alanna, but they're only a waste if we don't learn to avoid those things in the future."

"Yeah, I suppose you're correct," Alanna sighed. "I'll go prepare the greeting party."

"I'll see you momentarily."

The woman stepped out of the pavilion, waving to Tam and Badric. They embarked to the last bridge.

A sudden cold nipped the air. The wind rising from the river rippled the gates of linen around Payton's pavilion, and they blew deep into her space. She felt the air current crawl up the cliff from the south, away and out of sight from the last bridge.

Payton went to tie down the linen. A horrid scent stabbed her nostrils. She peered over the ledge, down which stretched a steep incline covered in heather, and found the smell, a distinct odor of sulfur. Just like the bogs. In the heather was a steaming heap of flesh. Another gust blew the steam into her face.

"Who's there?" she called.

The stinking body lay hidden from her camp in the city, for the heather had grown waist high. She edged closer and saw it. Behind the steam wavered the scarlet scarf, a tousled band of bloody worms.

"It's you," she realized.

This spook would haunt her ad nauseam, especially with this smell, if she made no end of this. However, he was wallowing the heather, devastated by an unseen mortal blow.

Payton dropped the linen behind her, stepped beyond it. Carefully, she inched down the sheer incline with her feet turned sideways so that they rested on small footholds in the heather. She clutched a dagger by her hip.

The man in the scarf was about fifteen paces from her pavilion's lip. Once in arm's reach, Payton crouched beside him, raised the knife, and readied for the end.

Then, a flash of his eyes, indistinct and yet present beneath the hanging hood, sent her to a knee. I know that face, she thought. Yes, yes, yes. That was the face. The face she'd wondered about since yesterday, the one she felt in the burning brothel last night. The face she thought she recognized in the cellar closet last night. There he was, and she had the name. But how, and how, and how?

The name distorted her vision; the ground and the pavilion, the past and the present melted into one. Back. Back back back she flew. Payton knew the night. It was so clear she could touch it. The memory's brick and mortar resembled the sound of drums, a hand across the cheek, and a caged cat craving the kill. There'd been no herald to that night when Payton Tallhart and Lord Leon Tallhart, honored guests of Lord Lanair Mavogar, had suddenly been deemed traitors, off with their heads, onward to Faedelin.

She'd been with Saewyn hours before. He knew. Those were the scrutinizing eyes that hadn't seen. They nagged her every moment of orgasm, for which there were invariable moments of sinking through bottomless basements beneath her belly, unmistakably lit by the gaze of the arraigning eyes. They'd lit the way from the drums. The beat that Mehsani had used to beat back the storm harmonized with her thumping chest. *Doom doom*, they sang, a sound that would resemble the four-letter synopsis for tonight: doom.

Her father's eyes lashed across her, the hand not far behind. Resolutely, she held her place and wrested the point of vantage from him, who was too sure of his unopposed authority and never saw the answer coming. The answer came, set him on his rear. The shocked face was the shattered vision of glass. "Fuck Faedelin," words that deepened the blow and sharpened the

339

edges of the jagged glass remnants. They were done. Their ornery reign had come crashing down, but she couldn't stay there to watch them wither away.

She took to the window, climbed the ivy lattice to Saewyn's room, and was sent to the screaming cells. Only after Jon, like a caged cat, prowled beneath the swaying bulb could she get the shards out of her memory.

"Payton Tallhart," croaked her father's ghost, red scarf loose around his throat.

"Leon," Payton breathed.

His body withered in the heather. She stared at her father's ghost for a few moments, while her thoughts paced over how he could be here. Increasingly throughout yesterday, Payton thought the spook had been Leon, for the words sounded more and more like they'd come from her father, though reason told her not to entertain that possibility. Reason faltered. There he was, fallen pitifully on the hillside of flowerless heather. His body steamed and melted like wax under the sun. His jaw drooped into heinous jowls, his brows and forehead sagged like intestines. Melted to the rocks beneath the heather, Leon's ghost couldn't move easily.

"How are you here?" she asked.

He emitted a hoarse, asthmatic wheeze.

"Pick your head up," Payton said, propping his head up with a small rock. He was real and palpable and there.

Leon's ghost pointed to his throat and the scarf. His fingers, fat as ropes and just as knotted, trembled in the effort to lift them from the ground. Leon gurgled. Again, he motioned to the scarf before his hand sank to the ground.

Payton began to unwind the scarf. A rush of stink came as she did. Beneath the scarf smiled a red grin with fangs sticking up and down. The Sumarans had made messy work when they cut his throat. His hand went clumsily to it. A gasp snuck out of his mouth when his fingers made contact. There. Know it, touch it, absorb it. She tossed the scarlet scarf aside.

"How?" he stuttered, his voice hoarse, though clearing up.

"Sumara," Payton replied. "I remember the night. Jon left the letter about the poison on the table, I told you to fuck off, and they cut your throat. Not any of our finest work."

Perhaps her eyes skipped a beat, but his forehead was now less like a pile of intestines and closer to a wrinkled dog. On his neck, the fatal cut was fading, too. Bloody and vermilion when Payton unwrapped it, the throat's scar congealed and lightened. Now he could speak.

"So strange, to be back," Leon uttered.

"No shit," Payton agreed. "How are you here?" Though he seemed on the mend, Leon was still too weary to sit up in the heather. The green shrub embraced him.

"I can't say. I'm not here for long, though. I feel myself vanishing again." He locked eyes with hers. "I wanted to prove you wrong, Payton. Faedelin comes first. That's something I could never get you to comprehend."

Payton kept herself out of reach from him. The image of his whirling blade in the brothel last night came back to her. She shook her head. First, he returns to order the death of an innocent courier, then he assaults her in the night, and finally he traps her in a nowhere cellar.

"You tried to kill me," she said.

He lazily waved her off. "I'd never kill you. I didn't even want to harm you," he claimed, coughing, "I only wanted to secure the plan. There's a plan in place; I've felt it. I only wanted to secure the plan. You see, Faedelin always comes first, my daughter. Before you, before me. That is why I gave my life in his name, rather than be jailed for the sake of my name."

"What plan?"

"One that keeps Faedelin first," he answered. Leon pushed up with his elbows, but they slipped weakly out from under him. "I tried to go into your pavilion last night, but something stopped me. Just after I approached Carrow, I was thrown back by your curtains."

"My curtains?" she asked.

"Once I touched them, I was thrown into the heather and became this," he explained, and he gestured to his melted, debilitated state.

CALYPSO SUN

Could the linen, which she intended as gates, have repulsed him? For now, he was not one of the superstitious, the group she hoped to ward away with the gates of linen, but he was part of superstition, an even viler threat, since he affirmed the superstitious. Perhaps her plan had worked. If it had, then she knew how her father had returned: the gates of linen were a facet of her imagination. By flinging back her father, while others came and went through the linen, the gates declared him another facet of her mind. He had no place in the pavilion anymore. As she determined the night earlier, the linen divided the mind and the calluses on her feet. He was of her mind. But the lawbreaker yesterday afternoon had seen him, he had set the brothel in real flames, and Jon had conversed with his apparition in Alaveren before Payton spoke to him. So Leon's ghost was of her mind, though it had somehow pervaded the real world as well. He could touch the land. He played a part, though he was dead. She allowed him that accidental reentry to the world.

"I let you return," Payton stated.

"Yes. That must be it," Leon agreed, laying down in her shadow. "A thing that isn't allowed to rest shall not stay at rest for long."

"All this time, I thought I had let you rest."

"By leaving me in Sumara to die?"

"I almost died, too. Yet I'm here. I survived."

Leon sighed. "I died before I could teach you what I wanted. What will House Tallhart become now? They ripped a monster from your womb, and now you're a faithless person trusted to lead a flock of the devout. What legacy could you possibly bequeath to the future?"

Payton stood in the heather. "Here I am, father. I am who I am. That has been enough so far. It'll be enough to secure our country."

"Keep Faedelin first, girl," he said. "Maybe Faedelin would've allowed that thing they took out of you to live if you'd have prayed more often."

"These things happen, but I won't pay vigil to them each morning." She placed her hand over her stomach. "In a few months, we'll see if my lack of prayer births another monster. I'm certain it won't."

Leon hid his eyes. "And what, Tam will father the future of this country? Some godless soldier?"

342

"There's nothing left for you to say, Leon," she said. "You're gone."

"You let me back. You let the past catch up."

Payton shrugged. "So I did. Now we can both move on."

"How?"

"Come."

Payton slid her hands beneath her father's shoulders and pulled him up the incline. He winced as his body went over the rocks and the stalks of heather slapped his face. Yet despite his discomfort, Payton noticed that the smell had gone. His forehead donned only wrinkles, no sagging flesh.

"Remember the time we docked in Calidum?" she asked. The ground rasped underneath them. A cloud of dust rolled down the hill. "You had a heart attack. I thought you were gone. But just as I thought you were fading, you pulled me close and kissed my forehead. Remember that?"

"Yes," he replied.

She propped her father against a rock. They were a pace away from her pavilion and the linen gates. From this height, they could see far south through the city and narrow strips of the valley beyond. It stretched a great length under the gray morning. They panted for air following the climb.

"So this is how I end," Leon muttered. "A quiet stumble, not a confident sprint."

"I'll remember that moment on the docks, Father," she said, partially ignoring him. There was work to be done. "You didn't deserve the death you got. You don't deserve to melt away down there, either. Rest, Leon. Your job is over."

"I was putting Faedelin first, Payton."

"I know."

"You must do that for me," he pleaded. "Try to put the Lord first."

"We'll be okay. Panic does no one a favor. We will be fine."

Payton took his hand, and a glowing cloud began to rise from him. She coaxed his face toward hers so their eyes could meet. The eyes must meet. His, quivering madly, watered when they finally acquiesced, bowed down, were mastered.

She placed his hand on her belly. "See? No brimstone, no locusts. That's my point. We'll be okay."

Leon's image was evaporating. The fine gray-blond strands detached from his pate, a yellow pall diffusing out of sight. The pieces of him, once jettisoned, were at that moment forever part of something else.

The pall started to draw on his shoulders, his arms, his legs. Only his face remained untouched. "Don't look away, Father. That's right. See me before you go."

As she spoke, the smiling scar on his neck that matched her navel scar, a sibling, not a twin, lost its pigmentation. The rosy red bleached into a white line. Then that faded. His neck was, as it always had been, complete.

She pursed her lips while bowing her head to the height of her father's shrunken frame. Payton tenderly placed the kiss on his forehead. On contact, Leon dissolved. The image that had been him collapsed into a phosphorescent billow of round lights that thronged around her, a school of honeybees flocking to a store of nectar. For a heartbeat it embraced her, and then the wind launched the cloud's ascent. It was no longer a part of him. It was part of the beginning and the end, those secret voids marked exit and enter. The school of honeybees floated away, faded from Payton's vision, and was gone.

After it vanished from the sky, Payton stood and stepped back into her pavilion. She began tying down the linen. A breeze caught her attention, for it loudly rustled the stalks of heather. While rustling, the flowerless heather began to bloom where her father had lain. In seconds, the plain, green stalks unfurled with purple flowers and formed a mound to commemorate the man who left. Smiling, Payton reached back out and plucked a purple petal. She retied the linen.

Once back inside, Payton retrieved her copy of *Old Braelandish Folklore*. The worn spine fanned out to the page with Leon's note to her. Payton placed the petal over his name, pressed the book shut, and tucked it away into her chest.

The noises beyond her pavilion came back to her ears. She nodded, regarded her blade on the desk, and noted the sense of balance that rose with the sun. Perhaps not everyone had felt it, for balance was difficult to detect, though it seemed to rise even clearer, brighter, with the spores of her father's ghost. The balance hadn't taken hold yet, but that didn't shake her. It was coming.

34

Kill the Damn Heron

The sun is a suspended dandelion in a bed of dew. It isn't like the carpet of dandelions that braced my fall last night. You see, those dandelions had lingered to the point of proliferation; as my body fell, it sent the orb of seeds onto the wind to spread one weed into innumerable. Once the weed manages to get to that point, it's dangerous. You can't control the spread. The spreading weeds recall Faedelin and Mehsani, Marosia and Ambrose, and their inability to stop the spread. They allowed the dandelion to turn white in old age and spread along the wind. But not this sun, hanging with a golden mane in a dewy sky. If you kill the dandelion now, at this stage, the spread stops. You master the contagion. The sun like a yellow dandelion tells me it's time to kill him. I know it's time. Pluck it now while the dandelion sits innocently in a bed of dew.

Lanair has assembled a small envoy to cross the bridge. The columns of two thousand men and woman line up in the streets of the western bank, waiting for Lanair to march across the river and into the shadow of the broken tower.

A nervous susurrus rustled through the Sumaran camp once a glowing cloud flew from Payton's pavilion. So unnerved were some they pissed themselves. Faed sorcery was afoot.

Last night was a short sleep packed with dreams. My last conversation with Royce sprinkled with a few other moments. Lanair and I meeting in Wilbraema once again. Lanair standing triumphant in the university's throne room following King Gareth's fall. Lanair.

He'd been an obelisk in a field of corpses. My old home was a graveyard lacking the headstones. In a mild night, the forerunners of Mehsani took the island city, an unprecedented, audacious feat, and in a red morning, the Mehsanics made quick work by carving out the weak sheep. Though Lanair's diversion at Wellfleet had opened the capitol to him, he regarded the bloodied city with bile bubbling in his throat. Regardless, he stood resolutely, buoyed by the prayers of his people.

But when Royce saw us, she glowered like I'd never seen her in my youth. I'd hoped she might understand, but ruefully I knew better on second consideration. She cornered Lanair after he'd taken the castle. Her scolding voice resounded throughout the building. She berated him over lost lessons; I overheard her wondering if he had listened to a single fucking word she ever uttered. When she finished with him, his knees began to wobble.

As she passed me on the way out of his study, she whispered, "I told you to avoid embers."

That was all Royce said to me.

Later that day, Lanair tossed the crown into the teardrop. I saw nausea whiten his face. He'd hear no words from me, perhaps already regretting his decision to slaughter Gareth and his men. Suddenly, all the words whispered in Sumara had materialized in carnage, and the flies would descend promptly.

Then once news broke that Payton took back her city, while Jon came for the capitol, he declared a small defeat. We fled.

I remember the flight south. We held the university for a week before Jon and Payton's army marched west from Wellfleet to liberate it. Lanair knew we'd have no chance of surviving a siege. He knew Alaveren was the only place to stake out.

Even that was taken from us. We stood no chance against Jon's stampede; we had to drop back across the river. We'd never be safe as long as he was hunting us, always thirsting for the blood of Lanair.

Jon is marooned on the island Ambrose spoke of. Laecuna. Like every other person trapped on the island of the goddess, he has amnesia. He forgets about the mainland he's left behind. He forgets he's even on that orbital island.

No matter what we say in the next few hours, it won't be a timeless discourse that saves Braeland. Our tongues can't form the dialogue necessary to do what must be done.

What must be done?

An end must be made. The Mother's voice said that the mote was the genesis; we're long removed from when the two siblings penned that book. So now we're mired in the sprawling forest they began. That's our fate.

It's only our fate as long as we refuse to notice the trees encasing us. These men and women, taking their first steps across the bridge toward Payton and her force at the other end, they accept no responsibility for the forest spreading like a virus. But the claiming of responsibility is what we must do.

Lanair has the procession commence across the bridge. Our men and women are silent. I feel the wind, but it makes no noise. The only score to the morning route is the clopping of several thousand hooves, amplified in the vacuum of the silence.

We've got to know the genesis, recognize the forest, beat it back, and unite the two siblings. And we should. The praeco never killed the raven, after all. Sad that we always have to flock back to that metaphor, so ashamed of ourselves for failing to uphold the dynamic between two birds.

I'm tired by this too-long dispute. It reduces us to little children in the guises of mature adults, bickering over which sibling ascended to the Light. We've posited a riddle with no answer. Perhaps that's been the secret all along, the one we've spent the past seven days searching for, the one that's eluded us for more than three hundred years. Nothing we say within the tower will solve it, either. The answer is that there is no answer, not within the framework of the question. Pretending to flirt with an answer is no substitute; comparing ourselves to two birds solves no riddles. We're lesser than the birds. We're more savage, more dumb, more stubborn. Even when we know we are, our attempts to better ourselves are futile, framed as such within the old context of the two brothers. Stuck in those old phases, how can we mature? How can we put words to the answer that is no answer?

Payton is up ahead, at the end of the bridge. She's the forerunner of an immobile ocean of soldiers, Faeds ready to euthanize the rabid dogs. Atop a horse, she sits next to her standard-bearers and a group of twelve people. The Lady of Wellfleet nods to me.

You can't tear down one sibling, for the survivor can't assume those refugees. One sibling can't rule, since the other will be a burr in their side. At present, though, the road between the two is disintegrating. Its shoulders sink into the encroaching mud. Weeds sprout in the cracks and drag the cobbles down. The only ones who traverse it are those who seek to be the gust of wind that knocks down the other sibling, to cast a trail of dandelion seeds into the wind.

With the fall of the dandelion, a proper question emerges, for the question was never to fight the praeco or the raven; there's an interloper in the equation. A black heron has weaseled in. His role is out of joint, for the equilibrium was breached at his incision, and it remains off kilter because of his presence.

No heron was ever welcome in this binary. That bird is cut out of the balance, a variable that refuses to submit to the raven and praeco. It's time someone truly remove this impediment, and the heron is at the primed stage.

Strange that a bird so dark as the heron should don the golden petals of the sun.

Lanair saw the answer, or thought he did, in the capitol. He thought a brave assault and successful siege would solve it. Took the city, took the country, and then fled all that he'd worked for. Nothing was answered; the question remained.

But now I see it. It's Jon, and always has been. To him, we'll be rabid dogs skulking across the last bridge. When we enter the tower, I expect him to be holding a leash.

What would Royce say to me?

The praeco never killed the raven, and the raven never slew the praeco. Yet then a third bird tries to hack his way into the conversation, ceaselessly turning his talons on both raven and praeco. There's no ending in that. That's an orbiting refrain that forces the praeco into an endless sprint and the heron into an insatiable hunt. They dance away and run and flee from the ending that must come, the thing that must be done.

To wander the forest ignorantly weathers our tolerance of the minute-to-minute thought, the day-to-day toil, so that each toil turns a day into a lifetime, and no thought can endure a second's run. The transient plays the unending. Then something breaks. The shards, if you were to place them neatly in order, would resemble a younger, firmer spirit. But there's no time for lamentation; the haggard soul paves a quick demise. I can feel it. The shadows of the forest weigh heavier than the trees casting them. I am in the day of a lifetime; my thoughts are jumbles of ticking seconds. I can feel it. The forest has me.

Beyond the idyllic kiss of the teardrop, an old adage loses its punch. What must be done?

Snap a golden dandelion in its prime. Punctuate the mortality of the genesis before it begins. Kill the damn heron.

35

Drowning the Miasmas

With his eyes wide shut, Jon could see the end. He drank the breeze that aroused the hairs on the back of his neck, little soldiers at the ready, little blond soldiers who were soldiers of a light. The broken tower, the blackened city, the dying fields, the greener valley, they linked him with the limit of the horizon. Below him the broken tower trembled in the morning breeze. The armies awakened and headed toward the courtyard below for a talk of peace. All the pieces were coming to him. They had peered inside his golden box, seen the teak interior, scoffed at his allegiance, cried beneath his words, and now they walked into it. Mehsani was right. They were sheep. Easy to forget the wooden walls beneath the gold lining once the sun glints in your periphery and draws you back out and blinds you to the coming end that Jon could see with his eyes wide shut.

He stretched out his hand, imagining the immense drop into the courtyard, one that would squash a man flat. His fingers pointed across the ruins of Alaveren, soared over the rumbling, waking armies, and challenged the great slate mountains to stare back. This high up the tower, the air was restless. He wavered in the wind. And he let himself oscillate dangerously close to the end and the incalculable drop.

The incalculable drop. How many layers in this cake of shit called the broken tower were there? Only now had Jon regained his breath from the countless stairs, some of which chipped away beneath his feet. Even the stone ones flaked away. Up the layers within the cake of shit called the broken tower he'd climbed. Jon ran through the numbers in his head, wondering how the brothers baked such an impressive cake with so much pressing down upon them in the Narrows. They planned and constructed and soared until the tower narrowed at the top where Jon stood holding his arm out over the edge, where there was room for only one brother to stand, so one gave the other a little shove. Down he went in the incalculable drop.

"My lord." The voice was Coyle's.

There was a feeling in the breeze. A faint nudge at this height should send a man tumbling down and down and down, good-bye Faedelin, so long Mehsani, until he splatters on the courtyard below. Yet the moving air planted him on the edge, seeming to say he was here to stay. Saying he had something to do, something in the works with his hand around the hilt that Payton had wrapped in blue sapphire.

Was this the mastery of the unstoppable stream? To exist in its flow, to venture into its realm and teeter on the edge flirting with its unquenchable thirst to drown you, only to plant yourself statuesque, and say no? Had he conquered the indomitable? Jon Carrow, the boatman of the unstoppable stream. Beneath its chugging inertia rested the bubbles encasing miasmas concealing the ghosts of the past. They threatened to explode. But the unstoppable stream drowned them, so long as the boatman of the stream mastered the rudder.

"Lord Carrow."

This was mastery. He felt it. Let it wash over you in the early morning as the sun mocks you in the shape of yolks, and then enough. He seized the rudder, and it was over. The stream was his. Mastery.

"Jon," Coyle whispered. The man's hand flicked Jon's shoulder.

"A man could fall this close, Coyle."

"Might as well come away then, eh?"

"Okay."

Jon's eyes opened. His toes wiggled in their boots like ten flags flying over the Holy City. He imagined the thousands of men and women far below kneeling to the flags and sigil of Jon Carrow the Ghost Lord. Bow down to the feet of the Ghost.

"Piper hasn't arrived," Coyle informed him.

"He will."

"My lord," Jasin began, clearing his throat, "you still haven't explained my purpose here."

Coyle ground his teeth. "You questioning your commander?"

"No," Jasin replied.

"Good."

"You're our sentinel," Jon murmured. "The Sentinel of the Light. You'll be remembered as a hero after today, Jasin. They'll raise toasts in your memory," he finished in a whisper. "Once Piper arrives."

Come quickly, Piper, you fool running around Alaveren like it's a schoolyard in the university we fought so hard for and now the fight for it hinges upon this day this morning this moment you threatened running around like a fool Piper come quickly.

Coyle paced the small floor of stones open to the sky. The tower's top floor was a square patch that was overgrown with weeds and blanketed in dust and soot. On three sides, stone walls boxed them in, while the side where Jon stood had crumbled away, so that a portion of the top of the tower was naked and visible, if not for the heavy morning mist. Jon heard the clanking armies below that gray mist blanket. A barren pole adorned the corner of the summit overlooking the courtyard. It called for a flag to fly. Jon eyed it.

"Jasin, did you bring the flag like I asked?"

"Yes, my lord. Don't know why you wanted it." The man fished in a satchel for several seconds before lifting an enormous banner with the Red Hook of Mehsani in the center. "We'd be hung carrying this thing around."

"You might," Jon replied while eyeing the naked pole. "Did you know this was where Mehsani hung from? Right there. Can you comprehend that? The Lord Mehsani took his final breaths at exactly this place. One second he was here; the next, he's dead. Nothing but a husk."

"Think the courier got spooked?" Coyle questioned him. His pacing evoked a dog whose bone has fallen beyond a gate that it can't reach through.

"Do you know why Mehsani lost?" Jon asked them. He turned to face the two men.

Coyle, in his pacing, shrugged slightly. Jasin frowned as his fingers traced the red hook on the massive flag.

"Mehsani lost because that's just the way it went. The Light didn't forsake him. He didn't take the apples without worms from Faedelin. He didn't profane some city. He just lost. Rope'll snap any neck." He sighed. Kneeling, he plucked a pebble near the precipice. Jon extended his arm over the edge once again. "And that's just the way it went; he fell." He dropped the pebble out of sight. "Honestly, who gives a fuck about Mehsani? But Faedelin must've been chosen. That much must be true."

The man must've been chosen, that much must be true, because maybe Faedelin saw the lantern light beneath the bogs like Jon did those two months ago. It tingled at his fingertips. The burning had been so omniscient, as though the sun seared him from within. And within him it meant something. When Jon slipped into the unending pool and the lantern burned him up, he knew it had to have been an omen, and a good one, but not until Leon's apparition visited him last night could he put a name on it, and its name was the four-letter panacea that Lanair had given him by holding his eyes so close to the candle. Kill. Leon's apparition said it meant Jon was chosen by Faedelin to end Mehsani's contagion. No, no. Time to end Lanair's.

But everything that must be done must be completed before handing her the chafing reins. For she wrapped the hilt in blue sapphire, but it shall mean nothing following the death of the hero and the handing of the reins. While he maintained them, he'd use them to fulfill the lantern's omen. Put things right. He'd hand her the reins with the added benefit of the hero he'll have invented for her. Then she could keep them, for all he cared.

Thanks to Nalda and his wordy letter designating Payton as family and Lanair as the last drop of Mehsani's blood, he knew that this was his window. He had assurance. He had the grain to cleave the rock. Separate Nalda and Tallhart, put things right. Simple as that. It was so clear Jon could see it with his eyes wide shut.

Heavy breathing came from the stairs. "Piper," Jon said.

"My lord," the froggish man replied. "Sorry. Had to be sure Tallhart's scouts wouldn't see me. Met one along the way."

"Okay. You ready?"

Piper nodded.

"What's he doing here?" Jasin asked.

"Rounding out old debts," Jon replied. He ripped his sword out of its sheath and cut Jasin's throat.

The man dropped the flag so he could clutch his spewing neck. He crumpled to the ground, twitching. Jon pinched the flag and peeled it out from under Jasin. He held it up in the sunlight. Red specks circled the red hook. The twitching stopped.

"Faedelin's balls," Piper breathed. The courier stared at the leaking man. Coyle remained still by the staircase, waiting for Jon's next command.

"Piper, look at me. Piper? Marc. Lookitme. Look. At. Me. You remember what I've told you?"

"Yes."

"Good. Thirty minutes, in and out." Jon balled up the Mehsanic flag and underhanded it to Piper.

He knelt down and listened. The unstoppable stream powered its way into a stranglehold of his mind and wrangled him into submission to the haunts of the past. The whipping when he was thirty. The room when he was nineteen. And the words. They had had the chance to drown him. Now it was his turn to master them. He wrestled the unstoppable stream into his grasp.

He listened. No ghost, no traitor, no fraternizer, no Sir Iayn Darrion, the Hero Knight of the North, arced in a graceful fall.

The wind wafted over the balcony as the blood ebbed around his feet. The sun beamed down upon the three men spattered in beet juice. Birds began to sing to them, but what was the song, what was the tune, where was the beauty?

Jon drew in a long breath. He pressed his lids together as he did to crush the thoughts like an anvil to an egg. But none came.

All was quiet.

"I did it."

"My lord?" Piper asked.

Jon got to his feet and said, "Do your job."

Piper was fumbling with the shepherd flag like a boy who was in danger of wetting himself. Even his puny legs danced nervously. "Half an hour, in and out, do my job. What then?" Piper asked.

Jon gulped another lungful of the brisk morning air. How he'd forgotten what fresh air tasted like. Without turning to regard Piper he offered one word of advice:

"Run."

The air tasted fresh. His mind was quiet. He could see the end.

36

The Light Through the Glass

Jem was coming across the river with Lanair and several thousand Sumarans behind him. Beneath them, innumerable hooves clopped on the last bridge. Already the eastern edge of the city felt crowded with men and their thoughts, like ants skittering around a constellation of crumbs. Finally, she'd gotten the ants pacified, stationary, vulnerable. Now here came the uncountable clopping beasts.

Jem nodded slightly at her. Careful, Jem. Behind you are the examiners, the inquisitors, the shepherds. They shouldn't see you nodding, innocent fool.

She returned a bob of her head, which rattled her vision. The pain radiated from the lump underneath her eye. A fingertip traced its orbit around the lump leaping away from the cheekbone underneath; when the orbiting tip grew too audacious and grazed the lump, the pain it germinated scintillated throughout her skull.

Lanair noticed the wound when he swung his leg over the brown leather saddle atop his horse. "From the battle?"

"No, my lord. An unexpected altercation last night."

"Hope all's well." He stepped from his retinue stretching far away, followed by Jem and the woman who had accompanied Jem to the riverbank. Tehsan, he'd called her. Her eyes were fierce, wound up in that scarecrow face of scars. She held her distance from Jem so that the three approached Payton in a disjointed, lopsided triangle with Lanair at the apex. Arm's length from her, he knelt, a performance that forced Tehsan to scowl. She wouldn't even show Payton the decency of a glance. Jem followed Lanair's lead.

When Lanair rose again, he said, "I suppose I should start calling you 'queen.'"

"Maybe we should focus on getting out of here."

His brows furrowed. "Haven't you discussed your coronation with Carrow? I assume the topic must've been taken up at some point, you being a Tallhart, the king being dead without an heir."

She shrugged. "I suppose I've you to thank for that, Lanair. The topic's come up. He's agreed to support me. So, you have given up, then?"

He grimaced. "'Giving up' is such a bland phrase. I've recognized the situation at hand, accepted my mistakes. Besides, I'd say razing Alaveren is no defeat."

"Once Jon signs it."

"I was told that you'd see to that," Lanair said curtly.

"Jon does as Jon pleases. I have faith he'll not screw today up, if only by margins. Too much hinges upon it." Lanair frowned, so she added, "Would I put Jem in harm's way?"

His frown deepened. As his mouth warped, his gaze combed across Payton's followers. "Where is he now?"

"He went up the tower. Said he placed a lookout named Jasin up there in order to deter any Sumaran spies."

His mouth went taut. "I never agreed to that term."

Again, she shrugged. "He's interim castellan. What could I do? He was convinced a spy of yours attacked me."

Lanair shot a heated glance at Jem, who frowned. The lord ruffled his black hair while a hot sigh billowed out of his mouth, a snake hissing when cornered. He paced two steps left, three to the right. Fists planted on his hips, he spat between his feet.

"You should've been the one to go up there. You're the true leader here, aren't you, Lady Tallhart?"

"Perhaps. Equal shares for now, you could say. Diplomacy relies on compromise. I had to give him the tower."

"You should've been the one," Lanair repeated.

"Can't do everything myself, though you'd be right for assuming I could."

He allowed a quick, bitter laugh.

"Maybe I don't trust him fully, either," she continued, "and he certainly doesn't trust me worth an inch. You make do with what you're given. I'm trying to prevent more dying."

Lanair stared away from her and Jem, a perpendicular gaze that tracked south where the running river hooked into ruin. "Part of the job, dying. Your father knew that more than anyone."

Payton bit back a retort, for she sensed only a wafer of malice in his remark. Instead, she said, "Look, I've got to ask: was Marc Piper in your employ?"

"Marc Piper?" he echoed.

"My courier."

Lanair nodded. "Ah. I remember. Nervous guy."

"He's the one who gave me this." She pointed to her welt.

"No," Jem replied. Lanair bowed his head in accord. "We never contacted anyone within your personal guard. Figured they'd be filled with fealty for you."

She glanced over her shoulder at Alanna, Badric, and Tam. The rest of the Harts were behind them. "They are."

"Which leaves the question," the Lord of Sumara began, eyeing her directly, "who did break the one who broke?"

"Maybe he was in it for himself," Payton suggested.

361

Jem cleared his throat. "Mmm, likely not. More likely, I think, is that a heron was in your midst, prowling around while you tried to find the good in a man whose good was gone."

"I'm aware Jon had reason to spy on me. Though roughly equals, he always tried to gain the upper hand on me. Feared people looking at him with one foot in the North, one in the South."

"Bad to trust him. When they put the crown on your head, make sure he's not clutching a string," Jem cautioned.

"I'll put the crown on my own head."

Lanair grimaced. "If you're a Tallhart, I've no doubt about that."

Payton looked up at the broken tower. "Jon might be a few minutes. Let's have a quick cup of tea."

"Tea?" Lanair echoed.

"A quick refresher before the business begins."

Jem cleared his throat. "Go on. I'll wait back here."

"You come, too, Jem," Payton replied. He looked at Lanair for permission, and the lord shrugged indifferently. Payton waved for the two men to follow her to the pavilion, only several paces away from the bridge. So quiet were the soldiers the whispering river bellowed at her. Tehsan, Alanna, Badric, and Tam took awkward perches at the entrance of the pavilion, while the enormous columns of men and women waited in place at the bridge.

Inside, Payton poured the tea she'd brewed before going to the greeting. The steam wafted toward her nostrils, reminding her of the days she had spent in the university. Handing two cups to Lanair and Jem, she told them how rare these herbs were in the South.

Lanair sniffed it. "Summer mint," he stated vaguely. His long face drank in the steam from the cup. Then he took a sip, placed it on the saucer beneath. He held his other hand in a fist behind his back.

"Jon has the treaty parchment. I saw him," she assured him. "The lookout is merely insurance. It doesn't change the words on the document."

"Do you know the man he placed up there?" Lanair questioned her.

Payton pinched her forehead. "No. Light, I thought you were going to smooth things over, Jem."

"I did," Jem replied, midsip. He flicked away a stray bead of tea from his lip. "But the Carrow situation troubles me, too. He was supposed to meet us. Now he's lurking about the tower. Especially in light of your courier's betrayal, I don't feel comfortable with him loose."

Payton snorted. "Want me to leash him? Should I dally in his wake when I have a country to fix? He's in the place to use the world, given how it has used him, I'm not surprised he's playing puppeteer. Quicker you sign that parchment, quicker you'll never have to deal with him again."

The men were silent, sipping their teas.

"Mistrust pervades this place," she said, mostly to break the quiet, "but we might as well start somewhere. Take the pitfalls as they come. Imbue tomorrow with a glint of change." Smacking her lips, she returned the teacup to the table still filled to the brim. Nothing would satisfy her thirst right now. Jem was nodding.

"Only way to break the refrain," he said.

"Hmm?" Payton asked.

"The refrain. Sometimes the thing that's the answer was something not even in the framework." Jem licked his bottom lip. He'd been impeccably balancing the saucer on the top of his stunted forearm. Years of practice with wounded instruments. "Sometimes that's the answer."

"What's the answer, Jem?" Lanair asked.

He'd get no answer: a horn blared to the east, near the broken tower. Payton peered toward the mouth of her pavilion where a young soldier sprinted up toward Alanna. He handed her a note. The woman nodded, patted him on the shoulder, and entered the pavilion. She extended the paper to Payton, who took it.

"'Lord Jon Carrow has entered the broken tower. He shall await Lord Lanair Mavogar's arrival,'" she read.

Lanair snorted, tossed his tea onto the table. "Arrogant swine," he muttered.

The Lord of Sumara marched past Payton, nearly clipping her shoulder as he did. Halting near the upward slope out of her pavilion, he spun around, finger in the air. She waited for him to speak.

"You should know, Lady Tallhart, that even in light of our peace talks today, I don't lament cutting your father's throat. I don't regret killing the king. If we're going to have any accord, I want you to taste the sourness in my mouth."

Payton clenched her jaw. "I'll accept that. If we can all leave here, fine."

"I'm swallowing a bigger bite of pride than you, Lady Tallhart. I just had to recognize the futility of it all. Listened to too many agitated voices. I was the fool," he continued, nodding. "I was the fool. I'm not sorry for fighting, but I lament not putting it to an end sooner. Should've seen it was unwinnable. Nothing's winnable in Braeland. Promise me this, Payton: when you and I rule, Braeland shall never face another Reaving."

"I agree, Lord Lanair."

At the second his name left her lips, he spun around and marched out of sight.

Jem was swirling his cup of tea, waiting for a moment alone with her. Instead of finishing it, he set it back on the table, sent it skating over the wooden finish. He finally looked at her.

"Carrow's your hound, Payton. You ready for that responsibility?"

"I've handled him so far, Jem."

"Yes?"

"I can handle Jon. You don't think I know he'd like to supplant me? I know what he thirsts for, now that's he's gotten a glimpse of what it's like to be the oppressor. Nonetheless, he could've left me in those dungeons under Sumara. I can't forget that."

Jem shook his head. "You were his absolution. Where'd he go without your power to stay his execution? He needed you."

"As I needed him to navigate north." Payton frowned. "I learned a few details about his past, about Lanair and what he did to Jon. I saw it last night. I don't think you understand. It runs deep, in ink. But I can handle him."

"So can I."

"Know what's harder to handle than Carrow? The maelstrom that'll follow any deviation. Sign the treaty, leave us, live on."

"He is the bane, Payton. I know it in my gut."

She turned away from him, lest he say anything more. He sighed. "Long way from pouring ink into the chancellor's tea."

"Mmm. Bet his teeth are still stained though," Payton joked.

A chuckle escaped him, surprised him. "Probably."

Payton embraced him for a moment. There was no warmth in him. It had been snuffed out, stowed away, obliterated. So much time in the South might do that to a man. Go there for the heat, you'll lose your warmth. His arms wrapped her briefly. She'd once told him they'd never lose their warmth for each other. Not the Fire Queen for her Spider King. Oh, heroes, where have you gone?

"You could be one of the heroes, Jem," she said. "All you have to do is follow the plan."

Jem frowned, shaking his head.

"I'm serious," Payton said. "Don't risk this on a moment of passion."

"Okay."

"Okay?"

Okay, okay, okay.

Don't risk it on a moment of passion, she says, but this is not a moment but a slow build of myriad instances reaching an inexorable finale. What's a hero, Payt? A dead man. A fallen woman. A cadaver snug in a vague but immaculate cloud. Though not all dead things become the immortal vague cloud; some dead things are simply husks, ghosts, heaps. That's the trick. To make not a hero, to spill the blood and contain it so the threads of it can't spin into a tapestry of dreams through the loom of legends. To not send the white seeds abroad. The moment of passion is merely the culmination of every pointless letter and lesson before it. It always comes, and all stories end.

I'm so, so sorry, Royce. You tried so hard to plug your lessons into my head. So much time spent staring at the doomed worm caught in the heat. You let it die. Is this so different? To hasten its dying? Your words, or some version of them, are hacking their way back to me. But this time I have to block them out. The time has come. All stories end.

I brush the pale area around the plum ripe beneath Payton's eye. She winces slightly but lets my hand go. "Good-bye, Payt."

"So long, Jem."

We walk in silence out of her pavilion. Lanair waits for me back at the bridge where a band of a hundred Mehsanics prepare to station in the courtyard. Lanair motions for the solemn procession to start. We, along with Payton and her hundred soldiers, filter into the square cobbled courtyard cowering in the eternal shadow of the broken tower.

The broken tower. A sharp ruin leaping out of a gray landscape. Its base, rotund and broad, gives the impression of a pillar to the stars. Toward the heavens it soared and slaked away gradually, a fallen wall here, an exposed floor there, until the thing peaked with a narrow turret barely distinguishable from the mist.

Our guards open the doors for us. They reveal the dilapidated throne room within. An enormous sunburst set in the floor barely shines through a thick kiss of dust. Red pillars, faded since their installation, margin the sunburst's path toward the opposite end. Those pillars frame the view of two stained-glass windows depicting the likenesses of Faedelin and Mehsani, the former triumphantly clutching a blade, the latter meekly wielding the wooden hook of a shepherd. In the middle of the glass, a cylinder of light stabs through a missing plate. Beneath the majesty sits the centerpiece. A throne, seemingly carved from a single stone block, stares us down, perfectly centered fifty yards away. Atop it lounges a man. He sits, legs crossed in leisure, pale skin like an earthworm buried deep in the soil. He thumbs his chin. From where he sits, the light through the glass draws a crown on his pate. Illuminated, his blond threads recall the golden petals of the sun.

37

Mischief's Deep

The heron king breaks his reverie. Carrow regards the three of us with a smirk and slowly leans back on the throne. As he does, the light through the glass dashes his face into oblivion. Now the gray sun engulfs the throne, hides the heron king. Playful laughter comes from Carrow, obscured by the sun.

"So you've chosen to end it at last," his voice says.

Lanair grunts and marches toward the table near the far side of the hall. Tehsan and I follow, part of a strange formation, since she insists on keeping her distance, and the doors slam shut behind us.

"You've been feeding us apples with worms for far too long to make jabs, Jon," Lanair replies. "Where's your third member?"

I study the far side of the room. Only a tall man with a stone chin accompanies Carrow; the man is dressed in armor so dingy it doesn't sparkle even when it wanders near the spear of light. Only two. There were supposed to be three. But Carrow shrugs.

"Needed a lookout atop the tower. Had to quell any mischief, Lanair."

367

The slow approach is made tense by Tehsan's swiveling head, a hyper owl searching for something hiding in the dim places between the faded columns. Her fingers pluck at unseen strings. They flirt with the spaces near her sword.

"Another condition I didn't consent to," Lanair notes.

Another shrug. "Did the math, figured if I had one up there, three down here, that'd be four. Then I'd outnumber you and break my accords. Damned if I did, damned if I didn't." Carrow's voice is inflected with feigned disappointment.

We reach the table, a roughly hewn relic with no sheen. Lanair drums his fingers on the chair adjacent to us. Tehsan plays the owl. I stare at Carrow, who lingers on the throne. The man beside him hasn't moved. Might not have breathed. Then he steps forward once Carrow claps his hands, springs up, and saunters toward the wooden table.

His pace is leisurely. Takes him almost a minute to pass the twenty yards between here and there. Impatient, Lanair removes his sword and sheath, and sits in his seat. When Carrow finally reaches us, he leans on the back of the chair, observing it but not sitting down. Then he drags the chair aside. Its scraping reverberates in the highest vaults of the ceiling. Rather than sitting, Carrow rests his fists on the table and glares at Lanair.

Just then, a cloud must've covered the sun. The light spear diffuses, and a rope of shadows crawls around the hall like a taupe noose.

Payton tapped the stirrup on her horse. It stood in the middle of the tight courtyard packed to the north with Mehsanics and to the south with Faeds, partitioned by a thin strip of bare stone perpendicular to the broken tower. Beyond the walls were the rest of the armies. A thin line of goldcoats had lined in front of the broken tower's doors to protect the lords within. Payton tapped quicker.

Badric and Alanna were obelisks on either side of her. Gwenaever waited beside Badric. The rest of the Harts were stationed around the tower grounds, near the hidden entrances to the tower.

Scowls seethed over them from one end of the yard to the other. Somehow the silence made it all worse.

The old knight cleared his throat. "Not even your father managed to break the might of Mehsani bloodlessly, Lady Tallhart. Be proud of this moment."

"No, he did not. This wasn't bloodless, either." She glanced at the closed doors of the tower. What she'd give to be in that room now, rather than out here, in her position of power where she felt absolutely none.

Badric scrunched his mouth and frowned at the return of his compliment. His shoulders leaned back, his back straightened. Good, let him know. This wasn't the drying of ink on paper.

"No, I'm telling you, that's it," a soldier her side of the yard murmured. He was about thirty, a little salt brushed in his beard. He was pointing up. "That's it," he repeated to the man beside him.

"My lady, did Lord Carrow estimate how long it'd take?" Alanna asked.

"Half an hour, he said. Can't be sure with him. He rambles. Then other times he's mute."

"No, no," the second man replied. "Can't be."

"You blind? That's *it*," the first soldier insisted.

"No, no. Shut up."

Payton heard Alanna slurp water from her flask, but she was watching the two men. The one who'd spoken first kept his finger skyward. The second man shifted uncomfortably. He was frowning. "Shut it," he told the other.

She glanced up at the broken tower. Climbing boldly into the gray morning mist, it loomed overhead, giving that sensation that it was falling perpetually upon an observer but never quite moving. The sun had moved behind it. Its rays struck the vapor, bloomed in a halo around the tower's zenith. Something might've been up there. She couldn't say. Old stones, more than anything.

"Come on," she said to Alanna. "I want to check in with the Harts. Badric, the courtyard's yours. Gwenaever is your second."

Badric nodded solemnly. Gwenaever mirrored his genuflection.

"Want me to go alone, my lady? You could stay here, keep the peace," Alanna offered.

Payton shook her head. "Sir Badric can keep it just fine."

"That's it!" the man insisted.

"Badric can keep it just fine," she repeated.

"Shut it!" the other soldier hissed.

Payton frowned. "I want to inspect the grounds. Who knows who's causing mischief round these parts."

✿ ✿ ✿

The scroll lies centered on the table between Carrow and Lanair. In haphazard scratch, it lists the stipulations we demanded. Partition the Narrows, raze Alaveren, a high lord in the South, a queen in the North. Below it are lines for signatures, but there's no pen. Carrow smiles smugly at Lanair.

Behind Carrow, the man with the iron cheekbones gazes over our heads. He never looks at Tehsan, at Lanair, or at me. His eyes are for the closed doors far behind us.

"Why here?" Lanair asks. "And not the thing about making amends that you told our emissary. Why here?"

"Don't you agree it's fitting? To come to the spot where it all went wrong to make it all right. All right, all right. Today's the day they'll say it all went right."

I clear my throat. "Where's the pen, Carrow?"

Dumbstruck, he stares at me.

"Where's the pen? You brought the paper, but where's the pen?"

Carrow breaks into a quick grin. "Do you remember that day we wrestled by the river, Lanair?"

"Sorry?"

"That day we wrestled, Lanair."

"Perhaps. It was twenty-two years ago."

Carrow splays his fingers wide. Palm open, he stares at each fingertip. "You beat me, pinned me down in the mud. Then you took your hand and put it like this." He moved his splayed hand toward his chest, clutching his breast with it. "Do you remember that?"

Lanair laughs nervously. "Okay. So I did. Are we here to sign a treaty or talk about wrestling?"

"I'm asking only because I want to know what changed."

"How do you mean?"

"You regarded me so tenderly that day. Then the day of the squirrels came."

Lanair scratches his hair. "The squirrels? Jon, what're you talking about?"

"Tell me you're not serious."

"Jon," he sighs.

"Meant that little to you, huh? You had this glimmer of contempt in your eyes all of a sudden, as if nothing we'd done mattered. 'The priests have spoken,' your father said. 'Mehsani has spoken.' Funny how dead men with broken necks keep speaking."

"Jon, get to the point."

"That *is* my point, Lanair. The world pivots on a ring of squirrels."

Tehsan spits. "Why are you talking about squirrels, for Mehsani's sake? Sign the parchment, Carrow!"

Carrow grins again. He stands straight, taking his weight off of the table. Even without the crown of light around his head, the heron king is completely comfortable with his position. I stroke my stump along the hilt.

"You really don't remember," Carrow states.

Lanair throws his hands up, an admission of guilt. They slap flat on the table. "Guess you caught me." He pushes himself several inches away from the table, out of Carrow's shadow. "Two years of fighting, and you want to discuss squirrels."

A scowl twitches on Carrow's face. Tehsan rocks on her feet. The man with the iron cheekbones cracks his neck.

371

"If I've learned anything, Lanair, since you ran me out of our home, it's that you have to know why you're doing a thing. I'm doing this because of the day with the squirrels."

"Doing what!" Lanair exclaims. "Signing this treaty?"

"No."

"What then?"

"Let me tell you what I think of your fucking treaty."

Tehsan gasps. "Mind your tongue! This is the blood of Mehsani!"

"Enough!" Lanair shouts. "Say your piece, Jon, and be gone."

Carrow plucks the parchment from the table and shreds it to pieces.

⊗ ⊗ ⊗

Though she'd rounded the tower halfway, Payton could feel the tension brewing back in the yard. Badric would have to hold it down. He could. He'd held most of her city while the world around it burned. He could hold a courtyard.

The first four Harts they'd met said they'd seen nothing suspicious. Thanet noted some footprints that didn't belong, but they led into grass, and he lost the trail. Gawaen saw nothing. Thanet and Tristam had cleared out a pack of feral dogs that'd climbed over the crumbling walls that boxed in the tower grounds. Other than that, silence.

Tam was the next one. He wouldn't be far up, just through this patch that had smacks of a garden. A few rusted trellises stood lonely. Behind them, a long glass building that might've been a shed. Two rusted rakes lay on the ground.

Alanna bounded up ahead as she had with the first four Harts. Wanted to make sure the path was clear. Of course it'd be clear. These were the Harts, Payton's trusted circle. No one in it could be compromised.

But the woman's gasp sparked an impulsive sprint. Before Payton reached her around the bend, she saw the pooling blood. Tam lay face down. The red trickle came from the man's head. Payton knelt down, touched his back. It rose coyly. She felt a knot in her stomach. Tears welled in her ducts.

372

His faint breathing soothed her, though, and she quickly refocused. He had a pulse; he'd persevere. However, something was afoot.

Alanna swore. She swore again and, waving her sword around, promised vengeance against the houses of Mehsani.

"Focus!" Payton hissed. "Keep it together!"

Alanna frowned, but she drew in a long breath and sighed it out.

"Good. Help me search the tower," Payton ordered.

The entrance Tam had been guarding led into a dim atrium, which soared until it vanished several floors above. With so little light, she could barely see her feet. Something snagged her foot. She went down. Luckily, mud braced her fall. In the mud was a precise trail of queer footprints stretching farther into the shadows. She instantly shot back to her feet.

"They a Mehsanic's?" Alanna asked.

"No. Too small. Couldn't be Piper's, either." Then she saw another trail of far larger prints running adjacent to the small prints. "But those could be."

Payton crept alongside the parallel trails. They'd been made with purpose, in haste. Eventually the prints ceased at the foot of a stairwell leading out of the atrium. It climbed out of sight.

Before Payton could go up, Gwenaever rushed into the atrium. "My lady! It's deteriorating. The courtyard, we couldn't stop it. Say they see something. I couldn't convince them otherwise."

Payton ran to her. The woman bit her fist as she stared at Tam. Her cheeks blushing purple, Gwenaever dropped to a knee. "Damn," she breathed.

"Follow me when you can, Gwenaever. Alanna, guard the entrance. No one comes in. Make sure no one gets out."

Alanna bowed her head. "On my life, no one will."

Payton nodded, burst out of the tower, and dashed for the courtyard.

✿ ✿ ✿

"You never cared for me after the squirrels. That was the day on which the world pivoted."

"Mehsani's ass, Jon," Lanair breathes. "How, how could you let a single day linger?"

"*That* was the only day that should linger!"

"Maybe I did care before, maybe I didn't after. I did see you as a brother. Then one day, I didn't." Lanair's voice grows breathless with the quality of searching for words that refuse to be found. "I left those things behind, Jon."

"All I wanted was a fucking home. You gave me nothing but pain. You let the words of priests and idiots cloud your judgment."

Lanair sighs and stands up. "Childish things belong in the nursery. Don't blame me if you couldn't learn that."

Face twitching manically, Carrow slams his hand on the table. It dominates the hall with its eruption. That face can't keep still.

"*Blame* you? You ruined me!"

"Did Payton Tallhart not give you a home?" I ask.

He stares at me again, this time irate.

"Tell me! Did Payton Tallhart not save your life? Did she not risk her own for you?"

"Agh," he spits. "And once she gets her throne, she'll toss me aside. I did my part. Like in the old world, there'll be no place in the new one for Jon Carrow. She'll toss me aside once I hand her the throne."

I snort. "You're in no place, Carrow." I edge closer to his side of the table.

"Who the fuck are you talking to? Me. I hold the pen, not Payton Tallhart."

"Where is the pen, Carrow?"

Lanair grunts and walks away from the table. He snaps for both Tehsan and me to follow him out of the hall. Neither of us budges.

"No." Carrow's voice was a low, booming command. "This is my window to set things right."

Lanair spins around. "Let's set it right. Could you actually do that, Jon? Let's put ink on the paper. Make it all go away."

"Ink on a page was the original sin," Carrow retorts. "That was the reason the squirrels meant something so awful I had to leave, and leave, and leave. Now I stand here, homeless and about to be homeless once more. Nobody cares about Jon Carrow. The only way to set it right is to do this."

Tehsan begins murmuring to herself. A prayer. Words for Mehsani.

"What then?" Lanair shouts. "What do you suggest we do? You agreed to these demands! Did you call me in here simply to fling childhood grievances at me?"

"This is my own window to make it right."

With his eyes fixed on Lanair, I swing my blade at Carrow's throat. In a flash, the man with the iron cheeks deflects my blade, knocks me on my ass. Carrow smiles.

"Jem, what are you thinking?" Lanair breathes.

Tehsan screams Mehsani's name as she pounces on Carrow with knives drawn.

"Tehsan!" Lanair gasps, utterly dazed.

Carrow, anticipating the lunge, falls fluidly with Tehsan, evading both knives and injury. His feet catapult her into the air. She rolls away toward the dim places between the columns.

I glance up to see Carrow and the man with the iron cheekbones smiling smugly at us. The latter wets his lips. Suddenly thrown into animation, he approaches assuredly.

"What have you done?" Lanair asks.

"This is my window," Carrow replies, thumping his chest.

Carrow upturns the table at Lanair.

❂ ❂ ❂

The two men were pointing up at the tower, and the soldiers huddled around them joined in. They were screaming, "It's the flag! It's it, I tell ya!" and spitting across the narrow strip at the Mehsanics, who were condensing into a coiled bunch ready to spring. A handful of her men had swords drawn. When she sprinted back into the fray, the cursing died off.

"What's the problem?" she demanded of Badric.

Frowning, he nodded, looking upward. "Look, Lady Tallhart. It's undeniable."

Payton whipped her head up and saw that the sun had receded slightly, the mist abated. For a moment, she thought they'd been complaining about a bunch of vapor, but then the flag came into focus as it undulated coyly in the gray sky. She couldn't make out the sigil. Could've been anything. Then the wind seemed to die up there, and the flag sagged. Before it shriveled up, the Red Hook of Mehsani stole a glance at her.

Fuck. Fuck fuck fuck. That was impossible, the Red Hook flying over the broken tower. They wouldn't've done it.

"Blood of the Usurper will out!" the Northerners screamed. "Fucking scabs! Kill 'em!"

What did that mean to these people? The Red Hook claiming the broken tower for itself.

"No," she said.

"Put these dogs down!"

"No!" she shouted.

"Fuck Mehsani!"

"No!"

The screaming trickled off, though some persisted. She held her ground between the two columns. They looked at her behind twisted, bestial visages.

"Enough! Lords Carrow and Mavogar are organizing a truce. We'll not besmirch that over some petty squabble. There is no betrayal. Only misunderstanding." Unseen cowards jeered her. For the most part, however, the mass was controlled. "We're going home. Today we'll be siblings in Braeland at long—"

A nauseating crunch silenced the courtyard. The subsequent spatter embarrassed the air, made it blush. The mist swelled up like a mushroom spore and partially masked the Mehsanics standing across from Payton. She shivered.

Silence permeated every soul within the foyer. Her eyes settled on the twisted mass of bone and blood. The man smiled two smiles: a snaggle one for his teeth, a red one for his throat.

❋ ❋ ❋

Carrow parries me and sidesteps, attempting to reach Lanair, but I block his path and he comes back and goes for the kill but I dodge him then he pursues Lanair waiting behind me. I chase him and try to distract him and here comes Tehsan to protect her lord but Lanair isn't taking out his sword why why take it out you fool the big man who'd been called Coyle yanks me into a headlock.

"Watch," Coyle utters. "Watch what happens, little lamb. This is who you're fucking with today. Jon Fucking Carrow. Watch him." Liquor's hot on his breath. Keeps my good arm contained, so I thwack him with my stump but it does little.

Tehsan lunges at Carrow but misses since he's an exemplary killer, a bulk of death that fidgets when it hasn't been put to use. She can't touch him. His tongue glides the split of a sick smile.

She falters and trips a beat, and he hamstrings her. Her cry pierces the hall. She goes down, clutching her thigh.

"Lanair," Carrow hisses.

"Kill me," Lanair replies. He unties his belt, sets aside his sword. He could be preparing for a nap, for all his serenity. Carrow's face slackens, as if disappointed with the ease of the prey. "Kill me. Kill me, and let my people go. I'll not hear another death cry while we bicker. If you want me to, I'll die for Mehsani's Word."

Coyle's body loosens as if he, too, were made small by Lanair's voice.

"Go on!" Lanair cries.

Carrow frowns at him. With Coyle transfixed, I jolt my head back. His nose shatters. The giant slumps to the ground, and I lash my foot across his face. He goes limp. Startled, Carrow readies himself for me. I lunge toward him.

✪ ✪ ✪

Breathlessly, Payton knelt beside the body. The heap leaked blood everywhere, sluicing down bones like white masts. Half the man's head was gone, but she could still recognize Carrow's sentinel. The Sunburst sparkled on his chest for all to see.

It was only seconds before the conflagration reignited and the furor crept back.

"Fucking scabs!"

"Traitors!"

The Mehsanics pushed for the tower. "Blood of Mehsani!" they cried. "To our lord! Blood of Mehsani!"

The Faed goldcoats held their rigid line. No one passed. They began to shove the Mehsanics back, who yelled, "Blood of Mehsani!"

"Wait," she said. Could've shouted, wouldn't have mattered. Would've been a mote between raging seas.

She didn't see the first spear, nor did she know who threw it. The next second, the seas awoke. One tidal wave crested, another arced. The waves collided headlong.

✪ ✪ ✪

"Meraxes," Carrow snarls. He talks through me, even as I stab at him relentlessly, for his words are for only Lanair.

"Jon," Lanair says.

"Meraxes."

"Jon, listen to me."

His blond bangs oscillate over icy pools. He stops me, nearly takes my hand, and my sword clatters away. I'm out.

"We can break Faedelin and Mehsani," Lanair says.

"Think of Meraxes," Carrow snarls. "I know, Lanair. There's nothing in your golden box. Nothing to bargain with. No reason for me to stop. I found the little grain in a letter. The little grain told me there's no glue with-

378

out you, Lanair. If you're dead, so is Mehsani's blood. Forever." Lanair eyes me. "There is nothing in the box but men's imagination. Well, I have been imagining a world without you."

Furor rages beyond the doors.

"And I like it better than this world."

Carrow backs Lanair toward the overturned table, towards a leg bent sideways from its fall, and it trips Lanair. He takes a fall. I pounce for my sword.

"Jon. You're not hearing me. The world will not remember Faedelin or Mehsani; they will know only Carrow and Mavogar."

Carrow holds me away with a flick of his hand. The blade hovers over Lanair.

"Jon."

"Mehsani was only an arm on the body, Mehsanism a finger on the hand."

"Jon."

"When an arm rots, you cut it off. Spite the arm to save the body," Carrow hisses. "The world will not know Mavogar. Not after I wipe that name off this earth."

"Jon."

"My hand is steady."

A red rain falls. Horrified screams pierce the chamber. I don't know if they come from me.

"Lanair, Lanair!"

The heron stands immobilized as he looks down at his prey. The rain drips insignificantly from his blade. Some fire's gone out of his face.

"No, no, Lanair!"

The noise nauseates me. Then I find myself screaming:

"Carrow!"

38

No Special Providence

The sparks flew outward on the burning air.

The banners of the fox had fallen, but the men who'd held them huddled within the portico of the courtyard, staving off the rushing wave of Faeds. In a tight mass they took in the swiping blows from Payton's force. She pushed back. Had to get to her horse. It whinnied madly, desperate to escape the roaring around it.

After the first few lines of men and women fell, the Mehsanics wore the Faeds into a grisly stasis. Their blades clunked the red shields, but no one fell. The hollering blared, shaking the broken tower at its stony roots.

The madness attracted the retainers beyond the yard. "Blood of Mehsani!" they called. "Burn the scabs!" was the answer.

The two columns of retainers bullied their way to the mouth of the courtyard. Bottlenecked, they lashed at one another. Ropes of red knifed across Payton. Fast. Quick. Had to get to the horse.

Badric had been knocked to the ground beside Payton's mount, and he was holding a welt on his head. Her mind throbbed; her own welt pulsed. She lifted the knight to his feet.

"We've got to drive the Mehsanics out of the yard! Else we're all dead!" she yelled.

"How?" he breathed.

Trick them, she thought. Make them believe in a pale monster not there. Spin the monster into their charge.

"Secure the door! We've got to drive them out." She grabbed the saddle and swung her legs up. "To your lord! Secure the Tower of the Light! To Lord Carrow!"

A cry went up in her force. The ranks of her people, which had dwindled after the bloody spat, formed a line in front of the tower's doors, shoving the Mehsanics back who hadn't bombarded the doors. Good, good. Let them believe in the monster.

Once the rows of men and women consolidated in front of the tower, felling the Mehsanics who tried to sprint there first, Payton drew her sword and pointed toward the bridge.

"For Faedelin!" she bellowed.

An echo repeated her. The sea lurched behind her and rushed toward the Mehsanics. The Southerners faltered, dropped back, were conquered. Beyond the mouth of the courtyard, the real fight awaited. For Faedelin. Who'd said those words?

Payton Tallhart charged out of the courtyard screaming. Behind her rushed the army, a tide of inexorable inertia fueled by the word Faedelin.

✪ ✪ ✪

Tehsan screams, but I'm already trying and can't touch him. He glides out of reach. His face is tight. No emotion in that slab of stone, little recognition of what he's done. I want to just put it there end the beating but it won't come close enough, so dance, dance, dance around the hall weaving through the red pillars like hardened cylinders of blood.

No, no; he mustn't have intended any treaty this day. This was it: the trap. We walked right into it, not shepherds but sheep.

The dance continues round and round, but how long have we been dancing? Sidestepping to the right, then to the left, then over him, arms spread wide and feet together, so peacefully not moving. Right, left. Over and over. The dance of life.

"It was preordained," he says, "that the blood of the second brother would eat apples with worms."

So it was.

Tehsan's screaming continues, underscored by her dragging herself on the floor either to him or to her weapon, but she's out, just rest, the thing is done, but not the next thing, the answer to the new question.

The heat of my heaving breath rubs down my chest with the trails of sweat plastering my tabard to me. We're nearing the back of the hall where the throne hosted the heron king minutes ago, the place where the taupe noose tightens.

"It was preordained," he repeats.

Those words are an empty grimace with no feet. He's drawing me back, back, back. Toward the place where the taupe noose tightens. Into the unknown haunts of the broken tower. He's leading me into the shadows, black heron that he is. The dim places of the broken tower yawn around him. He slinks backward into the noose. I follow him. The dance of life.

✪ ✪ ✪

Payton thundered toward the Mehsanics beyond the courtyard. Her retainers joined the fight and pounced upon the poor redshirts. The gradual slope downhill eased their purpose. "To the bridge!" she cried, drawing a path with her sword. They shoved the Mehsanics westward.

Arrows took down the men around her. Glancing up, she saw Southern archers dotting the roofs of the surrounding buildings. That held her force back. The Mehsanics regrouped in the boulevard to the last bridge. The front line held spears at attention. Behind them stretched innumerable compatriots, hardened by the fights long past, prepared for the battle rushing ahead. Their grim, ashen faces were interchangeable.

Mehsanics fought uphill toward their own flag, to the tower they conquered. Faeds claimed the tower, claiming the Mehsanics had betrayed them. The mischief stank.

Payton took her horse parallel along her front line. They straightened up in her coming, ceasing their spitting and consolidating the poses of true soldiers. She stared at the tense sea, its archers trained on her and hers. Payton held her sword high, opened her mouth.

"Cover," the Mehsanics shouted. They struggled as a mass to throw up their shields. Bewildered, Payton glanced around her. Then she saw them. A line of Faed renegades had taken the walls of the courtyard. They ignited their arrows, trained them on the huddled masses below. The firelight flirted with their sunbursts.

"No!" Payton screamed.

They loosed their arrows. A bow of fire crashed from the sky.

✿ ✿ ✿

Carrow pounds his chest. "It was me. It was Jon Carrow."

He's drawing me through the shadows hiding the rooms that'd been resting for the years under the dust beneath our feet. Our feet shuffle on the ground, disturbing the dust and kicking it up in each room we skulk through, doused in shadows.

"Mehsani was doomed when he turned against Faedelin."

Overturned tables and broken chairs and piles of putrid fruit and maggoty carcasses adorn the halls of the Light. They peek out of the shadows. The heron spreads his wings to blanket me in the shroud. Quick. Can't let the heron win today, not today of all days. This hallway's narrow. The Narrows.

"Sumara was doomed when it tethered itself to Mehsani."

To balance, I keep my legs wide. To fit through, I turn sideways. I pursue him warily, for this is the heron's ground.

Several ruts filter light into this corridor. The heron's head ducks in and out, in and out, of the beams, dissolving and reappearing every five steps. Torn tapestries droop in between each square rut. They tell the making of Braeland, from the days of the chasing corsairs, the hunting empire, the writing of the Way, the schism of the brothers. In dancing forward, we drag ourselves back. The dance of life.

The heron flies back into an enormous atrium soaring into the dimness that conceals the ceiling.

"Mavogar could not live as the House of Sumara. A house upon a compromised foundation is itself unsound."

There's more to this dance than our legs and feet. The cataclysm has joined the rear of the tower. Two soldiers fight where the standing wall has fallen, ripped naked the belly of the tower. A woman's blonde hair whips madly as she strikes savagely at the other with a large throat.

"Lanair signed his obituary when he took it from me."

Strange footprints are under mine; they're fresh in the soil blown in from beyond.

"Took it all. Everything. Left me a ghost."

The heron perches on the stairs where the footprints end. He rises up, an emblem of imminent death wrapped in a fleshy disguise.

"It was me, Jon Carrow."

He flies back up the stairs, challenging me to wade into his shadows. I chase him now, up, up, up, deeper into the void.

◎ ◎ ◎

Mehsani's Rock, they were called. They upheld that name. A tired mass of shields, they held their place at the foothill of fate as the raining fire challenged them to break. The rock sucked it in, let the archers grow tired as the rock lay in wait. Then it would erupt.

She knew she didn't have long. Like in the courtyard, only seconds before the peace would break. She would have to break the stasis, not let it crumble all around her in red spatter. It was hers to break.

She just needed the platform.

Payton's voice crescendoed: "Fire everything!"

The thrumming of the air, the denting of shields nearly deafened her. And yet the rock remained, nestled at the foothill of fate.

And yet here she stood, the flame atop the foothill. She searched for a place to break, for all rocks had a point of compromise. Had to get that compromise before the core of it erupted, targeted your point of frailty.

There.

Aloft on the wind was the Red Hook, shorn from its traitorous post on the broken tower. They'd know it was a sign. Payton gripped her spear, hurled it through the Hook. It planted several paces in front of the mass at the foothill. The rock let air out: the shields lowered an inch, the eyes widened a hair, the stance retreated a pace. The Sumarans regarded the fallen image of their hero pinned to the ground by the spear. They were betrayed. The fissure had opened.

Payton called another volley. It went up, descended. The little missiles snuck through the rock's fissures, made it stumble. The rock broke in animation, rushed backward across the bridge. Even the Mehsanics' retreat was organized, columns charging efficiently over the river. They ran from the mastered Hook, never looking back.

Now was the time. Had to get there before the rest, to stand alone in a moment of faith on the bridge. Payton called for another volley. Then she broke into a charge and left her host stunned by this moment of dauntless bravery. Payton pursued the host of Mehsani. A solitary monument beneath the falling fire.

❂ ❂ ❂

He pounds his chest again. "It was me," he grunts. "It was Jon Carrow. It was mine to build!"

Neither of us stand upright; we dance in a hunched stance, fighting the pull of the ground as much as the distance between us. Impossibly tired, challenging the magnetic drag of the ground. Carrow tugs at his collar in the moments intercutting our dance. In the dark I can see the sweat glisten.

"It was *me*," he wheezes.

We've danced near a balcony stretching across the broad side of the tower. It drops away before reaching the other hall. Hazy morning light blinds me.

Carrow backs out onto the balcony. The light engulfs him, vanishes him, destroys him completely. For a fleeting second, the monster is gone.

✪ ✪ ✪

Payton charged toward the bridge, past her pavilion, beyond the spot she'd kissed her father into memory. The host of Mehsani scattered before her. She felt the rush, the exhilaration of cheating the countless arrows. Each gallop took her a sentence deeper into legend.

She heard the Faeds ebb in answer to her dauntless bravery. She couldn't move quickly enough. They'd be on her like a tick.

The host of Mehsani, regrouping beyond the last bridge, formed an impenetrable garrison spiked with spears. The horde of Faedelin thundered in her footprints. Quick. To the center of the bridge, to the place of the pivot, to the core of legend.

Payton pulled up short, whipped her horse around, thrust the Red Lady banner skyward. Her voice filled up the gray sky. "Stop!"

The horde stumbled to a clumsy halt, falling over itself in some places. They gaped at her, mouths ajar and thirsting for more. A rogue arrow sliced through the banner and ignited its top half. The flames took hold of the Red Lady's sinuous hair, then refused to devour any more of Payton's sigil. Bewitched by the burning banner, her followers withdrew several yards.

She planted her sword into the bridge's stone and leveled the standard of the Harlot toward them. "Kneel!" she commanded.

Unsure, like children drawing near a serpent, they put down their weapons, held rapt by her voice. Spears clanked the ground behind her. They went to their knees, host of Mehsani, horde of Faedelin, bowing their heads, mastered utterly by the belief in the banner, in reverence of the one holding it.

☼ ☼ ☼

Sun rushes upon me, floods my eyes. I dart right. A *whoosh* passes on my left. He's near.

"It was mine!" he screams. "Mine to build!"

The furor of myriad swords below the tower deafens me.

"They trusted me! I was supposed to build it!"

I dodge him. My eyes have adjusted to the light. My calves are screaming. It's an effort just to stand.

"The bridge was mine to build!"

I stumble back. The balcony breaks off midway where it once reached another turret. It drops off ten paces away into jagged ruin. Into the bloody ruins and bloody battle below.

He's led me out of the shadows. The sun feels cold on my neck, like in early spring when its newfound height belies its emptiness. We turn, and in turning, dance around each other. His face falls into shadow. The dance of life.

Wincing, I keep him away. Ferocity burns in his eyes. Perhaps it's the moment of a man fearing he's wrong.

"It was mine!" he screams again. Carrow's voice has gone sheer, stripped of its humanity. It sounds like a shrieking, dying animal. "They gave it to me!"

"You didn't need to do it!" I shout back.

"There never would've been peace with him alive! Never."

"You were just too tired to fight for it."

Carrow's jaw screws up. Pouncing at me, he gnashes his teeth. Screams over and over and over that it was his. His to build. They gave it to him.

I draw him toward the edge. I pivot as I feel the chasm creeping up. Carrow lunges, nearly plummets. I wrap my stunted arm around his throat to subdue him. The recoil sends his sword clattering into oblivion. I draw him back.

A fire seems to have gone out in him. He wriggles but doesn't struggle.

I push him to the balcony's edge. Pressing his head over, I force him to look at it. The savagery stretches far away.

"Look," I demand. "Look at what you've done."

The banners in the courtyard have fallen. The Northerners push out of it to the west, purging the streets of shepherds. The last lines are falling back across the river. No banner flies for the fox.

"Look at it, Carrow." I can't stop the tears. My body goes limp against his, already slumped against the stone palisade. The tears are hot in the cold sun. "You've ruined us."

Carrow's breathing is soft beneath me. I have his throat firmly, but something tells me he wouldn't fight even if I didn't.

"Great smoking ruins. All of it."

The Faeds begin firing across the river. A few Southern legions flee beyond the city's limits.

He breathes hoarsely underneath me.

Two hollows husks, we observe the carnage below. I can't tell a fallen Northerner from a dead Southerner. Together they fall. Together they rest in a heap. Together their blood runs, innumerable rivulets within the cobbles racing toward a dead end.

"Just more ghosts to haunt us," I think aloud. Something tenses in him.

The soil crunches to our left. My head turns to find Dinian staring at us. Vaguely, I wonder what he's doing here. Standing there in the midst of this like a lost lamb.

Carrow snarls something: "Ghost." His breath steams on my forearm. But why the boy?

He lurches back. I feel the ground rush up. He's on me before I can blink. The pain is hot at first, but then it fades to a dull warmness, like a sip of summer mint in winter's heart. It's almost a relief.

I look up at him, and our eyes meet. His bangs bow down to kiss my forehead, and the crux of his elbow cradles my head. Something there is in his eyes. I can't describe it with any certainty, but the pools of blue ice are gone. Spring has come; a thaw has set in. The floods have rushed forth.

The salty droplets sprinkle my face, and I think I see the sea, changeable blue ridges dividing there and here. The island across the waters calls me. I go. In going, the things that evaded my tongue find their shape. They tell me how deaf I've been. Ears cannot do their duty when filled by the nymph's song, sultry and enthralling, an intoxicating tune that desires the blood of the heron. So I go. The mast, in my imagination, is flanked by a carmine sail, thin yet warm, that, if hoisted down, could wrap around us to make a red haze bordered by four pine pillars.

39

The Fall

Jon Carrow stood. The boy faced him from the doorway, a step beyond the shadows inside the tower. The space between them deepened. Jon wondered how he must look to the boy as he stood over Jem. It wasn't supposed to happen like this. His task grew more complex. How was he going to clear up the confusion now?

This morning was intended for the beginning of the new days. That was what the deal had intended. Though maybe Jon should've known, once he saw the sun rise as a yolk, that the days of youth, the days of agony, wouldn't die. They'd persevere.

He'd wanted to set right the things that went wrong. That is the thing Jon had planned. To set things right. Though, he realized this moment, the boy knew too little about the deal that began our story.

Wasn't that always the problem? he wondered. Too few of us ever know enough about one another. And too few of us will listen. Maybe telling the boy, finally clearing up the confusion over squirrels and foxes, once and for all silencing the omens of the superstitious, maybe that'll endear him back to me. The problem isn't any particular person; the gulf of unknowing between them creates the conflict.

So maybe that'll endear him back to me, Jon hoped. Perhaps once the unknowing is cleared, my boy will understand, and he will call me "Dad."

When Jon stepped forward, his boy drew back. Jon felt his mouth open, though he was dumb to anything he could say. He forgot his goal. What was I supposed to tell him? he wondered. I must convince him of something.

"You murdered them," his boy said, voice quivering.

I—I did, Jon realized. Light, it's so clear now that that's what happened. My brother, Payton's brother. They're gone.

"You murder everyone," his boy continued over Jon's silence. "Why do you destroy everyone?"

No, no, no. That's not what happens. Jon was aware his mouth still hung open. The words whirled in his mind, but they wouldn't come out.

No, no, no, he thought. I don't destroy everyone. I have been destroyed. I have been obliterated.

Jon took another step. His boy bolted.

No! I must explain the thing to my boy!

Jon raced after him. He heard his boy's footsteps echoing up the staircase, avoiding the battle below. Jon dashed up.

They put on a chase through the highest floors. They could feel the broken tower moaning beneath their feet. The space between them was deepening. At such a pace, they might narrow the gap, but would they have life remaining to close it completely? They would need the strength to save themselves.

When they came at last to the top of the tower, they paused to pant. The tower's peak offered little room, though the space between them was striking. They knew it. They were aware that this was the end.

At that instant, standing atop the broken tower, they were there as a product of misunderstanding and superstition, because of the fox who attacked the necklace of squirrels, because of other people not currently present who said, "Ghost," and because of the two brothers who fucked up a beautiful deal. Even so, in that instant, they were alone. The moment was for them, and it would end on their terms, not on the whims of the two brothers, or the names that were said, or the fox in the woods.

The man found his son eleven years ago. Eleven years. The man wished for eleven more. Though the morning wouldn't allow it. His dreams, which began during his son's infancy, were dashed irreversibly. The man had to let his son go.

His son backed away. His heels skirted the edge that earlier this morning the man's toes had wiggled over. The man held out his hand.

"Go away," his son said.

"Come away," the man replied.

"Go away!"

Why could his son not get it? Why did no one ever grasp the horrors that the man had been put through? The world cut him to pieces and then condemned him for not being complete.

His son backed up, went over the precipice. Instinctively, the man lunged after him, caught him by the wrist. They held each other, in their own ways, there at the end of all things.

"Jon."

Sometimes, a man must let go of the past. When nothing can be salvaged, a man must let it go.

"Jon!"

Dinian—

40

Coda of the Yolk

To be a yolk. Mmm, yes, to chase those unmarred days within the shell is the pursuit of happiness all men desire. But what would Jon be pursuing—happiness? Just a sunburned sun-kissed sun runner trapped on the nymph's damn island, which was his own fucking head, chasing after that sun, which was the yolk. Chase, chase, chase that fucking sun while the beguiling nymph watches. The old motions to the old days of the yolk, which laugh at him, since he's no yolk, he's a shell, he's a fucking ghost.

Jon rolled away from the jagged ledge. The weight of the boy falling from his grasp somehow seemed heavier after it had plummeted. The din of battle had subsided below, and the trick shepherd flag was gone from its post. Where had it gone? For several moments, he lay near the incalculable drop, ever more incomprehensibly vast following this new fall. He flattened his palms on the grains of stone.

Jon's breathing seemed to stall, and so did the world as if its heart entire paused to open his grieving space. Couldn't believe it happened. Or that he'd done it. But good-bye, Faedelin; so long, Mehsani. It ended in a great fall, as we end everything.

What had he been chasing? Was there a phrase he could use to express the confusion within? Was he just a sun runner chasing the sun, which was the yolk, which had fallen because he let a goddess, who was himself, trap him into the old motions of running, running, and running again?

He'd hoped to be so much more.

They're coming.

Jon clambered to his feet. The old ghost knew that he had nothing left. He felt the fatigue in his marrow. But though the battle waned, there were Mehsanics in the tower who were loath to let a fight die.

A handful of the pious ones confronted Jon near the top of the tower. He'd been wandering down the layers of shit cake called the broken tower and was eager to leave behind the incredulously immense fall. They got him by the balcony where Jem lay.

"We should've fucking known it was you, Ghost," they said.

"I suppose you should've," Jon agreed. "I suppose you should've."

Jon shuffled backward in a languid retreat. His heels skirted the ledge, where it broke off into the depths. Such a horribly dark word. Depths. Why did it leave a funny tickle in his head?

"You're a small consolation," they said. "Not enough for blood lost, but a small consolation."

"Yes," he mumbled. "Only a small consolation."

He turned toward the depths. It left such a tickle for a thing so silly. Only a word. Even though it was only a word, that word invoked the drop, the fall. It hewed a chasm inside of him. He coaxed his feet toward the precipice, where they tottered as though he had to piss. That's why it tickled. It encapsulated the interminable drop.

They're moving in.

What do you do, what did you do, what do you do, he wondered.

Jon lifted a foot over the abyss. "I am the singer and the sung," he said.

Then the burning started, and the light shone.

what…what…WHAT.

They saw it, too; he wasn't crazy. Just as he resolved to jump, the lantern from the bogs was burning again. He knew the burning and knew the light that was coming out of him. Oh, the burning, oh oh stop! Their eyes called him mad, but he wasn't mad. He was not mad. Not. Mad.

Poles of white light erupted from his chest, from his fingers, his eyes, and his mouth. It burned terribly. Oh Faedelin, make it stop.

Oh. Faedelin.

It was him. Jon couldn't have been sure at the bogs, and not even after Leon's spirit came to him last night, but now it was clear that this orb of light was a tangible vindication of all that he'd done. Jon Carrow, the boatman of the unstoppable stream, had been chosen. Let it burn these fucking scabs away, oh Faedelin, end this nightmare. Put down these dogs.

Those dogs stood transfixed by his mighty power. They gaped at the orb expanding and creeping toward them. It ballooned infinitely. Jon could feel it as if enlarging within his chest. His power was immense. And yet it terrified him.

The ever-expanding orb of white light touched the stunned Mehsanics, who began screaming when their flesh sizzled and dazzled like a stretch of road in midsummer. Blackened patches mottled the faces that screwed up in pain. The stench nauseated Jon.

He shielded his eyes from the light. Though it came from him and enveloped him, he did not burn. His flesh did not mottle.

A flash followed by a bang set Jon on his rear. The burning abated instantly, as it had so many summers ago in Sumara when he stepped too long on sun-drenched sand, then slipped his feet into the salty water. He uncovered his eyes.

An immaculate likeness of a star stained the spot where the Mehsanics had stood. Upward from the scorch floated wisps of red cloth. The air was quiet and unmoving.

Jon scratched his head. What under the sun had just transpired? He clasped his hands together and massaged the muscles that moments ago had suffered. The dogs were gone.

And yet a gnawing voice asked Jon if these had been dogs, then what was he? The light should've come from Faedelin. Should've vindicated Jon. But the gnawing voice gave a name to the pit sucking in Jon's intestines. It sucked them to the depths.

He placed a hand over his breast, the spot that had burned when the light went into him, the place that had seared when the light exited him. And that was the proper phrasing, mmm yes, it was the right phrasing. The light exited him. Jon kneaded his breast. Underneath the leather jerkin, layers below his mutilated flesh, within his ribcage where a flailing heart fluttered, there was emptiness. Moments before, Jon believed Faedelin had stepped in to save him from the Mehsanics, to stop him from leaping. The light had been so convincing. But he could feel it, the emptiness. Jon began to cry. No vindication had been handed down to him; he had gained only the loss of the light.

It was hopeless. Jon saw that now. He could not master the unstoppable stream, could not be the boatman, and could not capture the sun because once the depths sucked him in, they welcomed him as that little sun runner who wanted so bad to escape the goddess that he created, and to flee the island he imagined, and to ignore the sun he cherished. And though there was none of them, he continued to put stock in this dreamscape. What a biography to write for himself.

And even worse was the end to this story, Jon thought to himself as he collapsed. For Tomathy Carrow began the play by sending him to the depths. That was the overture to his sad ballad. This morning Jon sent the boy to a more precipitous depth. That was the coda he gave to his son. A macabre bookend that concluded the play he'd rather not have had any part in to begin with.

Oh, to be a yolk.

41

Great Smoking Ruins

The smoke was white as it ascended; the fires had been snuffed out. The flames had eaten away at the stones of the tower, and in their death, left behind sharp silhouettes printed with soot. Fire had cut through the armies after the fight. It started with the arrows. Then it took to the dry grass, the dead people, the wooden huts. Omniscient.

Payton left the place of the pivot, ordered a train of water from the river, and contained the fire chewing toward demise. It went out. White smoke, a sign of the death, signaled the rebirth. The foolish dance of eating life away had ended so those who'd escaped its steps could ask the questions. Cadaverous, anemic, pallid, the ones who'd welcomed the fire regarded one another from either end of the bridge. The white smoke blanketed the city on the seventh day.

Payton held the woman's hand, but by the time she'd reached her, the luster had already vanished from her eyes. As she knelt beside Alanna, she listened to Badric shuffling in the atrium as he muttered to himself. Said the madness the day had been made of. Wondered if it'd be the end. Oh, it'd be the end. Stroking the woman's blonde hair, Payton, with renewed determination, knew that it'd be the end.

She smelled the smoke across the tower's grounds. It wafted its way through the dark-green gardens, laced with burned flesh and charred wood. In a word, the odor encapsulated the day. Charred. Burned. Waste. It stung her nostrils, so she took breath in through her mouth. That left a queer stamp on her tongue.

Another set of footprints trampled the grass leading away from Alanna's body. They were flecked with maroon splotches. The splotches thinned into a segmented snake, one that pinpricked the moistened ground. The snake curved out of sight.

Following a final squeeze of the woman's hand, Payton took to the trail. It kept to the bend of the dormant gardens around the tower. The longer it stretched, the thinner the segmented snake grew, until only droplets ornamented the sloppy prints. At his feet, the droplets disappeared.

He was clutching his fat throat, a vain attempt at repairing the stab. The weeds had parted in his fall. As if in welcome, they parted, made a bed, and curled their bony, green fingers around his arms and legs. They'd swallow him up if he stayed there for long, and he'd become one of them, a noxious weed.

She hastened the transformation. Let noxious weeds lie with their fellows. Let them rest in bony tangled messes.

⊙ ⊙ ⊙

Once she followed the stairwell up through the veins of the broken tower, she came to the balcony. Falling away midway, the platform gave little room around the two bodies lying here. She stopped at the doorway; a golden patch

400

had scorched the stones several paces onto the balcony and was encircled by threads of red. Payton edged around the faint teeth of the golden scorch.

Jem stared up emptily. His good hand formed a crescent around the wound, a garish gash in his heart. She thought that perhaps tears would be appropriate; however, her eyes remained dry. Her body was numb.

Payton sank to her knee. She took her dagger, opened a nick in the red wrapping of her sword. She unfurled the tether until it dangled like a frizzled worm from her fingers. Pressing it gently on Jem's chest, she concealed the gash.

While she was repairing the wound, nurses eased Jon onto a cot. Soldiers lined either side of the doorway and saluted Jon's body as its chest dipped and rose. She shook her head and followed the regal procession as a pallbearer to Jem. The balcony became one with the light behind her.

Payton instructed the pallbearers to lay down Jem with Lanair in her pavilion. The Spider King and the Lord of Foxes. She smiled at them, shoulders kissing in their repose. Beyond the river she saw the tired masses packing up the camp. They'd want them in coffins sooner than later.

Five minutes later, Sumaran soldiers ushered Tehsan into her pavilion with a blushing bandage around her right thigh. Word was Jon had sliced her hamstring after she went crazy, charged at him and Edric Coyle. Scabs betray, after all. That'd been the plan all along. Coop up the guardians of the Light, locate and murder the Sentinel of the Light atop the tower, and try to squash the might of Faedelin with a single blow. Nothing had been squashed. Not according to that face screwed up with tension and tight with hate.

She scowled at Payton when the Sumarans rested her beside Jem and Lanair. From her lips a strand of saliva sailed toward Payton, who tilted her head to dodge the blow.

"Spirit stretches only so far, Lady Tehsan." Payton felt Tehsan's anger leaping off of the woman's heaving chest. Tehsan refused to look toward Jem and Lanair. "You're defeated."

Tehsan clenched the rods supporting her cot.

"Come get me," Payton dared.

Tehsan leaned away in surprise.

"No. Forget it. The thing's done. Take your people. Be gone."

"How can you expect us to go? Look at what you've done." Tehsan pointed to them.

"It happened. It's a tragedy. Time for the accord," Payton stated.

Tehsan's mouth hollowly hung open.

Payton continued: "Lords Carrow and Mavogar couldn't reach it. Maybe you and I can. An agreement was on the table."

"And the Ghost tore it up!" Tehsan shouted.

Payton bit her lip. "Word has it you attacked him while he tried to sign the thing."

Incredulity popped Tehsan's eyes.

"Of course, I know that's horseshit. The agreement was to partition the Narrows, raze this city. I'll sign it if you will. I imagine you'll be the ruler once everyone returns to Sumara. A bitter victory, I guess. Mine, too."

The woman still shook her head.

"Lanair has gone. So will Carrow after I speak to him. The board is clear."

"You suggest sacrilege," Tehsan uttered. "Mehsani intended this city for our inheritance."

"Intent." Payton crouched beside Tehsan's cot. "Old stones, broken bones. Ever hear it? Alaveren is an old heap of sand glued together by imagination."

She cupped soil in her hands and began passing it between them. "We've fought and fought and fought. We fall off course. We dribble away, little pebbles of little note. I think we've reached the point where we'll raze this place with intent or not. So I'm ordering it with intent."

Payton dropped the remaining sand.

"There'll always be something to fight," Tehsan promised.

"Not this. Not the Reaving."

"The Light of Faedelin won't outshine that of Mehsani."

Payton grimaced. "The period falls after the Light. No Faedelin, no Mehsani. Talk about intent; that's what I think was intended. And it's not Faedelin you'll face, but me. The might of Payton Tallhart." She rose from her crouch and cradled her chest. "Leave peacefully, Tehsan. Plenty here are still keen to skin a fox."

Tehsan slumped back onto her cot and clenched her jaw; whether in pain or in anguish, Payton didn't know. The woman's eyes averted, Payton moved her stool next to Jem and took her friend's hand. His palm was still warm. Then she felt her cheeks grow warm. Tears flooded over them, uncontrollably, unconditionally. They did not stop until long after the Southerners had departed, and Jem was truly gone.

❂ ❂ ❂

They'd wrapped his head in bandages, which concealed the left half of his face, so Tam regarded her nauseously with a solitary eye. Payton had him brought into her pavilion after Tehsan, Lanair, and Jem were shipped across the bridge. Tam had fallen asleep in waiting for her. When he awoke, he kept lamenting the courier's quiet feet that covered his approach. Never saw him coming. If he had, Alanna would be sitting there with them. Tower wouldn't have fallen. Mischief wouldn't have ran so deep.

Of course, if they were to draw the lines back to find the blame, wouldn't they end at the one who closed the gates of linen to let the phony playwright punctuate his last period? Didn't that allow the mischief to go deep? It was the running deep of the mischief that fell the tower; however, there sat thousands shepherds more.

Could things end as they began? The death of Mehsani, the fall of the sentinel. Were they the bookends, the former a wound, the latter a salve, the ignition and the extinguisher? Since the gates of linen peeled away and she took up the pen to commence the new narrative, the trick could work. Maybe Jon intended the death of his hero to end it. She'd make sure it did.

"Feeling better?" she asked Tam.

"Mmm. Need something to eat so I can keep up with vomiting," he quipped. "Love you, Payton."

"Got a fever or something?" she asked. Smiling, she kissed his bandaged forehead. "Love you, too, Tam. Stay quiet for a while, would you?"

Badric entered the pavilion, his shock of hair like snowy stalagmites. "My lady. Sir Tam. I have the tallies here. Not sure if you want to look at them now."

"No. Leave them on my desk."

He nodded. His face was condensed in a mess of wrinkles, some of fatigue, others of worry. The old knight thumbed the tally of bodies ruminatively before placing it on her desk.

"What's on your mind, Badric?"

The wrinkly mess avoided her. "Found a boy, in the wreckage. Lights gone out." Shook his head.

"There always will be. Go rest," she instructed. He nodded and left.

"I was a boy once," Tam mused aloud.

"I imagine you were."

"No, no." He smiled a dazed smile. "When I was a boy, once, a priest visited my village." His lips, chapped and split, smacked together. "Recall his face when I saw him on the dirt road. He smiled at me. I, uh, I don't remember much of him, I suppose. Left soon after."

Payton patted his shoulder and hoped he'd calm down, get some rest.

"When did you leave the church?" he asked.

"It was when an illusionist came to Wellfleet to perform for the spring feasts." A breathy laugh escaped her; suddenly the lights in the cool spring nighttime by the great forks of the rivers surrounding her home rushed back to her. The bards lost their voices singing in spring. "He greeted me with a small trick. Bobbed a cherry in his palms just before dinner. When it came down, it was an apple. Damn thing was a watermelon next. Balanced it on his pinky! What a sight," she said with a laugh.

"Took him to the stage, this illusionist character, and showed him to Leon's finest men. They loved him. Performed at our suppers throughout the festival. He made the pillars on city hall vanish so the pediment seemed to just hang there. But when the townsfolk started vanishing—my cousin's daughter, as it happened—we didn't feel so fondly for him.

"Leon called a trial and tried the invader." As Payton spoke, Tam continued smacking his lips. "We blamed the intruder for the girl's disappearance. He defended himself by claiming he couldn't vanish a human. He tried his magic on himself to prove it. Then, bewildered at the thing happening to him, the illusionist began to disappear. Right before my eyes. He couldn't stop it. Then he was gone."

Tam seemed to fall into a trance. Payton stroked his arm. Minutes later he perked back up.

"I never entered the church again. Stopped putting stock in magic tricks. That's the day I became Leon's godless swine. Honestly, how do you tell the illusionist from the illusion?"

Tam fell asleep.

Perhaps that could be the gist of her grand experiment. Payton gazed through the linen at the healing city, the Southerners leaving beyond the limits of Alaveren and the Northerners licking their wounds. She'd be no illusionist, no nymph. She'd be no Red Hart. Who was that, anyway? Her father, her ancestors? No. Nothing more could disappear.

Payton left Tam asleep on her bed, carefully drawing the linen curtains closed behind her.

With the Harts in tow, she stepped up the hill from her pavilion to where a throng of Northerners packed up in the dry dust. Her arrival made their weary faces perk up from the ground. Mutely, they formed a boulevard with deep margins. One by one each Northerner dropped to one knee.

"Payton the Dauntless!" a nearby soldier cried.

"Payton the Dauntless," echoed others in the vicinity.

She marched forward to the tune of this cry. It formed a susurrus that warmed the air surrounding her. Payton turned back to meet the gaze of the bowed ones, but their heads were still hung in solemn reflection.

❂ ❂ ❂

Coyle lay before Payton with a plum mound on his cheek, a cousin of her own throbbing lump. The cot they'd placed him on ended below his knees; his calves limply draped off, his feet brushed the stones. Couldn't be a comfortable way to recuperate. His hands were tucked under his buttocks. Shivers crept all over him. His jaw had broken, and it made speaking difficult.

"Lady," Coyle mumbled.

"How polite. Tell me what transpired in the broken tower this morning."

"Talk's hard," he quipped.

"I could have your head cut off, Coyle. I should've had it tossed from my tower in Wellfleet after you killed that boy."

"Not shepherd. Sheep."

"Did you kill that man on top of the tower? Or was that Marc Piper?"

"Didn't."

"Piper?" she asked.

"No."

"Mmm. Jon, then."

Coyle blinked at her.

"How long had you planned this? Must've been a while, no? Under my nose, no less. Light. Not again. I'll be no fool in Braeland."

"Enough around already."

Payton dragged a chair beside his cot. Beyond the tent flap, which rippled in the wind, Jon Carrow huddled atop a log, stoking the flames of a fire that his hunched body blocked from her view. The rippling flap peeked at him. Looking away, Payton touched Coyle's forearm. He squinted back.

"Did Jon plan to start a battle this morning?"

"End it," he replied.

"You went along with it."

"He could do it. He did."

"There are still over two thousand Sumarans across the river. Some ending."

"No leader. Fissures. Lost sheep."

"So Tehsan attacked only because Carrow threatened Lanair Mavogar. Did he intend to kill Jem and Tehsan as well?"

Coyle shrugged. He sniffed and readjusted his hands beneath his rear.

"Tehsan agreed to the parchment," she continued, "and the Sumarans will be gone by this afternoon. Alaveren is to be razed."

"Mmm."

"You think killing Lanair helped?"

"Maybe."

"Jon ever tell you about what happened to him in Sumara?"

Coyle sniffed. "Not really. His boy kidnapped. False shepherds whipped him."

"Did you murder Lanair?"

"No." The word plunged between them and silenced the tent. Coyle's lip quivered. Then he whispered, "He was a shepherd."

Payton leaned back in her chair. She propped her feet up on Coyle's cot, which coaxed him an inch closer to the far side. The injured man crossed his legs. As he did, she watched the figure hunched on the log beyond the flap, wool blanket coiled around him. He hadn't acknowledged Payton when she marched past him. Stared straight into the flames. She caught two words on his breath, "ghost" and "yolk," but she allowed him not a second longer before visiting Coyle. The man would have to wait, whether a minute or until his eyesight fried up in the firelight.

"Get rest, Coyle. It's a long way north."

"Dauntless."

"Hmm?"

"They say that. Payton. The Dauntless."

"Just a word."

"A good one. A great one, they might say. Does Payton the Dauntless take heads?" He was struggling to grind out each word from his broken jaw.

"Not now. You'll go back to your farm. I'm sure you've made enough for your boy to finish his lessons."

"What about Carrow?"

Payton the Dauntless narrowed her gaze. The man's shivers were visible, as if hyperbolic for a performance on the stage. Not even the fire could melt those tremors away.

"I'll see. Think he's too trapped in his own head." Payton pushed herself up.

"Aren't we all," Coyle murmured. "Aren't we all."

✪ ✪ ✪

The smoke wavered black.

Little was left to say to him. His visage seemed to upturn into the sickly fire, which clung to the logs melting into slivers. He weakly nudged them with his feet. The flames licked out to taste his knuckles, either adding to his frown or failing to break it.

"Ghost."

The dark plumes puffed up between him and Payton. She sat on the log opposite him.

"Yolk."

On and on and on went the murmuring. It opened small space for discourse. Little was left to say.

"Ghost."

"Quiet, Jon."

He perked up at the sound of her voice.

"I'm exiling you."

"W-what?"

Payton held up her hand. "What you did, Jon, it's punishable by far worse."

"You just don't understand."

"I do. You were right about trust. It's more precious than gold. Besides, aren't you tired of the lying?"

"Not lying. You can't do this to me. Please."

"I certainly can't execute you. Something in your bravery today framed you in a different light for the men."

"Radiant," he murmured, shaking his head and squeezing shut his eyes. "The Radiant Knight."

Payton frowned. "I feel sorry for you, Jon. How sad a life to suckle a fairy-tale box and to hope that no one looks inside."

Jon glared at her. "They ripped me out of my mom and handed it to me. Called it my birthright. Without that box I'd be a dead man." He spat at the fire. "And without that box, there'd be no sentinel, no hero to harden our resolve. How can you cut me out after I struck us this deal?"

"What happened on that balcony?"

He paused briefly. "The Light, Payton. It saved me."

Payton sighed.

"No! In the Mire, the thing went into me; it burned me up. It chose me. It chose me! Then it came back. The bulb burst out of my chest and stunned them all. Stunned me! I can't explain it. Faedelin. I think Faedelin picked me, Payton. It incinerated the men who tried to murder us."

Payton shook her head. "Jon Carrow, stop. Thirty-three years of lying. I'm putting an end to that."

"No. No, you're not. You're selling me, just like the rest. Knew it'd happen. Said as much to those fucking scabs. No place for Jon Carrow in the new world."

"Your sentence is commutable with a change in behavior. Show me you can live with us in this new order."

"Robert got to stay, and Lanair. The lot got to fucking stay."

She continued over him. "Show us you're not the devil that everyone claims you are. Perhaps after a few years you can come back."

"The world pivots on a ring of squirrels."

"I'm sending you to a place called Laecuna."

"No one ever cares for the Ghost."

"I want to see if you can come back from there."

"To be a yolk," he cried.

"Queen Kala will report to me," she said. "She'll let me know if you're in a condition to return to Braeland."

Between each sentence she spoke, Jon was muttering, "Only a Carrow when it's convenient. To be a yolk."

He glowered at her when she finished. "If only you knew what I did for this country, Payton Tallhart. If only you fucking knew."

"How much was for the country, and how much for you?"

Another glower was his response.

"You betrayed our confidences, Jon."

"I piss on your confidences. Did the legions of Mehsani not scatter when Lanair's death was announced? Did I not take out the one hindrance to your supremacy? Did the Faeds not raise toasts to the Sentinel of the Light? I did that. Me. Jon Fucking Carrow." A pound accompanied each name, first, middle, and last.

Payton rose. "The only toasts I've heard are to the Dauntless."

"What?"

Frowning, she replied, "Forget it. Exile's my final word."

"Bah. Final word. Fuck this blasted country. Burn its selfish, ignorant peasants. I'll make my own fucking way."

"I hope you do." Payton turned her back on Jon as he sat, still shivering like a stage performer, more an epileptic fit than a cold spell.

As she stepped away from the dying fire and its huddled man, a hollow bark sent chills down her legs. She craned her head toward a tree. An enormous raven sat on the lowest branch, cawing at the dead men and women who lay scattered below.

"Praeco," she whispered in recollection.

"What did you just say?" Jon's croaking voice made it a command, not a question.

"Nothing. It's just something I heard once down in Calidum. They call them praeco." She paused beneath the tree to look up at the bird. It blinked its onyx eyes. With a cock of its head, it observed Payton. "They think that they're actually birds of life." The raven barked at her. "It's nothing."

She heard Jon get to his feet. When Payton faced him, his melancholy stare fixated upon where the raven perched above her. Suddenly pacified, Jon's mouth formed a gaping oval ringed by coral lips.

"The praeco never killed the raven," he whispered, nodding solemnly as if finally grasping some elusive truth. "The praeco never killed the raven."

Payton's hair ruffled as the raven swooped off the branch and perched on her shoulder. She nearly swatted it away, but the bird seemed to be a fixture there. Its eyelids clapped over inky orbs. Tucking its wings away, the raven steadied itself on her shoulder, content in her company.

Roosting beside Payton's cheek, the bird's black orbs bored into Jon, who shrank under its encroaching, accusatory glare. The silhouette of its wings tattooed his face before casting a long, lightless column, into which Jon sank with his knees folded together. He searched for an answer from Payton. Her flat stare offered none. Then the raven beat its wings, dashed the fire, and soared into the sky. His mouth a gaping oval, Jon watched it mournfully. Payton looked overhead. The bird climbed into the overcast sky, a dense blanket blotting out the sun. Indifferent to those below, the raven ascended unceasingly, up and up and up, until it was lost in the gray mist of the morning.

ACKNOWLEDGMENTS

First and foremost, Heidi Frail deserves a nod. She read *Calypso Sun* when it was, as they say, in its alpha testing and a poor excuse for a coherent novel. Her suggestions and advice made it an objectively better text.

Also thanks to Philip Banaszek, whose input late in the process tinkered with some crucial elements and improved this story immensely.

To my grandparents, Eileen, Ken, and Joan, who listened to my ideas until my voice grew hoarse and their ears grew numb.

To Julia Sloan-Cullen, to Chris Brew, to Sydney Weinberg, to Spencer Jin, to Alex Karys, to Emefa Agawu, to Max Walsh, to Melissa Demeo, and innumerable more friends who gave me advice throughout this process.

And many thanks to my good friend Annelise Mahoney, who created the Dauntless logo.

Thanks to Tracey Doyle for the design of the cover and for help with the interior.

Immense thanks and gratitude to my copyeditors, Ivan and Christa, who treated an abstract experiment with surgical precision. Thank you for your input and your help.

Finally, I'd like to acknowledge Gabrielle Batchelder and Henk Rossouw. They were the teachers who truly encouraged me to pursue writing, especially when I was on the verge of quitting. Had they never counseled me, this book wouldn't exist. Thank you both.

ABOUT THE AUTHOR

Alexander Frail began writing when he was four years old and has rarely missed a day since. He enjoys trying out the snobbiest of craft beers and searching for the ultimate porter. A lifelong fan of bocce, Alex loves a long game on a dirt road down the Cape.

Alex lives outside of Boston, Massachuestts. *Calypso Sun* is his debut novel, and he's at work on his second. You can follow him on Twitter at @AlexanderFrail.

Made in the USA
Middletown, DE
09 September 2016